A bullet, a shrapnel
or a simple fragment of a shell
could have changed my destiny,
in the sense that
I would have had no destiny
and this book would never have seen the light.

Originally published in Italian as “L’Ardito - Romanzo storico”

Mail: roberto.nh.roseano@gmail.com
Facebook page: https://www.facebook.com/ArditiXXII
Cover, interior design, maps: Roberto Roseano

Independently published - Printed by KDP, an Amazon.com Company

ISBN-13: 979-8657639865
ISBN-10: 8657639865

ROBERTO ROSEANO

ARDITO

A VOLUNTEER IN AN ELITE UNIT DURING WW1

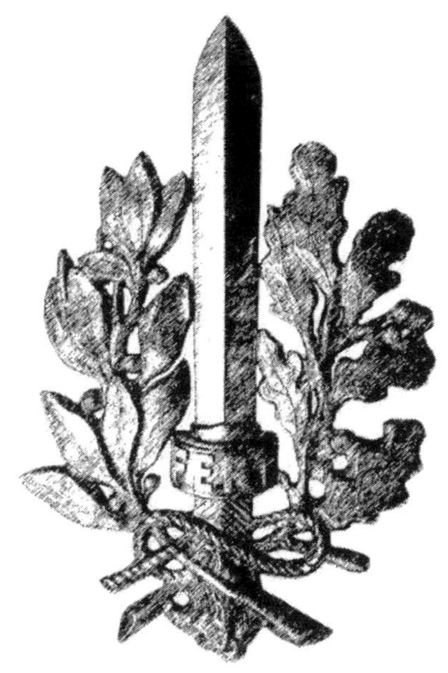

AD MMXV

WINNER OF
THE 50TH "ACQUI STORIA" AWARD
THE XI "GENERAL AMEDEO DE CIA" AWARD

After almost two years of war, a young sergeant decides to escape the bleak life of the trenches by volunteering for a newly created special unit of the Italian army. After a very hard training course he is selected, together with other men of proven courage, completely unaware that some privileges, such as higher wages, more leaves, no service in the trenches, will correspond to ever greater risks.

The command of the 2nd Army, in fact, intends to entrust these new units with the most difficult and dangerous enterprises, such as the conquest of Mount San Gabriele. Sergeant Pietro Roseano will experience firsthand the birth and epic of a legendary elite unit in the First World War, the Arditi: from the strenuous defense of the army in retreat after the Caporetto defeat to the victorious battles of 1918 on the Plateaus and the Piave river up to Vittorio Veneto.

A compelling narrative of those events through the eyes of one who lived them, risking his life.

CONTENTS

- PROLOGUE .... pag. 6
- 1st Part: CRISSCROSSING MEMORIES .... » 9
- 2nd Part: BLACK FLAMES .... » 127
- 3rd Part: TRAGIC AUTUMN .... » 175
- 4th Part: GREYGREEN REDEMPTION .... » 247
- 5th Part: VV .... » 325
- EPILOGUE .... » 398
- PHOTO BOOK .... » 400
- AKNOWLEDGEMENTS .... » 413
- BIBLIOGRAPHY .... » 415
- AUTHOR PROFILE .... » 418

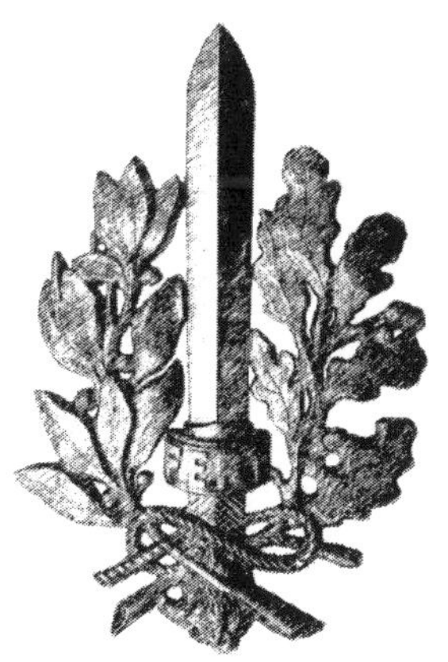

Prologue

Arditi?
Never heard of them.

Arditi?
Sorry, no idea.

Arditi?
Is it a surname?

Arditi?
Were they soldiers?

Arditi?
Fascists!

These were some of the answers I received when I asked the question:
«If I say the word Arditi, what comes to your mind?»

From the vast number of those who knew nothing, the most original answer was that of a friend who, after concentrating, said to me:
«Arditi? Wait a moment… I've got it!
Dante Alighieri - The Divine Comedy - The Circle of the Arditi.
In fact, in those days, boldness was considered a sin.»

At the other extreme, among the few who knew something about that word, another friend surprised me by intoning some verses of a song:

> *Mamma non piangere se c'è l'avanzata,*
> *tuo figlio è forte paura non ha*
> *asciuga il pianto della fidanzata,*
> *che nell'assalto si vince o si muor.*
> *Avanti Ardito, le Fiamme Nere*
> *son come simbolo delle tue schiere*
> *scavalca i monti, divora il piano*
> *pugnal fra i denti, le bombe a mano.*

This was one of the most famous songs in the Arditi repertoire.[1]

Apart from these two borderline cases, the results of my survey were rather disappointing: the vast majority of those questioned had absolutely no idea who the Arditi were.

Since I was aware of their exploits during the Great War, it seemed absolutely unbelievable and deeply unfair to me that their memory should have been completely lost.

I therefore determined to do something to bring the heroic deeds of these men to light and make them known to the circle of people I know, in the hope that they in turn would spread this knowledge.

This is one of the reasons that led me to undertake the writing of this book.

But it is not the only one.

---

[1] Mother don't cry if we have to advance,
your child is strong he has no fear
please dry my girlfriend's tears,
as in the assault we either win or we die.
Forward Ardito, the Black Flames
are a symbol of your ranks
climb over the mountains, devour the land
dagger between your teeth, grenades in hand.

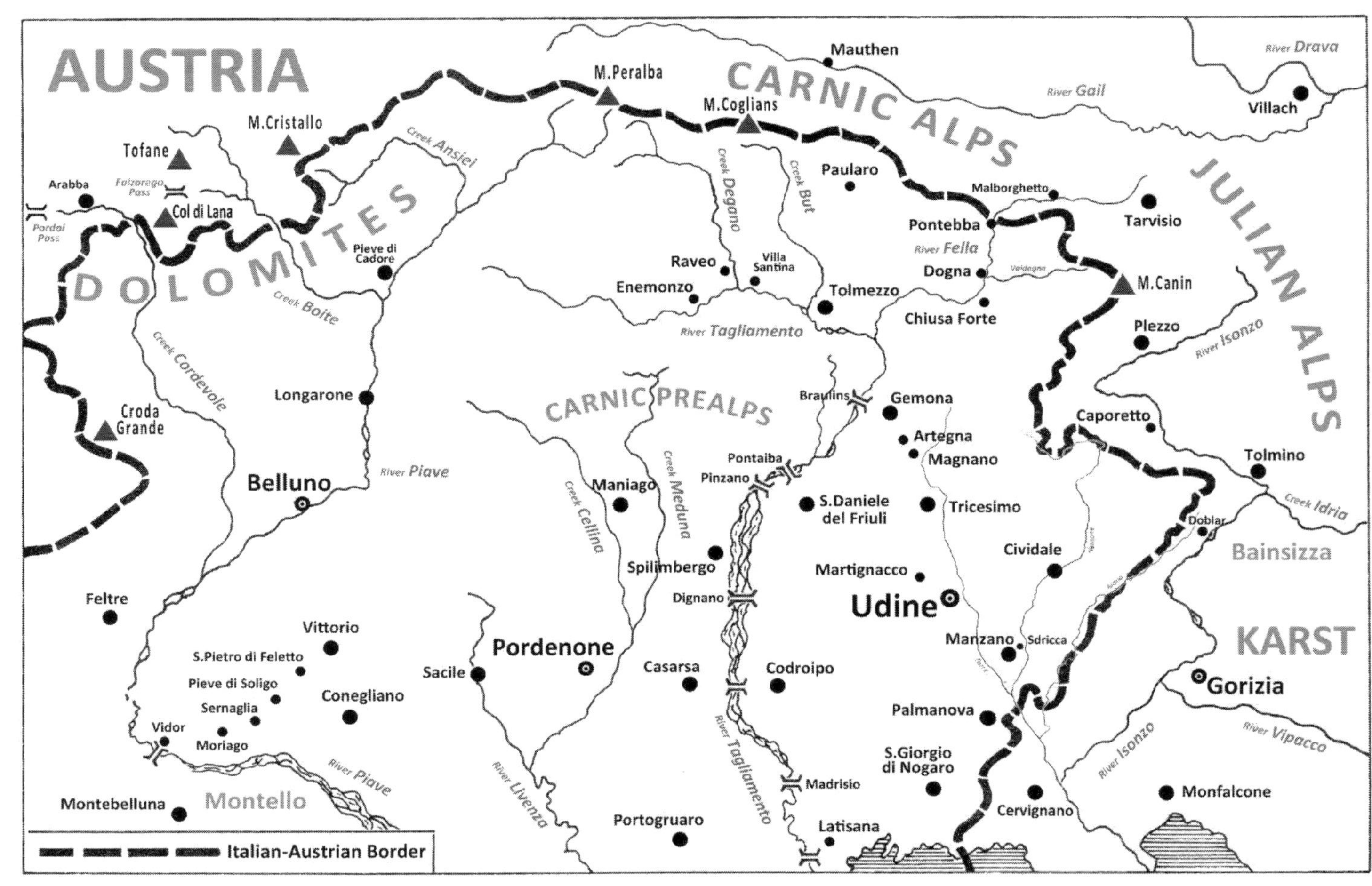
AUSTRIA
CARNIC ALPS
JULIAN ALPS
DOLOMITES
CARNIC PREALPS
KARST
Bainsizza
Montello
River Drava
River Gail
River Isonzo
River Vipacco
River Fella
River Tagliamento
River Piave
River Livenza
Creek Idria
Creek But
Creek Degano
Creek Meduna
Creek Cellina
Creek Ansiei
Creek Boite
Creek Cordevole
Mauthen
Villach
M.Peralba
M.Coglians
M.Cristallo
Tofane
Arabba
Falzarego Pass
Pordoi Pass
Col di Lana
Paularo
Malborghetto
Tarvisio
Pontebba
Dogna
Chiusa Forte
M.Canin
Plezzo
Pieve di Cadore
Raveo
Villa Santina
Enemonzo
Tolmezzo
Longarone
Croda Grande
Braulins
Gemona
Artegna
Magnano
Caporetto
Tolmino
Pontaiba
Pinzano
Belluno
Maniago
S.Daniele del Friuli
Tricesimo
Doblar
Cividale
Spilimbergo
Martignacco
Dignano
Udine
Feltre
Vittorio
S.Pietro di Feletto
Pieve di Soligo
Sernaglia
Conegliano
Vidor
Moriago
Sacile
Pordenone
Casarsa
Codroipo
Manzano
Sdricca
Gorizia
Palmanova
S.Giorgio di Nogaro
Madrisio
Cervignano
Monfalcone
Montebelluna
Portogruaro
Latisana
Italian-Austrian Border

1ST Part

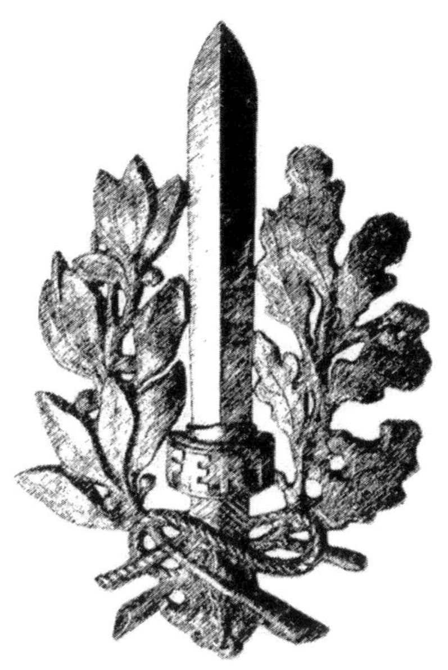

Crisscrossed Memories

Chapter 1.I

I'm writing not to think.
I'm writing slowly, one letter at a time, on this small piece of paper.
It's night.
I get a bit of light from a candle in a tin can.
Tomorrow is my birthday, but there won't be any birthday party.
I could die immediately or maybe at the end of our action.
Truly, I am surprised I'm still alive, after what happened last May at Zugna Torta and at the Buole Pass.
It was dreadful: thousands of dead and missing.
We repelled the attack.
Our flag received the bronze medal of valour.
Our Regiment was mentioned in the war bulletin of May 31st.
A piece of metal and a piece of paper as a tombstone for many men who are no longer here.
It's cloudy and very cold.
I'm used to it, but most of my comrades suffer from these low temperatures.
There have been many cases of frostbite.
Lots of them come from the south, where it is hot even in winter.
Few of them speak Italian well. Many of them struggle to understand it.
Orders are often given in dialect.
When someone is hit, though, the screams of pain are the same for everyone. Even those of the enemies.
If I get hit tomorrow, everyone will understand me even if I don't speak their dialect or their language.
Tomorrow, 1st December 1916, is my 20th birthday.

Chapter 2.I

So many memories have faded over time and then, perhaps irreparably, have been lost. Some of them have passed the test of time, however, and still remain alive in me. Among these, a memory that dates back to childhood stands out. It has often resurfaced in the forefront of my mind and influenced a part of my life on several occasions.
It was one of those typical summer afternoons when the air is still and everything seems suspended and motionless. Except the lively mind of a child, who in those moments is finally free to explore the most secret areas of the house, that of his grandparents.
Grandmother's slow and regular breathing, coming from the bedroom, was the much-awaited signal to begin the exploration planned for that day: the dark recesses of the basement. Leaving my coloured pencils on the table next to the drawing in progress, a battle between cowboys and Indians, I noiselessly opened the door, crossed the small terrace, descended four steps, turned left and went down the grassy slope leading to the back of the house where my objective was located.
The room was full of furniture, chairs, knick-knacks, lamps, boxes and unknown objects. Dust and cobwebs reigned supreme. The typical smell of old things hovered, a mixture of mold and humidity, which in this case instead of deflecting my curiosity, only increased it. I timidly opened a few cupboards, then a few drawers, without finding anything interesting.
Until my attention fell on a well-worn brown suitcase. After having placed it with some difficulty on the floor, with great ease I snapped open the two locks and lifted the lid.

Suddenly a whirlwind of light arose from that suitcase, dazzling my eyes, enveloping me and leaving me a little stunned. At least this is what my mind has established for me for that moment, admirably mixing facts with feelings.
In front of me was that indistinct something that I had hoped to find and that I was now actually seeing: a military uniform!
A beautiful one, with many golden buttons.
In my eyes it could only be the uniform of a general.

The sudden pride of being the grandson of a high-ranking officer immediately clashed with something equally unexpected and a bit disturbing.
Under that shiny uniform lay another, very rough and modest, grey-green in colour.
This couldn't have been the uniform of a general. I didn't understand how those two different uniforms could live together in the same suitcase.
The only interesting element of the "poor" uniform was a badge sewn on one of the two sleeves. It depicted a short, black sword surrounded by black floral decorations.
Fortunately, my perplexity was swept away by another discovery: a red plastic bag in one of the inside pockets of the suitcase. It contained several medals, some round and others in the shape of a cross, some silver and some dark, with beautiful coloured ribbons.
My pride could take flight once more at the thought that grandfather Pietro had been a hero, since he had earned so many medals.
There were also old yellowed sheets of paper full of writing, some printed and others written by hand. But I didn't know how to read well yet and they didn't interest me anyway.
In the side pocket there was another envelope, tied with string. It was heavy and to the touch it seemed full of other papers, so it wasn't worth opening. There was nothing else.
As I closed the suitcase, I felt that something had changed in me. I had discovered that I was the grandson of an Italian army commander, a highly decorated war hero.
Only one thing eluded me: the reason why that ugly gray-green uniform had been kept together with the other memorabilia.

Chapter 3.I

Yesterday our operation went better than expected.
Mainly because I saved my *ghirba* again.[2]
We moved before dawn. There was no moon, but the ground was illuminated by the reflections of the snow. Our dark shapes could be seen as we crawled through the rocks. This was my fear. But they didn't see us. So, taking advantage of the surprise, we stormed and conquered an enemy outpost without suffering losses. We captured two *Landesschützen.*[3]
We had to kill two of them, because they fought back. We had to use force to block one of ours, a Sicilian, nicknamed *Cuteddu*[4], who wanted to stab all of them with his bayonet. He lost two brothers on the Isonzo front and all opportunities are good for him to avenge them. Our sergeant, also from Sicily, said something to him in dialect and then he calmed down.
We tied up the two *mucs*[5] with a rope and then we divided the chocolate, spirits and cigarettes which we found on the spot. The bread was black and uneatable. Several times we responded to the enemy fire, which came from a nearby location. We used their rifles, to spare our cartridges. Our rifles seem better to me, but their coats are warmer than ours and so we took them to warm up.
In doing so I found my birthday present. In the inside pocket of the overcoat of one of the two dead soldiers there was a small notebook with a new pencil. He had written something on the first page, but his diary was finished before it started. Luckily my story continues.

---

[2] *Ghirba*, from the Arabic *qirba*, kirbeh in English, is a leather bag used for carrying water by African tribes. The word was brought to Italy by the Italian soldiers who fought the African War of 1895-96 and the Italian-Turkish war of 1911-12. It has remained in military language both to indicate the leather bag itself and to allude to human skin, as a metaphor for life.

[3] "Country shooters". They were a light infantry corps of Austrian mountain troops. As a rule, their men were enlisted only from Tyrol and Vorarlberg. On the left side of their caps was a tuft of black-and-white grouse feathers. When Italy declared war on Austria, these troops were moved from the Russian front to the Italian front in Lombardy, Trentino and Veneto. After 16th January 1917 they were renamed *Kaiserschützen*.

[4] It means knife in the Sicilian dialect.

[5] Literally it means billy goat. It is a derogatory term used in Friuli and Northern Veneto to indicate the Austrians.

Now I have many pages to write on.
When darkness fell, I and another soldier were ordered to bring the two prisoners down for interrogation. We were also supposed to ask for a machine gun to take up there to strengthen our position. The *mucs* will soon try to retake this piece of land.
I learned a bit of German while working with my father on construction sites in Switzerland. So I gave the two prisoners orders in their own language. They were amazed and my comrades were surprised, too.
I have shot at the Austrians many times, but this is the first time since the beginning of the war that I have spoken to them.
One was young, perhaps my age. The other was much older, in his forties. Both wore large, up-curving mustaches. The older man had a pissed-off look, perhaps he was thinking about running away at the first opportunity.
I told them I would shoot if anyone tried to sneak away.
The young man had a more resigned look. In a low voice he asked me where I was from, since I spoke his language. He comes from Mauthen[6].
I was about to reply that I come from a village not far from Mauthen in the *Canal del Ferro*[7], but the sergeant gave me a look as if he wanted to twist my warranty card[8] so I immediately shut up. We're not supposed to fraternize with the enemy. It is strictly prohibited.
Around 10:00 p.m. we went down with the two prisoners.
While I kept them within range of my '91[9], I thought about how strange this war is. When I hear some of my comrades talking, especially those from the south, I understand nothing. I understand a lot more when the enemy soldiers speak, especially since they only live a couple of kilometres from my village.
We handed the two *mucs* over to the lieutenant, who congratulated us on the success of the operation. He made a note of the due compensation which we will divide in equal parts: four rifles are worth 8 cents, while two prisoners make 20 cents. Then he took them to the captain of our company.
After, I never saw them again. For them the war is over.
I envy them a little.
For us, instead, the war goes on and it is not clear yet for how long.

---

[6] Kötschach-Mauthen is a town in Carinthia near the border with Italy.

[7] The Canal del Ferro is a rugged and narrow mountain valley in the province of Udine crossed by the river Fella, which separates the Carnic Alps from the Julian Alps.

[8] Military slang for harsh rebuke.

[9] The Carcano-Mannlicher Model 1891 rifle was adopted by the Italian army in 1892 to replace the Vetterli-Vitali after extensive design and testing work.

At the beginning of the year everyone thought it would end by summer.
But that did not happen.
Indeed, in August Italy declared war on Germany as well.
Many soldiers of my regiment are tired of fighting.
They want to go back to their villages.
Many of them have wives and children.
Most of them are farmers and want to go home to work the land.
We hope to end it by next spring.

CHAPTER 4.I

After my discovery that afternoon I stopped sketching fights between cowboys and Indians and began filling the pages of my notebooks with intricate battles between contemporary soldiers of unidentified armies.
I narrated the stories out loud as I drew them.
Rather than a story, though, I gave voice to a succession of onomatopoeic sounds: shotgun blasts, bomb explosions, cannon thunder and the moans of wounded soldiers.
This was how I spent most of my time at my paternal grandmother's house. Her name was Irma. My parents had decided to leave me with her that summer, perhaps to keep her company after my grandfather's death, in December of the previous year.
He died at night, in his sleep, without a whimper.
They first met in Pontebba, on the Austrian border, and got married in August of 1922 in Enemonzo, my grandmother's village.
After he had his first heart attack, a few years before I was born, my grandfather changed a lot. So they said.
He didn't go up to the mountains anymore, but most of all he quit going hunting. As I found out later.
He was always peaceful and relaxed at home when we went to visit them. I remember him sitting on the sofa in a short tan velvet dressing gown. His graying hair was combed smoothly back and his twinkling dark eyes shone out of two diagonal fissures. He was always smiling.
He had been retired for some years, after having worked as station master in various places in Friuli.
He passed away a few days after turning sixty-seven on December 10, 1963. Unfortunately, too soon to be named Knight of the Military Order of Vittorio Veneto, a national order founded in 1968. He was there though, in Vittorio Veneto, during the famous October of 1918.

I remember that once grandfather Pieri (as they called him) came to visit us in Marghera, near Venice.
To my immense joy he took me to the Mestre amusement park and bought me cotton candy.
On his head he wore an old gray flat cap, like the ones Sicilians wore.

I wore my inseparable green hat with the bird feathers.
More indistinct is the memory of what I did there.
My mother says that when we got home, my grandfather complained a little about me saying: «Ce ch'al trai chel frut! No rivavi adore a fermâlu.»[10]
I had asked to shoot at the coloured balloons.
At first grandfather was probably proud of his first male grandson, who, although still quite little, already wanted to shoot. Soon his pride must have turned to surprise and then to concern, though. Once I had the gun in my hands, I didn't want to stop and I kept on shooting and shooting at all the balloons in the booth, running up the bill we owed the carny.

I don't know how and when this passion for rifles was born in me.
Maybe I sensed that I belonged to a family of hunters. Even at the age of two I almost always used to go around with a small wooden rifle on my shoulder. This is documented in numerous black-and-white photographs.

On the other hand, no one had a clue as to why I developed a great passion for drawing at a very young age.
No one in my family had ever demonstrated that talent.

It often happens that male sons resemble the mother's father and daughters resemble the father's mother.
I too respected that rule and therefore I looked like my maternal grandfather. Unfortunately, however, I was not able to verify it in person nor compare myself to him, albeit taking into account the difference in ages: grandfather Silvio passed away many years before my birth.
He had gone to work in East Africa in the hope of making a fortune.
Instead he contracted malaria.
He managed to return to Italy, just in time to expire in his homeland at the Udine hospital in July of 1937.
He was only twenty-eight years old.

[10] «How he shoots, that boy! I couldn't get him to stop» translation from the Friulan language.

CHAPTER 5.I

I have to report a tragedy that happened in the outpost we had recently conquered. The comrades defended it well for several days, mainly thanks to the machine gun we had taken up there.
The *magnasego* attacked several times.[11]
Then the weather got worse and they stopped.
For almost two consecutive days there was a snowstorm.
It was also difficult to take rations up there.
Then a weak sun came out and we expected a new attack.
There were ten men on defense.
At any moment we were expecting to hear our Fiat sing.[12]
Instead suddenly we heard a strange noise, like a bellow, deep and very long. It wasn't a *Schützen cannonade.*
Our position was engulfed in a huge avalanche of snow, which completely buried my comrades. Snow and stones rolled down to our trench at the bottom.
We all stayed quiet waiting for some sign of life.
But there was only a great silence.
Nobody survived. *Ducj muarts*.[13]
During this time of year, more soldiers die from avalanches than from Austrians. They were silent too. We didn't hear them laugh or sing. Maybe some of them had died too.
The mountain had given us a hard lesson.

---

[11] *Magnasego*, literally tallow eaters, is a derogatory nickname, originally from the Italian Risorgimento, used to indicate the Austrians, since they made extensive use of tallow, a yellowish fat obtained from cattle, horses and sheep, both in their cooking and to maintain the upward curve of their mustaches.
[12] The Fiat Mod.14 machine gun was by far the automatic weapon most used by the Italian Royal Army in the Great War.
[13] "All dead" translation from the Friulan language.

CHAPTER 6.I

That summer, I returned to the dark room in the basement several times to take another look at my grandfather's medals and uniforms, but mostly to look for what certainly had to be kept somewhere and what was even more interesting for me: the weapons.
I rummaged almost everywhere, being careful not to get my clothes dirty.
It would have been difficult to explain it to grandmother.
I remember finding some unexpected things: an old typewriter, a telescope similar to the ones used by pirates, a golden trumpet and a big accordion.
Did anyone play in the family?
I found lots of books, some beautiful with black and white photographs of soldiers. However, to my disappointment, I didn't find what I was looking for. They had to be hidden somewhere.
I was almost sure they were in a wooden crate, which I hadn't opened yet.
It was blocked by some heavy pieces of furniture, which I could not move.
If they weren't there, they could only be in the attic.
Unfortunately, I had no way of getting up there alone.
I would have to take advantage of my friendship with Mr. Ugo, an elderly gentleman who lived on the second floor of the house together with his daughter Eva.
He liked me and I liked him.
I often met him when he came down to work in the garden and to feed his chickens and rabbits.
Poor things.
Occasionally I witnessed the killing of one of them: a twist of the neck for the hens, a blow on the head for the rabbits.
For Mr. Ugo it was quite natural for a child to witness such scenes, which he performed with extreme ease and in a didactic manner.
Just as naturally, he taught me how to drown "las pantianes" in a tub full of water. These were big mice that he captured by means of a trap, a cage with iron bars, methodically placed every evening in front of a hole in the garden. They died in the water and were then thrown into the fire, along with weeds and dry branches.
Thus the cycle of life was completed: earth, water, fire, air.

Mr. Ugo also grew silkworms in the attic.
It was only natural for me to demonstrate my curiosity for those strange creatures. I admit that it was really interesting to see how eagerly they munched on their mulberry leaves.
I must confess, however, that while Mr. Ugo was explaining the functioning of his strange hobby to me, my gaze was much more interested in studying the surroundings in order to figure out where the objects of my desire might be kept.
There was a world to explore in that attic.

CHAPTER 7.I

Our days were exhausting. We had to continually shovel snow to keep the path to our lower rear lines open and to keep our trenches clean.
At any rate snow is better than rain, which turns the trench into mud. It is very cold up here in the mountains, but at least there isn't the terrible stench of the Karst trenches and there aren't any mice. Some places are so filled with mice that you can hardly sleep because of them walking on you and even biting you. Besides, you can catch bad diseases. I learned that entire companies have been decimated by cholera[14]. However, we have fleas here too, which gives us a great hobby: picking them off.
Many soldiers are out of sorts and complaining, also because for a few weeks now they've reduced our rations of bread and meat.[15]
And not only that.
Our Command is also slow in relieving us from the line. This makes us nervous and impatient, because we are all due for a leave.
I have been away from home for over a year and I want to see my mother, my father, my brothers and sisters and my friends from the village, at least those who have not been displaced or gone to war. I hope to see my brother Noè for at least a few days. He was born in 1899. If the war does not end, his age class will be mobilized next year. I'd like to give him some advice. I hope they don't send him to the Isonzo front, because it's far more dangerous than here. It's a *beccheria.*[16]
After every battle there are thousands of dead and injured.[17]
Last June on the San Michele the Austrians launched asphyxiating gas against our trenches. Then the cruel barbarians of the *Honvéd* murdered our soldiers, either dying or just passed out, with iron clubs.[18]

---

[14] There were over 16,000 cases of cholera, most in 1915, with more than 4,300 deaths.
[15] In December 1916 the daily ration went from 750 to 600 grams of bread and from 375 to 250 grams of meat. This was not only due to difficulties in the supply chain, but also to the advice of some physiologists, who believed that the ration was too rich in protein and therefore too "luxurious".
[16] Dialectal word for a slaughterhouse.
[17] At the time, 9 major battles had already been fought, the so-called "shoulder shoves", with a very high number of casualties, but little territorial gain.
[18] Hungarian Royal Honvéd was the National Army of Hungary. The word *honvéd* means "defender of the homeland".

We will never forgive them for that. At the cost of losing our reward, we will no longer take Hungarians prisoner.
The High Command has also ordered that anyone found with an iron club in hand will be shot on the spot.[19]
I have many things to tell Noè. Things that other members of the family are better off not hearing. In my letters home I have always written that I am well and that I am in a fairly quiet area. I don't want them to worry.
Even our captain told us that we shouldn't say anything at home or reveal in which area our Regiment is located.
But how can you not say anything? They'll ask me a lot of questions.
Of course, it is better not to tell what I have seen and suffered in recent months. Either they wouldn't believe it, or they wouldn't be able to sleep anymore from worrying.
For sure I will tell them what happened today.
This morning I was called by the lieutenant of the 1st company. He comes from Valle d'Aosta and is a hunter like me. With his binoculars he had spotted a chamois. It seems there were quite a few in this area before the war. Then they migrated to quieter mountains.
It was an opportunity not to be missed. We could integrate our meat ration somewhat and have a little distraction, returning to our mutual passion for a few hours. With the captain's authorization, we went out to track that chamois and shoot it down.
We moved toward the rocky ridge where he had seen it.
We hoped it hadn't gone too far into the area controlled by the *mucs*.
We made our way with difficulty for about an hour.
We often had to crawl in the snow to prevent the enemy from seeing us.
Then, finally, we spotted our prey climbing among the rocks. It was alone.
That chamois looked like a beautiful specimen, even if it certainly weighed less than forty kilos. But it was too far away to try and shoot. In fact, we still couldn't see its eye clearly. We crept on until we were about two hundred and fifty metres away. At that point we knelt and got ready to shoot.
The shot was already in the barrel, as it always is when you go on patrol.
The lieutenant had the first shot.
If he didn't kill the chamois instantly, I was to shoot it right away.

---

[19] A circular issued by the General Staff on 13th August 1916 ordered that any enemy caught killing *"our wounded or unconscious soldiers by means of spiked clubs"* was to be shot on the spot. It must be said that the iron clubs for hand-to-hand combat in the trenches were already in use on the western front on both sides. Even entrenching tools, such as digging spades, however, were used in brutal close-quarter combat.

The chamois was up higher than we were, so we had to evaluate the trajectory well, so as to hit it right above its shoulder. That was difficult because it was very windy and we didn't have our own hunting rifles.
By now we had become rather skilled with the '91, but we had never attempted precision shooting.
We took aim with great care.
We were only waiting for the animal to stop for a moment to pull the trigger. A shot is much more effective and deadly when the muscles are relaxed than when they are tensed in the effort of the climb.
Suddenly the chamois stumbled slightly and we saw a cloud of smoke puff out of its chest. It dropped like a stone.
The echo of the shot reached our ears a fraction of a second later.
We stared at each other, amazed because neither of us had fired.
We carefully scanned the whole area to figure out from where that perfect shot had been fired and who had done it.
Nobody was in sight.
Then from a snowdrift above us, a figure dressed in white stood up. In his hand he held a rifle with a telescope. He looked at us, but he didn't point his weapon at us. He was a *Scharfschützen*, an Austrian sniper. We call them *cecchini*[20]. They are very dangerous. They blend into the environment and shoot at us from concealed positions with their high-precision rifles. They are capable of waiting hours for a soldier to appear in their high-magnification optics. And they infallibly shoot him dead. Their shots are always fatal, like the one which killed our chamois.
The lieutenant took off his helmet with a nod and so did I. The Austrian returned our greeting. Surely, he must either be a hunter or a gamekeeper.
He could have killed us both. Not just at that moment, but even more easily as we were approaching our prey. He spared us instead. Maybe he considered us to be his kind.
Immediately afterwards, two Austrian soldiers came out and headed towards the dead chamois. It was surely a nice addition to the *mucs'* chow today. Perhaps their high commanders, too, have decided to cut food rations. We sat down to smoke a cigarette. The sniper watched the recovery operation while smoking his pipe.
When they left with their prey, we walked back to our positions, in silence.
We returned without the chamois meat, but with our skins still intact.

---

[20] The word derives from Cecco Beppe, nickname that was given to the hated Francis Joseph I (18 August 1830 - 21 November 1916), emperor of Austria and King of Hungary. He had passed away a few days earlier, having reigned for nearly fifty years.

Chapter 8.I

I used the excuse of the silkworms to go up to the attic several times in the company of Mr. Ugo.
Until one day I decided to go up alone. The door was never locked. I still remember how excited I was on that summer afternoon. I was free to explore that new world, which promised incredible discoveries. There was so much stuff piled up that I didn't know where to start. I finally decided to start where there was more light.
The attic was high in the centre and sloping at the sides, where numerous windows opened more or less at floor level.
I don't know exactly at what point in my search the silkworms, in their tireless ruminations, saw my dreamy face as I opened the chest of wonders.
It was what I was looking for. Indeed, to tell the truth, it was much more than what I had hoped to find. Indeed, to tell the whole truth, it was something that I couldn't have even imagined finding.
As soon as I lifted the lid of the trunk, two visored caps resting on an old blanket appeared. The first was made of a gray fabric similar to the beautiful uniform I had found in the suitcase in the basement. The other was bright red, which to my eyes gave it a decidedly higher value. Of course, I immediately put the red one in my head (I had a passion for headgear) and continued the exploration, in spite of having my sight somewhat impaired by a cap much too large for me. Under the blanket there were many other surprises, starting with a large circular shield in black leather, with several engravings on the front.
A shield?
I didn't understand what a shield had to do with my grandfather.
Italian soldiers didn't carry shields.
Medieval warriors had shields, but they were very different.
I didn't understand.
Under the shield, however, there was much more: a dagger with a silver handle in a leather sheath and a long knife curved like a scimitar.
Saracen pirate weapons, probably.
The mystery grew deeper and deeper in my mind.
What did these things have to do with my grandfather?
And what about the two long rusty spearheads?

The coup de grace, however, lay in the bottom of the trunk, wrapped in a long piece of thick and wrinkled brown paper.
From the shape I immediately understood what it was.
I was beside myself with emotion.
I slowly unrolled it, until it re-emerged in all its fascination.
When I saw it, I thrown for a loop, a bit for the excitement of the discovery, but also for the lack of any clear link among all these weapons.
It was a rifle.
It was a Winchester.
It was Tex Willer's rifle and he was my favorite comic book hero!
That afternoon, some silkworms going about their business in the attic of a house in a small village in Friuli, saw a little boy beaming from ear to ear, in a red cap much too big for him, his head full of questions.
They heard him make shooting noises while pointing a Winchester rifle in all directions.

CHAPTER 9.I

San Cambio has finally arrived and we went back down to our rear for the long awaited *Santa Licenza*.[21]

After so many days in the trenches, sleeping on a cot and in a heated barrack is the most beautiful thing in the world. Just like wearing clean, dry clothing and walking between quarters with no fear of someone shooting you or throwing a grenade at you.

There is a lot going on. We are about to go home for our much-desired winter leave. We work with brush and comb. Some men are busy shaving, some are washing and removing lice, others are preparing their backpacks, still others are queuing up to get visa stamps on their travel papers or to get their hair cut by the *tosacani*.[22]

Those who are not leaving stay on the sidelines, letting the others get on with it, watching the preparations with envy. Their turn will come soon. It is only a matter of days.

As if by unspoken agreement, the war stops at this time of year. No major operations are planned. There are only a few desultory rifle fire skirmishes and a few cannon shots just to make it clear that everyone is monitoring the positions gained in the previous months.

When the war broke out in May 1914 we should have sided with the central empires, Austria-Hungary and Germany.

Italy had been allied with them for many years.

Instead we remained neutral.

The newspapers said the war would end in a few months. Things went differently. So differently, that a year later not only was the conflict still going on, but Italy had actually declared war on Austria-Hungary.

At that time, I was working on a construction site in Sankt Gallen in Switzerland. We Italians already were already seen in a bad light.

Even more after 24th May 1915.

The newspapers said that thanks to Italy's entry into the war, the conflict would resolve itself in a few months.

Four months later, however, I received a telegram from home.

---

[21] It was an ironic way to allude to the troop change in the frontline for a rest or a leave.

[22] Slang word for barber. It literally means dog shearers.

It said that I had to present myself to the military district of Udine, since my class, 1896, had been mobilized[23]. If I didn't go, I would be declared a deserter and punished by the Military Tribunal.
Washed, shaved and with hair cut short, on September 23rd, 1915, I had the medical examination.[24]
As I was of good constitution, healthy and unmarried, I was declared able and enlisted as a private 1st class.
Married and older men are in other categories.[25]
I thought they would send me to the mountain infantry, the Alpini[26], since I come from a mountain village. Instead, I was assigned to the 57th Infantry Regiment, 15th Division, "Abruzzi" Brigade, 5th Corps, located in Verona.
By early December I was already marching and practicing riflery (with sticks, since there was a shortage of rifles).
On March 25th, 1916, I finished training with the rank of corporal.
On April 1st, I arrived in territory in a state of war, the name of the village was Ala, about fifteen kilometres south of Rovereto, on the banks of the Adige river. I was part of the Reserves (Marche Battalion) of the 57th Regiment, commanded by Lieutenant. Gorbin.
This time we had real rifles, with bullets and bayonets.
On May 1st I was transferred to the "Taro" Brigade, 207th Infantry Regiment, 2nd company, commanded by Captain Fiore.[27]
Battalion commander was Major Binacchi.
The regimental commander was Colonel Danioni.
The commander of the Brigade was Colonel Brigadier Gualtieri.
Our job was to defend the left subsector Adige.
We were forced to do it almost immediately.
On May 15th there was a prolonged bombardment and immediately afterwards the Austrians attacked our lines in force.
We fought until July, when the offensive was blocked.[28]

---

[23] Over 5 million men belonging to 19 classes according to their year of birth, from 1881 to 1900, were enrolled in the Italian Royal Army throughout the war.

[24] The military letter specified that *"By orders of the high command, recruits must present themselves promptly, washed, with hair cut short and clean shaven"*.

[25] Men from 18 to 25 years of age were assigned to the permanent army, those from 26 to 29 to the reserves (mobile militia), those from 30 to 36 to the territorial militia.

[26] The Alpini are the Italian Army's special mountain infantry. Established in 1872, they are the oldest active mountain infantry in the world. During World War I the 26 peacetime battalions were increased by 62 battalions.

[27] The "Taro" Brigade was formed on April 6, 1916 with the 207th and 208th Regiments.

[28] Known as the "Battle of the Highlands" or *Strafexpedition*, a punitive offensive against Italy, a former ally accused of treachery, it was fought between 15 May and 27 June 1916.

I don't think I'll ever be able to reconstruct the events of those days.
Too many things were happening and there was too much confusion.
The sequence of attacks, retreats and counterattacks is no longer clear in my mind. My eyes still remember so many horrible scenes, however.
And as I saw them, death brushed by me in continuation.
I had never seen a man die violently before, except for a bricklayer who fell from a scaffold in Switzerland. In those days I saw scores of men die near me and in atrocious ways. Furthermore, in order to survive we had to kill. Sometimes even stab enemies with our bayonets.
Everyone was screaming, the living like wild animals, the dying like wounded animals. Amidst the screams, blasphemies were mixed with prayers to God, to the Virgin Mary and to our mothers.
I don't know if it is right to write these things down.
If I survive, I certainly won't need to reread these notes to remember the horrors I saw with my own eyes. In fact, I wish I could forget them. But I fear it will be impossible for me.

Now I just want to think about my leave.
I'm happy, but I'm kind of worried about the trip and the return home.
Most of the other soldiers can leave the war zone to go home. There are those who go to the regions of the Po Valley, others to central Italy and still others to the South. I, instead, first leave the front, going through Verona, Padua and Mestre. But then I have to re-enter the war zone.
I have to go to Udine, where the High Command of the Italian Royal Army is located. From there I'll have to go up to Gemona, Stazione della Carnia, Chiusa Forte and then finally to my village, Dogna[29]. The whole area is full of soldiers, because the border with Austria is very close.

Strongly promoted by Franz Conrad von Hötzendorf (11 November 1852-25 August 1925), Chief of Staff of the Austro-Hungarian army, it caused over 230,000 human losses. But this number is clearly incomplete. As for the 207th Regiment, it lost 9 officers dead and 41 missing, 82 dead in the ranks and 2,061 missing. Even if the offensive was blocked and disaster almost miraculously avoided, this battle provoked a serious political crisis in the Italian government. In addition, on the popular level, the psychosis of an enemy invasion was widespread and the deaths by execution of some of the most illustrious personalities of Irredentism, such as Cesare Battisti, Damiano Chiesa, Fabio Filzi and Nazario Sauro, caused a great sensation. The life and death of these figures, as well as that of Enrico Toti, inspired many of the recruitment campaigns and much of the propaganda literature of the following period.

[29] Dogna was the first village of a certain size that one encountered after crossing the Austrian border. In 1915 it had over 1,300 inhabitants, scattered among the various hamlets. Due to emigration, one hundred years later, there are fewer than 200.

In Val Dogna, instead of the old mule track, the Military Engineers have built a road to transport the artillery pieces. They've built tunnels, rest areas, shelters and installed a cableway.
In Dogna itself, at the beginning of the war, the Artillery installed two 305 mm howitzers to bomb Fort Hensel in Malborghetto. It seems that General Cadorna himself fired the first shot in early June 1915.
It took months of bombing and thousands of shells to destroy that Fort.
The howitzers' aim was guided by our observers on the ridges of the Due Pizzi and the Jôf of Miezegnot, where I used to go hunting.
The bells of Dogna always ring before firing starts.
It is a warning to the villagers, who open their windows to prevent the glass from shattering due to the air displacement.
All the houses in the village, including ours, quarter troops.
Many villagers preferred to leave as soon as the war broke out.
Even more left after an Austrian bombing raid.
They were trying to destroy our howitzers.
Instead, they hit homes causing a death and several injuries.
My family has decided to stay. Luckily our house is shielded from the enemy artillery fire, since it is located close to the mountain, one kilometre before Dogna, in a hamlet called Vidali.
Never would I have imagined that the places where I played as a child and where I went hunting as a boy would one day be a theater of war.

Chapter 10.I

After my incredible discoveries in the attic, my sketchbook began to fill up with improbable battles. Indians fighting pirates, modern soldiers machine gunning medieval knights, cowboys shooting at just about everyone.
To my eyes those strange mixtures had become absolutely legitimate.
My grandmother paid no attention to this sudden change of scenario but smiled good-naturedly on seeing my drawings and hearing my live commentary while I created them.
I don't remember if I ever asked her to tell me about when grandpa was a soldier. At the time I was unaware that he had fought in the First World War and that in the Second World War his first-born son, my father, had had to fight as well.
If I did, her answer didn't make much of an impression on me.
In either case, I really regret it today.
On the contrary I remember that one day my grandmother gave me a rag puppet, which she had made from the fabric of the sofa.
She had dressed it in a blue shirt and black knitted trousers.
From that moment on, my paper battles suddenly spread to the entire house, with the puppet playing all the parts: attacking and being attacked, shooting and being shot, hiding and being flushed out. I, simultaneously, was director, screenwriter and puppeteer. In the battles on the sofa, however, the puppet had only one role: to take my punches and fly from one arm to another.
I still preserve that puppet like a relic. It still holds the scent of my grandmother, of that house and of my childhood.
I remember too that on the days it rained I left the puppet on the sofa and became the sole hero of my stories.
I would leave the house and, hugging the walls, defy the bullets, or rather the raindrops falling from the eaves. If a drop hit me, I pretended I was wounded or even killed, depending on where my shirt became darker, and with a moan I would fall to the ground. I had become an excellent stuntman. The game inevitably ended when my whole shirt was wet. I preferred blue shirts, because you could better see where the shot had hit.

CHAPTER 11.I

I'm here in Udine waiting for a troop train to Carnia.
Up till now my journey has been unpleasant for many reasons.
We arrived at the Verona railway station on board a truck. Then everyone tried to take a train home. There was a terrible ruckus with hundreds of soldiers trying to get on or off the trains. You could see insignia of every colour from every regiment of our army, smells and dialects of all sorts, like a great Babel. There were also some scuffles between soldiers going home and others returning to the front, although the mass of bodies being pushed in different directions stopped them as soon as they broke out.
Pushing our way through, we finally got on the troop train to Padua. Our car was full of Venetian and Friulan soldiers returning from the Trentino front. More than once the Carabinieri[30] came by to check our travel documents. Some soldiers had to get off because they didn't have all the stamps and signatures needed to go on leave. Poor devils. Who knows if they can get home?
"Caproni" are never very popular among us soldiers.[31]
While we are risking our *ghirba* in the trenches, they are standing behind us with their rifles pointed, in case someone should refuse to fight. There are also plenty of them in the rear lines ready to check up on us and make things difficult when we return from the front. [32]
In Padua the train stopped. Since the next one would leave in a few hours we decided to go and visit the city centre. After so many months in the mountains we needed it.

---

[30] Inspired by the French Gendarmerie, the Carabinieri were created by King Victor Emmanuel I of Savoy with the aim of providing the Kingdom of Sardinia with a police corp.
[31] Due to the particular shape of their hats the Carabinieri were called "Airplanes" or "Caproni". This was the name of a famous Italian aircraft manufacturer, but literally it means big goats.
[32] The Military Penal Code was dated 1870. It provided for special powers, which were accentuated in wartime. In the case of trial, it was structured to demonstrate the guilt of the accused (inquisitory system), rather than ascertaining it (accusatory system). According to official statistics, declaredly incomplete, between 1915-18 the military courts pronounced over 3,600 death sentences, of which 750 were carried out, 311 not carried out, and 2,967 in absentia. Note that the death penalty was completely abolished by the Military Penal Code of war only in 1996.

It would have been much better had we stayed in the station!
We thought we would find a sober atmosphere and few people around, since we were at war. Instead the streets were crowded with people walking busily or strolling happily. Bars and cafes were full of men and women joking and laughing. There was even a queue to enter a theater!
I wasn't expecting it. Nor were the other soldiers with me.
Even worse was the number of men our age in civilian clothes that we saw.
We found out that not only are there *imboscati* in the army, such as those in the rear lines and offices. Padua is full of civilian *imboscati*.[33]
We are fighting in the trenches while they are enjoying themselves in the city! It was like a punch in the stomach. A healthy rain of punches was about to hit the face of one dandy in a café, who asked us impertinently: «*Ałòra, soldai, ve movè a vìnsar 'sta guèra?*».[34]
We had to stop a comrade from Treviso just in time from beating him up.
Every one of us would have gladly slapped that rotten *imboscato*, but just then we saw two *"Airplanes"* passing by.
From some other soldiers we met in another bar, we learned that we are not allowed sit at the tables outside, nor walk around with a woman at our side unless she is our mother, sister or wife.
Orders from higher up. Military discipline and demeanor in wartime.
But… why does it have to apply only to us?
We went back to the railway station with downcast faces.
We did not presume to be welcomed like heroes, but we did not expect people to ignore what is happening at the front and the sacrifices we are making for Italy and therefore for them as well.
Don't they read the war bulletins in the newspapers?
The clamor of those bars clashes badly with the sounds of fighting.
The sight of people strolling around the city offends the images of the dead and wounded imprinted on our eyes.
During the journey to Udine I noticed that many men had changed their expression and become serious. The joy of returning was gone. I'm sure you could see that change in my face, too.

---

[33] A derogatory term that literally means "hidden in the woods". It indicates both men who manage to be exempted from military service as well as enlisted men who manage to avoid being sent to the front, staying safe in the rear, hidden in offices, services or factories. There were many other derogatory words for them, such as *Filugelli*, *Ginocchi vuoti*, *Ciclamini*, *Depilati*, *Salesiani*.

[34] «Well, soldiers, when are you going to get a move on and win this war?» translation from the Venetian dialect.

Since the outbreak of the war Udine has changed completely from the city I knew. From what as I saw today, the city has even changed in comparison to September of last year, when I came here for my military examination.
It has become the seat of our Chief-of-Staff, General Cadorna, and his High Command.[35]
The streets are teeming with military, especially officers and senior officers with their families. Around the city there are few soldiers like me with shabby uniforms and worn-out boots. Instead, we see many soldiers from service, engineering and cavalry units with immaculate uniforms and shiny shoes. All these people have only seen the frontline through binoculars.
All around them are large numbers of *imboscati* and people who trade with the army. A quartermaster traveling in our coach told us that many are getting rich thanks to the war. He called them "sharks". Seeing the abundance in the shop windows and the quality of the clothes on the bourgeoisie, I begin to believe it too.
Speaking of "business", we met some Alpini in a tavern and they told us that Udine is full of brothels. Actually, I have never seen so many beautiful and well-dressed women around.
The Alpini had tried to enter a bordello in the centre of town, one with a blue light, but they got chased away and told to go to the one of those with a red light in the suburbs. The blue-light ones were reserved for officers and troops stationed in Udine. In short, for the pomaded and perfumed *filugelli* and the sharks.
A couple Alpini tried to enter anyway, but the madam and her sidekick threatened to call the Carabinieri. The two soldiers gave up, cursing heavily, but promised to return after the war to settle the score.
If they come back alive.

---

[35] The King of Italy, Vittorio Emanuele III (11 November 1869 - 28 December 1947), was formally the commander-in-chief of the Italian army. In practice, the actual commander was General Luigi Cadorna. He was appointed to that role on 27th July 1914 on the recommendation of the king to replace General Alberto Pollio, who had died of a heart attack a few days earlier.

CHAPTER 12.I

My passion for drawing grew even greater during the next four or five years, as did my passion for weapons.
My drawings became much more elaborate and continued to be war-themed. As for weapons, they ranged from miniature guns to toy guns (I remember two beautiful silver Colt revolvers my father's brother brought me from the USA).
I also had a bow and arrows and even a crossbow.
Small red-and-green firecrackers were my bread and butter.
My cult object, however, remained the rifle. Just seeing one gave me a thrill. For this reason, I had asked my father many times to take me hunting with him. I was excited to imagine him firing at a hare or pheasant.
One day he finally succumbed to my requests and even let me fire a shot with his double-barrel shotgun. My joy had no bounds, until it was surpassed by the discovery of the dark power called rifle recoil. It almost left me flat on my back.
And the Winchester I had seen in the trunk in the old attic?
After the death of my grandmother Irma in February of '68, some of her furniture and other objects had been moved to my other grandmother's house, in a neighboring village called Artegna, and the rest to another house in a village that I had never heard of : Dogna.
My father used to take us to Artegna almost every weekend. Then he would go to the mountains or to hunt. My mother helped grandmother Adele, who had a bar called "Impero" in via Villa.
In addition to the bar, there was a great big private house with a garden and terraced vegetable beds. For us children, namely me, my sister and my two cousins, this represented an immense territory for play and exploration. Not to mention the enormous advantages of a good and generous grandmother who had a bar. Ice creams, candies, pastries, crisps, fruit juices and drinks of all kinds were always guaranteed and at hand.
What grandmother Adele earned, in part, we ate and drank.
She was happy to see us happy. And we tried to make her even happier.
It didn't take me long to discover that the Winchester, still wrapped in its strange wrinkled paper, had been placed on top of a wardrobe in one of the many rooms.

Occasionally, when I was alone, I would take it down, unwrap it and spend a few minutes just looking at it. I also learned to arm it, using its characteristic handle, and disarm it by holding the hammer with my thumb after pulling the trigger. Only once did I let it freely click.
Luckily it didn't go off. It was unloaded.
I remember finding the bullets later in a box inside a drawer.
All the other weapons, the shield and the suitcase with grandfather's military uniforms must have been moved to Dogna, since I didn't find them anywhere in the house in Artegna. Frankly, that stuff interested me much less than the rifle, which, to my delight, was within reach.
My dream, however, was to have a gun of my own (the wooden one didn't really satisfy me). I had already spotted one in a toy shop in the same street as the bar. It was a small air gun.
The few savings I had were not enough to buy it, though.
So, with a certain entrepreneurial spirit, I had decided to make some money in every possible way. Every day and several times a day I would check the pinball machine in the bar lounge. Sometimes I'd find some coins jammed inside, which I could release by giving it a good smack with my fist or a karate chop in the right place. Another source of income was the "charity draw" that I organized among the bar-goers. The prizes were odds and ends of all sorts, found in the least frequented rooms of the house. To improve the prize pool, I even included the surprises that I had removed from the fancy Easter eggs on display in the bar window and replaced with stones wrapped up in tinfoil. It would have been interesting to see the reaction of the children and their parents when they opened those chocolate eggs!
Grandmother's bar was very popular with the infantrymen from the Artegna barracks. To get money out of them, I also devised a special kind of target shooting game. With my Meccano construction kit, I built a kind of cableway, which, using a crank, allowed me to slide pears hanging from the cable from one side of the garden to the other. For ten lire per shot, the soldiers tried to hit them with the arrows of my crossbow. Whoever hit the pear had the right... to take it and eat it!
Thanks to all these initiatives, in the end I was able to self-finance the purchase of the much-desired rifle, despite the fact that my mother and grandmother were not very enthusiastic.
The first use of that rifle was quite elaborate. Using Pongo, a kind of plastic clay that can be modeled with your hands, I had created about twenty toy soldiers, which I lined up ten against ten in our large playroom.

I then armed the rifle by bending the barrel and inserting a small red rubber bullet, but not before adding talcum powder. It wouldn't have seemed right to me without the characteristic puff of smoke.
I would lie on the ground on the side of the first group of fighters and shoot at the others. I immediately checked to see if and where I had hit, all the time giving a play-to-play description of the whole action as if it were the commentary of a football game. The game ended when I had pulped the Pongo limbs of all the soldiers, which I then proceeded to recompose for the next battle.
Unfortunately, the fun with my air rifle did not last long.
One Friday afternoon, taking advantage of the bar's weekly closure, my cousin, four years younger, and I had the unhappy idea of shooting at people walking along the street. One shot for him and one for me.
We were shooting through the half-closed shutters of the billiard room.
We aimed at the ankles.
I have to say that those rubber bullets were completely harmless and the pain of the blow was comparable to a pinch. So my cousin had said, when I shot him in the stomach as a test!
We did not hit many passersby. The trajectories of our bullets were far from straight. Some passersby probably did feel something strike their legs but continued on.
The tragedy took place when my cousin hit an elderly gentleman on a bicycle who, out of the corner of his eye, saw the barrel of the rifle disappear behind the shutters. Like an angry buffalo, the man dumped his bike in the street and, armed with an umbrella, began to beat furiously against the bar door. At that point we were already upstairs, hiding in the room farthest from the theater of war.
My aunt remembers going downstairs to see what was going on and being almost knocked over by an enraged individual who was swearing and looking for revenge. Still unaware of the real dynamics of the situation, she started laughing at this strange state of affairs, with the result of infuriating him even more. At some point, my mother and grandmother also intervened in order to understand what the stranger was complaining about.
From our hiding place, after a time that seemed interminable to us, we finally heard silence return. Shortly thereafter, however, our names rang out in the imperative voices of our mothers.
I remember nothing of what followed.
I only know that the rifle was taken from me and I never saw it again.

Chapter 13.1

Vidali, Friday, 29 December 1916
I'm finally home! This morning at dawn I jumped off the truck that took me to Chiusa Forte and with wings on my heels I devoured the four kilometres that separated me from home.
I have travelled that road many times in all seasons. But never before has it taken me so little time to get there, despite the snow and the traffic of men and vehicles. My heart leapt when I saw my house in the distance, tall and gray and, thank God, still intact. It used to stand alone on the left side but now it is completely surrounded by military barracks and shrouded in the smoke coming out of the chimneys.
«I live here», I said to two Bersaglieri[36] during the short climb that leads to the open space in front of the entrance.
A second later I had to throw myself to one side to let a captain come running down, followed by his lieutenants. My mother had written to me that a portion of our house, the part where my grandparents once lived, was now occupied by a command of the Bersaglieri.
As I knocked on the wooden door, I feared that the rest of the house had also been occupied and my family evacuated.
I trembled at the thought that some adjutant would open.
«*Cui isal?*»[37] asked a female voice from behind the door.
What a relief to hear those words.
«*Sei jò, Pieri, vierç che puarte*»[38] I replied.
As if it had been a password, the right one, the door was thrown open.
A wave of heat enveloped me and then the arms of my sister Margherita.
I didn't even have time to kiss her cheeks before she had pulled me inside, closed the door and started screaming at the top of her voice:
«*Al è rivât! Vignêit jù!*»[39]

---

[36] The Bersaglieri are a special unit of the Italian Army's infantry corps, created on 18 June 1836 to serve in the Army of the Kingdom of Sardinia. They can be recognized by their distinctive wide-brimmed hats, decorated with long black grouse feathers, worn with the dress uniform. The feathers are also attached to their combat helmets.
[37] «Who is it?» translation from the Friulan language.
[38] «It's me, Pietro, open the door.»
[39] «He's here! Come down!»

As I put my backpack and rifle down and took off my cap and cape, I heard a great bustle coming from the rooms upstairs and then descending the wooden staircase. There were my brothers, Agostino and Girardo, and my other sisters, Amabile, Attilia and Lucia. There was also my nephew Mattia, Amabile's son, born in 1909, the same year as Lucia. They are the youngest members of the family. They are about eight years old. We call them Lusiute and Matiuti. How they've grown!
They all jumped on me to hug me, kiss me and ask me how I was, everybody except Lusiute. Maybe she didn't recognize me anymore. She hadn't seen me in over a year. When finally she came near me and I picked her up, she grimaced and turned her head away. I stank. I smelled of trench.
So I asked Margherita to prepare the washtub with hot water for a bath.
On the other hand, Matiuti was thrilled by the sight of my rifle.
While Margherita was preparing the tub, Amabile and Attilia began to tell me what has been happening all these months. They are older than I am. Amabile was born in 1887 and Attilia in 1889.
We had two other siblings between us, Alice Luigia born in '92 and Niccolò in '94, but they died at an early age.
Our father is fine, but after Christmas he returned to Switzerland to work and Noè went with him. Too bad because I had hoped to see them both.
«*Vûstu alc di mangjâ?*» asked a voice behind my back. It was our mother, who now appeared as if from nowhere. «*Lat e crostis di polente, si tu vûs*».[40] I embraced and kissed her with affection.
«*Fati viodi*»[41] she said.
I stood to attention near the kitchen window, where there is more light even in winter. With a serious look she looked me over from head to toe. She gave a nod of approval and then said «*Gjave fûr che ròibe, laviti e dopo ven a mangjâ.*»[42]
Then she went out to the barn to feed the animals.
Evidently, I smelled worse than they did.
What a wonderful feeling to immerse yourself once again in the old wooden tub full of boiling water and to savor the smell of soap. How nice it was just to lie there soaking, in peace, without any hurry and without being surrounded by soldiers making a racket or scuffling for a piece of soap.
How nice to know that in the other room a bowl of milk with polenta crusts and a family happy at my return were waiting for me.

---

[40] «Do you want something to eat? Milk and polenta crusts, if you want.»
[41] «Let me see you.»
[42] «Take off those clothes, wash yourself and come eat afterwards.»

"They will ask me a lot of questions" I thought.
That was the most difficult part.
While I was thinking about what to say and what not to say, I saw the curtain at the entrance to the room move slightly and the curious face of Matiuti appear. Behind him there was Lusiute. Maybe she wanted to make sure I was washing myself well. With my soapy hand I motioned them to approach the tub. I put a little foam on my nose to make them laugh. They laughed, amused. When they were quite near, I suddenly surprised them with a great splash of water, drenching them completely.
«*Batòcjos!*»[43] I yelled, while they ran the other way.
I had decided to say nothing about the bad things I had seen and experienced. I would only tell them funny and harmless things.
I savored the polenta crusts, while everyone around me looked at me in silence. Then I started to narrate.
I said that I am in a company of soldiers who come from many regions of the Kingdom of Italy. Few can read and write.
So I immediately became famous because I read aloud the news in the newspapers that arrive in the trenches. I also read aloud the books that are passed on to us, such as *I promessi Sposi*, *Ettore Fieramosca*, *La Disfida di Barletta*, *I fratelli Karamazov*. The most popular book, however, is *Mimì Bluette*. I'm sick of reading it. I'd rather read my own novels by Salgari and Verne. Many soldiers ask me to write letters and postcards to their families, which someone else at home will read to them. I must also read the letters that come from their families, which are surely written for them by someone else.
It is a real chore every day, but at least this way I pass the time when am not busy on sentry duty, or handing out rations, or digging and arranging the trenches and so on.
It is not easy at all. Many soldiers speak only dialects and I don't understand them. Over time, however, I have learned a few words.
I have said some very strange ones, such as *pruvulazzu*, *alluccunutu*, *scafuniari*, *arriscigghersi*, *cufecchia* and *fetecchia*.
Every word makes them laugh and they try to guess the meaning but always get it wrong. They were only able to guess *cerasa* because it looks a lot like our *cjariesie*, or cherry.
In my platoon everyone has a nickname. I have two. They call me both *o' Professore* and *o' Scrittore*[44], even if I only finished elementary school.

[43] A good-natured way to say fool in Friulan language.
[44] The Professor and the Writer.

But for this job of scribbling I am respected almost more than the officers, even if I am only a corporal.
So I took the opportunity to say to all my brothers: «Do you see how useful it is to study and learn to read and write?»
«*Tros mucs âstu copât?*»[45] Agostino asked me point-blank, hoping to hear me say a large number.
«*Tros, tros?*»[46] Girardo insisted, followed closely by little Mattia.
«*Dîs mil*»[47] I replied, thinking that, by exaggerating, I would stop a topic I didn't want to talk about.
«*Mai avonde*»[48] said Agostino, shaking his head, while Girardo and Matiuti seemed satisfied.
My sisters, on the other hand, looked at me with disbelief.
In the village we have never had much sympathy for the *mucs*, but neither have we hated them.
If anything, we feel more antipathy toward *"chei di Sclûse"*.[49]
We feel that we belong to Dogna even if our house is in the municipality of Chiusa Forte. The stream behind the house, Rio Fornace, acts as a border.
I understand, though, that the upheavals of life brought on by the war, the bombings, the evacuation of the villagers and their relatives and the presence of soldiers everywhere have fed a grudge against them in a fifteen-year-old boy like Agostino.
To cut it short, I got up, gave him a benevolent pat on the head, mussing up his hair, and said I wanted to sleep in my bed again.
Margherita had already prepared it for me. I really needed to rest.
In the trenches you get used to sleeping during the day and keeping watch at night. Darkness is always dangerous.
Both we and the enemy always wait for darkness to fall to act.
My bed is in its usual place in the room on the second floor.
My books by Salgari and Verne are also in their places.
As for the bed, I had never found it so comfortable.
I didn't waste any time trying to find the most comfortable position.
I fell asleep immediately, while hearing muffled voices from below laughing and repeating the words *cufecchia* and *fetecchia*, again and again among themselves.

---

45 «How many Austrians did you kill?» translation from the Friulan language.
46 «How many? How many?»
47 «Ten thousand.»
48 «Never enough.»
49 "The villagers of Chiusa Forte".

Chapter 14.I

From the third to the fourth grade of primary school, my class, all male, changed teachers: from a gentle lady, slightly mustached, to an austere gentleman, always perfectly shaved.
He was tall and well built, with straight, very white hair always perfectly combed back. His voice did not match his appearance, but we were still afraid of him, both for his reputation as a very strict teacher and for the large gold ring set with a stone, which he wore on his finger.
It was said that he used it on the heads of unruly schoolchildren.
When he entered the classroom, we all had to leap to attention, as if he were a colonel and we were his troop.
We also wore uniforms, a blue jacket. I am sure it was he who taught us to sing our national anthem, the "Inno di Mameli".
In any case, he was an excellent teacher and we were a good class.
In fact, he never had to use his ring on our heads.
Perhaps, that might have been only a legend.
I will always remember what he assigned us to do in fifth grade: a research project with an exhibition at school on the First World War!
Fifty years had gone by since the end of that conflict.
Needless to say, that I was the one most excited by this, not so much for my love of history, but because it gave me an excellent excuse to sift through the attics and basements of relatives and acquaintances in Friuli in search of weapons and memorabilia.
Which I then did in a systematic and even a rather obsessive way, gathering up fragments of bombs, shrapnel, bullet casings, flasks, mess tins, shotgun barrels and so on.
All these objects seemed extremely interesting to me and worthy of being brought to the school exhibition. Luckily, I had had my tetanus shot, because the things were all very rusty.
With great regret I had to forego a German helmet which, nailed to a pole, was being used to empty the cesspool of a rural house. I consoled myself with an Italian "Adrian" helmet and the famous "Stahlhelm", the Austrian steel helmet with its characteristic side ventilation eyelets, which look like two small horns.

The best surprise came from a cousin of my grandmother, especially because it was totally unexpected. Struck by my enthusiasm, he pulled two swords with scabbards out of a closet and invited me to choose one.
I chose one and he gave it to me! They may not have had anything to do with the Great War, but I was happy all the same.
Needless to say, I was the pupil who, piece after piece, brought the most historical material for the exhibition, which was greatly appreciated by my teacher. The exhibition was inaugurated with great pomp and visited by the whole school, remaining installed in our classroom for almost the entire school year.
At the end of May, when the teacher decided it was time to dismantle it, I found myself having to lug home several kilos of rusty iron.
I don't know why, but instead of doing it a little at a time, I decided to do it all in one trip. I placed the two helmets one on top of the other on my head, I filled my schoolbag and the pockets of my trousers with metal fragments and shells, I carried two water bottles and a cartridge bag slung over my shoulder, I picked up the two gun barrels and, more encumbered than an infantrymen, I left for home with the sword sticking out from both sides of my schoolbag.
It was a hot sunny day.
I can only imagine the amazement of the school janitors and of the other people who saw that strange armored kid on the street. My mother, at the window, turned pale at seeing me arrive so loaded down with stuff.
I was drenched in sweat and distraught with fatigue, but proud to have accomplished a little act of heroism.
The next day I was in bed with a fever.

Chapter 15.I

Vidali, Friday 29, December 1916
A sudden and violent thunder yanked me from the sleep I was lost in.
I jumped up like a spring and tried to grab my helmet and rifle.
Panic engulfed me when I did not find them at my side.
At the same time, I was astonished to realize that I was warm and lying on something soft. By the second shot of a 305mm howitzer I finally realized that I was in my own room.
I got dressed quickly and with the roar of another *direttissimo*[50] I went down to the kitchen where the women were preparing dinner.
I had slept all day!
«*Minestron di fasui, polente e çuç, salam e sopis di cjaval come dolç. Vadie ben sior generâl?*»[51] the cooks announced with ladles in hand, to the joy of the kids, and mine too.
«*Nome vuei par festegjâ, però*»[52] our mother warned.
I smiled and sat down at the table.
Despite the joke I had played on her with the water and soap, Lusiute immediately came to sit on my lap. Now I didn't smell bad anymore.
After saying grace, we ate happily as our howitzers continued thundering, indifferent to the fact that somewhere in Austria their shells were perhaps destroying some families.
After dinner, when everyone else had gone to sleep, I was alone with my mother. She looked into my eyes with an intensity that I had rarely seen before. She let me understand that she imagined what I had suffered in those long months at the front and that she approved of my silence about the bad things.
Her gaze, however, was not enough to communicate what she wanted to say to me in words. She is worried about Noè. She is afraid that he too will be called up to the army next year and have to leave for the front.
I believe it is practically certain.

---

[50] Military slang to indicate the noise produced by a grenade similar to that of a big train rattling on the tracks.
[51] «Bean soup, polenta and cheese, salami and as a sweet, bread moistened in milk, fried and sugared. All right, mister general?» translation from the Friulan language.
[52] «Only today to celebrate, though.»

But I told her that Noè has always been lucky and that therefore the war will surely end sooner.
I don't think I convinced her.
She senses things.
However, after wishing me a good night, she seemed a little more relaxed.
Now I'm alone here in the kitchen writing these notes on my first day at home in a long time. I can still smell the good aroma of dinner, mixed with that of the Christmas tree.
Our howitzers are now silent.
The only sound is the crackle of the fire burning in the *spolert*.[53]

[53] A brick stove with a metal plate at the top, used for cooking and for heating water. It was common in the majority of houses in the north-east of Italy.

Chapter 16.1

The Great War exhibition also gave me the opportunity to ask a few questions about my grandfather.
Unfortunately, my father was unable to give me much information.
It seems that grandfather had always avoided talking about his "war efforts" (as they were called).
I pretended to be surprised when he told me that grandpa had been decorated with various medals. Of course, I remembered seeing them in the old suitcase together with the two uniforms. But I never told anyone.
Instead, I was greatly disappointed to discover that grandfather had not been a general and not even an officer during the First World War.
However, my father added something I did not know, underlining it with the facial expression and slightly trembling voice which he only used when he was exceptionally moved. Moments like that were very rare.
One was when he talked about the mountain climber Riccardo Cassin, or the conquest of K2 in 1954, in which his dear friend and best man Cirillo Floreanini had also participated.
So, with that mix of voice and facial expression my father revealed to me that «... grandpa was one of the Arditi.»
I had no idea what it meant but I sensed that it was very important. When he pronounced the word Arditi, I perceived an aura of respect and admiration hovering in the air, mixed with other things of an unspeakable nature.
Sensing my next question, my father completed the revelation with a phrase that left me stunned: «They attacked by throwing hand grenades and clenching daggers between their teeth.»
At that point I would have liked to know many other things, but the revelation stalled at that picturesque image, since grandfather had never wanted to tell anyone about his time in the war.
We only knew two things.
A few months after the end of the conflict he embarked for Libya, but the ship collided with a mine and almost sank, causing many deaths. Even if he came from the mountains, my grandfather knew how to swim and he saved one of his comrades, who did not know how to swim even though he came from a seaside resort, the island of Murano near Venice.

From that moment on, the two became as close as brothers, so much so that my father had often been a guest at the home of grandfather's comrade, in Murano.

The other story is that while they were waiting to embark on another ship for Libya, they chatted up a girl who worked in a bar there. Her relatives were not at all happy about this and so he and his comrades had to quickly decamp from that bar.

It seemed strange to me that these Arditi, so strong and bold, armed with daggers and hand grenades, had not dispatched that handful of relatives in seconds. I thought that the daggers and hand grenades must have sunk with the ship.

The other information about grandfather was related to the post-war period and therefore less interesting to me.

He had gone to work at the Italian Railways and climbed the career ladder until he became an esteemed stationmaster. In this capacity he worked in various stations in Friuli including Pontebba, Udine and, finally, Artegna.

The red cap, which I had imagined belonging to a general, was instead a stationmaster's cap.

When he retired, he moved to a nearby village, Magnano in Riviera, to the same house I had often visited as a child. I was even more interested in the fact that during the Second World War grandpa had been one of the few railroad men who had the courage to ride the trains on that line, in spite of the danger of bombardments.

There was no other relevant news, but by that time my curiosity had been quite satisfied. There was only one point left to clarify: the origin of the Winchester and, less importantly, the origin of the shield and the other bladed weapons.

Chapter 17.I

Vidali, Saturday, 30 December 1916
This morning I went out to take a look at the village. It was snowing.
I would have liked to take our hunting dogs. Unfortunately, they both are gone. They were used to rifle shots, but not to cannon shots. They got scared and ran away from home last year. They never came back. I'm so sorry. They were two very good dogs.
Outside there were groups of soldiers working to keep the road clear, as some trucks loaded with shells for our howitzers were expected.
The water of the Fella flowed quickly between its frozen banks, shining with an extraordinary turquoise.
I've always liked the colour of our river.
In the streets of Dogna I met only soldiers and no villagers.
I found the few who were around at the tavern. They were the old men of the village. When I opened the door, I saw everyone's eyes turn towards me through the thick smoke of their pipes and cigarettes. Compared to them, Yanez de Gomera is an amateur smoker.
I returned their attention with our typical greeting: «*Bundì a ducj.*»[54]
As I made my way to the counter, I heard the words «*Cui êse?*» and «*Cui ch'al è?*»[55] from among the tables.
I had been away for a long time and I was in uniform.
It was natural that they didn't recognize me right away.
Even the innkeeper, the old Vigjut[56], a giant despite the diminutive form of his name, looked me up and down, trying to understand who I was.
From a table finally someone asked: «*Setu Pieri, il fì di Matìe e di Perpetue?*»[57]
I turned around and after waiting a little while to answer I admitted with pride: «*Sei jò!*»
They all got up, some leaving their cards on the table, some their pipes, some an old newspaper.

---

[54] «Good morning everyone» translation from the Friulan language.
[55] Two different ways to ask «Who is it?»
[56] A diminutive of the Friulan name Vigj, equivalent to Luigi in Italian.
[57] «Are you Peter, the son of Matthew and Perpetua?»

Some sprightly and some less so, they came to greet me, patting me on the shoulders, exchanging hugs, handshakes, kisses on the cheeks and bombarding me with questions:
«*Cemût êse?*», «*Ce fatu chi?*», «*Setu in license?*», «*Di dulà vegnitu?*», «*Trop statu chi a Dogne?*», «*Satu alc di gno nevôd?*»[58]
«*Sumo, Vigjut, tire fûr la sgnape. Che buine!*»[59] proposed one of them and Vigjut did not need to hear it repeated twice.
So, between one round of grappa and the other, I had to tell those old villagers my stories from the war front. Even things that I shouldn't have said according to regulations. In exchange they updated me on the main happenings in Dogna: the shelling of the village, the dead and the wounded, the destroyed houses, the exodus of many families, the departure of young people for the front and the sad list of the wounded, mutilated, missing and dead through combat and illness. It was very hard to find out about the death of some of my friends and schoolmates.
They told me that during the bombing raids the villagers take refuge in the tunnel on the national road. However, the *ferade*[60], that is our railway, has never been hit by Austrian shells, despite their many attempts.
They told me about the completion of the carriageable road in Val Dogna that military engineers had started before the war, they described the great fortifications that had been built, they recounted the fighting in our mountains and in Val Saisera.
They also told me that the editor of the newspaper *"Il Popolo d'Italia"*, Benito Mussolini, a volunteer in the Bersaglieri of the 11th Regiment, was on duty here last summer.[61]

---

[58] «How's it going?», «How come you're here?», «Are you on leave?», «Where've you come from?», «How long will you be staying here in Dogna?», «Do you have any news of my nephew?»
[59] «Come on, Luigino, bring out the grappa. The good one!».
[60] The railway bridge, built in the second half of the nineteenth century, was a great engineering work. Two of the four arches fell in 1972 due to a flood.
[61] *May 1, 1916. Wake up at dawn. We take the road of Canal Dogna. A beautiful carriage road created from scratch. Before, there was only a primitive mule track. The work was started by the 4th company of the 5th engineer miners, continued and completed by Territorials and by teams of workers. This road is an achievement that should be seen by those who deny us Latins any capacity for organization and tenacity. This road which, tomorrow, will constitute an excellent commercial route between Dogna and Tarvisio, represents the "non plus ultra" of modernity. At every turn there are roadhouses guarded by sentries; tunnels, dug in the rock, would offer shelter to the troops in case of bombing the valley; there are drinking fountains; a cableway that shortens the portion of ramps. After seven kilometres of walking, having reached the altitude of 900-1,000, we stop. Here we*

Someone said that he took part in an assault along with the Alpini of the "Gemona" Battalion on the Jôf di Miezegnot.
But the opinions were conflicting.
Everyone asked me when this war will end, as if I had confidential information. I replied that we soldiers are expecting the decisive battle next spring, which we will surely win (I hope) because our weapons are better and the morale of the troops is very high (a lie).
«*A cualchidun a i displasarà ch'a finisi...*» commented acidly *barbe* Ustìn, so nicknamed for the large number of his nieces and nephews «... *cun cheste vuere a fasin i bês.*»[62]
He was not only referring to the big manufacturers and traders, who produce and supply weapons and materials to the army, but also to those who work in factories and the building sector.
He used as an example the workers building the fortifications and the carriageable road in Val Dogna. Their daily wages are much higher than those of us soldiers who live in the mud of the trenches, sleep on the ground and risk our lives.
My wages are 89 cents a day, but they detract 14 cents for maintenance and clothing, 38 cents for food and 27 cents for bread (although the rations have decreased in recent times). In practice, the take-home pay is 10 cents plus 40 cents of war bonus.
I earned more money when I was a bricklayer in Switzerland!
We soldiers are disheartened to know that the *imboscati* are not only safe and having fun in the city, as I saw in Padua, but they are also earning much more than we do.
«*Tu ses giovin, tu âs di difindi l'Italie*»[63] exclaimed Vigjut, gulping down another mouthful of grappa.
«*Sta cidin, osteòn, ch'i tu stâs fasind ancje tu i bês cun ducj i soldâts ch'a vegnin chi a mangjâ e bevi in ostarie*»[64] was the prompt reply of *barbe* Ustìn, to the approval of several rather vivid blasphemies from the onlookers.

---

are... Here the mountains are steeper than the ones we left in the Alto Degano area. We are face to face with the wall of Montasio, whose peak reaches 2,754 metres and is hooded in white. Benito Mussolini, "My war diary", Libreria del Littorio, Rome 1931

62 «Someone will be sorry to see the war end. With this war they are making money.» *Barbe* means uncle, while Ustìn is the diminutive of the Italian name Giusto.

63 «You are young, you have to defend Italy.»

64 «Shut up, since you're making money with all these soldiers who come to drink and eat here in the tavern.»

I pointed out that our war is not defensive, but offensive.
The goal of the High Command is to conquer Trento and Trieste.
At the moment we have only taken Gorizia.
«*Cjalait che chei là a stan mior cui todescs che coi 'talians*» sentenced Tin dal buinç, the oldest of the elders. «*Iò sei stât a lavorâ di ches bandes e ancje a Triést. Il lu soi ben, il lu soi. Scoltaimi me, scoltaimi.*»[65]
Almost everyone nodded at his words.
I don't know if it's true, as I've never been over there.
However, if the elders say so, it means that there is a bit of truth to it.
To us soldiers they have always said repeatedly: "we are fighting for a just cause, to free our Italian brothers living in Trento and Trieste from the Austrian yoke".
Many of my comrades don't even know where Trento and Trieste are!
We are at the front because they forced us. Those who refuse end up in front of a military court and risk very severe sentences or even execution by a firing squad.
At this point in the discussion, but above all to avoid another round of grappa, I took my leave, saying that I had to go home to help my mother in the barn with the animals.
«*Mandi, si viodin domàn, salude tô mari*»[66] they chorused goodbye.
As I closed the door behind me the discussion was shifting to the quality of Italian rifles compared to Austrian ones.
«*Par me a è miôr la sclope todescje...*»[67] was the last sentence I heard, blown away by a gust of wind.
It was still snowing.

---

[65] «Look, they are better off with the Austrians than with the Italians. I have worked there and also in Trieste. I well know. Listen to me.»
[66] «*Mandi*, see you tomorrow, say hello to your mother.»
Mandi is the typical Friulan greeting. There are various hypotheses on its etymology. For some it derives from the ancient *"m'arcomandi"* (I recommend) or *"mi racomandi a Diu"* (I recommend to God). For others it comes from the Latin *"manus Dei"* (hand of God, that is, may God protect you) or *"mane diu"* (stay long, that is, may you have a long life).
[67] «For me the Austrian rifle is better...»

CHAPTER 18.I

In the wake of my interest in grandfather's story, a few weeks later a cardboard box materialized on the table. It was full of other little boxes, which were in turn full of things that were wonderful to my eyes since they came from the past.
There were many chrome pen nibs with fine or truncated tips for writing with ink and their holders. There were stamps, some pencils, including the corrective ones of the past, half red and half blue. There was an album with a collection of postage stamps from all over the world. There were many coins from the 1930s, now out of circulation. Grandfather's medals were in there too: two in the shape of a cross with blue and white ribbon and four round ones with tricolor ribbons, green, white, and red. They were the ones I had seen in the old suitcase. There was a pocket watch with a chain, which grandfather had left me in his will. What a nice surprise!
But the biggest surprise of the day was kept in a tin box full of old black and white photographs.
In one photo, taken in the studio, there was grandfather dressed as a soldier together with two other comrades. His uniform was very similar to the one I had seen in the old suitcase. I recognized the badge with the black gladius (sword) and the floral decorations (laurel and oak branches). On the back was written "Camposanpiero". The photo had been roughly torn out of an album and the date could not be read, except for the year: 1918.
In another photo, taken outdoors, grandfather was in the middle of a group of soldiers and on the back was written "Tripoli 15-6-119".
Another in-studio photo showed grandfather with two of his fellow soldiers right after his return from Libya.
Strangely, there were no weapons shown in those photos. So my interest was quickly captured by other pictures in which the protagonist, armed with a dagger, wore a beautiful light-colored uniform with a dark shirt and tie and a colonial helmet. For the quality of the photos and the beauty of his face, they looked like images from a war movie.
In the next three photos the same man was shown in shirt sleeves on a white horse, with a rifle slung over his shoulder, next to an ostrich taller than he was, and with his prey, a large gazelle, hanging upside down.

The pictures were taken in 1936-37 in A.O.I. (Italian Eastern Africa, somewhere in Ethiopia, Eritrea or Somalia) and sent to my grandfather.
Who was that man?
«A l'è il Matìe» *replied my father.*
Mattia? A relative of ours?
«Ce po, al è il fì di une sûr di tô nono. Al è gno cusin dret.»[68]
My father often spoke to me in Friulan.
Mattia had done his military service in the infantry during the early 1930s, becoming a corporal major and a marksman. Then in 1936-37 he had been in A.O.I. and on his return to Italy he brought various souvenirs to my grandfather, including a shield made of hippopotamus skin, spear heads, a curved knife, a dagger and even a rifle! All war trophies.
This explained the origin of those weapons, which had nothing to do with the Great War.
Among the other photos in the box, one portrayed my grandfather, looking a bit overweight and rather old, together with three younger officers. In 1936 he had been recalled for a three-month course, at the end of which he earned the title of Second Lieutenant of Infantry, 2nd Regiment, in the "King" Brigade stationed in Udine. For me, the most important thing was recognizing the uniform with the golden buttons.
Finally, all the discoveries I had made as a child in that dark basement room and in the attic of the silkworms had been sorted out in my head.
There was nothing left to investigate.

---

[68] «Of course, he is the son of your grandfather's sister. He is my first cousin» translation from the Friulan language.

Chapter 19.I

Vidali, Sunday, 31 December 1916

Today is Sunday and the last day of 1916.

It has been a year that I will not be able to forget, although I would like to erase it from my memories. Maybe that's why these days at home with my family seem so beautiful to me, even if I'm not doing anything in particular.

I play with my brothers, I talk to my sisters, I help my mother in the barn, I see to the wood and keep the fire going. I don't even have to shovel the snow (a lot is falling), because the soldiers who live in the barracks around our house take care of it.

On the banks of the Fella, where I used to go to play and fish with friends as a child, there are now barracks, field kitchens and the two howitzers that shoot at enemy territory.

In the woods of Val Dogna and in Sella Somdogna, where my grandpa Pietro and my father Mattia taught me to hunt, armed patrols now roam instead of roe deer and chamois.

Military quarters have been positioned everywhere around the barns and alpine huts at Mincigos, Saletto, Visocco, Porto, Chiout, Chiout Zucuin, Chiout di Pupe, Chiout Pupin, Chiout Martin, Chiout di Gus and Goliz.[69] In Plans they have built an imposing fortified line, with trenches, walkways, tunnels and reinforced corridors. Even our King came to admire these military engineering works. For me, however, all of this is like the desecration of a temple.

The life of the village is no longer marked by the bells of the parish church, but by the thunder of the howitzers.

On the other hand, there are none of the unpleasant people around here that I saw in Padua and that bothered me so much.

I don't know if 1917 will be better. I don't know if there will be a decisive battle and if this war will finally end. I don't know if I will come back alive from what awaits me in the coming months. But I'm afraid that my village and my valley are unlikely to be the same as before.

---

[69] *Chiout* in Friulan usually refers to a pig sty. In the Dogna and Raccolana valleys it indicates a group of barns or a small hamlet. Most of the population of the municipality of Dogna was distributed in those small hamlets.

Vidali, Monday, 1st January 1917
Yesterday I went to mass in the Dogna church with the whole family.
There were the few villagers left and many soldiers. Some of them had organized a choir and a sergeant from the engineers accompanied them on the organ. They sang well. The only discordant note was the sermon from the military chaplain, who celebrated mass. He never stopped thundering against the Austro-Hungarian barbarians. He urged us soldiers to exterminate them without pity and without fear of death, because "dying for the Homeland is the best death you could wish for".
To stop him, the sergeant began playing the organ and the choir immediately followed him in song.
The chaplain of our regiment would have preached a very different sermon. During the fighting last May in Costa Violina and in the Buole Pass he was always among us, regardless of the danger. He gathered up and tended to the wounded. Twice he united soldiers left without officers and led them in an attack.[70]
I am sure that Don Annibale would never have made such a violent and war-mongering sermon on the last day of the year.
After the mass my mother and my brothers immediately returned home. I deflected to the tavern, already crowded with Alpini, Bersaglieri and Engineers. Here I encountered the sergeant who had played the organ, and I allowed myself to congratulate him for his splendid musical attack during the sermon.
«It was either shoot him or attack him with music» he replied seriously.
I offered him a drink and we started talking.
He told me he comes from Rovereto. When Austria started the war, he fled to Italy together with other mates living in Trentino.

---

[70] For those actions, Don Annibale Carletti, from Motta Baluffi (Cremona), assimilated lieutenant and military chaplain of the 207th Infantry Regiment of the "Taro" Brigade, was decorated with a Gold Medal of Military Valour with the following motivation:
"From the day he presented himself to the Regiment, with active and intelligent work, he knew how to inspire in all soldiers the most devoted feelings of faith, duty and love of country, giving constant proof of personal courage and contempt of danger in military action as well. In various battles, always the first where the fight raged the most, regardless of the serious dangers to which he was exposed, he incited the soldiers to carry out their duty to the end, also showing himself tireless in collecting and treating the wounded. Twice he brought together missing soldiers who were left without officers and taking advantage of the ascendancy he had been able to acquire among the soldiers, he organized them and led them to the assault. Ordered by the enemy to surrender, he resolutely refused and ordered and directed fire against the overwhelming forces of the adversary on whom he inflicted serious losses. Costa Violina, 15-17 May - Passo Buole, 30 May 1916"

Most men under the age of forty, however, were enlisted in the Austrian army and sent to fight against the Russians.[71]
He feels Italian and therefore volunteered to join our army.
This war is rather absurd. I have been sent to fight on the Trentino front, while he has been sent here near my home. Before that, though, he was stationed on the Isonzo front. It seems that High Command sends troops in need of rest and oxygenation both here and to Carnia, after their tribulations on the Karst.[72]
He told me with some pride about the fortification works in Val Dogna. For me, though, they had devastated the valley.
«Would you rather these lands fall into the hands of that hodgepodge of ethnic groups and religions of which the Austrian army is made? Serbs, Croats, Slovenians, Bosnians, Albanians, Bohemians, Slovaks, Poles, Romanians, Ruthenians, Tiroleans, Austrians and Hungarians!»
The very idea that Hungarians might go fishing in the Fella, or hunt on the slopes of Montasio[73] and then get drunk in this tavern made my blood boil. The thought that they might enter our house, sleep in our beds and touch my books triggered more aggressive feelings in me than any warmongering preacher or interventionist speech could have ever done.
I would like to stay here and defend my valley and not the Trentino.
«Here in Friuli, in the Trentino and on the Karst we have a reason to fight, given that the war is on the land where our families live» he continued. «Put yourself in the shoes of the ones who come from Turin, Milan, Bologna, Florence, Rome, Naples, Bari, Catanzaro, Palermo, Cagliari or from towns we have never heard of.»
He is right. What motive do they have to fight?
The discussion then passed on to the morale, rather low, of our troops. The too-rigid discipline. The soldiers who give themselves illnesses, injuries and wounds in order to get away from the front.
Better a hospital or a prison than a trench. There are some who pierced their eardrums with a nail, some who injected themselves with petrol, oil or piss, some who smashed a hand with a rock. It seems that some Sicilians put something in their eyes which left them blind.

---

[71] About 60,000 soldiers from the Trentino were sent to fight in the Carpathians and in Galicia against the Russian army. That mobilization deprived Trentino of its workforce and compromised all productive sectors, especially agriculture, which necessarily passed into female hands.
[72] From the point of view of military operations, the Carnia area was the quietest on the eastern front.
[73] Jôf di Montasio is one of the highest and most beautiful mountains in Friuli.

He also told me that some soldiers on the Karst shot themselves in the hand or foot. They fired through a loaf of bread to prevent the military doctor from noticing that the shot was at point-blank range.
Then there is the trick of keeping an arm up high, clearly visible outside the trench, so as to be hit by an enemy bullet. Those who are discovered, however, risk the firing squad.
He confirmed that the Carabinieri are hated on the Isonzo front as well.
It hasn't been printed in the newspapers, but it seems than some of them have had their throats cut in revenge. One was even found hanged.
We drank another glass of red wine to the *Caproni's* health.
I invited him to come and eat at my house tomorrow and he gladly accepted. We agreed not to talk about the war in the presence of my family.
At home everyone was happy about this invitation. My mother and sisters immediately started worrying about what to cook to make a good impression. Thank God there is no shortage of food. The harvest went pretty well and in November they slaughtered a nice pig.
In addition, the Bersaglieri command, quartered alongside, pays a small rent and my sisters are also paid to wash the officers' clothes and bedding and keep their rooms clean.
After lunch we played bingo. It is a tradition of my family on the first day of the year. We had a lot of fun. I kept the board and extracted the numbers from the bag. As a joke every now and then I called out numbers greater than 90. Or I called them normally, but in a southern dialect and nobody understood. I had to laugh at Lusiute, Matiuti and Girardo's expressions when they couldn't figure out on which number to put their corn kernels. Agostino, on the contrary, got angry because he wanted to win.
I tried to make sure everyone won something.
The prizes were walnuts, chestnuts and carobs.
For a few hours I completely forgot about the war.
Even the howitzers remained silent today.

Chapter 20.I

1968 was an unforgettable year for me.
The exhibition on the Great War at school was an authentic explosion of stimuli for me, both for the discovery of historical relics and as inspiration for my drawings. It also allowed me to learn many things about my family and to bring order to my childhood findings.
That innate interest in military affairs has also influenced other aspects of my life.
For example, it perfectly explains the paramilitary framework that I had given to my small band of "Black Grenadiers". We were competing with another gang of kids. Epic was the stone-throwing competition in the public gardens of Marghera, which earned us a negative note in conduct at school due to a head injury to one of our opponents.
Paradoxically, almost all of us "served" as altar boys at the parish of St. Anthony's, which was itself "regimented" by Father Bonaventura.
A Franciscan friar, he had succeeded in the miracle of rounding up dozens of boys, so many that at certain Sunday masses the forty black cassocks available were not enough for everyone. Those who arrived late had to wear one of the 4 scarlet cherub cassocks or, even worse, one of the two pageboy costumes with feathered beret, white tights and halberd.
My admiration for heroic deeds has maliciously turned into an overly competitive approach to study, play and sport. Whether it was an Italian essay or a math exercise, a football match in the street or in the oratory, a game of cards or bingo, I always wanted to win and be the best.
This is why I have always put the maximum effort into the things I do, but at the same time am sadly disappointed if the results are not what I expected. I immediately get myself back on track, though, because there are always new challenges to face and possibly win.
In the case of team competitions, I have always tried to infuse my energy into my occasional teammates.
I remember once in a summer camp in the mountains organized by my parish (Grest camp), all the activities were rewarded with points, from games to cleaning up the tent, from behaviour to jokes around the nightly campfire. Unfortunately for the other kids assigned to my tent I was the tent leader!

Despite their being among the least talented, athletically and competitively, I managed to make them work well, and earn valuable points for the team.
Needless to say, my own commitment was always the greatest on all fronts.
From among many adventures at that summer camp, I distinctly remember that of the dreaded night game. Woken by surprise at midnight and pulled out of our sleeping bags, we had to identify a spot somewhere in the woods from which rang out the sound of a horn and try to sneak into it without being caught by the older leaders. Instead of moving in a group with the other guys that night, I decided to do everything alone, moving in the woods like a commando, crawling in the grass, not turning on my flashlight but using only the moonlight. There were too many people guarding the base for me to sneak in, but I was not captured and tied to a tree, as were some others.
So I earned more points.
At the end of the two weeks our team ranked number two out of seven.
I was delighted at the result, given the level of the other guys on the team with me. Looking back today it seems truly incredible that the organizers of that camp (Franciscan Friars Minor) should have exposed children to such a varied series of dangers and ordeals. In addition to the night game in the woods, I remember hiking in the mountains from sunrise to sunset, crossing and bathing in icy streams, football games on steeply tilted pitches dotted with rocks, "mussa vegna" tournaments.[74]
Evidently at that time most parents did not keep their children in a bell jar. For that matter, my friends and I played football in the street almost every afternoon.
1968 will remain memorable for me for another reason as well: the unexpected turning point that occurred on a Saturday morning of a rainy autumn day.

---

[74] The members of a team lined up one behind the other, bent and grasped the hips of the teammate in front of them, braced to support the weight of the members of the opposing team who, one at a time, jumped on his back. The moment he took off running, each jumper first launched the shout *"Mussa"*, which means "female donkey" in Venetian dialect, followed by the answer *"Vegna"*, which means "come", by the challengers, and then *"Che ea vaca me tegna"*, which means "may the cow bear my weight". If the human chain did not collapse, but supported the weight of all jumpers, it had won the challenge.

Chapter 21.I

Vidali, Wednesday, 3 January 1917

The organ-playing sergeant, as I call him, came to lunch today.

He is a little older than me, as he was born in 1891 (just like our rifle, we have joked).

My cooks prepared delicious dishes, which were greatly appreciated.

It has been a long time since I have eaten so much and so well.

«I don't dare imagine what you would have prepared if General Cadorna himself had come to eat!» I said after lunch.

«*Cui isal chel sior?*»[75] Lusiute asked naively, sparking everyone's laughter, even from little Matiuti.

As we had agreed, the sergeant avoided talking about the war.

He told us about his life before he enlisted and in particular about his great passion for music. He was an organist in his parish church, but he also knows how to play other instruments, such as the piano and accordion.

The latter made him immediately interesting in the eyes of my sisters, who love dancing.

He is so passionate about music that he went to listen to concerts at the theater and even at the Arena in Verona. No one present, however, knew what the Arena was, except for me who had passed near it. At that point he made a beautiful drawing of it, which astonished everyone. He also spoke to us about symphonies and great composers, almost all of them with German names (to Agostino's disgust).

The sergeant understood that those were not very exciting topics for us.

So he cut it short and promised to come back with his accordion.

This immediately gained him an invitation to dinner for next Friday, when we will wait for Epiphany by lighting our *pignarûl*.[76]

It will be an opportunity for another nice meal and to hear the cheerful sound of the accordion.

To digest everything I had eaten, I accompanied the sergeant to his barrack, a little beyond Dogna. So we could speak freely.

---

[75] «Who's he?» translation from the Friulan language.

[76] The lighting of fire pyres on the eve of Epiphany is a tradition of Celtic origin widespread in Friuli. On the basis of the direction taken by the smoke and sparks, auspices are drawn for the new year.

We walked in the tracks in the snow left by the trucks.
He told me that some interventionists had arrived in the trenches on the Karst at the beginning of the war. A few days of mud, mice and lice had taken them down a peg, but they were still "raw". They had not yet experienced what it means to jump out of the trenches and go on the attack with a fixed bayonet.
I know what he meant, because I had had first-hand experience.
The incredible thing for the other soldiers was that those recruits couldn't wait to go on the attack. When the time came, they were the only ones who were happy. After the attack, though, those who returned to the trench were completely crestfallen. Many lost both their crests and their lives.
One of them, some days afterward, shot himself in the head with his rifle.
Of the many things the sergeant said to me, one struck me greatly.
I'll try to recall his words: «Whenever I hear the roar of our artillery, the crackle of our machine guns, or the crack of our rifles, I always think that one of those projectiles could kill a violinist, a pianist, a young symphonic composer, forced to wear the blue-gray uniform of the *Kaiserliche und Königliche Armee*[77]. Extraordinary musical talents were born in Austria and Hungary. This war is burying many other talented men before they can fully express their art.»
«The same goes for writers, painters or, for example, scientists fighting at the front» I observed.
«Quite right. Apart from the fact that scientists, unlike artists, are not sent to the front, all human lives are important. That's indisputable. I do believe, though, that the lives of certain men are more precious, because they could improve the existence of all the others. Their death makes this senseless slaughter even worse.»
Truly, it is a senseless slaughter.

---

[77] Imperial and Royal Austro-Hungarian Army.

CHAPTER 22.1

That autumn Saturday morning it was raining heavily.
I don't know why all the classes had been called together in the large atrium of the school, which was particularly dark that day. I don't even know whether as soon as I crossed the threshold, my gaze fell by chance or was magnetically captured by something in the midst of the mass of shouting pupils.
That something was, in truth, two somethings: two girls, side by side, one in a blue-grey coat and brown beret, the other in a gray coat and riding hat. Their hairstyles were also different, but their faces were very similar. Twins.
I had never noticed them before, even if I attended the same school.
I don't even know why this sudden vision had such a disruptive effect.
I know for sure that the following night I dreamed of the same scene.
In the following days I disbanded my small gang and my interest in weapons and soldiers quickly disappeared.
Shortly thereafter those two girls would become famous as "the Twins" and for some years they would exert an influence on the life, thoughts and works of many of my peers from Marghera, including me.
In June of 1969, after passing our fifth-grade examination, there were great expectations as to the make-up of our future classes in secondary school. I remember very well the crowd of kids in front of the window where the lists were posted. As the first lines retreated, leaving room for those behind, I could see expressions of great jubilation or extreme disappointment on their faces. I was among those beaming.
I was assigned to the 1st C, the "Twins" class!
Ironically, another set of twins had been assigned to our class.
They were males, though, mostly famous for their protruding ears.
After many years, I regret a little the radicality of that turning point in my interests. Nature takes its course, however, and young males fall victim to irrational forces, leaving them almost totally obsessed.
However, I very much regret that the inevitable turnaround did not happen a year later.

Chapter 23.I

Vidali, Saturday, 6 January 1917
Last night there was a nice party at our house.
We ate well and drank equally well.
The sergeant brought two flasks of excellent wine.
After dinner we moved the table and chairs to clear the centre of the room.
He sat on a stool and cheered us with the music of his accordion.
He is really good. I took turns dancing with my sisters, while the children imitated us by stamping their feet on the stone floor.
Seated a bit to one side, my mother sewed while looking after the fire of the *fogolâr* armed with a *tirebores*.[78]
Hearing the music, the soldiers quartered around our house came to see what was going on. From the windows of the kitchen we saw their faces pop up, one on top of the other. We would have liked to let them in, but the space in our room is modest. At the end of each song they clapped heartily.
At one point we heard an imperious knock on the door. When I opened it, I found myself faced with a second lieutenant of the Bersaglieri. He wanted to see what was going on, too. He is quartered in the house next door. We offered him coffee and grappa, which he drank happily. He asked us if the soldiers outside were bothering us. We said no and that, in fact, we were sorry not to be able to let them in as there was not enough space.
On taking his leave, he commented bitterly that our High Command, instead of always and only demanding the strictest discipline, should, if not promote, at least allow some recreational activity. Certainly, some music and some shows would help a lot in raising the morale of the troops.[79]

---

[78] *Fogolâr*, from Late Latin foculāris, from Latin focus, is the typical Friulan fireplace. *Tirebores* is a long iron pipe in which one blows to revive the fire.

[79] General Cadorna had imposed strict compliance with the Piedmontese codes of military discipline. Although total insensitivity to the suffering of soldiers on the front was typical of the commands of all the belligerent armies, he added a particular harshness in relations with collaborators and subordinates. Also due to the lack of authority of the Italian government, Cadorna was able to concentrate in his own hand powers and prerogatives completely unknown to the other allied commanders, so much so that his influence came to condition the work and guidelines of the Ministry of War. His practice of indiscriminate, even preventative, dismissals was notorious. Relieving from command for the most disparate reasons became such a widespread practice that it completely inhibited the spirit of

When the sergeant stopped playing and we stopped dancing, the faces pressed against the windows slowly disappeared in the dark, just as they had appeared.
Later, wearing sweaters and coats, we went out to light the *pignarûl*.
In the afternoon, the youngest members of the family had prepared a stack of wood and hay in the garden, supported in the centre by a stake with a figure made from rags, called the *vecje*, on the top. We all made a circle around it to admire the fire and calculate the direction of the smoke and sparks. I explained to the sergeant that if they blew to the west, it would be necessary to pack a backpack and roam the world in search of luck but if they blew to the east, there would be good luck in the months to come.
Our proverb says: «*Se il fum al va a soreli a mont, cjape il sac e va pal mont, se il fum al va a soreli jevât, cjape il sac e va al marcjât.*»
While singing traditional songs, I watched my mother out of the corner of my eye to perceive from her face how to interpret the trend the smoke.
It was not clear what direction it would take.
The wind blew it in all directions.
My mother's expression was impenetrable. I could only see her lips move.
When the *vecje* was completely burned and the small bonfire started its descending phase, we headed home.
«Ma'am, where did the smoke go?» asked the sergeant.
We all waited for my mother's response with curiosity and trepidation.
Her answer was lapidary and in Italian (something very rare):
«We will all do well to get our bags packed, sergeant.»

initiative of his officers at all levels. Each of them feared being dismissed by his direct superior for even the smallest failure. Historians agree that this practice seriously undermined the morale and will to fight of the Italian Royal Army. A shining example of historical nemesis, Cadorna himself was dismissed after the defeat at Caporetto.

CHAPTER 24.I

One fine day in the summer of 1969 my father decided to make a short visit to Dogna and take me along. I had heard Dogna mentioned sometimes at home, but I didn't know where it was or who lived there. We drove down a long paved road into a very green and very narrow valley, bordered by a river of enchanting colour.
«It's the Fella» explained my father. We pulled over to the left near a small group of houses leaning against the mountain, a bit above the road. This was Vidali, a hamlet of Dogna. The village itself was about a kilometre away, hidden by the mountains.
When we got out of the car, I immediately noticed a tall, wooden pole with a cord to raise a flag, although there was none there.
At the end of our small climb we were greeted by a beautiful black and white dog, wagging his tail happily, followed by an elderly gentleman with sparse white hair, small bright eyes and a friendly smile, albeit missing a few teeth. This was "Gjre", Uncle Girardo, grandfather's brother. He only hoisted a red flag on that flagpole on May 1st, his birthday. Above the front door of the house there was engraved in stone a date in Roman numerals: AD-MDCCLXXI.
He ushered us into a rather dark kitchen. The floor was dark and stone. On the far left was a sun-lit room in which a fogolâr could be glimpsed. Uncle put a bottle of wine on the table and to me he gave a syrup of rose petals, which he had just made. Unforgettable.
I immediately noticed that he was the classic smoker who lights his cigarette with the stub of the one that he has just finished smoking. At the time, I wasn't bothered by smoking. My father smoked and in my grandmother's bar I was used to being surrounded by smoke. It seemed completely natural to me. In any case, even at that first meeting, I realized that my uncle was overdoing it a little. Between one cigarette and another he prepared a great lunch for us. His stuffed tomatoes have remained in my mind ever since. He had worked in Genoa for many years. He had not married because he said he was too jealous to marry. Maybe that was the main reason why he had learned to cook.
After lunch, he took us to visit the garden and the back of the house, always in the company of trusty Lessie, his affectionate dog.

There was a small stream with a fast current of very cold water. A bridge allowed you to cross to the other side, from where, climbing up a steep lawn, you could reach the edge of the wood. From that wood at night "las ghirates", the dormice, descended, nibbling his food in the pantry. He was forced to set traps to catch them, but he later set them free. The location dominated the group of houses below and the Fella. The railway line running along the slopes of the mountain opposite, a little higher than the river, could be seen very clearly. Returning home, we met a lady who was filling her bucket from the fountain in the centre of the garden. To my surprise, she did not speak Friulan like everyone else. Her voice was very high and hoarse. This was "Elda", the wife of "Matìe", who immediately left his house to greet us and invite us to eat a slice of watermelon under the pergola. He spoke in Friulan in a low sweet voice. They were truly a strange couple. Even though he had grown old, I immediately recognized him as the man in the colonial pictures. His hair was still straight and black, a little graying at the temples, but always combed back. His face was still that of an actor. He vaguely reminded me of my grandfather. Two of his four sons arrived shortly thereafter. They appeared very different from each other, as did their parents. One was tall, thin and dark-skinned, the other was lighter, shorter and more robust. They were much older than me. Mattia's family lived in Chiasso, Switzerland, and came to Dogna during the summer.

After the watermelon, my uncle and Mattia took me to see the rabbit cages, down a very steep stone staircase.

Between Mattia's and uncle's houses was another house, very old and made of wood. The lower part was used as a stable. A ladder led to the living quarters on the upper floor. There lived an old woman named Flavia, small and with a curved back. It seemed strange to me that she was not a relative of ours there in the middle of our family houses; but at the same time, I was glad she wasn't, because I didn't like her. She looked like a witch. She hadn't even glanced at us when she entered the stable to feed her goats.

Before leaving, I took some pictures of my uncle and Lessie with my first camera, a plastic imitation of the Rolleiflex.

I still have them in an old album of photos.

Except for the old lady, I liked everything about that place. On the way home, I told my parents that I would like to return and spend some time with uncle Geraldo (Girardo was too difficult to pronounce).

A few weeks later I was back there to spend ten unforgettable days surrounded by nature and animals.

In one of the rooms of that ancient stone house there surely must have been the old worn suitcase that I had seen years before, but I was too enraptured by other things to start looking for it. Even worse, I failed to ask my uncle anything about his brother. At that particular moment I was more interested in dormice (we caught one), walks in the meadows and the woods with Lessie, fishing in the Fella, cooking lessons and Ritz crackers with condensed milk!

One of my uncle's stories made a great impression on me. After the Great War, when the rains were abundant, the Fella river carried a little of everything down from Val Dogna: rifles, bayonets, helmets, ammunition and once even a dead soldier. A few children from the village playing with unexploded shells had been seriously injured and maimed. Despite the horror of the injuries, I remember being envious of those children. From that story onwards, every time we went walking along the Fella, I scrutinized the ground very carefully in the hope of finding some war relic in the gravel.

The days passed quickly and that particular holiday was soon over. It was time to go back home. However, the displeasure of my departure was largely compensated by my enthusiasm for the start of the first year of secondary school, especially because the most beautiful girls in Marghera were in my class.

I bitterly regret not asking my uncle all the questions I would like to ask him today, as well as not searching for and bringing home my grandfather's suitcase with the military uniforms inside.

I regret it and I can't absolve myself, despite all the mitigating factors.

Every morning, from the first day of school on, there was a bunch of boys waiting for the Twins to leave their house and following them to school. I was among those who had the privilege of having them in my class and the luck of having one of them sitting at the desk in front of mine. It was an authentic apotheosis for me when their mother phoned mine asking if I would be so kind as to accompany them every day to school. She was a little worried by that crowd of admirers.

I did bodyguard duty throughout the first year, despite the fact that I soon realized that girls of that age, in addition to being more developed than their male peers, are more attracted to high school students. We were still too young to be interesting. Thus, already from the second year my interest in them gradually declined, albeit reluctantly. Fortunately, I didn't reactivate my gang of rascals, but turned my time and my passion to drawing and sport instead.

CHAPTER 25.I

Vidali, Monday, 8 January 1917

My home leave has come to an end.

Tomorrow morning I will have to get up really early to return to the regiment. I found a truck that will give me a lift to Udine. Then I will take the troop train to Verona.

My heart aches to leave.

As nice as it was to spend these days with my family, so it will be awful to have to shoulder my backpack again and travel back the way I came, knowing that I may never return. A bullet, a shrapnel or a simple fragment of a shell could kill me at any moment. Many young men from my village have already died. It's a miracle that things have gone well for me so far.

Today I did everything slowly because I wanted to enjoy every minute, one by one. Who knows when I will be able to hold Lusiute on my lap again and frighten her with the story of the *comparìtul*[80], play *smocâ*[81] with Matiuti, wrestle with Agostino and Girardo, joke with my sisters and savor their cooking? Who knows if I will see my father and Noè again?

I wonder if I will ever be able to embrace my mother again.

After dinner nobody wanted to go to sleep.

We were sitting around the *fogolâr*. Everyone was trying to speak as if it were an ordinary day, but there was a lot of sadness.

«*Cuant che tu tornis, Pieri?*»[82]

Lusiute's question broke that fragile balance.

Margherita got up with the excuse of going to get water.

Amabile and Attilia were no longer able to hold back their tears.

«*Parcé ch'a vain?*»[83] continued the little girl.

«*A i sarà lât alc in tal voli*»[84] said Girardo, with as much ingenuity.

«*A dutes dos?*»[85] Lusiute asked unconvinced.

---

[80] A mischievous goblin who ticks from under the pillow or in the corners of the room at night.

[81] A game with glass balls. *Smoco* is the big ball used to *smocâ*, that is to hit all the others in the game.

[82] «When are you coming back, Pietro?» translation from the Friulan language.

[83] «Why are they crying?»

[84] «Something must have gotten into their eye.»

[85] «To both of them?»

At that point I got to my feet and invited everyone to go to sleep, from the youngest to the oldest. It was difficult to say goodbye to each one with a smile on my lips and say goodbye, see you.
When? Soon.
When? Sooner or later.
Mandi e buine gnot.[86]
My last goodbye was to my mother. With a lump in her throat she reminded me to take the woolen clothes she had prepared for me.
I had a lump in my throat too.
Then, looking at me with her austere but affectionate gaze, she took my hands in hers. From the pocket of her skirt she took something out, put it on my palm and closed my hand.
«*Al è il grop di Salomon*»[87]. She had made it by weaving sprigs of hazel which were blessed on St. John's day.
«*Tenlu simpri cun te, ricuarditi.*»[88]
I promised to always keep it with me. I hope it brings me luck.
After a long hug, she kissed me on the cheeks, whispering:
«*Tu sês partît fantat, cumò tu sês un omp; ma tu sês simpri il gno frut.*»[89]
Then she went up to her room without looking back.
I confess that more than one tear streaked my face.
Now that I have finished writing I'll go out to smoke the last cigarette.
I hope the cold will stop the tears and make me feel a bit better.

P.S. I need to add this note before I go to sleep. In the open space just in front of the entrance to the house, I found a snowman with a *feldkappe* on his head, the Austrian field cap. Its figure, illuminated by the moon, was run through with several *raclis*, the sticks we use to hold up bean plants.
The work of Agostino and Girardo, for sure.
It is their good luck wish for me.

---

[86] Hello and goodnight.
[87] A typical amulet of upper Friuli, spherical in shape and with 12 points.
[88] «Always keep it with you, do remember.»
[89] «You left a boy, now you are a man; but you'll always be my baby.»

CHAPTER 26.I

I don't remember why, but I no longer went on vacation in Dogna with my uncle Geraldo in the following years.
I remember, though, that once he spent Christmas holidays with us in Artegna. One day he let me dress him up as a zombie with rags hanging from his arms and around his head. Looking like that he was supposed to suddenly pop out from behind a door and frighten the girl from Yugoslavia who worked in my grandmother's bar. It worked perfectly. The girl let out a shriek of terror and in two seconds bolted up the two flights of stairs leading to the upper floor where we lived, barricading herself behind a door. Today she would press charges.
Days later, the heart of that poor girl suffered another shock. Grandmother had finished her lunch and gone down to the bar to relieve her. As the girl sat down at the table, I started making strange speeches about the disappointments of life and the absolute uselessness of continuing. I consoled myself with a slice of cake. It might have been my last one. I don't know how much she understood me as she was gulping down her soup. She didn't speak much Italian. Anyway, she certainly understood that things were serious when she saw me pull out a gun from under the table, point it at my temple, fire a loud shot and drop like a stone from my chair. She let out the usual shriek of terror and in two seconds ran down the two flights of stairs leading down to the bar. When she came back upstairs, desperate, with my grandmother in tow, I was quietly sitting at the table intent on finishing my slice of cake.
Today she would press charges.
That bar was the Land of Plenty for us children. So you can well imagine our surprise and displeasure when we learned that grandmother was going to sell it. This was inconceivable to us. We tried several times to make her change her mind. But her decision was incontrovertible. Grandma had reached retirement age. It was the spring of 1971. My sister, my two cousins and I were so disappointed that we turned our wrath against the innocent buyer. For revenge, we made off with some crates of fruit juice, orangeade, soda and Coca-Cola from the cellar of the bar. In a short time, we had guzzled every drop until we were sick. We threw the glass bottles into a hole in the cellar floor. I don't know where they ended up.

Many years later I revealed our act of revenge to the incredulous amazement of my grandmother, the severe dismay of my uncles and parents, and the self-satisfied smiles of my two cousins and my sister.
In 1971, for the first time in our life, we didn't spend the summer at the "Impero" Bar, located on Villa Street in Artegna.
We had to resign ourselves to the idea that we had lost it forever.
Grandmother went to live in Udine. My parents rented a holiday home in grandmother's native village, Raveo in Carnia. My cousins' parents, on the other hand, decided to buy and refurbish an old house in another Carnic valley, near Misincinis, a fraction of Paularo, a village in which our grandmother had managed a hotel from '42 to '53.
The shield, the other weapons and the Winchester were taken to Marghera.
I remember the first time my parents left us at home to go to dinner with friends, I insisted on awaiting their return armed with the rifle. When they came back, they found me still awake and with the shotgun in my hands!
Even if there could be no comparison with the bar in Artegna, I slowly began to appreciate Raveo too. There were only about five hundred inhabitants, but most of them were relatives, all nice and interesting, and some cousins slightly older than me. Their doors were always open and they were always visiting back and forth to say good morning, to get eggs from the chicken coop or vegetables from the garden, to wish "bon apetit" for lunch, to have a chat in the afternoon, to eat or drink something and, at the end of the day, to say goodnight. I was fascinated to hear them speak a Friulan in an accent vastly different from that of Artegna.
The village was in a large valley in the midst of the mountains and consequently there were lots of possibilities for excursions and mushroom hunting with my father.
What excited me the most, however, was hunting for vipers armed with a club. I also carried a knife, which I hoped I would never have to use to cut myself to suck out the poison in the event of a bite. I was always successful. Every now and then I went proudly back to the village with a dead viper. I remember that one year the Municipality paid me one thousand lire for each viper killed and delivered.
Nevertheless, one day I decided to take a dangerous but beautiful horned viper and preserve it in a jar of formalin.
Before I did that, however, I arranged it artistically outside the front door and knocked, saying with a grin: «Someone is here for you, Grandma!»
Grandma came out.
Seeing no one, she gave me a questioning look.

With a roll of my eyes I indicated that she should look at the ground. When she saw the viper curled up a few centimetres from her feet she screamed and jumped back into the house. For security she even locked the door!
What a laugh!
Luckily, she forgave me almost immediately for that prank.
Sometimes we went to another village, Enemonzo, in a nearby valley, to visit other relatives: the family of the sister of my paternal grandmother. Her name was Elvira and she looked a lot like my grandmother. I liked to go to that old house to hear stories about her brothers, some of whom had emigrated abroad. Years earlier I had met one of them called Nêl, that is Daniel, when he returned to Italy from France for a short stay.
I could have asked that aunt too about my grandpa, her brother-in-law. Instead, I missed that opportunity as well.
The summer of 1973 was enlivened by the arrival of a group of new cousins in Raveo. Four females and one male. They were all younger than me. Two were blond and as light skinned as Scandinavians, the others dark and olive-skinned, like Mediterranean people. They came from Montecatini Terme, a city in Tuscany. In addition to their parents, there was their grandmother, named Iside, my great-grandfather Antonio's sister. We felt an immediate harmony with these new cousins and a beautiful friendship was born.
I was very surprised to find that a branch of the family came from Tuscany, since all the other members were from Friuli, including me (I was born in Gemona del Friuli).
Then my grandmother told me that in October 1917, following the Caporetto defeat, her parents had loaded her and all her siblings onto wagons and had fled to Tuscany. Other relatives had gone on that long journey with them. Many Friulans were displaced to that region as refugees, since the Municipality of Udine and, in turn, many other municipal administrations had moved their headquarters to Florence. I discovered this many years later.
They settled in Montecatini, after a dramatic journey: one brother, only a few months old, had died; another, Dante, had gotten lost in the crush in Padua, but then fortunately was found; my grandma contracted typhus, but recovered.
In that city, Aunt Iside met her future husband. So, at the end of the war, while everyone else had returned to Raveo, she remained, creating her own family. Once again and unexpectedly the Great War had returned to the fore in my life.

CHAPTER 27.I

War Zone, March 1917

I have started writing again after many weeks.

My return to the regiment was very sad.

All those who have returned from winter leave are out of sorts. Many are angry about what they saw during the trip and during the leave: most people in the country do not understand what is happening here at the front and the rear is full of *imboscati.*

What I saw in Padua and Udine was identical to what my comrades saw in their cities and in their villages. Someone even said that he preferred to stay at the front rather than stay home and see such goings-on.

Morale is very low.

Fortunately, we don't have to fight right now.

Who knows if the *mucs*' morale is as low as ours?

But there is another reason why I don't feel like writing.

I got a letter from Margherita, which made me very sad.

My friend, the organ-playing sergeant, as I called him, is dead.

He was buried together with some other engineers under an avalanche of snow in Val Dogna. He was supposed to return to pick up the accordion he had left with us on the eve of Epiphany.

After a week my mother went to ask about him and learned about the tragedy. Our whole family is grieved.

He was only with us twice, but everyone liked him.

He might have become a famous musician.

Instead, this war has buried him too.

I hope they can find his body when the snow melts and give him a worthy burial in our valley.

Chapter 28.I

I was at home in Marghera.
As usual, I had spent the afternoon studying. It was the end of the school year. I was attending the fourth year of Grammar school. Right after dinner I started drawing. I was drawing a comic book.
All of a sudden, I saw the living-room walls sway violently in all directions. Furniture and knick-knacks danced as if seized with an angry and irresistible fever. Frightened I called my mother, who was already in bed.
It was 9pm on May 6, 1976.
It was the first terrible shock, tenth degree on the Mercalli scale, of the earthquake that devastated Friuli.
From the TV news we immediately learned that the epicentre was near Gemona and Artegna. A series of telephone calls were immediately begun to relatives living in Friuli.
Thank goodness, apart from their fright, everyone was fine.
Meanwhile, the special editions of the news programs reported the proportions of the disaster. The jolt, felt throughout all of Northern Italy, had affected many communities both in Friuli and in the upper and middle Isonzo area. Buildings collapsing in towns close to the epicentre had caused an unknown number of victims. In the following days the death toll rose to 989 with more than 45,000 homeless.
Despite the distance from the earthquake's epicentre, many houses in Raveo were no longer habitable and many relatives had to move, first to caravans and then to prefabricated wooden houses. The ancient stone house of Dogna suffered numerous dangerous cracks.
New potent quakes in September undermined all the rebuilding work already completed by the all-too-diligent Friulans.
Our family homes in Raveo and Dogna had to be demolished and then rebuilt, erasing forever an important piece in the history of my two families.

CHAPTER 29.I

War Zone, April 1917

Nothing noteworthy has been happening up here in the mountains.

Snow and bad weather have blocked any action. The enemies we had to fight were not the *mucs*, but frost and avalanches.[90]

Many soldiers have had serious health problems due to the cold. Quite a few have had pneumonia and one has even died. Many have had problems with frostbite. In some cases, the doctors had to cut off their toes or even the whole foot. I ran a risk of this too. For many days I could no longer feel my toes.

Other soldiers died under avalanches of snow.

Now the weather is variable and it's not so cold, but after a few sunny days it often starts snowing again and the danger of avalanches increases.

We also have another enemy: boredom.

The days never end.

Fortunately, I keep busy reading the books and newspapers that arrive here, or as a scribe of other people's letters.

Now, though, I have to be more careful about what I write because the checks have increased a lot. All our letters and postcards pass through special offices where our private correspondence is read. If there is something unpatriotic or defeatist, according to the controllers, they cancel it by covering it with black ink.[91]

Censorship is creating significant delays in delivering the mail, which all of us eagerly await. This makes us even more angry.

It's useless to write negative comments about the war, the officers or the politicians. One letter even threatened Cadorna and the King with death!

At risk is not just a stroke of black ink on a few sentences.

At risk is a trial for the sender if the letter is confiscated.

It is even forbidden to indicate where we are located.

---

[90] All the soldiers remember the winter of 1916-17 as extremely severe.

[91] The Royal Decree of May 23, 1915 n.689 and the circular of July 28, 1915 introduced and regulated preventive control and censorship of the correspondence between soldiers and their families. All mail sent from the front was examined in Treviso and that sent from home in Bologna. The work was colossal in size: during the war almost 4 billion letters were exchanged between the front and the rest of Italy.

You always have to write “war zone”.
In spite of that, I sometimes have to quarrel with some soldier who wants me to write things that cannot be said.
What happens here on the front is quite different from what they write in the newspapers. We would gladly shoot some journalists.
If sometimes I was forced to give in to insistence, then I would write certain things under the postage stamp. It worked for a while, but then we realized that the letters were not arriving at their destination.
The censors had noticed the trick.
By now we’ve figured out that in those offices they read the entire text of the letters and not only the first lines, in which I write that health is excellent, morale is high, ration is abundant and other similar sentences.
A fellow soldier suggested that I use lemon juice if I really have to write about things forbidden by censorship.
I haven’t done it yet, but soon I’ll try that trick too.

The boredom of these months has been broken by two important pieces of news, which we read in the newspapers.
A revolution broke out in Russia in early March.
The czar had to abdicate.[92]
The Russians have proclaimed a Republic.
Many soldiers celebrated this news because they hope that the revolution will spread to other nations and end the war.
Someone, however, pointed out that if Russia asks for an armistice, the German and Austrian troops deployed on the eastern front will be moved not only to the western front, but also to ours.
And then it will be really hard to resist their impact.

---

[92] Russia was sorely tried by the war. The loss of Poland, Belarus, Lithuania, part of the Ukraine and Latvia were by no means offset by successes in Galicia and the Caucasus. The national economy and the army were in extreme difficulty. Tsar Nicholas II, inaccessible, distrustful and prey to alcoholism, refused to consider any reform of his autocratic regime. On March 12, 1917, according to the Julian calendar, the so-called “February Revolution” broke out, as the result of the largely spontaneous uprising of the population and the Petrograd garrison against the police. Eight months later, the “October Revolution” brought the Bolsheviks to power. In July 1918 the Tsar and his family were shot, hacked to pieces and dissolved in acid by a commando composed of former Austrian and Hungarian prisoners of war under the orders of the Ekaterinburg Soviet, in open conflict with Moscow. Trotsky, in fact, wanted to bring the Tsar to the capital to judge him in a showy trial, while his family was to be transferred abroad.

In return, however, there is another important news item: in early April the United States entered the war against the Central Empires.[93]
The United States is a very large and powerful country. So say the soldiers who worked there before returning to Italy for the war.[94]
The United States will furnish their Allies with lots of goods and ammunition. They will probably send their troops to the western front.
Most soldiers, however, hope that the war will end thanks to the Russian revolution rather than with the help of the Americans.
I also read in the paper that the editor of the *"Popolo d'Italia"* is in a very serious condition. Last February, during an exercise on the Karst, a Bettica torpedo launcher exploded in his hands.[95]
Those around him died on impact while he is said to be dying.
I feel sorry for the others, but not for him.

---

[93] At the beginning of the conflict, the United States had declared neutrality, also because its population was made up of ex-emigrants from both sides. As the war continued, however, a strong commercial link had been created with the Allies, who had asked the United States for ever more goods (weapons, food, etc.) and the financing to purchase those goods. The sinking of various merchant ships, including the transatlantic "Lusitania" (May 7, 1916), by a German U-Boot, began to worry American shipowners more and more. Exports to Great Britain and France now represented two thirds of all their trade. The prospect of a victory for the Central Empires was also a threat to the interests of bankers, who might not see the repayment of their loans to the Allies. Following the declaration of unconditional submarine warfare by the German General Staff (from February 1, 1917 any ship bound for Allied ports was considered a legitimate target), President Woodrow Wilson (28 December 1856 - 3 February 1924), who had been re-elected in November, authorized the arming of merchant ships and threatened to enter the war. The sinking of the "Vigilantia" on March 19 led to the Declaration of War on April 6. The United States entered the conflict as "associates", free to decide on their political future and maintaining the right to withdraw from the war at their discretion.
[94] At the outbreak of the war, about 6 million Italians lived abroad. Overall, just over 300,000 emigrants decided to return to fight (although no authority could force them). Over half of them came from the American continent. The influx was very strong at first (192,000 in 1915) but weakened almost immediately. Italian authorities did not produce adequate propaganda and showed absolute incomprehension for the specific problems of the emigrants. The latter received an economic treatment identical to residents and subsidies to disadvantaged families were inadequate, due to the unfavorable exchange rate and the different cost of living in the United States and Argentina. Lastly, and an element of not secondary importance, emigrants were not granted leave, since it was forbidden to cross the national borders to go home.
[95] This was a small bomb launcher, easily transportable, which was used to create openings in barbed wire. It was patented by a captain in the Engineers, Alberto Bettica. It was not entirely reliable since the bomb, called a Bettica tube, sometimes exploded inside the weapon causing serious damage to the users.

Serves him right!
He wanted Italy to go to war.[96]
Nevertheless, I have to admit that he had the guts to join up and go to the front. So I have more respect for him than for all those interventionist good-for-nothings and slackers who stay well behind the rear lines drinking and chatting in parlors and taverns.
We'd like to see them in the trenches for a few days too...

[96] Benito Mussolini (29 July 1883 - 28 April 1945). Editor of the socialist newspaper *"Avanti!"* he was a staunch anti-interventionist. In 1914, however, he radically changed his opinion, putting himself in stark contrast to the party line. After resigning, in November he founded *"Il Popolo d'Italia"*, aligned with interventionist positions. Shortly thereafter he was expelled from the Italian Socialist Party. At the outbreak of the war he volunteered, but his application was rejected. In the summer 1915 he was first enlisted in the XII and then in the XI Bersaglieri Regiment, where he reached the rank of corporal- major in August 1916. He published his war diary in the columns of his newspaper (end of December 1915 - February 13, 1917). During his convalescence following the accident with the Bettica launcher, he circulated two legends: one that he had refused anesthesia while the fragments were being extracted from his body; and the second that, considering him their most fearful enemy, the Austrians had tried to kill him by bombing the hospital in which he was. In December 1917 he published the article *"Trincerocracy"*, in which he claimed for veterans the right to govern Italy after the war and prefigured the fighters of the Great War as the aristocracy of tomorrow and the central nucleus of a new leadership. In 1919 he was discharged from the army.

CHAPTER 30.I

The catastrophe that hit Friuli in May 1976 has become a watershed.
When we talk about the past in our family, we always add a reference to before or after the earthquake.
For example, after the earthquake, our cousins from Montecatini no longer came to Raveo on holiday and we lost sight of each other for a while. The house we were renting had not been seriously damaged. So we made it available to two of my grandmother's sisters, until their home could be restored or rebuilt. Uncle Geraldo had to abandon Dogna and move to the home of his sister Lucia's daughter in Gemona. Unfortunately, I never had a chance to meet him again. He passed away in 1979.
At that time, I was studying Statistics at the University of Padua. My mind was almost totally absorbed in math and exercises of probability calculation. Having attended the Latin Grammar school, I had to make up the considerable gap with the scientific students.
I went to Padua every day and at the end of lessons I ran to catch the train to Mestre. I walked very fast, despite my briefcase full of books. I enjoyed counting the steps and the time it took me to get to the station. Every day I tried to set new speed records (traffic lights permitting).
I had chosen that university faculty not out of a sudden love of scientific subjects, but on the basis of simple reasoning. I sensed that the future would be dominated more by numbers than by letters. So, to have a better chance at a future job, I had to focus on numbers. Furthermore, I knew that the classrooms of other faculties were always crowded with students, while in Statistics it was like being in high school. I believed that greater proximity to the teachers guaranteed better learning.
I was right.
In the first year there were forty of us. During the following years I sometimes found myself alone in class with the teacher. Once I even found myself alone without the teacher!
Although my five years at the Franchetti Grammar school in Mestre were splendid, also thanks to my fantastic classmates in section E, my memories of my time at the university are not particularly brilliant.
Living only two minutes from the station and twenty-five minutes by train from Padua was definitely an advantage and very convenient.

However, it prevented me from fully immersing myself in the student atmosphere of that city. In retrospect I kind of envy the students who, coming from farther away, lived their university years in Padua. I only visited Prato della Valle and Saint Anthony's Basilica many years later, even though they were quite near my department.

I went to class, came home, studied all day and every once in a while took my exams, sometimes the same exam several times. Some were really tough and created on purpose to massacre students. It is no coincidence that there were always more veterans than novices at the Probability Calculation exam.

I did pretty well in it: I only had to repeat it four times before passing!

My only distractions were drawing and volleyball.

Already in high school I had given up football and elected volleyball as my favorite sport, like most of my circle of friends. I went to training two or three times a week for the game on Saturday. My role on the team was setter. For me each game was like a final, even in friendly matches. I hadn't changed. I remember that to psych ourselves up for a match, another setter and I listened to the intro of "Carmina Burana" by Carl Orff playing full blast in the car.

For some years now, music had become a vital element for me.

While attending my fourth year of gymnasium, I discovered that there was more to music than the jukebox songs from grandmother's bar or radio shows such as "Hit-Parade" and "Alto Gradimento".

My epiphany arrived in the form of a BASF green audio cassette, which a classmate had lent me: "Ummagumma" by Pink Floyd. Unexpectedly, the doors of a new world, rich and fascinating, opened wide.

A few years later another musical world, equally rich and fascinating, suddenly revealed itself to my eyes while watching Stanley Kubrik's movie "A Clockwork Orange". Thus, I discovered Beethoven and then, through subsequent connections, Bach, Mozart, Mahler, Schoenberg and many other German and Russian composers.

I was lucky enough to have a close friend who had lots of classical records. He was studying cello at the Venice Conservatory.

I remember that one evening, while I was drawing, I was literally electrified by the prelude to Richard Wagner's "Tristan and Isolde", broadcast by Radio Tre. The very next day I was knocking at my friend's house door to borrow the vinyl record of that prelude. When my friend, a bit surprised by my request, explained to me that it was a boxed set with four records, I was thrilled, although my joy was abruptly subdued by the news that the opera lasted over four hours.

I had always hated opera.
Nonetheless, I recorded the whole work on two 120-minute black BASF tapes with an orange label. My idea was to later record only the prelude and maybe some other orchestral parts.
Final result: I studied for my final high school exam accompanied twice a day by the "Tristan" and I became a great fan of opera, especially German and Russian. In my record collection there are now over two hundred operas.
During my university period, an unexpected link between volleyball and Arnold Schoenberg's dodecaphonic music paved the way for a series of various artistic collaborations with musicians from the Mestre area, which lasted for decades.
In those years, however, a complete oblivion had descended on grandfather and his military experience with the Arditi.
The Winchester, locked up in its strange paper sarcophagus, languished in the closet of my parents' bedroom. The hippopotamus-skin shield was hung on the door of our house basement and the other increasingly rusty weapons lay in a cardboard box along with the war relics I had collected in primary school for the Great War exhibition.
Another box protected grandfather's trumpet, accordion, spyglass and typewriter from dust.
The group of objects that I had discovered as a child in the attic and in the dark and dusty basement of my grandparents' house in Magnano in Riviera had almost been reunited.
Only the suitcase with the uniforms was missing, but I didn't miss it.
Indifference had taken the place of the wonder and curiosity of the past.
My life was now running on other tracks and toward other interests: study, sport, music, drawing and, big news, photography.

CHAPTER 31.I

War zone, May 1917
n.n.[97]

War Zone, June 1917
They wrote to me from home that Noè has been called to arms and enlisted in the Alpini of the "Gemona" Battalion.[98]
That boy is really lucky.
His Battalion is headquartered in Dogna!
My mother must have made him a fantastic amulet.
I am very lucky too, because my Brigade did not have to go fight on the Asiago Plateau. From what we are reading in the newspapers and war bulletins, things are not going well.[99]
There is a rumor going around, though, that we will soon be transferred to the Isonzo front. Between May and June there was another fierce battle there, but once again not the decisive one.[100]

---

[97] Nothing new (to report).
[98] The "Gemona" Battalion was part of the 8th Alpine Regiment, along with the "Arvenis", "Cividale", "Matajur", "Monte Canin", "Monte Nero", "Tolmezzo", "Val Fella", "Val Natisone" and "Val Tagliamento".
[99] The Italian attack by the 6th Army, led by General Ettore Mambretti, was, on one hand, intended to reduce enemy pressure on the 3rd Army front and, on the other, to retake the positions lost during the Austro-Hungarian offensive of May-June 1916, the so-called *Strafexpedition*. As these positions were facing the Venetian plain, the Imperials could have taken from behind the Italian troops deployed in Cadore, Carnia and on the Isonzo front. The battle fought between the 10th and the 29th June 1917, along a line of about 14 kilometres at an altitude varying between 1,000 and 2,000 metres, was extremely bloody. Despite a 3 to 1 ratio of forces, adverse weather conditions, difficult terrain, unfavorable positions and above all poor management by military commanders caused the repeated Italian attacks to be systematically repelled and in the end the objectives were not realized. The blood tribute was very high: 169 officers dead, 716 injured and 98 missing; 2,696 soldiers dead, 16,018 injured and 5,502 missing. Most of the casualties were suffered by the 52nd Division, in particular by the Alpine troops, in the fighting on Mount Ortigara.
[100] 10th Isonzo Battle: 12 May - 6 June 1917. After two and a half days of bombing from Tolmino to the Adriatic, the Italian infantry managed to cross the Isonzo and make some conquests (M. Kuk, the Vodice and the slopes of Monte Santo). There was bitter fighting in the southern Karst. But even that "push" was unable to definitively break through the

There have been many casualties and now they need fresh troops.
Actually, we are truly very "fresh" thanks to all the cold that we have suffered in recent months.
Now you can see snow only on the mountain tops.
Where we are, it has almost completely melted and therefore we have been very busy fixing the trenches and placing barbed-wire barriers.
We also tried to recover the bodies of our comrades buried under last December's avalanche in the outpost we conquered.
Unfortunately, this was impossible because the Austrians were strafing us.
Neither were they able to retake that position, though, because we were shooting at them.
One day we proposed a few hours' truce to bury the corpses. They shot at us, even though we had put a white rag on a stick. So the bodies of our dead and theirs remained there to rot and every now and then when the wind blows our way we can smell a terrible stench. The rations of the *mucs* smell pretty bad, too.
We have to be very careful how we move around in the trenches. There are snipers who keep us under fire and have already hit some of our comrades.
Surely among them there is the one that killed our chamois.
They use explosive bullets that leave no escape.
Our helmets are useless, even against normal bullets.[101]
I once saw a soldier from our company hit in the head by an explosive bullet. Awful!
We didn't dare remove his helmet. He was buried with it still on.
Now, though, we too have several marksmen and so the Austrians are not able to move around so freely either.
One of ours, who comes from the Abruzzo, showed me how many notches he has already put on the stock of his rifle. He is a hunter too. He told me he puts in the bullets upside-down to make them more deadly.[102]
Maybe I could be a sniper too.

---

front and open the way to Trieste, despite the heavy tribute of blood: 160,000 casualties (of whom 36,000 died). The Austro-Hungarians lost 125,000 men (of whom 17,000 died).

[101] The helmet supplied to the Italian Royal Army, Mod. 16, was a copy of the French one, Mod. 15 Adrian, named after its creator, General Louis Auguste Adrian. Made of thinner sheet metal, it was the least protective of all the helmets of the belligerent armies.

[102] The bullets were removed from their casing and reinserted with the tip upside-down. In this way, at the moment of impact with the target, the bullets ripped through flesh, causing wounds difficult to treat, like the infamous "dum-dum" bullets. In Italian military jargon, a soldier with his "balls turned upside-down" is highly aggressive and dangerous.

Nevertheless, I think that it is one thing to shoot a roe deer during a hunting trip and quite another to lurk around for hours and coldly shoot a man who has raised his head from the trench a bit too much or is doing his needs in the latrine.

That stuff is not for me.

A few days ago, one of our patrols came across two explorers in a wood in no man's land. The patrol leader did not have time to organize their capture before *Cuteddu* had jumped on them and killed them both with a knife.

The patrol leader gave him a tongue-lashing, but he didn't bat an eye.

He only hissed something in his dialect.

I don't know if it's true, but a soldier told me that he saw him clean the blood on the blade of his knife with his tongue.

I know for sure that I never want to pick a fight with him.

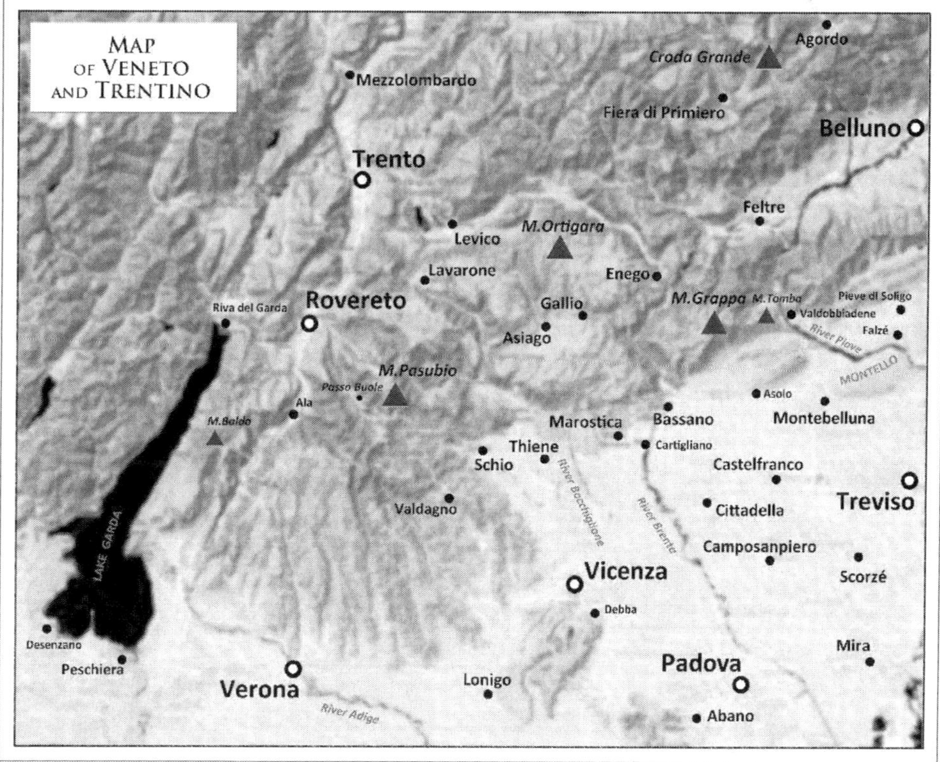

CHAPTER 32.1

September 21, 1984 saw me board the train to Rovigo.
For that special occasion I had cut the long hair and shaved the thick beard which several days earlier had earned me both the appellation of Jesus Christ and that of Barabbas, all within a few minutes!
Actually, I looked more like Garibaldi.
For the occasion, I was wearing a new jacket and tie. It was a completely unusual outfit for me. For the discussion of my thesis, on March 8, 1984, I had on a blue-on-blue sweater and dark blue velvet jeans.
That day in September, however, marked the beginning of a new adventure, full of unknowns, but also of hopes. From a certain point of view, it would be my last vacation before entering the working world. But it was an obligatory holiday, since I had chosen neither the destination nor the duration.
Thanks to my degree in Statistical Sciences, I was able to apply to and participate in a particularly tough physical and aptitude selection in Rome.
The first day was dedicated to medical visits and I remember the long line of candidates, in their underwear with urine sample in hand, which started in one building, continued through the courtyard, up a staircase and ended up inside another building, where a host of doctors visited and measured. At one point the queue halted and shouts were heard from the exam room. One of the candidates was scuffling with the doctors. He refused to admit that he was one centimetre shorter than the minimum allowed and he was loudly disputing the results of the measuring tape.
Rejected!
I remember that on the day of the psycho-aptitude tests, I was interviewed by the psychologist. He was full of compliments for the results of my tests of logic, but he was somewhat perplexed by a drawing I had made: it depicted a woman dressed in black rags, with exaggerated stiletto heels and an atomic-mushroom-shaped hairstyle, holding a large wrench in her hand. I explained to him that, since drawing was my hobby, I had copied one of my latest sketches (although, to avoid exaggerating, I had left out the mutant dwarfs with smashed heads dancing around the woman) and that he shouldn't jump to the wrong conclusions about me. "Out, out"! he said, shooing me away with his hand.

Day after day the number of candidates diminished visibly.
The fifth and final day was dedicated to the test dreaded by many. Athletics: the long jump, the high jump, the 100-metre sprint and rope climbing. Whoever failed two of these four trials was eliminated. Those who failed only one could make it up by running three laps around the track: over a kilometre under the hot June sun.
At the time I was in really good shape, and so for me those tests were just a game. Nevertheless, those trials were a source of concern and suffering for many candidates.
I can still see the ones who crashed into the bar even though it was placed only one metre high, the ones whose long jump was so short it didn't even reach the sandpit and lastly the poor wretch who had managed to climb up a bit of rope but instead of climbing further, tried to resist gravity by hanging on but instead slipped, slowly but inexorably, down to earth, skinning his hands in the process.
The final laps around the track, which the least physically gifted were forced to do, were tragicomic.
One guy actually passed out a few metres from the finish. Rejected!
The survivors of that long selection were then classified according to their graduating grades. Thanks to my 110 (the maximum) I was admitted to the XXI AUC training school of the Guardia di Finanza, located for the last time in the barracks at Rovigo.[103]
As military service was compulsory, I had looked for a solution that would not make me waste a year of my life. So, before starting the usual twelve months of service, I agreed to add three months of school. I could learn something new and then, once on duty as a 2nd lieutenant, I would earn a much more substantial salary than that of a private.
The training proved quite demanding at once.
For over ten days they forced us to wear camouflage and have no contact with the outside world. The instructors had to really brainwash us. How else could they have gotten a hundred top graduates in law, economics and statistics from all over Italy to fall in line?

---

103 AUC stands for Allievi Ufficiali Complemento, that is Official Reserve Cadets. The origins of the Guardia di Finanza (GdF) date back to October 5, 1774, when the "Light Troops Legion" was set up under the King of Sardinia, Victor Amadeus III. It was the first example in Italy of a special corps established and organized for financial surveillance duties along the borders, as well as for military defense. Nowadays the GdF is a militarized police force, forming a part of the Ministry of Economy and Finance, essentially responsible for dealing with financial crime and smuggling. It has also evolved into Italy's primary agency for suppressing the illegal drug trade.

I must say it worked.
Already after the first day there was no more talk about university, but only about how to put your beret on right, how to polish your shoes, how to salute your superiors and how to avoid wrinkles in the blue-and-white striped bedspread covering our beds.
Two months went by before most of us resumed talking about the fairer sex again!
Mornings were devoted to classroom lessons: eleven legal and military subjects. Afternoons were entirely dedicated to marching on the parade ground, holding the Beretta PM-12 9mm Parabellum submachine gun, which everyone kept in a trunk under his bed.
We had to learn to march well to music, in view of our ceremony of Oath of Allegiance to the Italian Republic, set for 11 November.
The company captain watched the progress of the three platoons remotely, each directed by a second lieutenant from previous classes. Wearing a peaked cap with a very steep visor (Japanese style), which hid his eyes, the captain instilled a holy fear in everyone.
Only after a few days did he materialize in the classroom and deign to speak to us, with razor-sharp imperative.
«Any questions?» he asked at the end of his precise explanations as to the nature of our training. There was nothing left to ask.
However, one colleague felt compelled to ask for a trivial clarification, «May I know how the final exam will proceed?»
After a studied silence, the captain's lapidary reply was: «Curiosity is feminine". At that point no one said another word.

Precisely this full immersion into military life made me want to pick up something where I had left it many years before: my search for information on grandfather's service in the Arditi troops.
I would do so on my first leave.
In the meantime, during the most difficult moments from a physical or psychological point of view, I began to think that my grandfather had certainly faced and overcome situations a thousand times more critical than mine. That simple thought gave me both the strength to resist during the hardest hours on the parade ground (especially when my feet were screaming in pain at being stuffed into too-small boots) and the energy to study eleven boring and unknown subjects, from Tax Law to Military Art, all in a short time.

Since that time, I have begun using the "Ardito" parameter, not so much to diminish the problems which I have had to face over time, but to face them and overcome them with even greater courage and determination.
That training course has become in my eyes a kind of surreal, comic and sometimes dramatic film, which I enjoyed in the double role of spectator and actor.
And so it was.
I worked very hard, but I also had a lot of fun.

Our first exit from the barracks was very theatrical.
One hundred perfectly clean-shaven and impeccable young men in jackets and ties emerged. Instead of walking, they marched in step with a proud mien, chins held exaggeratedly high, awkwardly brandishing briefcases (it was strictly forbidden to carry plastic bags).
The Captain gave us only two hours to do some shopping and communicate with our families. Upon our return our briefcases were searched and any food or drink confiscated.
Despite the strict ban on bringing food into the barracks, someone had filled his case with cold cuts, cheeses, bread and cans of beer. He was relentlessly intercepted and reprimanded.
Someone else, however, did elude the inspection and manage to bring something inside.
I can still see the scene: my colleague in the dormitory, hidden behind the wardrobe door, sucking greedily from a tube of condensed milk and watching himself in the mirror.
«This way I enjoy it twice!» was his ecstatic justification.

CHAPTER 33.I

War Zone, Friday, 13 July 1917
On 10 July, the Alpini relieved us on the front line.[104]
We finally descended to the valley and we quartered between Ala, Marani, Schincheri and Santa Margherita.
The next day I was promoted to corporal.
I am proud of my new rank, but I am also very worried.
Tomorrow morning we have to leave for the Isonzo front.
None of us are happy, not even the officers.
That front is like a slaughterhouse.
Our army has been trying to break through since the beginning of the war, but the defenses are very strong. So far we have conquered Gorizia and little else.
However, it is one thing to be unhappy, quite another to be insubordinate.
Lately, some soldiers from our Regiment have tried to convince our fellow soldiers to refuse to march against the enemy, to desert and even to shoot our officers and the colonel. They say that the war would end sooner.
I don't know if this is true, because nobody has talked to me about it.
It was reported by a few Carabinieri, who had mixed in with the troops, disguised as infantrymen so as not to be recognized.
Those soldiers have been arrested and now their necks are on the block.[105]
It was wrong of them to say those things, but those *Airplanes* have also become hateful spies.

Monday, 16 July 1917
We have arrived in Udine. It is a bedlam of men and vehicles.
It's very hot.

Sunday, 22 July 1917
n.n.
Exercises every day. Unbearable heat.

---

[104] "Exilles", "Monte Suello", "Val Cenischia" and "Val Maira" Battalions.
[105] Judgement, always very rapid, was passed soon after: a 22-year-old from Palermo was sentenced to life imprisonment; five other soldiers from various provinces of Italy were condemned to 20 years in prison.

Tuesday, 7 August 1917

I haven't written much lately, because there's been nothing new.

At the moment, we are located in Purgessimo, just north of Cividale.

In the last few days we have talked to soldiers who have returned well "cooked" from the front line on the Karst.

What they told us was worse than we imagined.

Shelling for hours, wiping out everything on the ground. Having to attack outside the trenches by running over the bodies of the dead and wounded, while machine guns mercilessly mow everything down; bodies ripped apart; human pieces scattered everywhere; earth soaked in blood; corpses entangled in the barb-wire as if hung out to dry; the nauseating smell of gunpowder and rotting bodies; mice, fleas and disease.

We fought a terrible battle in the mountains too and saw terrible things. But what is happening here is frightening.

They suggested that we keep a piece of paper in our pockets with two lines written on it:

B I P ZI R 16

C ch ZI P S S.

It seems that it brings good luck.

So we did, even if everyone already has his own amulets and lucky charms. Some men wear a little bag containing soil from their villages on their chests. Others keep three peas, each broken into three pieces, in three bags, which they move into three different pockets each day. Many wear pictures of Saints or of the Virgin Mary under their shirts. One man keeps a horse-shoe in his belt and is never separated from it.

Before a fighting or a foot patrol, it is customary to touch your nose, the stars on your collar and your groin with thumb, forefinger and middle finger together.

So far it's worked for me, but not for many others.

Yet we keep on doing it.

I have the Solomon's knot, the amulet my mother made for me.

I pray to heaven that it works now that I am about to cross the threshold of hell.

CHAPTER 34.I

After a few weeks we were finally given the "Drop", the gray uniform of the Guardia di Finanza.
From that moment on, we were only permitted to leave the barracks in uniform, and we had to walk or "march" in a way suitable to our dress. Of course, our behaviour had to be appropriate, too. For example, our cap with the golden flame could only be removed inside public places and then only when seated. Idem the gloves.
During our first city leave, we slipped into a restaurant to eat something other than the usual sad evening rations. I'll never forget the giant bowl of shrimps in an iced pink sauce.
At some point in the dinner we began to reminisce about our selection exams in Rome.
«V'à ricurdat e chill capellon barbut c'à magliett e cazunciell curt Addidas russ?» *asked my desk-mate, from Benevento, with a sardonic smile.*
«Teneva n'aspetto atletico, zumpava, curreva, saglieva a fun, ma po' l'hanno segato. Magari era pure nu poc drogato.»[106]
And we all fell about laughing, myself included.
I waited for the middle of the laugh to intervene point-blank:
«My friend, you would be a disaster as a detective. Look me in the face. That bearded longhair was me!»
Even if some of us feigned indifference, for better or worse we were all proud to wear the uniform and to be part of the one hundred "elite" of the XXI AUC class. Proof of this are the countless souvenir photos which I had to take, both of individuals and of groups, especially when we were celebrating the arrival of our uniforms.
By now I had become the official photographer of the class.
On the evening of the "Drop party" I understood just how much I had moved away from my old world and how deeply I had immersed myself in this new reality, full of strange disciplinary rules.

---

[106] «Do you remember that guy with a long beard and long hair wearing a red Adidas t-shirt and shorts?». «He looked like an athlete, he jumped and ran and climbed the rope, but in the end, they threw him out. He was probably a drug addict, too», translation from the Neapolitan dialect.

We always had to run from the classroom to the dormitories and back again, because walking was strictly prohibited, as was keeping your hands in your pockets.
Every evening, in pajamas and standing to attention, we had to wait for the instructor to verify the correct placement on a chair of all the elements of our uniform, after which he would authorize us simultaneously to go to bed. Just to give a couple of examples.
And so, on the evening of the "Drop party" a colleague sat down at the piano of the officers' club. I expected him to strum some sentimental melody or some regional song. Instead, he attacked "Firth of Fifth" from "Selling England by the pound" by the prog group Genesis, the real ones, the ones with Peter Gabriel. It was like an electric shock.
The unexpected intersection of my two worlds left an indelible trace in my memory file, a very big file, due to the many things that happened in those three months of training.
The Oath of Allegiance ceremony in front of the commanding general of the Academy, but especially in the presence of parents and relatives, practicing with pistol, rifle and submachine gun at the shooting range, exercising with sabers, throwing hand grenades, projecting my artistic slides (a great success among the cadets as the slides were all pictures of beautiful models), preparing for the live-fire exercise, the trip to Rome by pullman and live-fire exercises at Pian di Spille near Civitavecchia, my photographic documentation of the line of fire and of the exercises themselves, a great party in Rovigo with lots of girls and the nocturnal return trip to Venice. For all these events and for many others there would be many stories to tell, some more or less comic, some more or less singular.
For example, it was certainly a twist of fate that one of the girls subsequently married one of the career officers she met on that evening in Rovigo. She was one of the ten girls I had invited at the party.
Surprisingly, I have no memory of the final exam. Total blackout.
Perhaps for each of the eleven subjects I only had to answer a series of questions in multiple choice. For sure I copied some answers from those sitting next to me. However, adding my military grade to that of the exam, I ranked 14th in my class. This is one of my lucky numbers, like all those that add up to five. So there was a pretty good chance of being sent to one of the destinations I had requested: either the Alpine school at Predazzo, where I could ski and go to the mountains, or Udine, where I had many relatives, including my grandmother.
The region of origin was strictly excluded.

Conclusion: I was assigned to Bergamo, at the Training and Study Office of the Guardia di Finanza Academy, which had just moved there from Rome.
The captain had decided to bring with him a group of trusted second lieutenants who would add prestige to the AUC training school, which was moving from Rovigo to Bergamo.
That decision gave my life another important turn.

Chapter 35.I

Monday, 13 August 1917
We're not going to the Karst!
They're sending us further north.
Praise the Lord!
A great offensive is being prepared.
Many vehicles and troops are arriving. These movements take place at night so as not to be seen by enemy observers and *Draken*.[107]
We all hope that this offensive will go better than the one last May.
Everyone hopes to survive it safe and sound or get hit by a "smart" bullet.[108]
In the meantime, we are enjoying the sunny days, after the terrible cold of last winter.

Monday, 20 August 1917
After several transfers, our Brigade moved to Val Doblar.
We have set up camp at Case Bertini, while the 208th is near Drenchia.
Colonel Tiby commands our Regiment.
Brigade Commander is Colonel Brigadier Danioni.
Since the afternoon of the 17th all our artillery has been firing at enemy lines beyond the Isonzo river.[109]
The Austrians respond in kind.
It's one continuous, powerful, deafening roar. Day and night.
You can see large clouds of smoke and dust on the other side.
For sure we will be ordered to cross the river tomorrow.

---

[107] These were tethered balloons which spied on the Italian lines from an elevated position. The balloons used hydrogen as their lifting gas and were restrained by one or more tethers attached to the ground so that they could not float freely.
[108] This is how we called the minor wounds, which allowed one to leave the front line for some time or even definitively. British soldiers called them "Blighty" wounds.
[109] After a series of ranging shots, at 4:00 p.m. on 17 August the artillery of the 2nd Army intensified its rhythm until it reached a frequency close to bombardment. At dawn on the 18th, all Italian artillery, over 3,000 pieces of various caliber, went into action from the mountains to the sea along a front of over 70 kilometres. It was the beginning of the 11th Battle of the Isonzo, the most awesome for the volume of resources employed (between the middle and lower Isonzo more than 600 battalions were assembled out of 887 active) and the most tragic for casualties.

Easy to figure out: we got a ration more abundant than usual and lots of cognac, our "petrol".
After crossing the Isonzo river we'll have to go up a very steep and wooded slope, which leads to the Bainsizza plateau.
I had never heard of that place before the war.
We will have to head toward the 549-607-640 level lines and reach 509.
The III/208th will be supporting us.[110]
The other two battalions of the 208th will act as reserves.
I was assigned to an assault platoon.
It's like a *bassa* to the next world.[111]
My whole body is one continuous tremor.
I feel it and I can see it in my handwriting.
I have never written so badly in this notebook, but I can't help myself.
I am very sad because today I had to write letters and postcards on behalf of many comrades. These letters might be the last ones their families will receive and the last ones written by me.
I wrote home too.
May the Lord protect us.
If we really have to die, I hope at least that this may be the decisive battle and this damned war will end.

---

[110] Indicates the third Battalion of the 208th Regiment.
[111] In a figurative sense, this indicates a high-risk assignment. It derives from the word *bassa*, the lower part of the accompanying document, appropriately stamped, that soldiers always had to carry with them in transfers from one unit to another or upon entering the hospital.

Chapter 36.I

January 1985.
We said our last goodbyes in the snowy car park of the Rovigo barracks. After more than three months of living under one roof, our destinies were divided again, in most cases forever, projecting our lives towards destinations scattered throughout Italy.
The prevailing sentiment was happiness tempered with a touch of sadness since we were leaving behind some friendships born during the training (and seasoned with a bit of regret for our detachment from the inseparable PM-12).
Unforgettable scene: the classmate who scattered all the bullets of his Beretta pistol in the snow when he pulled out his handkerchief. We had been recommended to take the utmost care and not to lose the bullets. Despite all the training, some of us hadn't improved much. Months earlier, during an arms practice lesson in the classroom, that same classmate made us laugh by holding the gun as if it were a rifle! He didn't do it on purpose. He had never held a pistol before. He simply duplicated what he had learned days before during the rifle lesson. It was said that he was destined for a brilliant career as a magistrate, however.
During the Christmas holidays I had to satisfy all the curiosity of friends and relatives about my military experience. I had at least two thousand things to tell. On seeing me clean-shaven and in uniform, some people hadn't even recognized me.
Partly because of the limited time available and partly because of the many things to do and to tell, I ended up postponing once again my search for information on grandpa's service in the Arditi.
My leave ended quickly.
I arrived in Bergamo by car, driven by a classmate, on the night of February 17th, 1985. The Swearing-in before the Academy commander was scheduled for the following morning. We were very surprised to see so many people around at night. At that hour in Mestre most people had already been at home for several hours. In the main streets were lots of expensive high-powered cars which we rarely saw at home.
Bergamo presented itself to us as a rich and lively city.

The following months were wonderful and intense.
I was in charge of equipping the first computer room in the Academy, and providing photo-video coverage of all the main events (ceremonies, oaths, change of command between generals, athletic competitions between military academies, live-fire exercises, and parties, like the one in the castle of Urgnano for the Mak Π 100 of the 83rd training course, etc.).
Outside the Academy I also resumed my photographic business with numerous models from Bergamo.
However, on my scale of values none of that could compare in the slightest with the degree of intensity and uniqueness of my training in Rovigo.
Before summer came, I had already started thinking about the future.
I had already ruled out the possibility of "signing on" and staying in the Guardia di Finanza. I was interested in working in the marketing or advertising department of a company.
Among all the applications I posted (there were no e-mails at the time), only two led to job interviews: one with an advertising agency in Milan and another with a well-known clothing company in Ponzano Veneto, near Treviso.
Both interviews went well.
However, between working in the centre of Milan or in the Treviso countryside, I had no doubts. Milan also offered me the opportunity to become a professional photographer.
So, even before finishing my military service, I already had a job and had found a place to live in the centre of Bergamo, where I now felt at home.
The lion of San Marco represented on many of the city's buildings, especially the ancient one on the hill, made me feel still connected to Venice.
If I hadn't put down roots I would have gone back to Mestre.
A year of work in Milan made the rhythms of Mestre seem as slow as the movements of a sloth to me.
I began to perceive a strong Venetian accent in my friends.
Each time I took the train to Venice was like going back decades.
There was no doubt: I had put down roots.

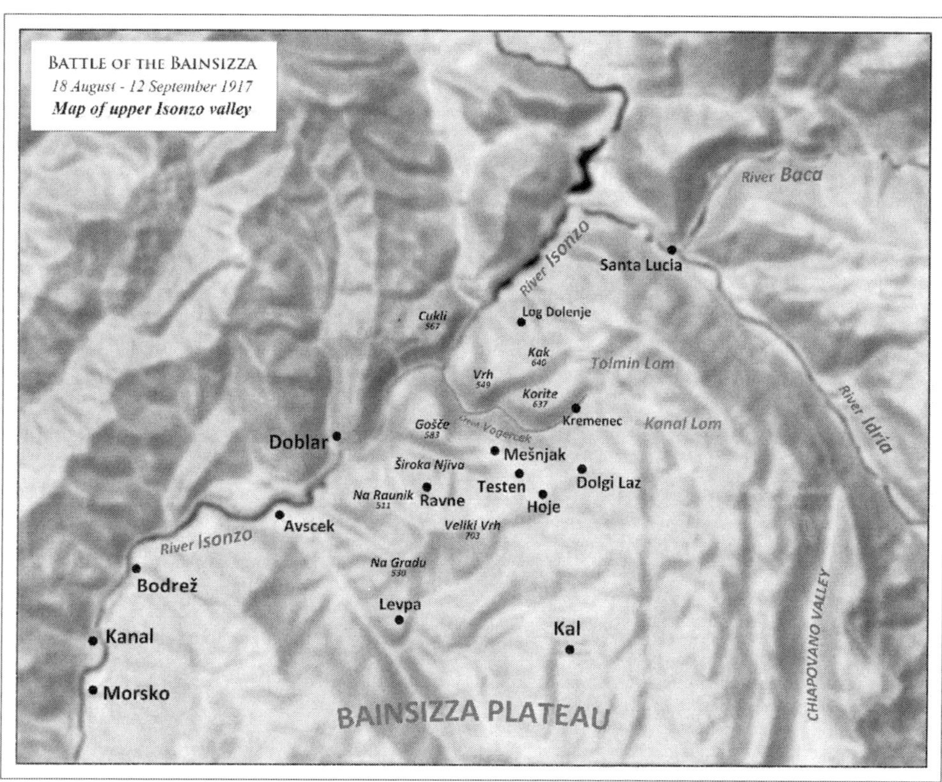

CHAPTER 37.I

Tuesday, 21 August 1917

Thank goodness I'm still alive.

This morning we made the crossing where the Doblar stream flows into the Isonzo river. There was a pontoon bridge set up by our bridge-builders.

The Austrians were shooting at us from high up on the hill.

The guns on the other side of the river, instead, were silent because they had been wiped out in the previous days.

To avoid being hit, we divided up into small groups. When the captain blew his whistle, we had to run like hell across the bridge and take shelter under the rocks. I made it with no problems.
As I waited for the others to arrive, I gazed at the river, which is a beautiful emerald green colour. In the current I first saw the corpse of an Austrian soldier float by and then that of a mule.
As soon as our platoon was back together, we started to climb through the thick underbrush. The ascent was also difficult due to the weight of our backpacks and ammunition. Continuous machine gun bursts flew through the woods, breaking off branches and ricocheting off rocks.
Luckily nobody was hit.
I wondered how the *mucs* could still be alive after all those days of heavy shelling and after the Alpini had already climbed the plateau the day before.
In fact, our artillery kept firing shot after shot.
When we reached the edge of the slope, our eyes fell upon a broad and terrible scenario. The ground was punctured by hundreds, perhaps thousands of shell-holes, and littered with corpses. It looked as if a terrible hailstorm had just passed.
In the distance the hills were dotted everywhere with clouds of smoke and dirt, so fierce was the shelling of our artillery.
We went right toward those hills.[112]
The heat was suffocating.
It is still very hot, even though it's evening now.
While we were descending into a valley we were attacked by a small group of Austrians, who shot our front ranks. As there were many more of us, we managed to surround them. We were in a very dense wood, so we did not use hand grenades, only rifles. They defended themselves to the end without ever giving up. Despite the heat, they wore heavy greatcoats. Their faces were thin and hollow, as if they hadn't eaten in a long time.
Some of our soldiers, who had already run out of water, took their water bottles. But they were empty. We left them there in that wood, without burying them. There was no time.
To go up again, we had to advance out in the open, trying to avoid the mortar shots. In that confusion, however, it was impossible to distinguish the hiss of incoming shells.

---

[112] After crossing the Isonzo river, the three Battalions of 207th and III/208th climbed the northwest slopes of Na Raunik, heading towards the hills south of the Široka Njiva valley, beyond which they were to occupy the levels 545-550 on the right side of the valley.

A lot of planes were skimming over us.
I held my rifle in one hand and in the other I clutched my mother's amulet.
Thank goodness I wasn't hit.
Towards evening we halted behind two hills inside enemy trenches, which our soldiers had already cleaned up.[113]
Now I'm here.
There are several bodies scattered around, both Italian and Austrian.
I see soldiers eating their rations right next to them as if it were completely normal.
As I write, the clamor of weapons does not cease.
Tonight we will have to advance again.

Wednesday, 22 August 1917
In the early hours of the morning we started moving forward again, but very slowly because of the difficulty of carving a path through such thick woods. Our faces and hands were full of scratches. We swore at almost every step. Our voices, however, were covered by the roar of artillery, which in these days never stops.
The difficulty increased when the terrain started going downhill. The wood was so dense that those who slipped or stumbled did not end up at the bottom of the valley but were held back by bushes.
On our right we heard heavy machine gun and rifle fire. Our Alpini were over there. They too were descending towards the bottom of the valley, where there is a creek called Vogercek. We hoped to find water, because our canteens were almost empty.
The fire from the machine guns began to slowly shift towards us.
At one point the bullets penetrated the forest like hail. The Austrians understood that we were coming and knew that we had to go through there.
We were ordered to stop and find shelter.
Our commander called for the intervention of the artillery, which started firing with increasing violence. The machine guns stopped persecuting us almost immediately.
After a couple of hours of that treatment, we assumed that we could proceed with greater peace of mind. Instead, we heard the voice of *Schwarzlose*[114] again in the area occupied by the Alpini.

---

[113] The two front-line Battalions of the 207th occupied the crests of the levels 545-550 on the right side of the Široka Njiva valley. On the right they were attached to the V Alpine Group and on the left to the III/208th, reinforced by the 1240th machine gun company.

All our shells had failed to silence them. The Alpini were also firing.
We stood still waiting to know what to do.
At dawn, we understood that another day of sun and heat was waiting for us. This worried us a lot, if the water supply did not arrive soon.
Later the order came to return to our starting positions.
The Alpini had not managed to prevail over the Austrians on the other side of the Vogercek and then attack level 633. Therefore, our assault on level 549 no longer made sense.
Much faster, we moved back to where we started.
Our hopes of finding food and water, however, were disappointed.
Instead, we had to turn out the trenches dug by the Austrians and bury their dead in holes created by our shells.
A task both pitiful and monstrous.
The command of our Brigade has established that tomorrow we will have to take levels 549 and 607, then Mount Kak and a hilltop west of another mountain.[115]
If we weren't able to do it today, how can we possibly achieve all four objectives tomorrow?

Thursday, 23 August 1917
Our command is sending out many patrols to check out the terrain in the valley that descends to the Vogercek creek then goes upwards to the hill that we have to take away from the Austrians.
I volunteered to lead a patrol.
I was too thirsty and I was hoping to find water in that stream.
We repeated yesterday's trek and passed the point where we had stopped.
The sounds of a battle echoed not far from us.

---

[114] Designed by the Prussian firearms designer Andreas Wilhelm Schwarzlose and manufactured by Steyr Arms, it was the main machine gun of the Austro-Hungarian army. It was fed by a 250-round cloth belt, mounted on a tripod and served by a crew of at least 3 soldiers. It had a range of 2,400 steps and a remarkable rate of fire (over 400 rounds/minute). Due to the significant amount of heat released during operation, the servers had to periodically replace the cooling water. In addition to the standard 500 rounds, each weapon was equipped with 9,500 ready-to-use rounds and another 10,000 were packed into ammunition boxes.
[115] It was from Mount Kak, now called Kuk or Cucco, that the Austrians prevented the advance of the "Taro" Brigade and the V Alpini Group. The other mountain was the Cukle Vrh.

The passage down to the valley floor was difficult, both for the slope and for the presence of rocks, which sometimes fell straight down the cliff.
When we got down, we had the unhappy surprise of discovering that the torrent was dry, except for a few undrinkable puddles of muddy water.
We cautiously started climbing up the opposite slope.
It was just as difficult as the downhill.
For safety I ordered the men to crawl on the ground. We advanced a few hundred metres very slowly, alternating between stopping and moving, until I thought I heard something and I ordered the patrol to stop.
After about a minute an Austrian came out from behind a tree on our left.
He was unarmed and was adjusting his trousers. He certainly had just moved his bowels. We kept our eyes on him until he suddenly vanished, just as if he had fallen into a hole.
It was a trench camouflaged in the woods.
I thought I had heard voices coming from there.
It might be a machine gun nest.
I took note of its position and then we silently retraced our steps.
Their *squarc' l'oss*[116] could have mowed us all down in seconds.
As I was crawling backwards, a viper passed beside me.
It would have been ironic to escape the Austrians and then be bitten by a poisonous snake!
We reported the location of the machine gun nest and the considerable difficulty of the path both downhill and uphill to the command.
We also reported that the stream is unfortunately dry.
We are all thirsty, even the officers.
The soil up here doesn't retain water and therefore there are no sources of water. We are all missing the climate of Trentino. Now, in exchange for a handful of fresh snow, the men who were complaining so about the cold would gladly give their entire *cinquina*.[117]
Some of them were even desperate enough to drink machine gun cooling water but were prevented by the officers.
Today we received the news that General Vanzo, commander of our Army Corps, the XXVII, has been dismissed by the High Command and replaced with General Badoglio.[118]

---

[116] It literally means "bone-ripper". It was a deliberately distorted way of calling the *Schwarzlose* machine gun in Italian.
[117] Military jargon indicating the pay that was given to soldiers every five days.
[118] General Luigi Capello (April 14, 1859 - June 25, 1941), commander of the 2nd Army, was very irritated at the lack of progress and the failure to conquer the Lom area, which would have allowed him to attack the important bridgehead of Tolmin. He asked and ob-

Instead of this news, we would have preferred to receive food supplies and especially water.
Everyone thinks that this new general will want to show Cadorna how much better he is than the other.
So soon we will have to start advancing again.
At all costs.
For now, however, operations are suspended and we have to reinforce our positions.[119]

tained from Cadorna the exemption of General Vanzo, commander of the XXVII Army Corps.

[119] The decision to temporarily suspend operations included the entire attack front. It was a serious mistake because at that moment the enemy was going through a grave crisis, especially in the centre of the Bainsizza plateau, where General Caviglia's XXIV Army Corps operated. Years later he wrote: *"The lesson that we failed to give the Austrians on August 23, was given to us by the Austrian-German 14th Army on October 24".*

Chapter 38.I

My grandfather had three sons: my father Sergio, Silvano, who for some unknown reason everyone called Bruno, and Mario.
During the Second World War, tragic circumstances led to the deportation of Bruno to a German concentration camp where he apparently died of pneumonia. His mortal remains have never been found, despite numerous searches by my grandfather.
My father had two children, me and my sister. My uncle had two daughters. For some strange reason since childhood I have taken on the responsibility of "carrying on" the family surname.
Once, a priest, seeing me serving mass so often as an altar boy, suggested that I enter the seminary.
I remember looking at him as if he had blasphemed in church!
Didn't he understand that I was racking up points to arrive first in Father Bonaventura's ranking of altar boys? I preferred to point out the other thing he didn't understand. I had a mission, that of adding branches to my family's family tree.
For many years I lived convinced that this was my mission, which no one had ever dreamed of assigning to me, even as a joke.
By the time I reached the age of reason, the prospect of having children had become a possibility, but, over the years, the likelihood of this happening has become ever more remote and is no longer even very attractive.
In any case, I liked to imagine that, consistent with the family trend, any future child would have to look for work five hundred kilometres from Bergamo, more or less in France. From Dogna my grandfather had gone to work in Udine and then to Artegna. My father had increased the range of travel: one hundred and fifty kilometres from Artegna to Marghera. I had moved another two hundred and fifty kilometres further west to live in Bergamo and work in Milan. My son should take a further leap west.
What if fate had reserved only daughters for me?
All this was too premature.
I had just started working in Milan. Now I had to build a career in the advertising world, not the one of the "stars" (i.e. the creatives), but the one of "the numbers" (i.e. the media).

What's more, I wanted to take up my historical research again.
Grandfather had never told his family anything about his military service.
My father had told me this several times.
My uncle Mario had confirmed it to me.
So there was obviously no point in asking other relatives.
Moreover, the only ones who might have known something, Noè and Geraldo, my grandpa's two brothers, had died respectively in 1960 and 1979. Mattia might have known something too. He was a pupil of my grandfather's and he too had long been a soldier. Grandfather might have confided something to him. Unfortunately, Mattia was also dead. One of my grandfather's sisters, Margherita, born in 1903, was still alive. But the idea of getting in touch with her after decades of silence among our families was complicated for me. For some obscure reason my grandfather had reduced relations with his Dogna family, preferring that of his wife from Enemonzo. My father had followed in his footsteps, preferring my mom's family, originally from Raveo (a stone's throw from Enemonzo).
Even the room inherited in the house of Dogna house had been ceded by my father and uncle to my grandfather's youngest sister Lucia's daughter. She and her family had been the only ones to visit that house assiduously, until it became uninhabitable after the 1976 earthquake. She had then hosted her uncle Geraldo at her home in Gemona del Friuli and, afterwards, she and her husband worked to make the house habitable again.
All I could do was try to recover the old suitcase which I had found as a child and which contained two of my grandfather's uniforms, in particular the Arditi one. Many years ago, that one had seemed very ugly.
Now, it was of inestimable value to me.
What could have happened to it?

CHAPTER 39.I

Friday, 24 August 1917
The day had started out in the best way.
At the first light of dawn I was awakened by the violent roar of our artillery, which then kept on firing with great intensity for several hours.
Strangely, the Austrians did not fire back as usual.
While we were waiting for our new orders, we found out that our enemies had abandoned their positions during the night.
Maybe they were in retreat!
Immediately a great wave of enthusiasm among all of us.
In one moment we forgot our hunger, thirst and tiredness.
By the late morning there were rumors that our troops had conquered the top of Veliki Vrh and even Monte Santo.[120]
Everyone was smiling and shouts of "hurrà!" arrived from all points of the plateau as the news spread.
We were eager to set off immediately in pursuit of the Austrians, but we had to wait until 2:00 p.m. before moving forward. We of the 207th had to ascend from Vogercek to level 633, head for the Lom of Tolmin and then to Ravne. Simultaneously, two Battalions of the 208th were to move to the left towards level 549, then to level 607, west of the Kak, and finally to level 770, north of Ravne.
We were told that the *mucs* were retreating and that only small rearguards were left. It was a nasty surprise to discover that in our area they were still very aggressive.[121]

---

[120] Together with Sabotino and San Gabriele, Monte Santo was one of the mountain peaks around Gorizia where fighting was more intense.
[121] Fearing a ruinous collapse of his troops, the commander of the Isonzo-Armeé, general Svezotar Boroević von Bojna (13 December 1856 - 23 May 1920), decided to vacate the entire Bainsizza plateau. However, at 4 o'clock in the morning he rescinded that order and commanded a fast retreat over the line proposed by General Ludwig Goiginger: Mešnjak-Hoje-Kal-Vrhovec-Madoni-Zagorje-Monte San Gabriele. This valiant general's intuition, both simple and ingenious, was that the new line would be beyond the reach of the Italian artillery. There were other advantages as well: a shorter defense line, fewer supply problems, the presence of cave shelters, water tanks, barracks and rolling roads. A further advantage was that of avoiding the difficult crossing of the Chiapovano valley for the artillery.

Just as we had almost reached the torrent at the bottom of the valley, we were hit with sudden bursts of machine gun fire. Two soldiers near me had their legs broken by those bullets. I was unharmed thanks to a tree trunk that acted as a shield. Other soldiers had also been hit. I could hear many cries of pain coming from all directions in that bush.
We responded to the fire with rifles and submachine guns, firing towards the other side, but as we were unable to see where our enemies were hidden, the chance of hitting the machine gunners was very poor. Again we requested help from the artillery, praying to heaven that it wouldn't hit us. For some reason the support of our cannons has not arrived, so we are still pinned down here.
We can't get past Vogercek and reach our objectives.
Anyone who tried was immediately repelled by the *Schwarzlose* fire.
Our enthusiasm of this morning has completely vanished.

Saturday, 25 August 1917
I'm really tired.
I hiked for many hours with my patrol to reestablish the connection on the left with the 208th Regiment.
While we werc in the middle of the woods, we almost shot their chaplain and his attendant. They were trying to regain contact with the troop. They had just escaped being shot by an Austrian patrol. Together with them we crossed that damned torrent without being targeted by a sniper or machine gun.
We only found a miserable puddle. Our thirst had reached such a point that we would have drunk even that putrid water, but all we could do was to wet rags to moisten our heads and necks.
We could hear the sound of gunfire from an ongoing battle coming from above. It was the 208th trying to conquer level 549. We went up the slope until we came across signs of the firefight. There was a strong smell of gunpowder, wood and burnt flesh. Many branches and shrubs were broken. Blood on the leaves of the undergrowth.
Then the sequence of the dead began. They were ours.
The chaplain took note of the names on their dog tags.
Impossible to bury them or take them with us.
There were too many of them.
To defend their position, the enemies had even employed some poachers' traps.

We saw one dead soldier with his leg crushed by a trap and some "wolf holes" into which someone, unfortunately, had fallen.[122]
A little further on we found a barbed wire fence put up among the trees. Other bodies lay dead nearby. In many places, however, the barbed wire had been cut. Our comrades had passed through.
Beyond the wire there were the trenches.
There were some Austrians inside. We searched to see if anyone was still alive. We found one man who still seemed to be breathing, but his face was horribly torn up. His lower jaw was missing. We only heard a kind of gurgling coming out of that bloody mask. Out of pity we put an end to his suffering.
Before noon we made contact with the rear of the 208th. We were told that during the morning they had conquered level 549 and taken prisoners, including an officer.
We continued the ascent to the crest. Everywhere men lay on the ground exhausted. Everyone complained about the absence of water. Food stocks were also getting low. I had a few biscuits and a tin of meat left. From the crest I saw the other hills which we will have to take away from the Austrians. I felt sick!
I reported to the 208th command, who gave me a message for our commander.
In the early afternoon we started the descent to go back to Vogercek.
Soldiers were recovering our dead. As we passed close by the Austrian trench, the hum of thousands of flies could be heard, already attacking the corpses. I hope I won't end up that way too, some day.
When we finally arrived at the command of the 207th we learned that not even today had our Regiment been able to take level 633. To think that they had told us the enemy was pulling back, maybe even in rout.

Sunday, 26 August 1917
Last night was very busy.
And the rest of the day didn't kid around either!
Around 10:00 p.m. we heard furious rifle fire and hand grenade bursts on level 549, defended by the 208th. We found out later that some Austrians had penetrated our lines with a very cowardly trick.

---

[122] This is a conical pit about 2 m deep and 1.2 to 2 m wide at the top, camouflaged on the surface, with sharp points of wood or iron set in the bottom. Sometimes infectious agents, such as feces or rotten meat, were smeared onto the points to make the victim's wounds more serious.

They spoke Italian and wore our uniforms.
They said they were prisoners, who had managed to escape.
When they were found out all hell broke loose.
Lurking behind them was an assault unit.
The *mucs* were eventually beaten back, but there were many casualties. One of these was a captain of the 7th company, silver medal of valour during the fighting of May 1916.[123]
Those criminals killed him with a stab in the back of his neck.
Seven of the rats who used our uniforms dishonourably were captured.
Colonel Casini was infuriated[124].
After a hasty interrogation he had them shot by our machine gunners.
On the 26th, a violent storm broke out in the middle of the night.
For us it was a blessing from heaven.
We had been waiting for this in order to cool off and quench our thirst after so many days of torrid heat. We stood in the rain with faces upturned and mouths wide open to drink the rain as it fell. With upturned helmets and mess tins, we collected as much water as possible for our water bottles. So much rain has fallen that we have filled them well.
The ground, though, has become muddy and slippery.
In fact, when we moved off to Kremenec in the morning, we had a hard time staying on our feet.
Then there were the Austrians who were shooting at us from level 633.
Luckily our commander, Colonel Tiby, didn't send us out to be massacred.
Given the situation, he revoked the order to attack.
God bless him!
The Brigade commander, however, was not of the same opinion and replaced him. In the late afternoon he sent Lieutenant Colonel Geloso to take over. The first thing he did was to reposition our three Battalions. He ordered us to deploy in the small valley that runs down to the Vogercek, to keep watch over it and to make contact with the 208th through patrols.

---

[123] Italo Stegher, made captain at only 23 years old. In an attempt to stem the night attack, he was surrounded by enemies and shot because he refused to surrender. He was awarded the Gold Medal of Military Valour with the following motivation: *In several days of fierce fighting, he cooperated effectively with the company under his command and conquered an important position. Counterattacked without warning by an enemy unit at night, he reacted quickly, and with his men, stemmed the raid restoring the continuity of the line already crossed by enemy factions. Surrounded by surprise and seized by an enemy who denied him the material impossibility of reacting, he disdainfully refused to surrender, and was killed. Bainsizza, level 549.*
[124] He was the commander of the 208th Regiment of the "Taro" Brigade.

We got moving through the rain and the fire of the Austrian machine guns. It was a really busy day.[125]

Monday, 27 August 1917

For those of us from the 1st Battalion today was a fairly peaceful day, but not for the rest of the Regiment.
All night the Austrians tormented the 208th, first with rifles and machine guns, then with a violent shelling of level 549 and finally with an attack, which our comrades managed to repel.

With the infantrymen of the "Belluno", the II/207th was engaged in dislodging the enemies from what remains of Mešnjak and apparently they succeeded.[126]

The III/207th attacked, as always together with the 274th, the rubble and rocks of Testen, but things didn't go well. Many dead and wounded.
Today four artillery batteries came to our support.
We hope that now the enemy defenses can be eliminated more easily, since they are very tenacious here.[127]

---

[125] Other notable events happened that same day. Cadorna moved 400 pieces of artillery from the 2nd to the 3rd Army to launch an unexpected assault on the Karst, substantially ending the victorious advance on Bainsizza. Reluctantly, Emperor Charles I of Habsburg (17 August 1887 - 1 April 1922) was forced to send a request for help to his ally, Kaiser Wilhelm II (27 January 1859 - 4 June 1941), since his army could not resist a 12th battle on the Isonzo front. German support would make it possible to launch a massive offensive against the Italians, who would then have been forced to sue for an armistice. Once the Italian front was closed, the Austro-German troops could move on to the western front and this would have favored the end of the war.
August 26th is also remembered because during the night a divisional band, directed by Arturo Toscanini (25 March 1867 - 16 January 1957), played the Royal March and the Anthem of Mameli on the conquered peak of Monte Santo. The Austrians responded with cannon shots. The Maestro gained further fame and a silver medal from General Capello.

[126] On the 26th during the fighting in Mešnjak the commander of the 274th Regiment of the "Belluno" Brigade, Colonel Alceo Cattalochino, was shot in the chest and died the following day in a field hospital. He was awarded the Gold Medal of Military Valour with the following motivation: *"Destined to command a Brigade, he asked and obtained permission to remain in command of the Regiment for an imminent action, and, with skill and enthusiasm, he prepared his troops for an attack on the enemy position, against which three previous attacks had been unsuccessful for three days in succession. He then directed his units against the position itself, and, as the first waves were unable to progress due to the intense enemy fire of artillery and machine guns, he forged ahead with his reserve units, and, placing himself at the head of the troops, he drove them to the attack, reaching the objective. With victory already in sight, he was shot to death."*

Tuesday, 28 August 1917
Today the III/207th bled to death in the conquest of Testen and the stone quarry above it. There have been violent hand-to-hand fights!
Only a few men from the entire Battalion remain sound.
They lost all their captains and the commander too.
I will forever thank heaven that I wasn't assigned to that Battalion.
And so will all my comrades.
The only one who regrets not having taken part in the slaughter is the Sicilian, who always wants to avenge his brothers.
I am afraid that very soon we too from I/207th will be called to combat, unfortunately.

Wednesday, 29 August 1917
Since the early morning our artillery has been unleashing a violent fire of destruction against the Austrians' defenses, situated near a village called Hoje.
Then, as is usual, some of our Brigades attacked.
But from the machine gun and rifle fire, which we can still hear, the enemy has not been destroyed by our gun shells.[128]
We have been ordered to be on thc alert to take action against Kremenec and then head towards the Tolmin Lom.

5:40 p.m.
We received the order to head towards Dolgi Laz following a mule track that starts north of Mešnjak.
As I write, machine gun fire is still coming from Hoje.

---

[127] It should be noted that at 11:00 a.m. on that day a very serious event occurred in Udine. It is believed that a saboteur blew up the ammunition dump of Sant'Osvaldo, the largest of the Royal Army in war territory. Houses in a large surrounding area were destroyed and many civilians died. For some hours, panic spread among the population due to the presence of chemical explosives. A further consequence of this explosion was the inability to adequately supply the troops engaged in the 11th Battle of the Isonzo with ammunition.

[128] Artillery fire was effective only behind the lines, while the machine guns placed in the front line remained intact and ready to provide deadly crossfire. The repeated assaults by the infantrymen of "Belluno", "Trapani" and above all "Pescara" resulted in a massacre. Even the commander of the "Pescara" Brigade, Major General Ernesto De Marchi, was seriously wounded (a shell fragment hit his jaw and a bullet hit his elbow).

CHAPTER 40.I

I got in touch with my relatives in Dogna.
They were the only ones who might have known something about the suitcase. Too bad they didn't remember it at all.
They did remember, though, that they had had to clear out all of the rooms after the house had become unsafe following the earthquake.
Everything had been piled up in various warehouses and even in the rectory of the church, all mixed up with household goods from the other damaged houses.
It had all been crammed in there until the house was repaired. In the general confusion, however, many things had been lost or thrown away.
I learned from a cousin that in the uproar of those days even the photographic plates and negatives of a famous Carnic photographer had ended up among the rubble thrown into the gravel of the river by a bulldozer.
Disconsolate, I decided to give up.
So more time went by, until I decided to make one final attempt: I contacted the parish priest of Dogna and organized an inspection of those improvised storerooms. I explained the whole story to him and with great kindness he agreed to accompany me.
«I can't guarantee you will find what you're looking for» he felt compelled to tell me just before ending the call.
I knew that very well, but I couldn't help making this extreme attempt before resigning myself to the idea of having lost the Ardito uniform kept in that old suitcase forever.
On the agreed day we met in the parish.
I told him the story again, enriching it with some other details.
«I can't guarantee you will find what you are looking for» he repeated to me with a touch of genuine displeasure. He was already imagining my disappointed expression at the end of the inspection.
When the parish priest opened the warehouse door, armed with an old rusty key, I felt a kind of déjà vu.
The large room was filled with furniture, chairs, knick-knacks, lamps, boxes. Dust and cobwebs reigned everywhere. The typical smell of old things hung overall, a mixture of mold and humidity, but instead of disappointing me it actually raised my hopes of finding what I was looking for.

To avoid getting dirty I moved around in that chaos like a contortionist. Every time I touched something, however, a smear of gray powder inexorably smudged my clothes or my hands.
Then, in the depths of that intricate mass of objects, I seemed to glimpse something that vaguely resembled a group of suitcases. I turned on my pocket flashlight to shed some light on that dark corner.
They actually were suitcases.
To reach them I gave up any idea of not getting dust all over me.
Removing the suitcases from where they were placed was like drawing the sword from the Stone.
The parish priest waited in the doorway with his hands clasped and his chin resting on the tips of his fingers. Maybe he was praying for a happy outcome to my search or maybe it was a simple professional pose.
Swearing under my breath I managed to extract the first suitcase.
In the light, I immediately saw that it was not my grandfather's. The label bore the name of another family. The other suitcases were easier to pull out, but it was not so easy to put them where there was more light and more space to examine them.
Even the second suitcase was not the desired one. And neither was the third nor the fourth. The fifth, however, resembled the one I vaguely remembered. My heart leapt when I recognized my surname on the label attached to the handle. I looked the parish priest intensely in the eyes so that he would understand that I intended to open it.
«Ese chê?»[129] *he asked me with his hands still clasped below his chin, but with the astonished gaze of someone who is about to witness a kind of miracle.*
Snapping open the two locks, I saw again for a moment that bright whirlwind that had dazzled my childish eyes, surrounding me and leaving me a little stunned. The suitcase, however, was still closed.
I held my breath and then, with a determined move, I opened it.

---

[129] «Is that it?» translation from the Friulan language.

CHAPTER 41.I

Saturday, 1st September 1917
It's a miracle I'm still alive!
Around 8:00 p.m. on August 29th we started advancing towards Dolgi Laz. We were backup to the 2nd Battalion.
It was easy to see which way to go because the village was in flames, hit by the incendiary bullets fired by our artillery from beyond the Isonzo.
It was not easy to move forward because the brush was thick, so much so that at some point we lost contact with the II°.
Luckily, we were protected from the sight of the *mucs*, who were shooting blindly from the surrounding hills into that tangle of vegetation with both cannons and machine guns.
Many times I felt the ground tremble under my feet due to exploding shells and many times I heard the crack of branches broken by the bullets of the *Schwarzlose* and the *Shrapnels*.[130]
Every step could be my last, if a random bullet or ball guessed where I was. I thought about it with every step.
After more than two hours of difficult and risky march, we arrived half a kilometre from the village, which was on fire in several places.
The *mucs* were waiting for us. They didn't shoot right away. They waited a while and then they targeted us with intense machine and gun fire.
Just then something horrible happened, something I will never forget.
A cannon shot at and hit a group of soldiers just in front of my platoon at head height. Pieces of them hit us in full. All of us were drenched in blood and other liquids. Some guys had to vomit from disgust.
In the meantime, others of us were hit by machine guns.
We immediately sought shelter.
An older soldier from my company, a father with a family, started to cry like a child.

---

[130] This is an artillery shell that, exploding before impact with the ground, projects its contents all around it: dozens of lead or steel spheres with potentially lethal effects. It was conceived and developed in 1784 by British Lieutenant Henry Shrapnel. Considered a secret weapon, it was used for the first time in 1808 against Napoleonic troops in the battle of Vimeiro and was also a protagonist in the battle of Waterloo (June 15, 1815). During WW1, this shell, no longer secret, was widely used by the artillery of all armies.

In my role as corporal major, I had to slap him to make him stop, even though I had a lump in my throat.
To go any further in that open field would be suicide.
The Austrians were well entrenched behind the walls and the ruins of the houses.
Luckily our command didn't send us to the slaughter.
I know well that other commanders did that in order to earn a medal.
Ours, however, suspended the attack and requested the intervention of the artillery.
During the night there was a violent thunderstorm and so we were able to wash some of the blood off of us.
At around 3 in the morning on August 30, an order came through to be prepared for a new attack. "This is it, I'm afraid" I thought.
The fires had gone out and so the Austrians continued launching coloured flares to light up the ground and prevent us from attacking under cover of darkness. We made a couple of attempts, but it was as if in front of us there was a wall of lead defending the ruins of Dolgi Laz.
Before dawn we were ordered to return to Mešnjak.
In the position we were in and in the light of day, the enemy artillery could have wiped us out in a short time.
In the ruins of Mešnjak our chaplain celebrated mass, even if it was not Sunday. Plenty of us attended it. We understood that something important was about to happen in our lives.
At 11 the order we feared arrived: the 1st and 2nd Battalions had to attack and take that village.
For the generals, sitting in the shade in their safe shelters miles away from real danger, Dolgi Laz was just a dot on a map.
For us it was the entrance to hell.
Two hours later we were back in that damned thicket.
Absolute silence reigned. There was only the hum of insects between one cannon shot and another.
A bad feeling lingered in all of us
We all had a bad feeling, similar to what animals feel when they understand they are being taken to the slaughterhouse. Unlike animals, we were armed and could theoretically kill the butcher. Unlike the slaughterhouse, though, the butcher here had howitzers and machine guns.
I believe that in those moments we were all thinking the same thing: I will never see my family or my home again. At best, my body will be mutilated somewhere and I'll be disfigured. It's probably better to die instantly.

I was clutching my amulet so tightly in the palm of my hand that I didn't notice that the spikes had entered my flesh.

In silence we exchanged letters. We had done it before. The survivors will send letters to the families of the fallen. I too have given copies of my letter to the comrades I feel closest to and I've received just as many.

They all say more or less the same thing: messages of love for wives, children, mothers and fathers; declarations of having done our duty with honour for them and for Italy.

A soldier came up to me. Instead of giving me his letter, he whispered in my ear that he and some other guys had decided to shoot our officers if they sent us to the attack.

I asked him if he was crazy. I told him that he and the others would be shot in the back together with other innocent people drawn at random from the Battalion. Our enemy is in Dolgi Laz.

His reply was that the real enemy lay behind us, in the headquarters and in the rear lines. They want all of us dead.

I told him to remember what had happened to us in early July and also the "Catanzaro" soldiers.[131]

He told me to go to hell and went away cursing. It was neither the time nor the place to slap him. But I would keep an eye on him from now on. If he made the slightest attempt to aim his rifle at our captain, I would shoot him dead on the spot with my '91.

---

[131] The "Catanzaro" Brigade had shown courage and value in many battles, in particular that of Mount Mosciagh on the Asiago plateau (May 1916), so much so that the flag of the 141st received the Gold Medal of Military Valour awarded by the King in *motu proprio*. However, in July 1917 news that there might be a new and early redeployment to the frontline trenches triggered a revolt in the camp at Santa Maria la Longa. After a night of clashes with 11 dead and 27 wounded, the riot was quelled. The commander ordered that 16 infantrymen caught in the act be shot. The 6th company of the 142nd Regiment mutinied *en masse* and was decimated after 12 soldiers, drawn by lot, were shot and the rest arrested and imprisoned. After these serious events the Brigade continued to fight with discipline, deserving a mention in the war bulletin of 25 August 1917 for having distinguished itself for boldness and tenacity in the fighting on the Karst. It is useful to remember some passages of the Cadorna circular: *"Everyone must know that anyone who tries ignominiously to surrender or retreat will be shot before he disgraces himself either by the summary justice of lead in the rear lines or by that of the carabinieri in charge of policing the rear of the troops. [...] I remind you that there is no other suitable means of repressing collective crimes than that of immediately shooting the main offenders, and when the ascertainment of the personal identities of those responsible is not possible, the commanders remain entitled and duty-bound to randomly extract some of the soldiers from among the suspects and punish them with the death penalty."*

Five minutes later that same soldier was face down, hit by rifle fire during our first rush forward. He had changed his mind.
At the officers' whistle, a first wave of soldiers came out of the woods shouting "Savoia!", or the more blasphemous "...boia!"[132]
From experience I had decided to go out among the first.
I was counting on the fact that the machine gunners had to line up their shots at the beginning and therefore were not always very precise. In fact, I and some other soldiers managed to run forward for about a hundred metres without being hit. Then, when the aim became more precise, we threw ourselves into some shell holes. Those who came out in the following waves had worse luck. Only a few managed to throw themselves unharmed into the pits in the ground.
Crawling from hole to hole we gained more metres. But at that point we were increasingly cut off from the rest of the Battalion and pinned down in a very dangerous position.
The worst came when they began shelling in the space between the woods and the village. It felt like being in the end of the world. A shell fell into a hole full of soldiers. I saw them tossed into the sky like cloth dummies. They were all my unfortunate assault comrades. A horrible sight.
I hate my backpack, but this time I blessed it because it cushioned the blows from the stones that rained down on me. Those backpacks, however, did not shelter us from a hail of *Shrapnel* bullets, which injured many of those around me. I escaped with only a glancing hit to my helmet.
In the midst of that tumult, all you could do was lie prone inside the shell holes and recommend yourself to God.
In every single instant of those interminable moments, I was afraid of finding myself suddenly torn to pieces by the explosion of a shell.
I prayed for it not to happen. Like everybody else.
I was trembling like a leaf and the vibrations of the ground increased my trembling. It seemed as if a volcano was getting ready to erupt below us. Squeezing the arms of the two soldiers beside me helped to give me a bit of courage. Only when I could hear that the explosions were getting farther and farther away, did I have the nerve to slightly raise my head, half-buried in the dirt. In the midst of the clouds of smoke and dust I glimpsed black silhouettes emerging from the ruins of the village.
I thought I was hearing something.
My ears hurt from all those close bursts.
The *mucs* were shouting "hurrà!".

---

[132] Similar to "Damn!" but much stronger.

They had emerged from their hiding places and were counter attacking!
I shook the arms of the two soldiers on either side of me to warn them of the danger. The one on the right raised his head and looked at me as if he had seen a ghost. The one on the left no longer had a head.
At this point all my fear suddenly turned into rage and I started shooting and cursing with hatred against those black figures. If I could have, I would have stabbed them all to death with my bayonet.
The survivors in the other shell holes started shooting at the Austrians.
Some fell to the ground under the shots of our rifles, but others kept on approaching menacingly, shooting and brandishing their hand grenades.
We drew out and threw our own SIPEs.[133]
Then suddenly in the general uproar I heard the familiar "raspberry sound" of our FIAT machine guns start up and I saw lots of our enemies fall like leaves.[134]
That was the moment to find a better position. I started running towards the nearest trees, followed by other men. Breathlessly I threw myself on the ground behind a large tree trunk. My temples were throbbing and it seemed to me that my heart was about to explode. I confess I yelled out a blasphemy, but it was actually a thank you. From behind the trees our men were firing furiously.
I took out my canteen to drink the little water I had left, but it was empty. A *Shrapnel* bullet had pierced it through and through.
I tried to see who had followed me. I recognized some faces, in spite of their being disfigured by the tension, exhausted from the race and filthy with soil and blood. A cadet patted me on the shoulder, saying «Good job, corporal». Another officer might have accused me of running away from the enemy.
I didn't know it yet, but in that assault we lost the battalion commanders and almost all the company commanders.
We stayed in that position for a long time, holding back the Austrian counterattacks and hoping for the support of the II/208th. That Battalion was supposed to join the attack after it crossed the Vogercek.

---

[133] This was the hand grenade supplied to the Royal Army, produced by the Italian Exploding Products Company of Milan. After unscrewing the protective cap, the head was rubbed against the special lighter or, in case of high humidity, it could be directly ignited by an open flame or a cigar. It had a 7-second fuse which allowed a safe launch from about 35-40 metres away. The cast iron splinters had a range of about 35 m.

[134] The providential intervention of the 518th machine gun company, located on the eastern edge of the forest near Dolgi Laz, blocked the Austrian counterattack, which tried to slip between the right flank of the 207th and Mešnjak, cutting off the Regiment.

When the news arrived that the 208th could not help us and that the survivors of the III/207th had been sent in its place, we lost all hope of taking Dolgi Laz.

The Austrians continued to hammer our left flank and so rather than attacking, we had to defend ourselves.

At around 19, after almost five hours of fighting, the order came to fall back to Mešnjak. Our two Battalions were reduced to about four hundred men. On the way back I was happy to have saved my skin, but I was appalled at what I had gone through and all the carnage I had seen.

A friend joined me on the march. Wordlessly, he handed me the letter I had given him. It was a little stained with blood. Both of his hands were injured and bandaged roughly. I gave him back his own with a pat on the back.

I will have to send most of the other letters to the families.

I was unable to sleep that night, even though I was destroyed by fatigue. Every time I closed my eyes I was immediately awakened by hideous visions and I leapt up with every gun shot.

I staggered around like a drunk yesterday morning. But I wasn't the only one in that state. We are dirty, unshaven and our uniforms are in tatters.

The Officers are no better. We are really scary to look at, in the sense that we are really pitiful.

My mouth still tastes like the dirt I had to eat and my nostrils can still smell the stink of burning and gunpowder that I had to breathe.

Many soldiers have been wounded. In spite of this, the doctors and the Carabinieri are sending them right back to fight.

We, however, have been ordered to strengthen our positions and to lay barbed wire. That means that the "Taro" attack is over. Now we have to defend the ground we have conquered.

I feel better today and so had the strength to write my account of the last few days.

I also feel better because of the good news that tonight we will be relieved by the 75th Regiment of the "Napoli" Brigade. From tomorrow on, it will be up to them to defend these walls and these ruined and burnt houses.

We will descend to and cross the Isonzo again heading for Drenchia to clean up and mend both wounds and uniforms.

The 208th will have to spend one more day up here, before they can be replaced by the 76th Regiment of the "Napoli".

P.S. I was appointed sergeant.
(my pay increases from 40 cents to 1 lira)

Chapter 42.I

I opened my eyes with my heart beating faster than usual.
This time, however, I saw no whirlwind emanate from the suitcase. On the contrary, I felt a dark force of gravity affix itself on my gaze as it fell on a series of discolored and insignificant objects.
I must have looked at the parish priest with the expression of a beaten and abandoned dog.
«A no è chê?»[135] *he asked me with his hands always clasped under his chin, but with the look of someone who hasn't seen a miracle.*
«There are a lot of people with your surname here in Dogna» he emphasized in Italian to make up for my lack of success, while I closed the suitcase. I sadly got up and prepared to put the five suitcases back in their dark lair. The parish priest spared me this sad task, as if this could compensate for the huge disappointment I was feeling right then. I had left home with very few expectations, but for a brief moment I had got my hopes up.
To try and make me feel better, he invited me to have a drink at the village tavern.
«Doi tais di neri, un par me e un par il sior ch'al è vignût fin cà di Bergamo»[136] *he told the young barman.*
«Do you understand Friulan?» he finally felt compelled to ask me.
«Avonde»[137] *I replied. «I understand almost everything because I've always heard it in the family, but I'm not used to speaking it.»*
«It is considered a language, not a dialect. Did you know that?» continued the priest.
«Yes, I know. I always say so, and with a touch of pride, when discussing languages and dialects with friends. The same goes for Sardinian. To change the subject, as long as I am here, could I have a look at the parish registers to reconstruct the dates of birth of my grandfather's brothers?»
As the parish priest nodded, I noticed an old photograph hanging on the wall. I went closer to get a better look.

---

[135] «Isn't that it?» translation from the Friulan language.
[136] «Two glasses of red wine, one for me and one for the gentleman who came here all the way from Bergamo.»
[137] «Pretty well.»

It showed a rather elderly gentleman.
«He was the innkeeper of this tavern for many years. He was a great big man, but they called him Vigjut. Probably your grandfather knew him.»
The photo was dated 1921.
«Yes, probably. Indeed, almost certainly» I replied, as I punished myself by drinking the whole glass of red wine in one breath and on an empty stomach.
At heart I blamed myself bitterly for not having searched for and recovered that suitcase many years before, now that its contents had become so unique and precious to me.

CHAPTER 43.I

Drenchia, Tuesday, 4 September 1917
It's like being in heaven here, even if we are only a few kilometres away from Bainsizza and the thunder of artillery is continuous.
In the fighting of these past days our Regiment lost over 170 dead or missing and had over 350 wounded.
It was much worse for the 208th: over 450 dead and missing and nearly 700 wounded. Those poor guys endured one final shelling before being relieved by the 76th Regiment.
I suppose the other Brigades involved in this battle have shed just as much blood. High Command states that it was a great victory, but the war continues unfortunately.[138]
The Pope's statement to the newspapers made a great impression.
He called it a "senseless slaughter".[139]
I remember that the organ-playing sergeant too had defined it this way.

All companies were called to muster this morning.
Our captain informed us that the 2nd Army Command is looking for volunteers for some new units that are being formed. He added, and this made everyone's ears prick up, that there are a lot of advantages: higher pay, better food, more leave opportunities and no fatigue duty at all.
No more trenches?
Is it possible?
Why all this sudden generosity?
What do they want in return?
What's the catch?
All these questions were going through our heads while we stood there, lined up and silent.
After a long pause, the captain revealed the mystery.

---

[138] Cadorna had deployed three quarters of his troops along a front that went from Tolmin to the Adriatic Sea: 600 Battalions in 52 Divisions with 5,200 artillery pieces. At the end of the Battle of Bainsizza (17-31 August 1917) the Royal Army counted 30,000 dead, 110,000 wounded and 20,000 missing or prisoners. Among the Austro-Hungarian ranks there were 20,000 dead, 50,000 wounded, 30,000 missing and 20,000 prisoners.
[139] The Pope was Benedetto XV (21 November 1854 - 22 January 1922).

Volunteers will first have to undergo very hard training, and then they will be employed in a new type of war action requiring great daring, as it is extremely dangerous.
«Volunteers step forward!» he ordered.
Dying in the mud of the trenches in the company of mice and lice, or dying after enjoying a good meal, with special leaves, and being better paid and quartered in the rear lines? The latter is certainly a better choice.
A lot of people must have thought so, since the majority took a step forward, myself included. At that point the captain passed through the line, looking each of us straight in the eye. By now he knows us all well.
Then he turned around and ordered:
«Married men or men with children step back!»
More than half of the volunteers returned to the ranks.
The captain walked around again, looking at us one by one.
At the end of the inspection he turned about-face once more, and then, at a brisk pace and, based on who-knows-what criterion, he clapped his hand on the shoulder of some soldiers saying «Selected!»
I am in that group!
We have filled out an application with the request to enlist as volunteers in these new units. Immediate departure for Manzano, Sdricca.
We will go through a training period and then there will be a kind of examination.
Those of us who do not pass will have to return to the Regiment.

Chapter 44.I

When I opened the gate to my house, I glimpsed something in the mailbox. Nowadays, only advertising flyers and bills arrive in the mail.
Bills invariably arrive when it rains, like it did that day. And in my mailbox they always find a way to get wet.
This time, however, it was not a utility bill but a very damp notification to pick up a registered letter. I've always thoroughly detested the arrival of that kind of letter ever since our post office was decentralized to an area far from where I live in Bergamo.
Climbing the stairs, in the angry rain of that summer storm, I tried to read the sender's name, so I could swear at him a little. But there was only a number. It's not very satisfying to swear at a number. Especially for someone who has based his professional career on numbers.

The following Saturday, very reluctantly, I walked to the post office.
Between one thing and another I would be wasting half a morning.
Just as I had imagined, in addition to the trip, I had to put up with a queue that started outside the office door.
When my turn finally came and the employee handed me the letter, I immediately looked for the name of the sender, so I could finally swear at him. To my surprise, though, it was a notary firm in Udine. The content of the registered letter was nothing but an invitation to present myself there for unspecified personal communications.
"A swindle or some kind of scam" I thought.
On returning home, I tried to imagine what kind of scam was most likely. In any case it was an annoyance.
That afternoon, I checked on the internet to see if this firm actually existed and if by chance it was related to the keyword "swindle".
It was apparently all right.
After the digital verification I switched to the analog one. I phoned a cousin from Udine to find out if she had heard of it, at least by name.
Affirmative. It was an old notary firm, renowned for its seriousness.
«Thanks, I'll be coming to visit you in Udine soon.»

During the trip I tried to avoid speculating about what I might hear at the notary office. I limited my cerebral faculties to the pure contemplation of what was quickly going by out of the window: the Lombard countryside, Brescia, Lake Garda, the Venetian countryside, the Adige river, the Vicenza hills, the Brenta river, the Venetian countryside, the Piave river, again the Venetian countryside, the Tagliamento river, the Friulan plain.
Like the landscape, the seasons too had gone by very quickly for me: every now and then the window reflected my thoughtful face with a beard turned white.

Udine.
A classic secretary, classically dressed, opened the door and invited me to sit in the typical waiting room of a vintage notary's office. Shortly thereafter, a man appeared, who introduced himself as a notary, although he looked anything but classic. He was wearing a small gold earring and a Maori tattoo emerged from the collar of his shirt. After sitting down in his study, exchanging the ritual pleasantries and having ascertained my identity, he came to the point.
He began by reassuring me that it was nothing bad, on the contrary. He was carrying out a disposition that had been passed on to him by his father, who had died a few years earlier. His father had received this assignment in the 60's of the past century: he was to give me a sealed package which had lain for over fifty years in one of their safes.
Now it was there on his table.
Rarely in my life have I experienced a loss of lucidity, although sometimes I would have liked to. However, as soon as I saw what was written on that yellowed envelope, the room began to twirl faster and faster around me, as if I were both axle and motor rotating together. Internally, however, I seemed to sink into a bottomless void, while at the same time projecting myself into an endless sky, like an astronaut thrown from his spacecraft. If it was not quite the Kubrick's vision of the journey to Jupiter and beyond, it was pretty close.
The entire experience lasted less than a second.
Physical contact with that old envelope immediately brought me back to the correct space-time dimension. On the back it was glued shut and sealed with sealing wax. On the front, written in a beautifully ornate calligraphy, was a handwritten inscription: "For my grandson Roberto".
The notary watched silently, concealing his curiosity to find out the contents of that letter, entrusted to his office many years earlier.

I have always opened parcels and envelopes with great care so as not to damage the paper. Even more so now did I open this envelope with religious respect, almost as if it were a relic, using the letter opener that the diligent notary handed me.
Inside the package were three notebooks, held together with a silk ribbon, one of which had a very worn leather cover.
There was also a small envelope addressed to me. Inside the envelope a few words written with the beautiful calligraphy of the past.

"In memory of your grandfather Pietro, in the hope that the years of your youth were better than mine."

Once again, I lost my space-time coordinates in a sort of vertigo.
«Are you all right?» asked the notary, who was desperately trying to understand what was going on.
«It's a memento from my grandfather» I said, as my eyes fell on a little piece of paper attached to the first page of the notebook with the leather cover. They were already beginning to fill with tears.

"I'm writing not to think..."
These are the first words I managed to read.

I was in Udine.
It was July 28th, 2014.

•

Chapter 45.I

Reading my grandfather's diary gave me very powerful emotions.
It would be completely futile to try and describe them in words.
Instead, I thought about sharing his writings, even though I was aware that they were unlikely to produce on others the same effect they have had on me.
I also thought about adding historical notes both to explain things that were well known to my grandfather and his comrades (names of commanders, weapons and locations) as well as to frame some events in the more general context of the conflict. Although he wrote in good Italian, also thanks to his passion for Salgari and Verne, I have taken the liberty of making some corrections to render the reading more fluid.
Precisely because of the influence of those authors, I believe that at a certain point grandfather decided to write his diary as if it were a novel, inserting dialogue and using his characters' dialect, as if it were an exoticism.
Once again, I have taken the liberty of correcting the words in dialect, which he transcribed more or less as he had heard them.
Finally, it seemed interesting to me to interweave part of his diary, which unfolds slowly over three years, with a diary in retrospect which, however, embraces almost an entire life, mine.
I hope this juxtaposition of memoirs is useful for at least two reasons.
On one hand I want to show how this diary came into my possession and the value it has for me. I have always lived with the myth of a grandfather whom I was able to enjoy for far too brief a time. As a child, I would have liked to ask him: «Grandpa, please, tell me a story»[140] *like other Friulan children did. When I grew up, I would have asked him lots of questions about his experiences as a young man, hoping that he would have confided in me. Instead, I was still too young when he left us.*
On the other hand, I want to underline even more clearly what we often forget: the great good fortune that my generation and the following ones have had in comparison to my grandfather's.
The fortune of living in a period of peace.

---

[140] «Grandpa, please, tell me a story» translation from the Friulan language.

2ND PART

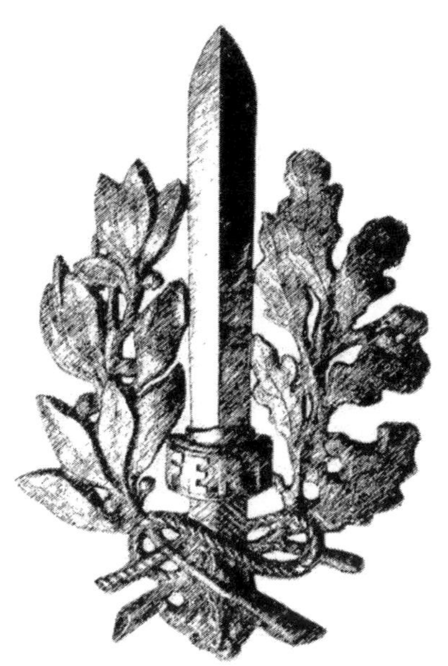

BLACK FLAMES

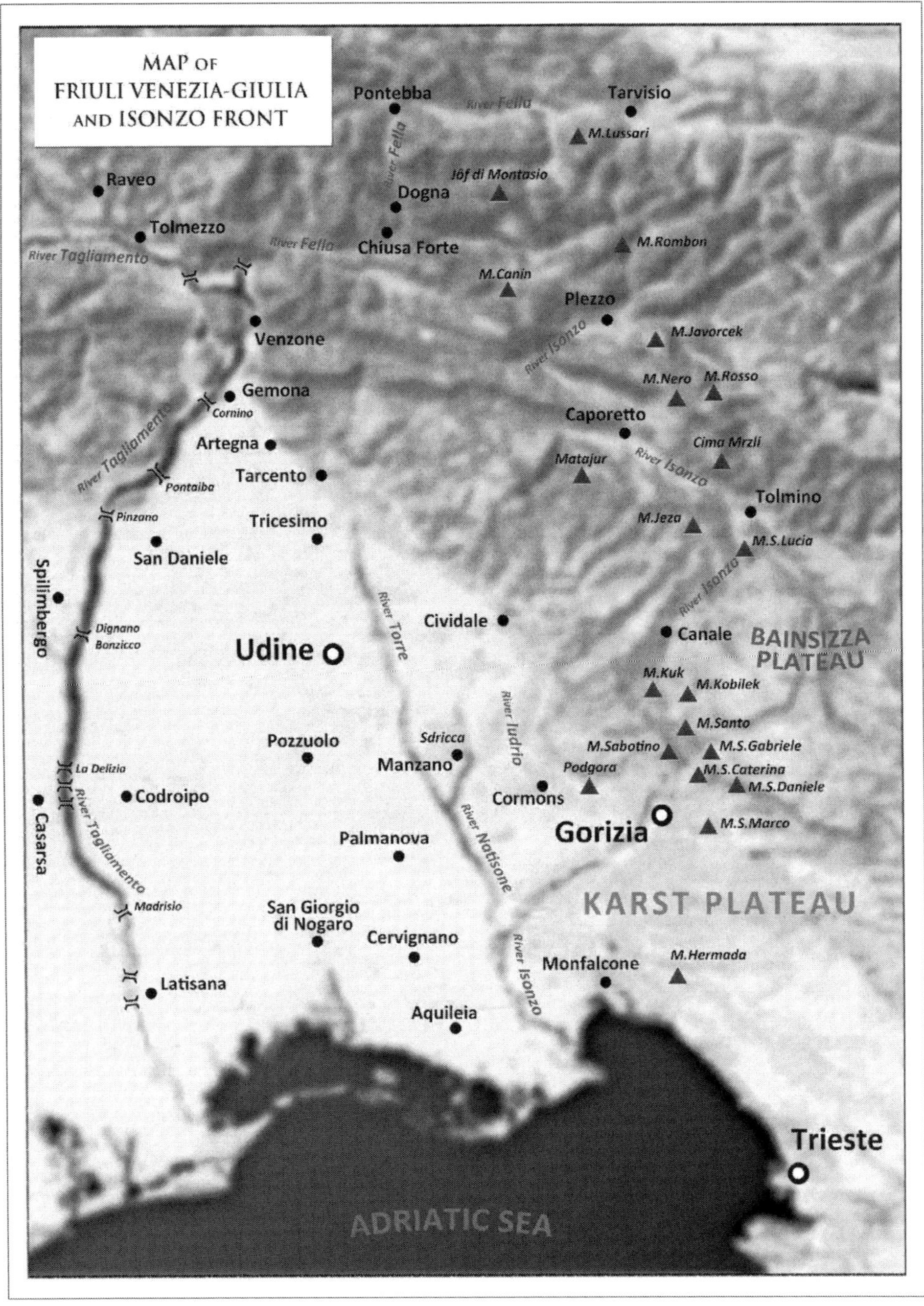
MAP OF
FRIULI VENEZIA-GIULIA
AND ISONZO FRONT
Pontebba
Tarvisio
M.Lussari
River Fella
Jôf di Montasio
Raveo
Dogna
Tolmezzo
River Fella
Chiusa Forte
M.Rombon
River Tagliamento
M.Canin
Plezzo
Venzone
M.Javorcek
River Isonzo
M.Nero
M.Rosso
Gemona
Cornino
Caporetto
Artegna
Cima Mrzli
Matajur
River Isonzo
River Tagliamento
Tarcento
Pontaiba
Tolmino
Pinzano
Tricesimo
M.Jeza
M.S.Lucia
San Daniele
Spilimbergo
River Isonzo
River Torre
Cividale
Dignano
Bonzicco
Udine
Canale
BAINSIZZA
PLATEAU
M.Kuk
M.Kobilek
River Iudrio
M.Santo
Pozzuolo
Sdricca
M.Sabotino
M.S.Gabriele
La Delizia
Manzano
Podgora
M.S.Caterina
M.S.Daniele
Codroipo
Cormons
Casarsa
River Tagliamento
River Natisone
Gorizia
M.S.Marco
Palmanova
KARST PLATEAU
Madrisio
San Giorgio
di Nogaro
Cervignano
River Isonzo
Monfalcone
M.Hermada
Latisana
Aquileia
Trieste
ADRIATIC SEA

Chapter 1.II

Sdricca di Manzano, Sunday, 9 September 1917
I am writing so as not to forget.
I am writing quickly because I have little free time.
We will soon go down to Manzano on leave.
I have only been at the training camp for a few days, but many things have happened that deserve to be written down.
I arrived in Manzano last Wednesday with the other volunteers from the "Taro" Brigade. On the road that leads from the village up to Sdricca there were a great many comings and goings: many soldiers from other 2nd Army Brigades going up and some French and English officers going down. Among them there were also some journalists, who greeted us and wished us good luck. This surprised us. Then we learned that the day before three companies from these new units had accomplished a heroic feat that no one else had managed to perform before: they had conquered the mountain called San Gabriele! [141]

---

[141] On the morning of September 4, 1917, after a short but heavy artillery barrage, the companies 2nd, 3rd and 4th of the I Assault Unit conquered Mount San Gabriele in a few hours and defended it vigorously all day until the arrival of backup troops. From the observatory on Mount Sabotino, the King, Generals Cadorna and Capello, the Franco-English military mission and some journalists watched the action. Among the many victories of the Arditi, that of San Gabriele is considered the best and the most representative of the new fighting techniques. Before then, every attempt by the Royal Army had ended in a bloodbath, despite the forces deployed. Out of about 500 men the Black Flames sustained 61 dead, including the commander of the 4th company, Lieutenant Stefanoni, and 200 wounded, including the commander of the 2nd company, Lieutenant Crisanti. More than 3,000 prisoners, 55 machine guns and 26 trench artillery pieces were captured.
A few excerpts from General Capello's message, read to the Arditi by their commander, Lieutenant-Colonel Bassi, just before the attack, are worth mentioning:
"Arditi! I have kept for you the boldest and biggest undertaking of the war. You will meet the enemy, who both knows you and fears you. I am sure you will return, as from the glorious days of Bainsizza, victorious. I am entrusting to the blades of your daggers, to the strength of your arms, to the unsurpassable courage of your breasts, an enormous task. For our army and for Italy you will conquer the mountain blocking the way to Trieste. [...] Know that this mountain, up till now, has been impregnable. The military art of our adversaries, assisted by nature, has made it a truly unsurpassed masterpiece of defence. Our attack Brigades have hurled themselves against it in the most powerful attempts in history

At the beginning of the road to Sdricca, there is a signboard with the inscription "Assault School". Below that is the drawing of a skull.
Despite that somewhat macabre sign, the landscape is very beautiful. There are no signs of war as on the Bainsizza plateau. The fields are green and cultivated. There are many vines and many cypresses, poplars, willows and acacias. The continuous rumble of artillery is not heard as in the past few weeks. This increases the sense of peace of this place. The war seems far away, if it were not for the column of us soldiers.
The old road ends at a small group of houses. In the fields, the farmers are busy working. This is Sdricca. From here starts the new road leading up to the training camp.
Just before we got there, sentries stopped us to check our documents.
They were wearing a uniform that I had never seen before.
Unlike ours, their tunic opens in the front with reversed lapels. In place of stripes, on the collar there are large flames, like those of the Bersaglieri or the Alpini. Rather than crimson or green, they are black in colour. On the left sleeve is sewn a badge embroidered in black, which I had never seen: a short sword surrounded by the leaves of some kind of plant.[142]
I asked a sentry what it was.
«It is the Arditi badge, Sergeant, a Roman gladius between oak and laurel branches. Only those who pass the School's tests of courage have the honour of wearing it on their arm and the black flames on their collar» he replied, proudly, in a strong Tuscan accent.
«And then there's this!» he added, suddenly unsheathing a dagger which he carried in his belt, putting it sideways in his mouth and grinding his teeth like a ferocious dog.
"He's crazy" I thought to myself as I moved on.
«*Chist' è nu pazz*»[143] whispered a corporal from the Bersaglieri near me, tapping his temple with a forefinger.

---

but their superb efforts, their brilliant valour, their sublime sacrifice, have unfortunately been crushed. To you goes the honour of victory in this most perilous trial. [...]
In a matter of days, all Italy, the dead from all our wars, men from every epoch will look to you. I am sure that from the crest of that mountain you will either return victorious or you will never return*."*

142 The Roman gladius, symbol of honour and courage, had a lion's head knob, symbol of strength, or an eagle's head, symbol of power. It was encircled by a laurel wreath, symbol of victory, and an oak frond, symbol of loyalty and strength. The Savoy knot tied the branches to the weapon on whose crossbar was the motto "FERT", another reference to the ruling house.

143 «He's crazy» translation from the Neapolitan dialect.

The base is located on a wide plateau, with low hills on the left and an escarpment on the right, below which flows the Natisone river.
There are barracks and many tents scattered here and there. Some are very large, for military mess and warehouses.
In a small enclosure, four poles surrounded by barbed wire, there was a shirtless soldier. One of the poles had a sign with the word "Troublemakers" in huge letters. We learned later that this is the prison.
The School Commander is Lieutenant-Colonel Bassi.
He is revered by the instructors and Arditi of the I and II Assault Units.
I was pleased to find out that he is a native of Friuli like me.[144]
After some paperwork, they immediately gave us the uniform of the school, but without the black flames and with no badge on the sleeve.[145]
For now, we will keep the collar patches of the brigades we come from.
It's a very comfortable uniform.
The trousers are like the Alpini ones, that is knee-length, and the hobnail boots are the same, too. The crewneck sweater is that of the Bersaglieri cyclists. The tunic is open in the front with two waist pockets and large hunting-style pockets on the back for storing hand grenades. Not SIPEs, but Thévenots.[146] They are petards that make a lot of noise and produce small splinters that are harmless, apart from the firing pin. Yesterday we started throwing them from various positions, both standing still and running. Our instructors explained that they are fundamental for this new type of assault.

---

[144] Giuseppe Bassi, (Udine, 21 January 1884 - Naples, 11 June 1959) is the founder of the Assault Units. After earning the Silver Medal of Military Valour twice, he proposed a new form of combat to the Commanders and effectively put it into practice in the actions of June 7, 1917. He received a reprimand for that initiative, but all the same was given the opportunity to experiment his technique with the creation of a special assault school. After several surveys he chose Sdricca as it offered the most suitable terrain for the complex needs of the new type of training (July 15, 1917).

[145] The uniform, designed by Bassi to be both comfortable and immediately recognizable, was initially opposed by the High Command because its shape was too similar to civilian jackets. It was approved thanks to the intervention of the King. The double flames were similar to those of Alpini and Bersaglieri. The black colour was in memory of one of his ancestors, Pietro Fortunato Calvi, a Risorgimental hero. Calvi used to wear a black tie, the revolutionary symbol of the Venetian Carbonari, who freed Manin and proclaimed the Venetian Republic. Captured by the Austrians, he was hanged in Mantua in 1855 for having spearheaded yet another attempt at revolt in the Veneto.

[146] The Thévenot type AL offensive petard was not dangerous for those who threw it, having a range of action of about 10 metres, but it was dangerous for those who were close to the explosion point in consideration of the high-power charge (170 grams of explosive "Echo"). It weighed only 400 grams so soldiers could carry more of them and they were easier to throw.

We will get lots of practice in this new technique on one of the hills at the base. They call it the "dummy hill" or "the hot zone".
We will have to overcome obstacles and hurl ourselves forward by throwing these bombs against a trench and attacking it, all under a hail of machine gun bullets and gun fire.
It seems that at every practice session there are men wounded and one soldier even died. The instructor said it was the soldier's own fault: he made the mistake of standing up and was hit. Those who make mistakes pay.
That's all.
The instructor also explained to us that during the assault we have to clench the dagger between our teeth in order to have both hands free. Then we'll use it to eliminate enemies.[147]
The Bersaglieri corporal, a Neapolitan, and I exchanged a look halfway between the amused and the worried.
"These guys are really nuts" we both thought.
I looked at *Cuteddu* (he is here too).
He was grinning under his moustache.
A lot of crazy things happen in this school.
One of these is the test they had us undergo on the second day.
They took us to one of the firing ranges and ordered us to stand at attention, whatever happened. We stayed in that position for several minutes, until some veterans from the II Unit arrived. They started running and then suddenly, at a whistle, they launched Thévenots only a few metres from us. Some comrades were frightened and fell onto the ground. I got a splinter in my thigh (they call them "butterflies"), but I kept standing at attention, like most of the platoon.
Our instructor yelled at those who had moved, threatening to kick them out of the course for lack of discipline and courage.
Then he approached me, looking me up and down.
«Your left thigh is bleeding, sergeant» he said.
«Yes, sir» I replied.
«Do you want to bleed to death on this firing range?»

---

[147] The dagger supplied to the Arditi was obtained from the long bayonets of the Vetterli rifle 1870/87, which had become unsuitable for this new type of combat. Two 28 cm daggers (with 18 cm blade) were made from each bayonet. It was also possible to adapt the sheath of the old bayonets to the new daggers. Other types of bayonets were transformed into daggers: those of Austrian war spoils and those of the 1891 TS (Special Troops) carbine. Many Arditi, especially officers and enlisted men, were free to use personal daggers, including those captured from the enemy, in particular from the Hungarian troops, or to carry knives typical of their own regions.

«No, sir.»
«Then staunch the wound with a handkerchief and go to the infirmary. Then get some clean pants and come back here.»
«Yes, sir» I replied, quickly executing his order.
To avoid further remarks, I ran to the infirmary.
Meanwhile I heard his sharp voice exclaiming: «Your hand is bleeding, soldier. Do you want to bleed to death here on this firing range?»
The medical officer found that my wound wasn't serious.
While extracting the splinter he explained to me that it is a very common accident here at the school.
If that splinter had hit my eye, I would have been left with only one eye, I told him, while two other bleeding comrades lined up outside the tent.
«If the striker had hit you, it could have broken your thigh bone. If it had hit you in the heart, we would be burying you now. If you weren't here right now, a 305mm shell could have hit you and blown you up into a thousand pieces. And no doctor that I know of, could have stitched you up. If, if, if...» he placidly commented, while cleaning and closing the wound.
"If I didn't always have my mother's amulet with me..." I thought, comforting myself with the idea that it really could protect me.
They're calling me.
Now I have to go.
I don't know when I will be able to go on with my account of these days at the Arditi School.[148]

[148] The Arditi School was officially inaugurated on July 29, 1917, in the presence of King Vittorio Emanuele III, the Prince of Wales, the Crown Prince of Belgium, General Luigi Cadorna, General Luigi Capello, the commander of the 3rd Army, Emanuele Filiberto, Duke of Aosta (13 January 1869 - 4 July 1931), Italian and foreign officers assigned to the High Command and many journalists. Under the orders of Captain Maggiorino Radicati di Primeglio, the 1st company of the I Assault Unit demonstrated the new fighting technique with the conquest of the "dummy hill" and a cave with an outflanking move, evoking the admiration of all those present.

Chapter 2.II

Sdricca, Tuesday, 11 September 1917

Today I received my black flames.

I'm very proud. Tonight, I will have to "wet the flames" and offer the veterans a drink on me, but it's worth it. I've been assigned to the VI Assault Unit, commanded by Major Ambrogi, a Tuscan from Lucca.

Some of the volunteers who had arrived with me last Wednesday have been sent back to their Regiments. Including two of the comrades who fell to the ground when the veterans launched petards near us.

Other men, though, have asked to leave. The meals are abundant, the cots are comfortable, the pay is good[149], and there are no fatigue duties, but it's clear from stories recounted by the veterans that the risks are far higher in these new shock troops than in the trenches.

Physical training is tough. Captain Racchi and his instructors keep an attentive and inflexible eye on us.[150]

We have to run all the time. They make us jump long and high. Lots of us are able to do somersaults, too. We have to clamber over walls, hedges, tree trunks, *chevaux-de-frise* and piles of bags full of earth. We get over the barbed wire barriers by using a pole as a lever.

Of all the physical tests, the one that ruined me the most is playing tug of war. I skinned my hands and even lost money. This is a contest between twelve men on each side. There is always a cash prize at stake for the winners. Sometimes even some officers take part in these competitions. In particular a tall and very strong lieutenant from San Giorgio di Nogaro, whose name is Max di Montegnacco.

They say he is a count, but he pulls the rope like a bull.[151]

---

[149] There was extra pay of 20 cents per day for soldiers and corporals, 30 cents for sergeants, between 1 lira and 2.50 lire for non-commissioned officers according to their rank. Soldiers in the war zone received additional 40 cents as a war allowance. To get an idea of the purchasing power of the lira in 1917, a kilo of bread cost 55 cents, one litre of wine 1 lira and 20 cents, ten cigarettes 36 cents.

[150] Giovanni Racchi was well known in the sports and military environment. In 1896 he published a book on military gymnastics. He was sent to Sdricca by the command of the 2nd Army to oversee the physical education of the Black Flames. He was assisted by two of his students as teachers, Sebastiano Milanesio and Eugenio Ferrante.

Despite my injured hands I tried to do my best in the dagger exercises. We are supposed to pounce upon sheaves of compressed straw and plunge the dagger in from the top, from the bottom, from the right or from the left, depending on the instructor's command. The same exercise must be done starting from a kneeling position, or flat on the ground, or by surmounting various obstacles placed in front of the target. It's easy with the hay but I dread the moment I will have to do it to a man.
In our spare time, some of the Sicilians show us what a duel with a knife to hurt or kill is really like. *Cuteddu* has become a highly respected teacher, especially after he taught a good lesson to a Calabrian guy who claimed to be better than him. To prevent them from actually slaughtering each other, our instructor forced them to face each other with blunt wooden daggers. The Calabrian was not bad, but *Cuteddu* would have killed him even with the wooden dagger, if three of us hadn't intervened to block him.
I don't know what he mumbled in dialect to his opponent, but it was certainly nothing good. The Calabrian, instead of shutting up, answered with something equally incomprehensible to us.
At which point five of us had to intervene to block *Cuteddu's* anger. Four others carried the Calabrian away. Firstly, they beat him up and then they put him in the "Troublemakers" enclosure with the instructor's approval.
Captain Racchi says that a dagger attack is not like a rustic duel. You must immediately pounce on your opponent already knowing just where to strike in order to kill him at the first blow. Instantly break away from your victim, eventually finish him off, and move on. Nobody dared to ask the Captain if he had ever done it personally, but some veterans confirmed that it actually works that way.
According to them it is much better to attack with a dagger rather than with a bayonet fixed on the rifle, because in the confined space of the trenches it is completely impractical.
Spuafogo, one of the veterans in the flamethrower section, likes to say: «*Mi go meio farli rosti.*»[152] He always carries a very sharp stiletto with him.
«*Par coparme se i me ciapa*»[153] he adds.
Mucs are not at all tender when they get a *rotisseur*. Neither are we.

---

[151] Massimiliano, called Max, count of Montegnacco (1892-1939) commanded a heroic platoon of the 3rd company of the I Assault Unit, which conquered Mount San Gabriele. He took part in numerous very risky actions both during the Great War (and in Eastern Africa.) He was killed in mysterious circumstances during the Spanish Civil War, hit by a hand grenade thrown by "Republicanos" militiamen.
[152] «I prefer to roast them» translation from the Venetian dialect.
[153] «To kill myself if they get me.»

CHAPTER 3.II

Sdricca, Sunday, September 16, 1917
This week has also been very intense and eventful.
Every morning at 6:00 a.m. the wake-up call is given by two gunshots.
We have to jump to our feet immediately and run and wash in the Natisone river. There is no time for playing around in the water because we have to hurry back to the field for physical exercises. Then each group alternates in the different training areas until 10.00, when we have our morning meal, which is really excellent and abundant.
Training resumes again from 15.30 to 18.30.
Then for half an hour an instructor or chaplain gives us a lecture, which they call "moral education".
After, we have our evening meal, much more interesting.
After dinner, the multi-sports field comes alive with competitions in various disciplines. The football tournament between the six Units attracted lots of people from Manzano, San Giovanni and Oleis.[154]
We trainees have put up a good team and we've won two games out of two. One of our guys is a very strong striker. I play defence and I don't let anyone through, unless he wants to have his leg broken.
Every evening there are also boxing matches between veteran Arditi and trainees and bets flock here. Now we have real boxing gloves, but until a few weeks ago they used to punch each other with their hands taped.
The other evening a French instructor, who had recently arrived at the camp, showed up. He challenged one of our strongest and most formidable boxers, an Italo-American.
Almost everyone bet on our comrade and therefore there was little to win.

---

[154] In Oleis was the airfield used by the then-captain Francesco Baracca, the most famous pilot in Italian aviation during the Great War (two silver medals and one gold medal of military valour). Fascinated by an aerial demonstration, in 1912 he switched from cavalry to aviation, obtaining his pilot license n.1037 in the same year and soon distinguished himself for his exceptional acrobatic ability. At the beginning of the conflict he was employed on patrol duties. On April 7, 1916, he shot down his first plane, the first such victory ever for the Italian air force. Back on the ground, he sportingly shook hands with one of the two pilots he had shot down. Baracca used to say: *«I aim at the aircraft, not at the man»*.

«He's a braggart, like all Frenchmen» was the least offensive comment that circulated among us.
Someone proposed to bet on how many minutes the guy would remain standing, but it was too late, since the match had already started.
Our comrade started like a fury by raining a hail of blows on the Frenchman, who nevertheless dodged them with a skill and speed never seen before. Then with equal speed he kicked our boxer twice, grabbed him by an arm and threw him down in the dust. He jumped on him, blocking his arms with his legs, and pretended to hit him repeatedly in the face and throat, stopping his fists a few centimetres from the target.
We all fell silent in the face of that rapid and unexpected action.
Our champion was even more dumbfounded.
«C'mon guys! Pay up, please» the voice of Captain Abbondanza, commander of the II Assault Unit, broke the silence, closely followed by the other officers, who had all bet on the French officer.
Evidently, they knew him and knew they were betting on the safe side.
«Victory is achieved with speed and with a fighting technique unknown and unexpected by the opponent. Just like we did on Mount San Gabriele, Belpoggio and Mount Fratta»[155] said captain Radicati, commander of the I Assault Unit.
A huge "hurrà!" came out of our throats, even though they had just fleeced us of quite a few lire.
«The fighting technique, which you have just seen, comes from Japan. It's called Ju-Jitsu. Harness the opponent's strength in such a way that it backfires. From tomorrow we will teach you some chops» concluded Captain Racchi.
We went back to our tents singing one of the most popular songs in the field (we sing a lot and very often):

---

[155] On August 19, 1917, the 3rd company of the I Assault Unit (Captain Pedercini) conquered the barren hill of Belpoggio, an offshoot of Mount San Marco near Gorizia, strongly defended by the Austrians. On the night between August 18th and 19th, in the early stages of the Battle of Bainsizza, the 1st company of the I Assault Unit (Captain Radicati) crossed the Isonzo on boats piloted by the bridge-builders of the 4th Battalion and established a bridgehead near Loga, taking many prisoners. Then they conquered and defended Mount Fratta while waiting to be relieved by the Bersaglieri of the 47th Division. The 2nd company ran into greater difficulty in crossing the Isonzo near Auzza. They even lost their commander, Captain Porcari, who was shot to death and replaced by Lieutenant Farina. The crossing was successful via a makeshift walkway. The Arditi wiped out the Austrian defenses on the other side and then conquered the northern part of Mount Fratta. The survivors of the two companies met up among the ruins of Ronzina, acclaimed by Colonel Bassi.

Se non ci conoscete guardateci dall'alto,
noi siam le Fiamme Nere dei battaglion d'assalto!
Bombe a man e colpi di pugnal!
Se non ci conoscete guardateci i vestiti,
noi siam le Fiamme Nere dei battaglion arditi!
Bombe a man e colpi di pugnal!
Se vuoi trovar l'Arcangelo da fante travestito,
ricercalo a Manzano e troverai l'ardito!
Bombe a man e colpi di pugnal!
Se Pecori Giraldi vuol fare un'avanzata,
ricorrerà agli Arditi della seconda armata!
Bombe a man e colpi di pugnal!
Se non ci conoscete guardateci dai passi
noi siamo gli arditissimi del colonnello Bassi![156]

After the evening games, we usually go down to Manzano and San Giovanni. We must be cleaned up, well-shaven, and with uniforms in order. We will be expected to go into combat in the same condition.
One evening we had to buy drinks for some Arditi of the 2nd company of the I Assault Unit, who in return told us about the Mount San Gabriele feat. A corporal was holding the stage.
«*Gera e sinque e quarantasinque quando che nialtri semo andai al'asalto. Ła artiieria gaveva inisià da poco a bombardar el San Gabriełe. I todeschi se gera rintanai ne łe caverne. Quel monte xe tuto sbusà de cunicoi e gałerie come un toco de groviera, ciò. Nialtri se semo sbarasai in un lampo de łe vedete lasae in prima linea e semo balsai ai ingresi de łe caverne.*

---

[156] The original text in Italian cannot be properly rhymed in English:
If you don't know who we are, look down upon us from above,
we are the Black Flames of the assault battalions!
Hand grenades and slashing daggers!
If you don't know who we are, look at our clothes,
we are the Black Flames of the Arditi battalions!
Hand grenades and slashing daggers!
If you want to find the Archangel disguised as a soldier,
look for him in Manzano and you will find the Ardito!
Hand grenades and slashing daggers!
If Pecori Giraldi wants to advance,
He'll turn to the Arditi of the second corps!
Hand grenades and slashing daggers!
If you don't know who we are, watch us march by,
we are the daredevils of Colonel Bassi!

Łori pensava che, come al solito, el bombardamento saria durà tante ore prima del ataco. E invese dea corvè col cafè semo rivai nialtri coi łancia-fiame e i petardi, ciò. Spuafogo ghe ne ga rostìo un casin de quei che no voeva arenderse. Ae sie e trenta gerimo già in veta e gavemo isà ła nostra bandiera su un fusil todesco come asta.»[157]

The corporal's entire narrative was interspersed with Venetian curses and sips of the red wine offered by us trainees.

While a Sardinian guy, unaccustomed certainly to the Venetian dialect, was asking his companion to translate what the corporal had said, a soldier from Rome asked: «*Capora' raccontece de Colacci.*»[158]

«*Chel cancaro del Coeaci la ga fata bea, ciò*»[159] the corporal promptly continued, tossing back another glass of red.

«*Gaveva apena perso do dei dea man e i stava sercando par tera quando che se ga scontrà co un general todesco pien de medaie, ciò. El general ga tirà fora la pistoea e ga sparà. Ma ghe vol altro par butar zo el Coeaci, che ło ga copà a corteae, ciò. Zio beo, deme n'altra ombra che ve conto come xe finìa*»[160] demanded the thirsty corporal, as his glass was immediately filled.

«*El stava tornando indrìo con do pałotoe de pistoea in corpo quando che el ga incontrà do ufisiai todeschi, ciò. El Coeaci se ga butà dosso de łori come un cavron incassà e i ga butai zo e disarmai. E sti do se ga cagà dosso e se ga areso coe man alsae. Bono taliano, bono taliano, i diseva coe man alsae. I gà da aver teror de nialtri i todeschi, Zio beo*»[161] the corporal went on.

---

[157] «It was five forty-five when we started the attack. The artillery had just begun to shell San Gabriele. The Austrians had holed up in the caves. That mountain is pierced through and through with wells and tunnels like a piece of Swiss cheese. Right away we took out the sentries on the front line and hurled ourselves at the entrance of the caves. The enemy thought that the shelling would last several hours before the actual attack as usual. Instead of the coffee service, we arrived with flamethrowers and hand grenades. *Sputafuoco* roasted the ones who didn't want to surrender. At six thirty we had already reached the top and we hoisted our flag using an Austrian rifle as a pole» transl. from the Venetian dialect.

[158] «Corporal, tell us about Colacci» translation from the Roman dialect.

[159] «That devil of a Colacci, he did a great thing» translation from the Venetian dialect.

[160] «He had just lost two fingers of one hand and was searching for them on the ground when he ran into an Austrian general full of medals. The general pulled out his gun and shot him. But it takes much more to knock Colacci out, instead he stabbed him to death. For God's sake, give me another glass of wine so I can tell you how the story ended.»

[161] «He was returning with two pistol bullets in his body, when he met two Austrian officers. Colacci charged at them like an angry billy goat, threw them down and disarmed them. They actually shit themselves, raising their hands in surrender. Italian good, Italian

Now completely inebriated by the wine, he began to sing at the top of his lungs a verse from the song of the I Assault Unit:

Il ventinove luglio, quando si taglia il grano
è nato un fiero Ardito con un petardo in mano![162]

At that point we started singing too:

Passiamo come fulmini sul campo di battaglia,
mentre il cannone tuona e scroscia la mitraglia!
Bombe a man e colpi di pugnal!
Il battaglion d'assalto è battaglion di morte,
avanti a tutti quanti è sempre il più forte!
Bombe a man e colpi di pugnal!
Abbiamo una bandiera che è nera di colore,
abbiam le Fiamme Nere e la speranza in core!
Bombe a man e colpi di pugnal!
Quando si va all'assalto con i petardi in mano,
par che l'inferno passi, che passi l'uragano!
Bombe a man e colpi di pugnal!
Se non ci conoscete guardateci dai passi,
noi siamo gli arditissimi del colonnello Bassi![163]

The curfew to return to camp is set at 10 p.m., but it isn't always respected. The officers, however, turn a blind eye and sometimes even two.

---

good, they said, raising their hands. Those Austrians were scared to death of us Italians, for God's sake» translation from the Venetian dialect.

[162] *On the twenty-ninth of July, when the wheat is reaped*
a proud Ardito was born with a petard in his hand!

[163] *We fly around the battlefield like lightning,*
while cannons thunder and machine guns roar!
Hand grenades and slashing daggers!
The assault battalion is a death battalion,
always ahead and always the strongest!
Hand grenades and slashing daggers!
Our flag is black in colour,
we have Black Flames and hope in our hearts!
Hand grenades and slashing daggers!
When we go on the attack with petards in hand,
it's like hell or a hurricane sweeping through!
Hand grenades and slashing daggers!
If you don't know us, watch us march by,
we are the daredevils of Colonel Bassi!

Some Arditi even return late at night. They boast about making love to some girls from Manzano. In fact, I have noticed that our uniforms have a great effect on women.
However, whatever the time of return, the important thing is to be present and well awake in the morning when the gun "rings" its two shots.

CHAPTER 4.II

Sdricca, Wednesday, 19 September 1917

I received a postcard from home.

They are all well. Even Noè, who is still based near Dogna. I replied that I am fine too, but I did not say that I had entered this training school.

I don't want them to worry about me.

If they only knew the tests of courage, we are subjected to every day...

I had to pass the knife-throwing test too. Even if you know the throwers are good, it makes an impression to see a knife coming at you and feel it penetrate just a few centimetres from your head. Then there is always one of the launchers pretending to be cross-eyed or drunk before he throws.

Better to keep still, because if you move there is the risk of meeting up with the trajectory of the knife. The test ends when all the knives have been planted around you.

Another test of courage is to hold a live bomb in your hand until just before it explodes.

But the strangest test of courage is one devised by Captain Racchi.

It's called "the Swing". It is one of the tests to obtain the Ardito badge.

Many officers come, both Italian and foreign, to watch its use.

The structure is that of a swing. But what moves like a pendulum is a large block of wood. The test consists in standing to attention at a point set by the captain. The point is different, based on the soldier's height. At the captain's nod, an assistant, positioned on the opposite side, throws the stump, which arrives at full speed towards the soldier's head. Usually the block knocks the soldier's cap off, if he doesn't duck or flinch. But if he ducks, he risks being expelled from the school. The bravest, of whom there are few, face the test more than once. In that case, the captain modifies their position slightly so that the block not only knocks their cap off but also parts their hair!

I will have to submit to this test soon.

I am sure that I will not be asking for an encore.

In addition to our physical exercises and tests of courage, we are learning how to use the weapons supplied to our enemies: the *Stielhandgranade*, the *Mannlicher* rifle and the *Schwarzlose* machine gun. We must be able to turn those weapons against them if we run out of ammunition.

Every day we do countless exercises in throwing petards so that they fall perpendicularly into a trench or between two walkways. These throws are done individually, then in pairs and finally in teams (5 or 6 pairs).
Speaking of pairs, a characteristic of the School is that each of us had to choose a partner with whom to share everything, including spare time.
If one partner is wounded in action, the other must see to dressing his wound or to carrying him. There are no stretcher bearers in our Units.
My partner is a Sardinian corporal major, who comes from the "Sassari" Brigade, 151st Regiment. He is a man of few words, but very reliable. He throws petards like few others. He seems born expressly for that. His battle name is *Carestia*[164]. When an instructor praises him for the distance and accuracy of his throwing he always replies seriously in the same way:
«I just do what I can, sir.»
One of the drills in pairs consists in running towards numbered dummies, lined up in a semicircle, but positioned at different distances. At his discretion, the instructor yells out the number of the target we have to throw the petards at. Then we have to run forward, hoping not to be hit by splinters, and stab the dummy. Then we do the same thing in teams with moving dummies.
Another very important lesson is how to capture a machine gun.
God only knows how many victims the *Schwarzlose* has killed.
The team runs towards the machine gun. At two hundred metres away, the team leader and his mate throw phosphorus hand grenades, which produce a very dense smoke which blinds the machine gunners. Another pair have to crawl forward and continue launching smoke grenades to mask the outflanking move by other pairs in the team. Once they are positioned on the flanks, the attack is triggered, the machine gunners and their servers are eliminated and the weapon is captured.
Veterans have confirmed that this technique works almost always, proof of which is the large quantity of machine guns captured.
To make the exercise more realistic, the machine gun actually does fire at our teams, but high enough so that it goes over the men's heads. Very soon my team will be ready for the live-fire exercise on the "dummy hill".
Several days ago work began on the barracks that will take the place of our tents. By November they will be well-equipped and heated. Ours are near the entrance to the School, between those of the IV and the V.
Units I, II and III are located at the bottom of the hills near the Command.

---

[164] In Italian it literally means famine.

They are also planning to erect a big canopy to cover the sports field and a wooden bridge over the Natisone. That way we can also train over on the plain of Oleis. It seems they want to bring drinkable water to the camp and build a road connecting it directly to the road of the Val Natisone.

P.S. Yesterday in the football final we beat 3 to 2 the *nonni* from the 1st company of the II Unit commanded by Captain Abbondanza.
Tonight we'll celebrate in Manzano with fish in… "Abundance", that we caught ourselves in the Natisone. No rods or bait, only the petards kindly provided by Sergeant Pace, who will be a welcome guest at our dinner.

Chapter 5.II

Sdricca, Thursday, 20 September 1917

Last night at the restaurant the fish was excellent and so was the wine.

We sang and drank until late. We were celebrating our victory in the football tournament and learning by heart the new Arditi hymn, which was composed right here in Sdricca recently.

The music is very beautiful and fills the soul with energy.

The words of the first verse are:

Del pugnale al fiero lampo, della bomba al gran fragore
su compagni tutti al campo, là si vince o si muore,
sono giovane e son forte, non mi trema in petto il cor
sorridendo vo' alla morte, pria d'andar al disonor!

The chorus follows:

Giovinezza, giovinezza, primavera di bellezza
della vita nell'ebbrezza il tuo canto squillerà.

Second verse:

Allorché dalla trincera, suona l'ora di battaglia
sarà pria la Fiamma Nera che terribile si scaglia
col pugnale nella mano, con la fede dentro il core
ei s'avanza e va lontano pien di gloria e di valor!

Refrain:

Giovinezza, giovinezza, primavera di bellezza
della vita nell'ebbrezza il tuo canto squillerà.

Third verse (if I remember it correctly):

Di Pontida il giuramento, feci un dì per la mia terra
esclamando guerra, guerra all'austriaco invasore
sono Ardito, Ardito e fiero con la bomba e col pugnal
guai per l'orrido straniero, che mi attende e che mi assal!

Refrain:

Giovinezza, giovinezza, primavera di bellezza
della vita nell'ebbrezza il tuo canto squillerà.

Fourth and final verse:
Dell'Orsini ho qui la bomba, ho il pugnale del terrore
pur se l'obice rimbomba, non mi trema in petto il core
la mia splendida bandiera è di un unico color
è una fiamma tutta nera che divampa in ogni cor!

Refrain:
Giovinezza, giovinezza, primavera di bellezza
della vita nell'ebbrezza il tuo canto squillerà.[165]

I think that my friend, the organ-playing sergeant, would have appreciated this song too.[166]

---

[165] *At the fierce flash of the dagger, at the loud blast of the bomb*
Let's go, comrades, everybody onto the field, where you either win or die,
I am young and strong, my heart is firm in my breast
I go to death with a smile, rather than live with dishonour!
Refrain: *Youth, youth, springtime of beauty,*
in the thrill of life your song will ring.

When the hour of battle blares out from the trench
the feared Black Flame will be the first to launch himself forward
with dagger in hand and heart full of faith
he advances and goes far, full of glory and valour!
Refrain
The oath of Pontida, I swore for my land
declaring war, war against the Austrian invader
I am bold, bold and proud with bomb and dagger
woe to the vile foreigner who waits to attack me!
Refrain
I've got the Orsini here, I've got the dagger of terror
even if the howitzer echoes, my heart is firm in my breast
my beautiful flag is all of one colour
it's an all-black flame blazing in every heart!
Refrain

[166] Originally this song, entitled "Il Commiato" ("The Farewell" in English), was born in Turin in 1909 as a joyful song of farewell to university studies to music by Giuseppe Blanc and text by Nino Oxilia (killed by the fragment of a grenade on Mount Tomba in November 1917). In 1910, Blanc, at the time a second lieutenant in the Engineers Unit, successfully performed it in front of an audience of officers and Alpine troops at the end of a ski course. They chose it as "The Skiers' Hymn" and imported it into their units. In 1911, the Alpine Corps elected it as its official anthem. Once inside the military world, the text of the song was modified during the Libyan campaign and again during the Great War. The commander of the Sdricca School, Lieutenant Colonel Bassi, had commissioned several musicians and poets to compose an official hymn for his assault units, but in the meantime, some soldiers at the camp, including Marcello Manni, wrote their own text to

Blanc's music. Thus, the Hymn of the Arditi was born, with its origins in the very tents of the soldiers. During the three-year period 1919-21 other versions saw the light, including that of the fascist squadrons edited by Manni himself, who published it as an original creation, prompting Blanc to take legal action which, however, was not successful. Finally, in 1925 the definitive version of "Youth" became the official Hymn of the National Fascist Party, and the unofficial national Anthem, with text by Salvatore Gotta.

Chapter 6.II

Sdricca, Sunday, 23 September 1917

Almost three weeks have passed since I got here.

Three hard weeks, in which I've strengthened my body a lot thanks to the excellent food and daily training. I've even learned to swim well. As a boy I used to jump into the frozen pools of the Fella river but then I'd scramble out right away. The Natisone river is not as cold but quite deep, so that you can go for long swims even against the current.

I have also bolstered my morale. In the regiment I was surrounded by depressed and disheartened soldiers. Together with these new comrades, strong and courageous, and with the support of these officers, who live among us and don't stay hidden in the rear lines, I think that no obstacle can stop us.

Every day numerous officers come to study our drills in order to apply the same methods. Other Arditi Schools are opening or have already been opened in the other army corps.[167]

If they succeed in bringing together men like the ones here at Sdricca, then, with the new combat techniques, we really can defeat the Austrians and put an end to this war.

I have met many volunteers in the past weeks.

They are of all different types.

There are those like me, the majority, who came here because they were promised better treatment. No trenches, no corvée, abundant rations guaranteed twice a day, higher pay, frequent leave. Almost everyone in my team, including *Carestia*, is of this kind. If you are destined to die, it is better to do so as an Ardito rather than down in the trenches.

Then there are the firebrands who are spoiling for a fight at any cost, who seek adventure and hope to earn medals. Some of them call themselves "Death Riders".

I put *Cuteddu* in the second group, even if he is unique: he is not interested in medals, he only wants to avenge his brothers killed on the Karst.

---

[167] On August 10, 1917, the High Command ordered all Armies to send their officers to Sdricca to be trained as instructors for the establishment of new schools, which would form their Assault Units.

There is also a small group motivated instead by a strong sense of duty towards Italy, an authentic patriotic spirit. They are soldiers who mostly come from big cities, students and educated people. Some of them were already interventionists in 1914.
Finally, there are what we call the "in-volunteers", because they have been sent here by their commanders. Most are experienced soldiers who have shown courage. Some, on the other hand, are discards or no-goods whom the commanders wanted to get rid of. The latter were immediately sent back to their senders.[168]
After the newspapers wrote an account of the Arditi enterprises on the Bainsizza, Belpoggio and Mount San Gabriele, a lot of "maffiosi" began to appear here at the camp[169]. Fortunately, after the tests of courage many of them were sent home with a kick in the rear.
For several days I have been commanding a team of ten men.[170]
To get to know them better, I asked each one where he had fought.
When his turn came, *Carestia* limited himself to saying: «With the Sassari fought I» and continued whittling a stick with his particular switchblade knife, which he calls *s'arresoja*. What he said was more than enough. The "Sassari" Brigade covered itself with glory both on the Karst and on the plateaus. The flags of the two regiments (151st and 152nd) received the gold medal for military valour. I wouldn't be surprised if he himself had been decorated, but he is too modest to say so. He did not even want to sew the decoration for wounds suffered in combat onto his tunic. We have counted the many scars on his body when we wash in the river.
To compensate for my partner's few words is *O'pazzo*, the corporal of the Bersaglieri, whom I met the day I arrived. He calls almost everybody in this school crazy.

---

[168] The High Command strictly forbade enrolling common criminals in the Assault Units. However, the presence of men prosecuted for infringements of the Military Code cannot be excluded, given the high number of soldiers who had run-ins with military justice (a late return from leave was considered mutiny). The Arditi themselves fuelled the rumour that there were murderers and criminals among them, in the verses of one of their songs:
In the national prisons there are no more bandits, because they all joined the Arditi units.
If you want to make war with good soldiers, go to the jail and round up the prisoners.
With a six-year sentence, he can be a corporal, with a life sentence, he can be promoted to general.
[169] In military jargon *"fare la maffia"* meant showing off. At the beginning, many volunteers were attracted by the appeal of the new uniform and the aura of adventure surrounding these new units.
[170] Each platoon was made up of an assault team, two flanking teams armed with submachine guns, and one covering or rearguard team. Each team consisted of 5-6 pairs of men.

If you ask him the reason for his nickname, he replies: «*Chistu è 'o contranomme mio*»[171] as if it were the most normal thing in the world.
He is paired with *Mandulino*, another Neapolitan, so they can freely speak the same dialect. He can play both guitar and mandolin, but he can also shoot very well with the machine gun.
Another pair is made up of a native of Bergamo and a guy from Brescia. Despite the historical rivalry between the two cities, they get along well (perhaps because they are both mountain men like me). We nicknamed them *il Gat* and *il Vólp*.[172]
Bracciodiferro and *Pugnodiferro* make up another team[173]. The former was a dockworker at the port of Genoa. He has incredible strength in his arms. Nobody at the camp has ever been able to beat him at arm wrestling.
The latter is a Florentine, a butcher, a former boxer, a bravado, but a nice chap. He has made himself a personal dagger, the handle of which incorporates a brass knuckle[174]. He boasts about having torn it from the hands of an Austrian from the *Stürmtruppen*.[175]
Finally, the last pair is made up of two men named Salvatore, *Cuteddu* and *Biunnu*[176], one of his countrymen, the only one who can calm him down when he has one of his temper tantrums. Everyone now knows that if you speak to a Sicilian, it is better not to use his nickname, because otherwise he will get offended, give you dirty looks and not answer you. I've learned that in their dialect nicknames are called *li ngiurii*, that is, insults.
As far as I'm concerned, no one here calls me *O'Professore* or *O'Scrittore* anymore, like they did in my old Regiment.
Here my men just call me *Sergente*.

---

171 «That's just my nickname» translation from the Neapolitan dialect.

172 *The Cat* and *the Fox*.

173 *Iron-arm* and *Ironfist* are the literal translations of these nicknames.

174 An improper weapon made up of four rings welded together with a piece of iron. One holds it by inserting his fingers in the rings. It hugely amplifies the bludgeoning power of a punch.

175 These were the assault units of the Austro-Hungarian army, made up of the youngest, most physically gifted, most morally reliable and best trained elements. The Arditi represented the Italian response to that type of troops, from which they certainly drew the initial inspiration, going on to develop autonomously and originally, completely different from the Infantry and with an autonomous role in battle.

176 It literally means *Blond* in the Sicilian dialect.

Chapter 7.II

Sdricca, Friday, 28 September 1917

Again, this week many things happened that are worth remembering.

Last Tuesday some of the neighboring farmers complained to our commander about the disappearance of three hens. For sure, some of our people had made a "coup de main" to supplement their rations. The investigations conducted by the officers did not lead to the discovery of the culprits. So Colonel Bassi decided to punish everyone, including the officers.

Instead of our evening liberty, we had to stand for four hours in the centre of the multi-sports field all lined up and loaded down with backpacks and weapons. Fortunately, our equipment is lighter than that of the poor infantrymen.[177]

In the following days we tried to discover the culprits of the crime.

Nobody has yet been able to figure it out.

On Wednesday I faced Captain Racchi's swing. I was the last of my squad. Nobody ducked. It's truly unnerving to see a block of wood of that size coming toward you at such great speed[178]. At the last moment it rises and, instead of smashing your face, makes your cap fly off.

«Would you like to drink another one, sergeant?» the captain asked me with a dare in his voice. Instead of looking the other way as I put my cap back on my head I replied: «Thanks, sir. Today I am very thirsty.»

I would have gladly avoided accepting his challenge. But I wanted the men of my squad to know what their commander is made of.

«Alright, sergeant, now I will try and quench your damned thirst» was the captain's not-very-reassuring announcement, as he grabbed my shoulders, moving me a little closer to the frame of "the Swing".

I was counting on his precision in handling that contraption.

At his whistle the assistant let the block fly.

---

[177] To ensure maximum speed of action Bassi studied a lighter set of equipment: 15.100 kg. for the Arditi compared to 22.850 kg. for infantrymen. The elimination of the backpack, detested by all soldiers, was considered an authentic privilege. Since the Arditi returned to their quarters at the end of each action, a haversack with the bare essentials was sufficient.

[178] It was one metre by 60 centimetres in diameter and 1 quintal heavy.

I saw it right in my face! At the last second, however, it rose up, making my cap fly. This time I felt it part my hair.
I really don't know why I acted the way I did, but instead of picking up my cap and leaving, when the captain asked if I had quenched my thirst sufficiently, I couldn't help saying: «My throat's still a bit dry, sir.»
From under the visor of his cap, he shot me a withering glance and with a hiss said: «Come here, sergeant, come here and let me quench your thirst for once and for all.»
Planting his steel fingers in my shoulders, he positioned me damnably close to "the Swing". Meanwhile lots of Arditi and trainees had gathered around, curious to see how this challenge would end.
"If it already touched my hair the first time, this time it'll hit my forehead" I thought. I was cornered. There was only one dignified way out. I waited until very last second and then I stooped down just enough to give the block the satisfaction of making my cap fly off.
I heard an explosion of "hurràs!" from my team and all those present, while the captain whispered in my ear: «If you hadn't stooped a little, this time it would have hit you in full. Never take a risk if you haven't got at least one way out in mind.»
On the way back to our tents everyone complimented me except *Carestia*, who said to me «Don't do it again.»
He wasn't only talking about "the Swing".

Yesterday there was a lot of excitement at camp for the arrival of a delegation of senior foreign officers accompanied by a minister.[179]
They wanted to watch the assault on the "dummy hill" by the III Unit.[180]
At the end of the exercise, the Black Flames of the III sang our new hymn, accompanied by the Army band. We were all very proud.

This morning I witnessed a scene that could only happen here at the Arditi School. Sudden shouts and rifle shots arose from the area of the headquarters of the II Assault Unit, commanded by Captain Abbondanza.

---

[179] This was the minister without portfolio of the Boselli government, Ubaldo Comandini, accompanying an Anglo-French military-political committee to Sdricca.
[180] Most of the School's activities were organized around this massive exercise, which simulated an actual attack with the covering fire of machine guns and support from the artillery. Each time, between 12 and 15 thousand petards were consumed, 30 to 40 thousand bullets, and 5 to 6 thousand grenades. These assaults were repeated both in daylight and at night under spotlights in order to assimilate the movements of the new combat techniques and accustom the soldiers to the danger and noise of weapons.

Grabbing our weapons on the fly, we rushed out of our tents to see what was happening. It was the Arditi of the 1st company of Captain Signorelli, who were marching around the field, as exalted as ever, with their banners streaming in the wind, their daggers unsheathed, with petards in hand and some smoking muskets.
When they passed by us, we understood that they were off to a war action.
I saw incredible joy in their eyes, as if they were going to a dance party rather than a bout with death. I was very moved.
How different it was from my old regiment. The announcement of an action was always greeted by us soldiers like a sentence to the gallows.
We felt like animals sent to the slaughterhouse.
On the contrary, those Arditi seemed happy to put into practice everything they had learned and to give Colonel Bassi more satisfaction.
The whole camp got into line behind them and joined in the festive march to the colonel's barrack.
When he appeared, he didn't indulge in a long speech.
He simply said: «Be worthy of honour!»
This was enough to trigger a roar.
We lined up along the road and when our comrades passed by in the trucks of the 6th auto-column, the so called "flying column", we said goodbye to them, shouting out loudly and repeatedly, "hip-hip-hip-hurrà!".
They responded by firing several shots in the air.
During that day, more than one comrade was sorry not to be part of that company.
If I have to be honest, I also felt a bit of envy at the bottom of my heart.

CHAPTER 8.II

Sdricca, Sunday, 30 September 1917

Last night my team played a joke on *il Gat* and *il Vólp*.

Instead of coming with us on liberty to Manzano, the two cronies preferred to go to Udine. Someone saw them get on a truck (drivers never pick up infantrymen, but they always willingly give a ride to us Arditi).

They didn't say so, but they most probably wanted to pay a visit to some brothels in the outskirts of the city.

We went down to Manzano.

When we got back to the tent, *O'pazzo*, *Mandulino* and *Bracciodiferro* hid their cots, replacing them with bags on the ground filled with a bit of straw.

Around three in the morning *il Gat* and *il Vólp* came back to the tent. So as not to wake us, they headed towards their bunks in the dark. While the first one felt around in vain in the void to find his cot, the other one, however, threw himself on it, dead weight.

We heard a string of oaths never before heard in the Brescia dialect, followed by a volley of curses in the Bergamo dialect.

Il Gat lit a sulphur stick and discovered that his cot had also disappeared.

We all burst out laughing.

In the dark someone said: «Have you been reclining on something soft in Udine? Well, now you'll have to lie on something harder.»

I cannot repeat what the two unfortunate comrades replied, because it was completely incomprehensible.

In the afternoon, before going down to Manzano, we had fun experimenting. On a pole, we stuck an Austrian "chamber pot" and one of our Adrian helmets, which are lighter.[181]

Then we shot at them with our muskets from a distance of about two hundred metres. When we went to see, our helmet was all riddled with bullets, while the enemy one had only a few holes and many dents.

---

[181] The Italian Adrian helmet was certainly more elegant, but the sheet metal was less thick than the Austrian Berndorfer and the German M16 (0.7 vs 1.0 mm). It weighed less (700-800 vs 1,150-1,400 grams) but gave little protection to the neck and was more deformable on impact with a ratio of 1 to 3.

After having examined the effect of our bullets *Pugnodiferro* started singing the famous song:

L'elmetto è quella cosa - che la testa ti protegge
dalle palle e dalle schegge - dagli Shrapnels e dai granat.
Ma se palla ovvero scheggia - ti colpiscon per davvero
ti saluto bel guerriero - te ne vai all'altro mond.[182]

«You know what?» concluded *Bracciodiferro*. «At our next attack I'll wear one of their "buckets of coal" under my helmet.»
«First you have to snatch it from a *Crucco*[183] with a head as big as yours» *Pugnodiferro* snickered under his moustache.
«*Tu si pazz. Lascia perder 'sti strunzate, guagliò. Può tenè pure a nà curazz e ferr, ma se sta scritt ca' e murì, na' schegg o nu cunfiett te po' accider in ogni mument. È tutta na fatalità*»[184] *O'pazzo* pronounced seriously.
«*È tutta na fatalità*» echoed *Mandulino* and told us this story.
«*Rinto a cumpagnia mia ce stev nu capural ca durante a nù bumbardament invec e se n'e fuji rint a qualch rifugi s'è mettette a girà pà trincea fumann a pippa. Ricev c'a si steva segnat c'aveva murì chill juorn ò colp l'avrebb cogliuto arò stev stev, pure rinto a nù fifàus. Quindi era inutil nascondèrs.*»[185]
«Did you scrape him up with a spoon at the end of the shelling?» I asked him.
«*No. L'avimmà truvat c'a fumav ancor a pippa!*»[186]
«*Can da l'ostie! A i plaseve mateâ cul fûc*»[187] I said.
«*Chillo steva tutt pazzo rint a cervello...*»[188] added *O'pazzo*, repeatedly touching his temple with his index finger.

---

[182] *The helmet is that thing - that protects your head*
from bullets and shards - from Shrapnel and grenades.
But if a bullet or a shard - really hits you
I salute you, beautiful warrior - you're going to the other world.
[183] *Crucco* is another nickname for Austro-Hungarian soldiers. It comes from the word "kruh", that is bread, asked for by hungry Croatian and Slovenian prisoners to their jailers.
[184] «You're nuts. Forget about these ideas, man. You can even be wearing iron armour, but if it is fated that you have to die, a shell fragment or a bullet can kill you at any moment. It's all up to fate» translation from the Neapolitan dialect.
[185] «There was a corporal in my company who, during the shelling, instead of going to the shelters, walked around the trench smoking his pipe. He said that if he was destined to die that day, the bullet would reach him anywhere, even inside a *fifàus*. So there was no point in hiding». In military jargon *fifàus* was a deep and safe shelter for commanders.
[186] «No. We found him still smoking his pipe!»
[187] «What a scoundrel! He liked playing with fire» translation from the Friulan language.

«*Chillo ha fatto accussì dint a tutt'e bumbardament*»[189] continued *Mandulino*.
«*...ma tenev pure ò mazz*»[190] concluded *O'pazzo*.
«Until one day we heard a whistle and an isolated "muffler" hit the latrine in full. *E chi ci steva dinta a latrin proprio a chillu mumento? O' capural!*»[191]
«*Te l'aggio ritt, è tutta na fatalità!*»[192] *O'pazzo* reiterated, rolling his eyes.
«Bad luck» said *Carestia*. «Something much worse happened to us in June. We were all ready to attack Mount Zebio. Six battalions. Suddenly the artillery started shelling us. Our own! A massacre, I can't begin to describe it. In the end, only four companies attacked.»
«*Maremma impestata*, you were commanded by general...» *Pugnodiferro* snapped.
«Don't say that name!» *Carestia* ordered him.
«*Chill'è nu jettatore. Sciò, sciò ciucciuè!*»[193] exclaimed *O'pazzo*, touching all his amulets.
All of us hurried to touch wood.
Cadorna dismissed that general after the battle. He should have done it sooner. The offensive on the plateau and on Mount Ortigara was said to have been a disaster because that general is a jinx.[194]

---

[188] «He must have lost his marbles» translation from the Neapolitan dialect.
[189] «He always behaved like that during all the shelling.»
[190] «...he was really lucky.»
[191] «Who was inside the latrine at that moment? The corporal!»
[192] «I told you it's all fate!»
[193] «He's a jinx. Shoo, shoo, screech-owl!»
[194] The 6th Army offensive in the Asiago plateau (June 1917) resulted in a bloodbath: over 25,000 casualties among the dead, wounded and missing, with no results. Things went wrong from the start, when a mine exploded prematurely on Mount Zebio, killing 180 men from the engineers, infantrymen and officers of the "Catania" Brigade. Among the numerous negative events, there was also the short shelling by the Italian artillery on the trenches where the "Sassari" had paused, waiting for the attack on the nearby enemy trenches. The losses were considerable, especially among the ranks of the 151st Regiment. The commander of the 3rd Battalion, Major Fresini, was also seriously wounded. His place was taken by Captain Emilio Lussu, who later described what happened in his famous book *"A year on the plateau"*. Both for the negative outcome of the battle and for the persistent rumour that he brought bad luck, Cadorna dismissed the commander of the 6th Army, General Ettore Mambretti (5 January 1859 - 12 November 1948). In a private letter, Cadorna wrote: *"When the soldiers see Mambretti they touch wood. In Italy, unfortunately, this prejudice constitutes a strong negative power"*. In spite of this, after the war Mambretti was promoted to Army general (1923) and in 1929 he ran for office and was elected Senator of the Kingdom.

Chapter 9.II

Sdricca, Monday, 1st October 1917

Last night we had a party in Manzano. We were celebrating the heroes of the II Assault Unit for the great victory they won over the "Bean".[195]

They took 2,500 prisoners, including 49 officers, and captured 25 machine guns, 6 bomb launchers and 2 trench cannons.

We toasted our dead and the wounded, who included Lieutenant Bonanni and Lieutenants Lionti and Falcone. We also toasted the regimental Arditi of the valiant "Venice" Brigade (their captain died) and the gunners of the 89th mountain battery (their commander lost his right hand).

Lieutenant Bonanni's orderly told us all the details.[196]

«At six in the morning our artillery opens fire. There were at least five hundred pieces firing on the "Bean". After about two hours we move forward divided into three columns. I was in the left one, commanded by Lieutenant Bonanni. The bulk of the responsibility lay on our shoulders because we were coordinating the others. As soon as we reach the first line of trenches, we see five *tognìt*[197] waving white rags. They want to surrender, we think, and so we don't shoot 'em. But as soon as we get close to them, those bloody bastards start throwing hand grenades at us...»

I can't transcribe the curses that spewed from the mouths of everyone who was listening, including some civilians from Manzano, who were there in the tavern.

«Luckily, they don't explode, except one that hits the lieutenant. He is dead, I think. It drives me crazy. Together with the others I throw myself on those bastards and we avenge him with our daggers. Instead, like Lazarus in the parable of the Gospel, he gets up. It's a miracle, I think. He's bleeding from one eye, from his arms and legs. Grenade fragments. Anyway, he keeps on going like it was nothing. So we go forward too. Just at the sight of us lots of enemies surrender and we keep going forward to-

---

195 It was the name given to an entrenchment, level 800 and south-east of Madoni on the Bainsizza plateau. The action took place on 29 September 1917.

196 Each official had an "orderly" to take care of his needs and carry his properties.

197 *Tognìt* or *Tognino* was a derogatory way, mainly in Lombardy, to indicate Austrian soldiers since the times of the Lombard-Veneto Kingdom (1815-1859). It would derive from (An)tonio, which in the Lombard dialects assumed the meaning of "gross". Toni was the typical name of the clown, a big, tall, simpleton with a red nose, who in the circuses entertained the spectators between one act and another.

gether with him up to the third order of trenches. And there, what do I see?»
We all waited to hear what he had seen.
«Doesn't one of the prisoners, a bastard, pull up his rifle and start shooting at the lieutenant?»
«*E ło ga ciapà?*»[198] asked a Venetian comrade anxious to know how the story ended.
«*No. Lo go ciapà prima mi. Co' questo…*»[199] the lieutenant's orderly, although he's from Calabria, replied in Venetian dialect, unsheathing and brandishing his dagger. A burst of applause, fist punches on the tables and clinking of blades on glasses and bottles echoed in the tavern.
«The enemy understands that there is no joking with us. When the wounded lead the prisoners away, we go ahead. Even if he is losing a lot of blood, the lieutenant doesn't want to go back. Then we go back down the other side of the "Bean", where the *tognìt* are holed up in caves. We clean them out one by one, until we've used up all our petards, and only have a few cartridges left and the flamethrowers are almost empty. So we start using the enemy's own grenades and rifles. Meanwhile, the men of the "Venice" arrive to help us. We are always in the lead, forward, forward towards the Chiapovano valley...»
«This guy is capable of reaching Trieste» said a Sicilian dryly, silenced immediately by the others.
«At some point one machine gun starts firing, then two, then three. We take out the first, then the second, but at the third the bastard gunner hits the captain of the "Venice" right in the throat. Dead.[200] He doesn't get up again. Those machine gunners, however, won't have the chance to talk about it at home."
Another round of "hurrà!".
«We notice two other caves. We go to see what's there. The lieutenant is in front with his pistol in hand half empty. We too have only a few more shots. What do we find in those caves? A major, seven officers and eighty-five Austrian soldiers. All prisoners!»
Another round of "hurrà!".
«We find cases of ammo and machine guns. A blessing from Heaven, I think. In fact, other *tognìt* arrive to try and do us in. And we shoot them

---

[198] «Did he hit him?» translation from the Venetian dialect.
[199] «No. I hit him first. With this…» translation from the Venetian dialect.
[200] It was Captain Mario Merlin, commander of the Arditi regimental company of the "Venice" Brigade.

with their own weapons. Three times they attack and three times we drive them back. They preferred to avoid a fourth attack.»
Another round of "hurrà!".
«Your lieutenant? Was he still standing?»
«He was always on his feet. But he lost so much blood that he was staggering. He was full of shards. His eye was swollen shut. So we loaded him on our shoulders and carried him to Madoni to have him medicated. Captain Abbondanza was there with tears in his eyes. He embraced him. The general commander of "Venice" was there, too. Then we took him on a stretcher to a nearby hospital. Even General Papa[201] wanted to see him to compliment him. That evening the general lent us a car to take us back to Sdricca. Yesterday I accompanied the lieutenant to field hospital number 66 where a doctor removed the shard from his right eye. The doctor decided to send him to the Piacenza hospital. I came back here.»[202]
If we could have, we would have exploded some petards in that tavern to properly celebrate this feat. We limited ourselves to draining a dozen flasks of wine and performing the entire repertoire of our songs.
When we got back to our tent in the middle of the night, we threw ourselves dead tired into bed.
Suddenly, however, some of us jumped up, cursing.
Something was pricking our feet.
Someone had placed bunches of nettles at the bottom of our beds.
Among the string of curses, the satisfied voices of *il Gat* and *il Vólp* could be heard: «*L'è ü pensér di s-cète de Ùdine... chèle bröte porsèle!*»[203]

---

[201] General Achille Papa, commander of the 44th Division, was killed by an Austrian sniper a few days later (October 5, 1917), in the exact same position that had been conquered by the Arditi. Unlike many other generals, he used to do front-line reconnaissance, to personally understand the situation and avoid unnecessary losses.
[202] For that action, Lieutenant Armando Bonanni proposed his orderly, Cosimo Chiurco, for a medal of military valour. Both were decorated with the silver medal in 1919. The lieutenant was wounded a second time during the assault on Monte Valbella (28 January 1918), obtaining another silver. Then he fought both the Battle of the Solstice in June and the Battle of Vittorio Veneto, in Moriago (27 October 1918), earning his third silver medal. In the year 1919 he took part in the mission to Libya and then followed d'Annunzio in the Fiume Exploit. He participated in the March on Rome (1922). He died in 1923.
[203] «It's a gift from the girls of Udine... those ugly sluts!» translation from the Bergamo dialect.

Chapter 10.II

Sdricca, Wednesday, 3 October 1917
Some trouble has broken out, upsetting the happiness of the school.
Yesterday in Udine the Carabinieri stopped nine of our comrades because they were without permits. They could have let them come back to camp, where they would have been justly punished and thrown into the "Troublemakers" enclosure. But no, they took them to Manzano handcuffed like criminals.
In the afternoon, Colonel Bassi met up with the Carabinieri as they were coming up to Sdricca. He ordered that the prisoners to be handed over to the IV Unit guards, who are headquartered right at the edge of the camp, right before where we of the VI are. He wanted to prevent the Carabinieri from entering too far inside the school so as to avoid the sight of them triggering the wrath of some Ardito. There is bad blood between us and the *Caproni*.
For this reason, the guard officer, cadet Guaia, requested that only the deputy brigadier with the arrest papers remain. He invited the others to leave. But by now it was too late. Some men from the IV Unit had noticed the arrival of our comrades, handcuffed and escorted by those six *Caproni*. In a few minutes the squad was surrounded by several shouting Arditi.
If you put petrol near a fire, then a big blaze will break out for sure.
In fact, the Carabinieri soon had to run away chased by our comrades and also a couple of stones.
Hearing the shouting we of the VI went to see what was going on. We crossed paths with some of the IV who were coming back to their tents to pick up sticks and petards. Meanwhile the Carabinieri had taken refuge in a farmhouse. On seeing more and more Arditi arrive, the *Airplanes* decided to take off towards Manzano.
The most agitated of us chased them, throwing stones and even some petards, but it only made them fly faster. In retaliation, those bastards fired their muskets and hit two Arditi. One is seriously wounded in the abdomen. This made us really mad.
If they had not found refuge in another farmhouse and if artillery lieutenant Meli, who was nearby, had not intervened, I do not know what would have happened. Definitely ugly.

The lieutenant tried to calm people down and invited the Carabinieri to lay down their arms. Second lieutenants Erò and Punzoni, both of the IV Unit, also arrived to give him support. While negotiations to avoid the worst were going on, someone shouted: «They're getting away, the *Caproni* are getting away! Let's get them!»
Two Carabinieri had jumped out of a back window and were sneaking away through the hedges. A bunch of us gave chase, while the bulk of our group overwhelmed the officers and entered the farmhouse. *Bracciodiferro*, *Pugnodiferro* and *Biunnu were among them*. I wouldn't have wanted to be in the shoes of those Carabinieri. Fortunately for them, Major Mannacio, commander of the IV Unit, arrived a few minutes later and with his authority restored order, along with his gun.
My three brawlers left the farm visibly disappointed at not being able to complete the job.
«There were too many of us in there. There was no room to teach those goats a lesson» said *Bracciodiferro* bitterly.
«At least I landed a couple of punches» said *Pugnodiferro* with more satisfaction, massaging his knuckles.
«I wonder if anyone got the two who escaped from the window. In the woods there are no officers to defend them...» added *Bracciodiferro*.
«*Chisti cuomu cunigghi sinni fuieru. Chisti 'nfinu a Uddene sinni ieru*»[204] said *Biunnu*.
«*Miôr! Si ju cjàpin, ju còpin*»[205] I replied in Friulan.
Biunnu gave me a questioning look.
«I said: that's better, because if they catch them, they'll kill them. Learn to speak in Italian if you want to make yourself understood.»
Returning to our tents, we continued talking about what had just happened and above all the consequences, which were not long in coming. There was no liberty for anyone that evening.
At 9 p.m. the "fall in" was called, all six units, fully equipped and lined up, with their officers, at the multi-sports field. The nine Arditi found in Udine without permission were already in the "Troublemakers" enclosure.
There was total silence.
Only the rustling of the wind in the leaves and the occasional cry of some nocturnal bird could be heard. We remained like that, in silence, for four hours. It was clear that we were in big trouble.

---

[204] «They ran away like rabbits. They're already in Udine» translation from the Sicilian dialect.
[205] «Better! If they catch them, they'll kill them» translation from the Friulan language.

The ones who had not participated in the clash were pissed off, but they certainly didn't hold it against us, because they would have acted in the same way.
At one in the morning the "fall out" order broke the silence. We went to bed without the usual racket and a little worried about the following day.
In fact, instead of dismissing the matter, the *Airplanes* had run to whine about us to their commanders, who in turn complained to Colonel Bassi and asked for the heads of the nine Arditi.
The following morning, October 3, the "fall in" was called again.
Captain Pedercini, commander of the 3rd company of the I Unit, took the floor. These more or less were his words:
«At eight o'clock this morning an extraordinary war Tribunal will meet to judge the Arditi guilty of yesterday's very serious incident. All troops must attend the trial. Unarmed. I repeat. Unarmed! Fall out!»
At eight o'clock we were all lined up in a square around the area of the trial. A long table and several chairs had been placed in the middle. More than one Ardito had stowed petards in his jacket.
«If they condemn them, I'll blow up the Tribunal» a corporal of the IV confided to me, patting a bag full of Thévenots.
The court was chaired by an infantry colonel, flanked by other officers. To the left of the table were the nine defendants, guarded by some Arditi armed with muskets. The interrogation was quick.
Then a colonel of the Carabinieri with thick black eyebrows and moustaches strutted in. Attention! rang out. We promptly performed it but accompanied it with low kind of howl.
When Colonel Bassi arrived to testify, the "Attention!" was perfect and in unison. I had never heard him talk for so long. His tone was calm and his words measured.
Then it was the turn of the prosecuting attorney. He had an unpleasant voice. After a few words of introduction, he asked that our nine comrades face the firing squad. Right away I looked for the corporal of the IV with his bag stuffed with petards and from his face I realized that he was ready to use them if the request had been accepted.
In their defense, Lieutenant Cao di San Marco gave a beautiful speech. He is Sardinian and a lawyer as a civilian. He said that the discipline of the Black Flames is boundless, not the discipline of the barracks, but the discipline which renders us conscious of risking our lives for the good of Italy.
If the Carabinieri had understood this difference, they should have asked the nine Arditi to return to Sdricca and they would have immediately obeyed, without needing to be accompanied in handcuffs.

«Bravo! Very good!» someone shouted from our ranks, immediately silenced by the President of the Court.
At the end the judges consulted with each other.
I was quite worried about what could happen if they were sentenced to be shot. How would many of my comrades react at that sentence?
Would they throw petards at the officers, creating an even more serious incident than the first one?
And what was I supposed to do?
Attempt to quell the revolt or take part in it?
As the judges prepared to pass the sentence, I had decided what I would do.
I had enlisted in the Arditi so as not to rot in the trenches.
Ruining everything now seemed silly to me.
Colonel Bassi and his officers would certainly intervene to quell a possible uprising. And so would I.
In that same instant the President of the Tribunal took the floor:
«In the name of His Majesty Vittorio Emanuele III, King of Italy by the will of God and of the nation...»
We were all in suspense.
The nine Arditi listened to attention, eyes wide.
«... we condemn them to twenty years of military imprisonment...»
As these words spread through the air, I felt a great sigh of relief travel through our lines.
Someone started to sing our song:
Se non ci conoscete guardateci dai passi...
And the whole field responded with a thunderous chorus like thunder:
Noi siamo gli arditissimi del colonnello Bassi!
Bombe a man e colpi di pugnal! [206]

Just as well.
The judges may have figured out that in the event of a death sentence, the first ones to lose their *ghirba* would be them.
None of us were fond of the *Caproni* even before this trouble. During these years of war, they have always pointed their muskets against Italian soldiers and never against the *magnasego*.
Now we hate them ever more.

---

[206] *If you don't know us, watch us march by...*
We are the daredevils of Colonel Bassi!
Hand grenades and slashing daggers!

CHAPTER 11.II

Sdricca, Sunday, 7 October 1917
After a month of training, they awarded me the Ardito badge.
After the black flames on the lapels, there is now on the left sleeve of my tunic the Roman gladius, surrounded by oak and laurel leaves, tied together with the Savoy knot. On the sword is the word FERT. It seems to be the King's motto, but nobody knows exactly what it means.
«Fittorio Emanuele Re di Talia» I said, jokingly.
«*Belìn*[207], they can't spell: the King's name is Vittorio and not Fittorio» pointed out *Bracciodiferro*, who hadn't understood my joke.
«They are really ignorant. They should have written VERI, because Italy starts with an I and not a T!» I went on.
«*Te gh'é resù, Sergènt*» muttered *il Gat.*[208]
According to *il Vólp* it means "Fusil Explosive Revolver Thévenot".
«*Te gh'é resù, Vólp*» muttered *il Gat.*
«Where's our dagger, have they forgotten it?» I said.
«*Òstia, Vólp, a l' gh'à resù 'l Sergènt*» *il Gat* muttered again.
«Fanteria Esercito Regio Trionferà» said *Carestia* instead.[209]
«*Chèsta l'è pròpre bèla*»[210] agreed both *il Gat* and *il Vólp*.
«*Guagliù ve state sbaglianno tutt'quann*» intervened *O'pazzo*, who until then had been strangely silent. «*O vero significato è n'ato, ma nun voglio c'à se vene a sapè. Io ò saccio, ma è meglio c'à nun v'ò dico.*»[211]
«Tell us, tell us» we all asked.
«*Scusate, scusate, ma è meglio c'à nun v'ò dico*» he kept repeating, raising his chin.[212]
Finally, *Pugnodiferro* intervened: «Either you tell us right away or you won't be sleeping the next few nights. Do you understand *chicchiricchì*?» [213]

---

[207] A typical swearword from Liguria, equivalent to "Fuck!"
[208] «You're right, *Sergente*» translation from the Bergamo dialect.
[209] «Royal Army Infantry Will Triumph» translation from Italian.
[210] «This is really good» translation from the Bergamo dialect.
[211] «Guys, you're all wrong. The true meaning is another, but I don't want anyone to find it out. I know it, but I better not tell you» translation from the Neapolitan dialect.
[212] «Sorry, sorry, but I'd better not tell you.»
[213] A joking name for the Bersaglieri because of the plumage on their hats.

«Vabbuò guagliù, se proprio insistit ve dico ò significato segreto di chesta parola, ma nun ò dicito a nisciuno. Giuratelo ncopp a capa e Cadorna» *O'pazzo* said cautiously.[214]
«Come on, Napoli, say it and forget that shithead.»
«Dìl, dìl dóca!»[215] *il Gat* and *il Vólp* chimed in.
«O significato segreto è chisto: Fessi E Rincoglioniti Tutti!»[216]
Pugnodiferro, *il Gat*, *il Vólp* and also *Mandulino* chased *O'pazzo* all over the tented camp, throwing water bombs at him.
We guessed at the meaning of FERT for a little while longer.
We even asked some of the veterans, but nobody knows the meaning of the word we carry on our arm.

The other day my unit too had to go where it is "hot", the hill of fire.
It was like being in the midst of a war action. We overcame all obstacles with our daggers between our teeth, throwing petards and running forward, unheeding splinters and wounds under the arc of our artillery grenades. Machine-gun bullets skillfully directed by Lieutenant Bravi also whistled over our heads (may God keep his hand steady for a long time).
We attacked the enemy redoubts, circumvented and stormed various machine gun nests, laying waste to all the trenches on our way, cleaned out the caves and chased our foes down the back of the hill. The whole action lasted over an hour, an hour of continuous fire.
Nobody died.
That's the only difference from a real action.
The following day we had no evening liberty, because we repeated the same action at night.
A beam of light from a large reflector guided us. Again, the action was well conducted by everyone.
The officers were very satisfied.

Last night in Manzano the VI Assault Unit celebrated with a tour of all the taverns. However, we were very sorry to hear the news of the death of General Papa. He was killed in the very same location recently conquered by the Arditi of the II.
We toasted his memory numerous times.

---

[214] «Okay, guys, if you really insist, I'll tell you the secret meaning of this word, but don't tell anyone. Swear it on Cadorna's head» translation from the Neapolitan dialect.
[215] «Say it, say it then!» translation from the Bergamo dialect.
[216] «The secret meaning is this: Fools And Numbnuts All!»

P.S. In these days I am rereading everything I've written in my notebook. I'm realising how many things have happened in such a short time.

I have long thought about the story that *Mandulino* told us and about the death of General Papa.
If the Arditi had not recaptured level 800, the general would not have gone to inspect "the Bean", the *mucs* would not have put that walkway under observation and the sniper would not have shot him.
It really is all about fatality.
Last year I too saw a very strange thing.
I was still with the 207th Regiment. It was night. We were in a trench.
A fellow soldier of mine had decided to move half a metre or so. He got up for just a moment to stretch his legs. Just then an Austrian decided to fire a random shot in the dark toward our trench. That stray bullet passed through my friend's neck. We weren't able to save him. The bullet had severed his jugular vein, just like what happened to Archduke Francis Ferdinand of Habsburg in Sarajevo. So the medical lieutenant said.
It gives me goose bumps to think that perhaps all the events in the lives of those two men, from their very birth, were only a build-up to that fatal junction.
I hope that no *muc* was born, grew up and came to the front line on purpose to get my *ghirba*.

CHAPTER 12.II

Sdricca, Monday, 8 October 1917

Today two new Arditi joined my squad.

One comes from Cesena, the other from Turin.

Both have a score to settle with Military Justice, so they prefer to be here rather than rotting in a trench or in a cell. Both have passed various examinations in this training school, including "the Swing".

This was enough to welcome them into our team.

However, during the break after the morning drill, they had to challenge *Bracciodiferro*, who defeated them in seconds. Then they had to face dagger fencing with *Cuteddu*, who stabbed them both without problems with the wooden knife. Finally, they had to box barehanded with *Pugnodiferro*, who good-naturedly knocked them around a bit.

After these tests, *O'pazzo* felt obliged to ask on behalf of the team: «*Guagliù, ma vuje che sapit fà?*»[217]

«*Napoli*, give me a cent and I'll show you what I can do» the guy from Turin replied promptly. The Bersagliere attempted to deflect the challenge thrown at him saying: «*Guagliò tu si' pazz. Chist ten voglia 'e pazzià.*»[218]

Our good manners convinced him that he could no longer back out.

Reluctantly he pulled a cent out of his pocket, while the challenger rolled up the sleeves of his sweater. He took the coin in the palm of his right hand and, placing it on his left arm, began to rub it up and down pronouncing mysterious sentences.

Then he blew on his hand and the coin was gone.

We were all amazed.

«*Fall n'ata vot*»[219] asked *O'pazzo*, offering him another cent.

We watched his movements even more carefully.

The guy made exactly the same gestures, this time changing hands.

The result was the same. Puff, a breath and the cent was gone.

«*Chistu è nu mago...*» declared *O'pazzo* «*...e accussì ce futte tutto l'argià.*»[220]

---

[217] «Guys, but what do you know how to do?» translation from the Neapolitan dialect.

[218] «Boy, you're crazy. This guy wants to joke.»

[219] «Do it again.»

[220] «He is a magician... and he's taking all our money.»

«I'm not stealing anything from you, Napoli. Look where your cent is...» continued the guy, reaching behind the Bersagliere's ear and magically extracting the coin.
«*Te n'aggio rat duje. L'at addò sta?*»[221] asked *O'pazzo*, bewildered by the magic, but alert as always.
«Unfortunately, in this magic, one cent always gets lost. It is my pact with the devil» said the Turin guy with a snicker.
Needless to say, his nickname became *Mago*.
«*Óter che l'artiglierìa! Ol comando a l' gh'avrèss de mandàt té 'n di trincée di tugnì, issé intàt che ti spènet e ti fé passà bambòss coi tò magée, a m' rìa nóter a fenì 'l laurére col töi fò de mès öna ólta per töte!*»[222] suggested *il Vólp*, eliciting our laughter.
Almost everyone experienced his magic. He managed to score least twenty cents without any of us figuring out where the trick was.
«And what can you do?» I asked the other newcomer before the Turin magician made off with our entire day's wages.
In response, he grabbed a wooden stool that was in the tent and he too began to roll up his sweater sleeves.
«*N'ata magia?*»[223] immediately asked *O'pazzo*.
The guy from Cesena continued undaunted, laying his open hand on the stool and extracting, from I don't know where, a switchblade knife.
He triggered the blade and passed it quickly in front of our faces, looking us in the eye. Then he threw the knife up high, grabbed it in one hand like a dagger and with impressive speed began stabbing it between one finger and the other of the hand resting on the stool.
At the end of the performance we could not help applauding him.
«Don't try to do it yourself. Otherwise you're risking your fingers» he warned us.
«*Mandóm inante pò a' lü insèma al Mago a desavià i tugnì de la prima lìnia, cósa m' ne disì?*»[224] suggested *il Gat*.
«*Chest nun è na squadra, chist è nu circ!*»[225] *O'pazzo burst out.*

---

[221] «I gave you two coins. Where is the other one?» translation from the Neapolitan dialect.
[222] «Better than artillery! The command should send you to the Austrian trenches, so that while you're fleecing them and stupefying them with your magic, we can arrive to complete the job and get rid of them once and for all» translation from the Bergamo dialect.
[223] «Another magic trick?» translation from the Neapolitan dialect.
[224] «Let's send him together with the Magician to distract the Austrians in the front line. What do you say?» translation from Bergamo dialect.
[225] «This isn't a squad. It's a circus!» translation from the Neapolitan dialect.

«It might be a circus but... come on and I'll show you something else.»
Moving along in single file we followed him out of the tent.
He led us up to a tree. Picking a flower from the ground he stuck it in the bark about one and a half metres up.
Then he took a dozen steps away.
I have no idea from where he pulled out another knife.
He quickly took aim and threw it in the direction of the trunk, severing the flower from its stem.
«*Fall n'ata vota*» asked *O'pazzo*.[226]
«If you give me a cent, I'll do it again» was the playful reply.
«*Aggio già rato. Non s'o mica na banca.*»[227]
While *O'pazzo* continued to grumble, *Cuteddu* came over and gave him a cent. Instead of standing on the side and witnessing that test of skill again, he went over to the tree, put a small piece of wood on his head and hissed:
«*Jecca si cciai l'ardiri.*»[228]
«*Chist so' tutt pazz*»[229] exclaimed the Neapolitan, wide-eyed.
The other did not blink, he took aim and launched.
Cuteddu did not move an inch nor close his eyes for a moment. The knife fully centred the piece of wood, cutting it in two and sticking in the tree trunk. *Cuteddu* extracted the knife, examined it carefully and then returned it to its owner, congratulating him (which is very rare) and in turn receiving compliments from *Trepugnali*, as we decided to baptize him.
Back in the tent, *Trepugnali* told us about his troubles with Military Justice. A lieutenant in his company had targeted him and continued to torment him with duties and insults.
One day he decided to retaliate (with words, not with his knives).
The lieutenant went on a rampage and started lashing him with a whip. That was the last straw. *Trepugnali* sprang on the officer, threw him to the ground, took out one of his knives and made the gesture of cutting his throat.
«Now shut up or I'll cut your throat for real» he whispered in his ear.
They sentenced him twenty years in prison.
Twenty years to be served after the war, if he survives.

---

[226] «Do it again» translation from the Neapolitan dialect
[227] «I've already given. I'm not a bank.»
[228] «Throw if you dare» translation from the Sicilian dialect.
[229] «They are all crazy» translation from the Neapolitan dialect.

«Since I'll have to spend many years in jail, I want to enjoy life now. I am sorry for you guys and for Italy, but I hope this war lasts a long time» he concluded his story with a bitter smile.
«So what happened to you?» someone asked the magician.
With a hint of embarrassment in his eyes, the guy from Turin confessed to being punished for having eaten his spare ration without the officer's permission: some biscuits and a little tin of meat.
«*Nun putev fa' accumparì a scatulett appriss a recchia e chillu strunz?*» asked *O'pazzo*.
Without giving him time to reply, he put an end to the matter, saying:
«*Allor tu sì... nu miezz Mago!*»[230]
Mezzomago is the nickname we gave him before leaving the tent for the afternoon drill.

---

[230] «Couldn't you make the can reappear from behind that asshole's ear? Then you're a just a... half wizard!» translation from the Neapolitan dialect.

CHAPTER 13.II

Sdricca, Sunday, 14 October 1917
Last night we went down to Manzano to eat in a good trattoria.
We wanted to have a party for *O'pazzo*.
It was his twentieth birthday. I asked the cook to prepare a Friulan specialty, which he had never eaten: fresh sauerkraut and *frico*.[231]
I confess that I was hungry for it too, since I hadn't eaten it in a long time.
The innkeeper brought three, since there were twelve of us.
Everyone ate a quarter.
«So, do you like *frico*?» I asked *O'pazzo*.
«*Bùono, sì. Ma vulite metter a pizza c'à mozzarella e bufala e a pummarola n' copp?*»[232] he replied, rolling his eyes.
We all looked at him not understanding what he was talking about and then everyone asked a question:
«Pizza?»
«What is mozzarella?»
«Do you have buffaloes in Naples?»
«Cup of… what?»
«*Guagliù, ita venì a Napule si vulite mangia' verammente bùono*»[233] replied *O'pazzo*, who then explained what Neapolitan pizza is. He also told us that in 1889 a chef dedicated a pizza with the three colours of the Italian flag to Queen Margherita of Savoy: red tomato, white mozzarella and green basil.
Then he went on to extol many other culinary specialties.
I only remember the *babàs* and the *friarielli*.
All these delights made us hungry again, except for *il Gat*, who mumbled:
«*A mé me piàs la polènta taragna, chèla con dét ol formài di Brans e con sura ol bötér rüstìt co l'èrba sàlvia. Chèsta sé che l'è öna lecardìsia, mia i òste paströgnade…*»[234]

---

[231] A typical dish of the Friulan tradition made of potatoes and cheese.
[232] «Yes, it's tasty. But it can't compare to a pizza with buffalo mozzarella and tomato on top» translation from the Neapolitan dialect.
[233] «Guys, you have to come to Naples if you want to eat really well.»
[234] «I like "polenta taragna", the one with Branzi cheese inside and with brown butter and sage poured on top. That is a real delicacy, not like your weird foods...» translation from the Bergamo dialect.

«Did you eat all this stuff at home?» *Carestia* asked *O'pazzo*.
«*Magari, guagliù, magari. Ogni tanto, quanno si puteva. Quanno si teneva l'argià.*»[235]

I hope one day we can all go to Naples and eat pizza margherita.
Right now, we can only dream about those delicacies, because something is moving on the front.
Days ago, in a nocturnal action near Tolmin a platoon of the III Unit took many prisoners, including some officers.
On the night of the 8th, two teams from II Unit took more prisoners on Bainsizza.
From what the prisoners have said, it seems that the Austrians are preparing a great offensive on the Isonzo front with the support of German troops and artillery.
This is credible.
Now they can send our way the Divisions that until a few months ago were employed on the Russian front.
We have stepped up our daytime and nightime drills.
It seems that the "Butcher"[236] wants to head off their offensive with an attack on the plateau of Bainsizza and Ternova.[237]
Good. We can't wait to show the Germans what the Arditi from Sdricca are made of.

---

235 «I wish, guys, I wish. Every once in a while, when we could. When we had enough money» translation from the Neapolitan dialect.
236 This was the nickname the soldiers gave to General Luigi Capello, commander of the 2nd Army, for the ruthless and often irresponsible way in which he ordered his troops to attack even the most impregnable defenses.
237 The news gathered by the information office was confirmed by those prisoners. On October 21, 1917 General Capello learned from some Romanian deserters of an impending attack on a front reaching from Plezzo to the sea. General Cadorna, however, did not believe this information and prevented Capello from making a violent counterattack on Bainsizza in order to weaken the enemy offensive, denying him the resources he had requested. Capello in turn did not take the defensive measures that would have been necessary, should the feared enemy have attacked in force.

Chapter 14.II

I literally devoured the pages of my grandfather's diary.
I knew about the Arditi special training from books.
Reading about it, written in his own hand, however, had a great effect on me.

What struck me the most, however, was something else.
It was something that in an infinitely smaller way I experienced myself during the Guardia di Finanza officers' training: the power of the surrounding environment to change a person.
We may quite rightly speak of brainwashing.

In my grandfather's case, his training, cohabitation with other bold comrades and the example set by his commanders changed his attitude towards the war.
As an infantryman he was resigned and passive in the face of events.
At the Arditi School he became more aware and determined to fight to contribute to victory and end the conflict.
Subsequent events strengthened this will in him.

I am very sorry that there are no pictures of the grandfather with his comrades at Sdricca.
Some of them are certainly present in the photo taken in Tripoli on June 15, 1919. Every time I pick it up, I look at those faces in an attempt to recognize someone. I may have detected one.
I have two more photos of my grandfather when he was with the Arditi.
One was taken on his return from Libya. There is the date, August 24, 1919, but there are no names for the two fellow soldiers with him.
The other was taken in 1918 in Camposanpiero, north of Padua.
Again, he is with two fellow soldiers and there are no names on the back.
However, thanks to the following pages of the diary it was possible to identify them. I even managed to find and contact the descendants of one of them! They had saved a copy of that photo too.

3RD PART

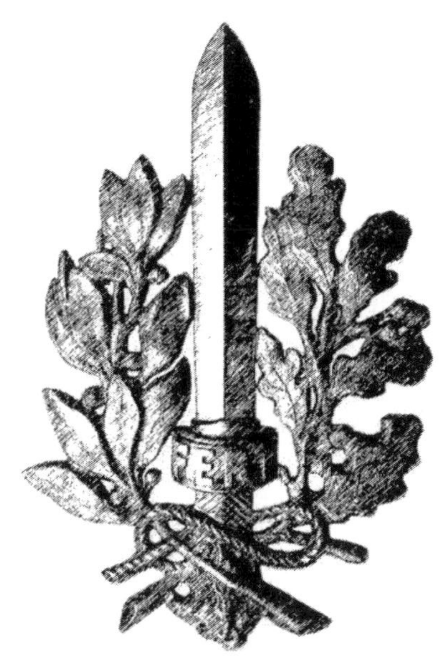

TRAGIC AUTUMN

CHAPTER 1.III

Sdricca, Tuesday, 23 October 1917

The other day the V Unit was mobilized for an action in the sector of Lake Misurina.

Objective: to recapture some positions conquered by the enemy.[238]

As always before an action the camp erupted in shouts of enthusiasm, rifle shots and petard bursts.

When our one hundred and eighty comrades sped away on the trucks, we bid them farewell with joy, but also with a little envy.[239]

«*Sergente*, when it will be our turn?» *Trepugnali* asked me with shining eyes.

«Our turn will come soon, perhaps already in the next action» I reassured him.

I'm sure of it, also because something is happening at the front.

We hear rumbling as if a storm were approaching and we see a reddish glow on the horizon as if there were a big fire, despite the pouring rain that has been falling since afternoon.

«*Sergente*, is it us or is it the *tognìt*?» my men asked several times, as if I had some confidential information.

«It must be the *tognìt*. I don't think the 2nd Army would be attacking without us.»

«*Incö ó ést i üficiài assé preocüpàcc e pò a' 'l colonèl*»[240] added *il Vólp* with a serious look.

«*Miezumago, fa' na magia, dimme caddà succedere*» intervened *O'pazzo*. «*Facimm accussì, guagliò, si adduvin torn... mago.*»[241]

---

[238] The enemy had attacked the Italian positions on Mount Piana and occupied some trench sections important for the defensive system. It was a diverting manoeuvre to draw away attention from the Isonzo front.

[239] At dawn on October 23, after fierce fighting begun the previous day, the V Assault Unit, led by Captain Anchise Pomponi, managed to liberate the trenches of Mount Piana occupied by the Austro-Germans. The losses were huge: 3 officers and 52 Arditi dead or wounded.

[240] «Today I noticed that the officers were quite worried and the colonel, too» translation from the Bergamo dialect.

Mezzomago continued scanning the horizon like all of us, and then said: «I'm a magician not a fortune teller. However, I have the feeling that a storm is about to break out and we will deal with it... hand grenades and slashing daggers!»
The whole squad began to sing and our singing spread from tent to tent throughout the camp.

It's night.
It's still raining.
I'm writing these notes while we are awaiting orders.
I have two very different sensations.
On one hand, I feel full of energy and want to put into practice what I've learned here at the school. With these troops we can defeat the enemy and win the war.
On the other hand, I am very uneasy.

---

[241] «*Mezzomago*, do some magic and tell me what will happen. Let's make a deal, boy. If your prediction is correct, we'll call you… Wizard once again» translation from the Neapolitan dialect.

CHAPTER 2.III

Sdricca, Wednesday, 24 October 1917

At two in the morning I woke up with a start.

I had fallen asleep with the distant roar of artillery.

Suddenly that rumble had increased in intensity, so as to wake up my other tent-mates, too.

We exchanged opinions, but we had no doubts.

It was a destructive shelling! That type of shelling is always a prelude to a major attack and for certain it was the Austrians who were attacking.

We left the tent. Outside there were already many other comrades scanning the horizon. But there was nothing to be seen because of the low clouds and the heavy rain.[242]

Why were we still lying in bed?

Why weren't we on the trucks ready to leave for the front?

How were the Austrians able to attack with all this rain? [243]

We spent more than an hour outside in the cold, trying to find an answer to these questions. Just like so many others, judging by the lit cigarettes that could be seen in every angle of the camp. The whole camp was in turmoil. From our command, however, no orders arrived and so little by little everyone went back to their tents.

I tried to go back to sleep, but I was unable to.

---

[242] At two o'clock the Austro-German artillery began bombing the Italian lines. In addition to grenades, a thousand gas tubes launched two thousand 15-litre cylinders of a new deadly mixture of toxic gases, created by German chemists, into the Plezzo basin. A dense, whitish cloud filled the valley floor, mixing with the fog. The wind pushed it towards the frontline trenches manned by two battalions of the "Friuli" Brigade. When the soldiers of the 22nd *Schützen* Division and the 3rd *Edelweiss* Division attacked those trenches, they found approximately eight hundred Italians killed by the gas, together with mice, horses, mules, cows and birds. The anti-gas alarm had not been sounded. In any case, these men would have died because the diphenylchloroarsine (marked with a blue cross) which created vomiting and a sense of suffocation would have forced them to remove their masks. At that point the phosgene (green cross) would have corroded their lungs. The same fate befell the gunners on the hills surrounding Tolmin. For a couple of hours everything was engulfed in the vapours of the toxic gas.

[243] Military doctrine required offensives to be launched in favourable weather conditions. As had happened until then on the Italian front.

Not so much for the sound of the bombing, multiplied by the echo of the mountains, but for the nerves that were grabbing my stomach.
Someone was already snoring.
At around four in the morning the bombing stopped.
I must have fallen asleep shortly after.
My sleep was again broken by the simultaneous thunder of thousands of pieces of artillery, at the very moment when our own gun fired the morning wake-up call.
It was six o'clock.
The deafening roar lasted at least three hours.
Then it died down a bit.[244]
Today our exercises have been suspended. The commanders have confirmed that an offensive is underway along the entire Isonzo front.
All units have been ordered to prepare for departure, tonight.
Everyone except us.
We will have to garrison the School.
Many Arditi of the VI Unit are grumbling and are disappointed that they cannot fight right now.
Cuteddu is like a rabid dog.
Fortunately, *Biunnu* is there to calm him down.
«*Sergente*, but why are we always the last?» *Trepugnali* asked me.
«Someone has to watch over the camp. As long as there isn't a VII Assault Unit, we will always remain the last unit. It's mathematics» I replied.

---

[244] At eight, artillery fire was extended to hit the rear lines and destroy communications. At the same time, under cover of the fog, the infantry began its attack on the Italian first and second lines.

Chapter 3.III

Sdricca, Thursday, 25 October 1917
We are the only ones left to guard the School.
Last night at 11 p.m. the other five units started marching off to Cividale, singing our hymns and waving our banners.
At their head was Colonel Bassi.
Toward the end of the night a very strong wind blew up and this morning the sun is finally shining.
The mountaintops are whitewashed with snow.
Today again exercises are suspended.
The war bulletin of October 24th contains little news and says nothing in particular.
It confirms the rumour circulating in camp: the Austrians began their offensive with the help of German troops.
Not even the newspapers say much about this attack.[245]
Even so it seems to us that something serious is happening.
We have seen numerous planes fly over the field going east.
The artillery continues to grumble in the distance.
The most important news reached us tonight.
The "Butcher" is no longer in command of the 2nd Army!
Health reasons.
Now the command is in the hands of General Montuori.[246]

---

[245] The High Command war bulletin of 24th read as follows:
Thanks to the heavy contribution of German troops and vehicles, the Austrians have concentrated numerous forces on our front for offensive purposes. Their impact finds us steadfast and well prepared. Last night, the intensified shooting on various stretches of the Giulia front and a brutal bombing with wide use of special gas shells between Mount Rombon and the northern region of the Bainsizza plateau marked the beginning of the expected attack, but towards dawn, due to bad weather, the enemy fire waned in intensity. With that the violent bursts of our batteries in response slowed down.

[246] At 18.00 on 25 October, General Capello sent a circular phonogram to the field commanders in which he communicated the transfer of command to his deputy, General Luca Montuori (18 February 1859 - 8 March 1952). For some time Capello had been suffering from nephritis and the doctors had advised that he be hospitalized immediately in Verona. Cadorna was happy to get rid of an officer who was overly ambitious, bad-tempered and not much in line with his dictates.

CHAPTER 4.III

Sdricca, Friday, 26 October 1917

Something very serious is afoot.

This morning Major Ambrogi ordered us to load all the weapons and ammunition boxes from the depot onto the trucks. We filled other trucks to capacity with food. We also dismantled all the tents, except ours, which were kept for last. Everything not on the trucks will have to be destroyed before we leave.

We also filled backpacks with food, ammunition and petards. We had hoped we would never again have to carry them on our shoulders.[247]

There is a great deal of sadness in hastily packing up our School and a great deal of anxiety over what the next few days will hold for us.

The men who accompanied the major down to Manzano say that people are leaving their homes and that the village is full of long lines of soldiers fleeing from the Isonzo front.

Many soldiers have no collar patches and are unarmed!

They're saying that the Germans have swept away and destroyed all our lines and that their commanders have either fled or been taken prisoner.

Some of them are yelling loudly that the war is over and that they are going to go home.

Then again, today's war bulletin says the attack has been repelled.[248]

---

[247] The Arditi considered it a great privilege not to have to carry a backpack.

[248] The war bulletin of General Cadorna, written on the evening of October 25 to appear in the newspapers of the 26th, concealed the harsh truth, since no barrage had taken place and the defenses at the Saga narrow passageway had already collapsed: *"Yesterday morning, after a few hours of rest, the enemy reopened violent artillery fire on the entire frontline, which took on the purpose of destruction between the southern slopes of Rombon and the northern region of Bainsizza, where, afterwards, great masses of infantry were launched in attack against our positions. The Saga passageway resisted the enemy impact, but further south, favoured by the dense fog that rendered the effects of our barrage null, the enemy managed to overcome our advanced lines on the left of the Isonzo and, leveraging on the offensive outlets of his bridgeheads of Santa Maria and Santa Lucia, he carried the fight to the slopes of the right bank of the river."*

The telegram that Cadorna sent shortly after to the government was rather more dramatic: *"The enemy offensive has resumed on the Saga-Stol-Luico front and on the Lom plateau. The enemy attack succeeded in Luico and Auzza. The losses in terms of missing soldiers*

It says that the enemy managed to pass over to the right bank of the Isonzo in some places, favoured by the fog.
This sounds strange to me since yesterday was a beautiful day.

---

and artillery pieces are very serious. Roughly ten regiments surrendered en masse without fighting. I foresee a disaster, against which I will fight to the last."
As we see, Cadorna began to insinuate the thesis according to which this defeat was caused by the lack of resistance of some of his troops. That morning he had written the following order-of-the-day for the army to be issued down to the company commands:
"The first impact, launched by the Austrian and German forces on a sector of our front, gave the enemy results beyond their own expectations. The sudden collapse of our line at a vital point, through the work of opposing troops although not superior in numbers, can only be explained as the consequence of a moral breakdown whose terrible effects weigh on those who have felt their responsibility as men and soldiers. But today the dismay of those men who were incapable of fighting must not spread like a depressing spirit in those who fight with valour. A false sense of enemy superiority must not generate a false sense of weakness and of our inability to resist. The hour is grave. The Homeland is in danger, but the real danger lies not in the strength of the enemy but in the soul of those who are ready to believe that his strength is invincible. I appeal to the conscience and honour of every man, so that, as in equally serious days of the past year, each one, reaffirming his own moral energies, may become worthy of the Homeland again. Let every fighter remember that there are only two ways open for him and for the country: either victory or death. No hesitation, no tolerance. Let the commanders be ironclad. Every weakness must be mercilessly suppressed. Let all shame be purified with iron and fire. I hold all commanders responsible for the unyielding exercise of wartime justice in order to keep the Army firm. Whoever does not feel that we either win or we die on the line established for resistance is not fit to live. However, I make this supreme appeal to the generous hearts of those soldiers of whom for the past two years I have known the valour, the serene and patient endurance of sacrifices, the heroism of which the nation is proud. Today they must prove themselves worthy of their brothers who, at the Passo Buole, on the Novegno, on the Asiago plateau, said to the enemy: "no one passes here". When their leaders tell them that they must resist, let them feel that they are defending all that is most sacred and dear to them. Let them hear in the voice of their commanders the voice itself of their living and of their dead, asking them to save Italy.
October 26, 1917 - The Army Chief of Staff - Cadorna."

CHAPTER 5.III

Sant'Osvaldo, Saturday, 27 October 1917

Today something happened that nobody could imagine.

We abandoned Sdricca after destroying everything that we couldn't load on trucks or take with us. We left without the usual songs. We had to go to Cussignacco. It was raining.

As soon as we got to the Manzano road we saw an endless column of trucks, carriages, tractors, guns, animals and soldiers marching towards the west. A very slow march, worse than a funeral procession.

The High Command has given orders to fall back to the Tagliamento.[249]

The enemy appears to have broken through our front in several places.

Our troops are in disarray and in retreat.

In just a few hours we lost everything that had been won in over two years of war and at the cost of many sacrifices and many deaths.

I saw large numbers of civilians, women, children and the elderly mixed in with the soldiers. On their carts, pulled by oxen, donkeys or horses, was everything they had managed to salvage from their homes.

It was a bleak sight, made even worse by the torrential rain.

Roads and fields are a sea of mud today.

I thought of my family with anguish.

Are they also on the run?

Are they also in a column of refugees on some clogged and muddy road?

Is my father with them or is he still in Switzerland?

What about my brother Noè?

What about our house?

In the midst of all this confusion I don't know who to ask for news.

Suddenly my mother's words on the eve of epiphany came back to me: «We will do well to get our bags packed.»

---

[249] Finally realizing that the breach opened by the XIV Army of the German General Otto von Below (18 January 1857 - 15 March 1944) was irreparable, between two and three in the morning of October 27, Cadorna ordered the retreat to the Tagliamento river. The assurance of being able to resist, given by the new commander of the 2nd Army, General Montuori, and his generals, served to avoid their dismissal, but delayed fallback by two days, thus resulting in serious logistical consequences and significant material and human losses.

A shiver passed through me. This was what she had seen in the smoke curls of our *pignarûl*. She had said so to that poor sergeant.
In Manzano almost all the inhabitants had already fled.
A farmer, whom I know by sight, was loading his cart. He said with tears in his eyes: «*A rivin i boborosso. I scugnin scjampâ.*»[250]
I could not blame him. I was ashamed of our army, running away from the enemy and no longer defending our land.
The doors of the houses stood open and inside were soldiers sheltering from the rain or looking for food. As we passed by a tavern, where we had spent many happy evenings, we heard shouting and singing. We went inside to see what was going on. There were drunken soldiers who were guzzling everything the innkeeper had not been able to take away.
Some were yelling: «The war is over! Let's go home! Long live peace! Long live Russia! Long live the Pope!»
Others were singing "The International".[251]
The smell of wine mixed with the stink of dirty, wet men was unbearable. Beastly screams came from the cellar. Soldiers in uniforms filthy with mud and drenched in wine were destroying the barrels and drinking directly from the gashes.
«What the hell are you doing?» asked *Carestia*.
«We don't want to leave anything for those German stinkers» replied the least drunk of the group. As he saw that we were armed, he started shouting at us: «Dirty blacklegs! Drop your weapons!»
He did not have time to say it again.
Pugnodiferro threw a punch in his face that made him topple to the ground amid splashes of wine.
The rest of them started shouting all sorts of curses and insults against us. The shouting did not last long, because in a few moments they were all lying on the floor, stunned by our fists and half drowned in a sludge of wine, vomit and blood.

---

[250]«The *Boborosso* are coming. We must get away» translation from the Friulan language. *Boborosso* and *Babau* are terms equivalent to Boogeyman, or evil beings to be afraid of. In those years, German troops were much feared for the atrocities they were said to have perpetrated in Belgium: cutting off hands, gouging out eyes and deaths inflicted amidst unspeakable torments. The German command gave orders not to treat the civilian population badly, expecting in return the *jus praedae*, i.e. the freedom to sack their houses. Nonetheless, there was no shortage of violence and abuse against civilians in the occupied territories.

[251] A socialist song since the late nineteenth century, when the Second International adopted it as its official anthem.

As we emerged from the cellar to deal with the other soldiers, our lieutenant appeared and ordered us to forget about that scum, get out of there immediately and join up with the rest of the company.
There was no time to waste.
As we were reaching the others, I saw soldiers, who had put on civilian clothes, but were still wearing military boots, come out of a house.
We didn't have time to stop and teach them the same lesson.
Getting to the bridge over the Torre river was a difficult undertaking.
The road was clogged with every kind of conveyance and a multitude of people. To make our way through the soldiers, we did not hesitate to use sticks or rifle butts. Some of us would have liked to use daggers and petards, especially against those who were insulting us or applauding the end of the war.
But if the war is really over, why were they running away in the rain?
Why were the civilians fleeing?
Is the war really over?
Who said so?
Cadorna?
These were the questions hammering in my head with each step. I also wondered if those soldiers had actually fought or if, instead, they had run away from the enemy, throwing away their rifles.
Several of the stragglers left the column to rummage through broken crates from vehicles lying on the sides of the road. They were looking for food and dry clothes.
One small group, which had found something in the wreckage, began to squabble rabidly. They looked like hyenas fighting over the corpse of an animal. That brawl drew the attention of other desperate people, who threw themselves into the struggle to divide up the spoils.
It was impossible to proceed quickly near the bridge on the Torre. The crush of people filled every space between trucks, wagons, artillery pieces and pack animals. And there was no one to regulate that hellish traffic.
Our commander directed us to the railway bridge, which was mobbed, especially by soldiers. So it was easier for us to make our way by force. To make everyone understand us we fired some shots in the air, drew our daggers and started shouting: «The Arditi are passing through! If you don't know us, watch us march by, we are the sixth of Colonel Bassi!»
We managed to get through, although not without a struggle, or without having to beat up some stragglers, who still did not know us well.
Someone even ended up in the water. But in the end, we passed through.

In Cussignacco, a runner informed us that we were to continue on to Santo Osvaldo, on the southern outskirts of Udine, where the other units were also converging.[252]
We arrived in the late afternoon, in the middle of a violent storm. Thunder and lightning mingled with the roar and flashes of artillery behind us.
We camped near the former insane asylum in houses damaged by the explosion of an ammunition dump last August.
As I write a great bonfire is warming us and trying to dry our sodden clothes. The men of my squad are dazed by everything that's going on.
It seems like a nightmare.
I am worried about my family.
Where are they now?
I clutch my mother's amulet closer than ever.
I hope she too has a good one to protect her and my brothers and sisters.

---

[252] In the meantime, General Cadorna left by car from Udine to Treviso, where he had decided to move the High Command (a transfer that had already begun the previous night with trucks coming and going between the two cities). He was closely followed by the officers of the 2nd Army who were supposed to guarantee resistance. In the morning the mayor of Udine had a poster put up in order to reassure the citizens. In the afternoon he discovered that the offices of the High Command were empty and the soldiers fled. Meanwhile chaos was spreading among the population, as the roar of artillery fire was getting closer to the city.

CHAPTER 6.III

Sant'Osvaldo, Sunday, 28 October 1917, 9:30 a.m.

I slept very badly.

I had very bad dreams. I don't remember them, but they left me with an unpleasant feeling. In any case, reality doesn't seem much better.

You can hear artillery fire approaching and shooting from Udine.

It is still raining, but at least our clothes have dried out a bit.

We are waiting for the arrival of the other units to leave again.

Soldiers and civilians continue passing on the main road.

I watch those wagons in the hope of seeing someone I know or, by heaven's leave, my family. I have asked a lot of people where they came from, but none came from the villages of Carnia and the Canal del Ferro.

The men from my squad try to cheer me up.

«I'll do anything to take back this land, *Sergente*» said *Carestia*, patting me on the back and then embracing me fraternally. The others have also sworn to fight to the death to drive the Austrians and Germans back beyond the Isonzo river.

Fall in! I have to go.

Martignacco, Sunday, 28 October 1917, 9:00 p.m.

Colonel Bassi gave a brief speech to all six units this morning.

We were lined up in a field in the rain.

All the I Assault Unit and some platoons of the II were commanded to go to San Gottardo, east of Udine, to block the German advance units, which are heading directly towards Udine on the road from Cividale. The rest of the II Unit and a company of the IV were ordered to go to Codroipo at the disposal of the general in charge of defending the bridges at La Delizia.[253]

---

[253] The High Command reserved the bridges at La Delizia, Madrisio and Latisana for the 3rd Army, which, in a frantic race against time was trying to escape being surrounded by the Austro-German troops. Cornino, Pinzano and Dignano-Bonzicco, the northern bridges, were reserved for the retreat of the 2nd Army. Not everything went according to orders. When the fury of the Tagliamento in flood destroyed the bridge of Dignano, many troops headed south towards the bridges of La Delizia. At 5 o'clock on 29 October, Emanuele Filiberto di Savoia, commander of the 3rd Army, specified: *"I confirm the peremptory order that all civil and military elements of the 2nd Army be inexorably transferred to their northernmost passages."*

The V Unit was tasked with establishing a liaison with the troops of the XXVII Army Corps. All the others were to go to Martignacco, along the Udine ring road.
We left at 10.30.
At the head of our column was General Badoglio, on horseback, with other officers of the XXVII Army Corps.[254]
Colonel Bassi was with us of the VI. We acted as the extreme rear guard.
During the march, especially in the afternoon, we were kept busy by continuous German patrol raids. They have light machine guns and can move quickly.
If they have already arrived here, it means that, unfortunately, they have succeeded in entering Udine.[255]
Towards evening we arrived in Martignacco always in the rain.
Our command and that of the XXVII Army Corps have been set up at the "Savoia" tavern, open and deserted.
We have taken possession of some houses abandoned by their owners.
Inside we found everything they hadn't been able to put on their wagons.
We were able to supplement our rations with salami, cheese, fruit and abundant wine. This made everyone a little happier, but I my heart aches to see the columns of smoke rising from Udine.
The idea that a large part of Friuli is occupied by the enemy makes such a lump in my throat that I can't drink or eat.
The idea that Hungarians or Slavs are devastating my home right now makes my blood boil.
What will become of my books?
They've probably already used them to light a fire.
If only I knew how my family is doing.

---

[254] Pietro Badoglio (28 September 1871 - 1 November 1956) commanded the XXVII Army Corps at the time of the events narrated here. Although he was one of the parties mainly responsible for the Caporetto defeat, good fortune guaranteed him a dazzling military and political career even in the years following the conflict and until the end of the Second World War.
[255] On 28 October the Germans began to infiltrate Udine, defended by only a few thousand men, including the Arditi leaded by the Captain Maggiorino Radicati da Primeglio.

CHAPTER 7.III

San Daniele, Monday, 29 October 1917

This has been another very hard day.

Before leaving Martignacco this morning, General Badoglio ordered us to act as rear guard to the troops of the 2nd Army, who have to cross the Tagliamento on the Pinzano bridge.[256]

On the road to Fagagna there was the usual slow procession of vehicles and wagons. At least it wasn't raining today. The road, however, was very muddy and this helped to slow down the march. To go faster, we took the roads in the fields, impracticable for vehicles. Mud almost up to our knees.

The men of the V Unit joined us. They had returned in the night without making contact with the XXVII Army Corps.

In Fagagna I saw a very painful scene. A woman was looking for one of her children, who had gotten lost in the midst of all the commotion. She was desperate and in tears. I felt sorry for her.

I don't know where my family is either in this commotion.[257]

Again, today I asked the civilians on the wagons which villages they came from, in the hope of getting some news about the Dogna refugees. Nothing. They all came from the Friuli lowlands.

Then an old man driving a cart, pulled by a mule, opened my eyes and took away any hope of finding someone from up there among these fugitives: *«Cjale, frut, i cjargnei e chei dal Cjanal dal Fier e àn miôr a fâ il puint di Braulins dongje a Glemone.»*[258]

I hope they cross that bridge before the engineers blow it up. We left the V Unit to defend Fagagna. We heard they had a tough fight with the Germans, but they didn't let them through.

We and the others continued on to San Daniele.

Here too many inhabitants are fleeing and slowing down the military columns. But how can you blame them? Firstly, they saw the officers run away, then the *imboscati* together with the local officials and now they see our troops retreating, along with the people from the villages further east.

---

[256] It was the bridge along the Fagagna-San Daniele route.

[257] The loss of children or the separation of family members was a further drama for many refugees.

[258] «Look, boy, for the people of Carnia and Canal del Ferro it's better to use the Braulins bridge near Gemona» translation from the Friulan language.

What are they supposed to do? Stay here and wait for the arrival of the Germans, who are far more cruel and brutal than the Austro-Hungarians?
Together with the 2nd Cavalry Division of General Filippini, we tried to regulate at least a little bit the infernal traffic moving towards the Pinzano bridge. We managed to let a column of three hundred trucks loaded with food and ammunition pass. Just in time because the Germans next launched a series of increasingly violent attacks against our bridgeheads.
Il Gat took a "sugared almond", which fortunately came out the other side without damage, in his leg. He cursed in Turkish, I mean his dialect.
Mezzomago lost a finger and I don't know if he will still be able to do his magic with his right hand. He is very angry, but for a few centimetres, instead of his finger, he could have lost his *ghirba*.
Thank goodness, the III, IV, V Units plus two companies from the II have come to our aid and so we have loosened the grip of the Germans.[259]
Transit on the bridge is continuing even now that it is dark.
We have been relieved and now we are in a group of abandoned farmhouses in the countryside. Unfortunately, they are empty and we have nothing to eat.
Carestia asked me how I could write in these conditions.
I replied that writing helps me not to think.
He already knows that if I die, he will have to take my notebook and send it to someone in my family. If he should die too, *Bracciodiferro* will take over the job.
«*Sergè, e si murimm accis ogn'un?*»[260] *O'pazzo* asked me a few weeks ago.
«On the first page I put a piece of paper in Italian and German asking whoever finds this notebook to deliver it to my family. If it gets lost, it means fate wanted it that way.»
I remember that *O'pazzo* started singing a Neapolitan song about fate, *a fatalità* as he calls it. We were at Sdricca.
It seems a long time ago and yet only a few days have passed.

---

[259] They were the 200th Division of General von Hofacker's Army Corps. The original plan was for Austro-German troops to advance to the mouth of the mountains. However, since the momentum of the offensive was going very well, the generals decided to move beyond the Tagliamento to continue the pursuit. Therefore, on October 27, they gave the order to occupy the bridges over the Tagliamento as soon as possible. Due to the flood it had become a major obstacle to the transit of the imperial troops.
[260] «*Sergente*, what if we are all killed?» a translation from the Neapolitan dialect.

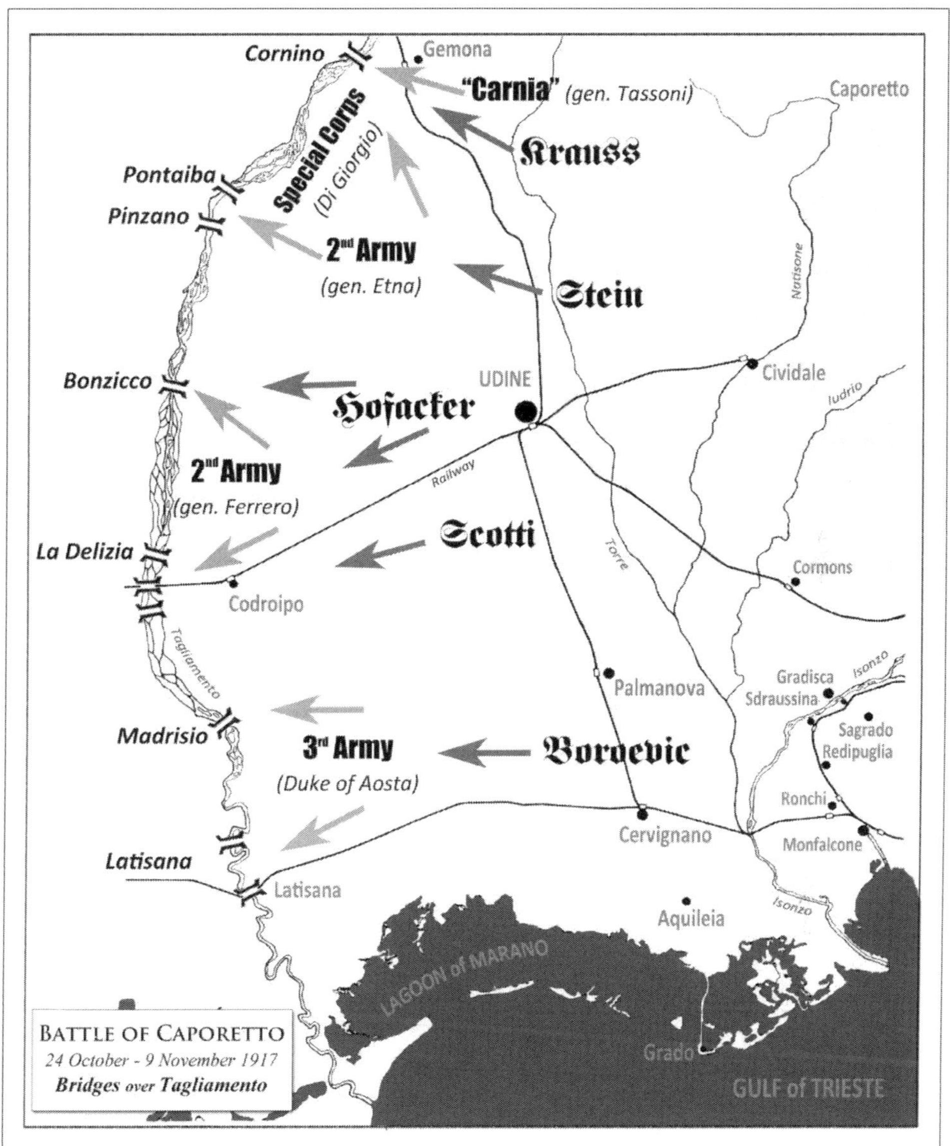

BATTLE OF CAPORETTO
24 October - 9 November 1917
Bridges** over **Tagliamento

CHAPTER 8.III

Pinzano, Tuesday, 30 October 1917

Tonight, I write these notes with great difficulty.

I'd rather fall asleep and for a few hours forget about the situation I'm in.

Last night it started raining again and the storm raged on all morning.

Together with other troops, under the downpour, we defended the bridgehead of Pinzano from the constant German attacks.

During these firefights *Pugnodiferro* and *Trepugnali* were slightly wounded. Unfortunately, *il Vólp* was killed outright, hit in the head.

Our helmets are of little use against bullets.

We buried him together with other comrades, each with his cross.

We are all very sad, but also determined to avenge him, especially *il Gat.*

We are also saddened by what we read on the leaflets that a plane with the black cross dropped on our heads this afternoon. They say that General Cadorna has accused the soldiers of this debacle. They say that he did it to excuse himself from blame.

It's been several days since we had the chance to read the war report and therefore we are unaware of what the High Command has actually written.[261]

---

[261] The theory of betrayal developed by Cadorna to hide the mistakes and shortcomings of the High Command, or rather of his own, was made public in the war bulletin of October 28, which appeared in all newspapers on the morning of the following day: *"The lack of resistance from units of the 2nd Army cowardly retreating without fighting, or ignominiously surrendering to the enemy, allowed the Austro-German forces to break our left wing on the Giulia front. The valiant efforts of the other troops failed to prevent the enemy from penetrating the sacred soil of the Homeland. Our line withdrew according to the established plan. The warehouses and stores of the vacated villages have been destroyed. The valour shown by our soldiers in many memorable battles fought and won during two and a half years of war allows the High Command to have faith that this time too the army, entrusted with the honour and salvation of the country, will know how to accomplish its duty. General Cadorna."*

More to cover up the scandal than for the love of truth, still unknown, the President of the Government, Vittorio Emanuele Orlando, ordered that all newspapers be confiscated and a new edition printed in which the war bulletin was modified as follows: *"The violence of the attack and the inadequate resistance of certain units of the 2nd Army allowed the Austro-German forces to break our left wing, etc."*

Rumour has it that Cadorna and other generals in the 2nd Army have been removed and will be tried. According to others, Cadorna has shot himself in the head. Nevertheless, if that were true, the Germans would have written it in their leaflet.[262]
Furthermore, yesterday morning General Badoglio was in Martignacco with us. Hardly removed and on trial!
However, we still do not know for sure what happened on the Isonzo front on 24 and 25 October.
We only know that we Arditi are still here, fighting and dying in the mud.
We have to tighten our belts. With this confusion, no food can get in and so we have to find it ourselves.
This afternoon *Pugnodiferro* made himself useful with what he knew how to do before he signed up, that is, butchering.

The original bulletin, however, had already been circulated abroad from the High Command's new headquarters, which had hastily been transferred from Udine to Treviso.
On the evening of 29th, other, harsher, versions of the bulletin began to circulate, both in the daily provincial press and on mimeographed sheets, in which the names of the "traitor" units were specified, varying according to the city and the edition. For example:
"Due to the strong pressure of the enemy but even more due to the ignoble betrayal of some units of the 2nd Army and more precisely of the Brigades Rome, Pesaro, Foggia and Elba, the foe was able to invade the sacred soil of the Homeland. May God and the Homeland curse them and mud and shame cover them forever."
The explanation of the betrayal was believed around the country and allowed the population to better face the dramatic situation. Knowing the real causes would have caused a dangerous distrust of political and military power, leading to even more serious consequences.
262 The Austro-Germans were not at all satisfied with the official Italian explanations. In their own bulletins they underlined the difficulties of their advance due to the obstacles put up by nature and the tenacious resistance of the Italian soldiers. On 30 October, on the heads of the retreating columns along the muddy roads of Friuli, their planes dropped thousands of leaflets exposing Cadorna's allegation: *"Italians, Italians! General Cadorna's press release of October 28 will have opened your eyes to the huge catastrophe that has befallen your army. In this very serious moment for your nation, your "generalissimo" resorts to a strange expedient to excuse the debacle. He has the audacity to accuse your army which so often his orders have launched in useless and desperate attacks! This is the reward for your valour! You have shed your blood in so many fights, we your enemy do not deny you the esteem due to valiant foes. Yet your "generalissimo" dishonours you, he insults you so as to exculpate himself."*
In an interview at the end of November, General Boroević called "unfair and incorrect" the accusations of cowardice by Italian troops. In his opinion, the cause of the debacle was the fact that the soldiers *"had felt the command slipping away"*.

«Hey Arditi, are you hungry?» he asked us, already knowing the answer. «*Sergente*, *Bracciodiferro*, *Carestia* come with me. Let's go get some food. In the meantime, you guys look for something to make a nice fire.»
We followed him, without understanding what he intended to do.
We walked around the fields for a while, getting wet up to our calves, until he stopped. «Here they are!» he exclaimed pointing to a grove.
There were a few cattle that had escaped from their stable.
«I saw them running around the countryside an hour ago.»
When we got close enough, *Pugnodiferro* aimed his rifle at a calf and shot it in the forehead. The animal toppled like a stone. The other ones ran off at a gallop.
«Here's our dinner» he said, looking at us smiling.
Then with his dagger he began to quarter it, skin it and masterfully carve some pieces of meat, which we wrapped up in a piece of tent cloth.
We knew he had finished when he cleaned off his dagger in the wet grass.
«I took the best parts. It will be enough for two days. Let's go.»
When we got back the fire was already lit.
We had found shelter in a small abandoned farmhouse.
«What is there to eat?» everyone asked.
«Fillet and sirloin!» *Pugnodiferro* exclaimed. «Still, we need a grill to cook the meat on.»
There were no grills around.
So we dismantled an iron gate. *Pugnodiferro* let that *"grill"* heat up and then put on the meat for everyone.
«Turn your piece over in two or three minutes, but don't puncture it! Someone go and see if there is any rosemary around here.»
We had a great meal of tender rare meat.
Too bad we had no wine.
Too bad that *il Vólp* was no longer with us.

Chapter 9.III

Sacile, Thursday, 1st November 1917

Yesterday I was unable to write.

I resume doing it now.

On the night of the 30th we were ordered to leave the bridgehead of Pinzano and to follow the columns directed toward Spilimbergo.

Beyond the bridge, only the "Bologna" Brigade remained in defense in the trenches of Mount Ragogna in front of San Daniele. Ill-fated men!

We learned that today the Engineers blew up the Pinzano bridge without giving those soldiers time to cross the Tagliamento.[263]

So they too have gone to swell the ranks of the prisoners.[264]

At Spilimbergo new orders arrived: all the assault units were to converge as soon as possible on Sacile.

The other troops had been given the same orders: the road was invaded by a multitude of soldiers marching towards Sacile.

Like a horde of grasshoppers, they were hunting down everything that could be eaten.

We were, too.

However, while it is one thing to look for food in an abandoned house, it is quite another to bluster into inhabited houses to steal food, wine and tobacco. More than once we had to step in and beat up the good-for-nothings who were preying on the poor people.

Moreover, on the outskirts of Pordenone we settled a scuffle between some Arditi and a group of infantrymen. They had called our comrades cowards because they were headed to Sacile rather than the Tagliamento.

It is a real miracle that no one was killed.

---

[263] The "Bologna" Brigade, used as reserves by the High Command, was sacrificed to delay the enemy advance. No longer able to cross the river, those 3,000 men were finally forced to surrender. Quite unusually, the Austro-Germans gave them military honours in a parade, attended by generals von Stein, Krafft von Dellmensingen and von Below. The latter in his war diary wrote that they personally consoled the Italian commander, Colonel Brigadier Carlo Rocca, and praised his troops for their valiant resistance.

[264] In the days of the Caporetto defeat, roughly 300,000 Italian soldiers were taken prisoner. Such a mass of men created considerable problems for the invaders and consequently for the prisoners themselves.

On the other hand, *Bracciodiferro* and *Pugnodiferro* floored several of them. In that fray, however, I got a punch in the face.
I'm still swollen and my jaw aches.
The knuckles of my fingers are all skinned from the punches I gave to calm down those troublemakers.
Yesterday I couldn't even hold the pencil in my hand.
We arrived in Sacile this morning.
Finally, you can begin to see some signs of order.
At the crossroads there are signs to show the soldiers what direction to take to find their own units.
We are headquartered in a large barracks.
During the day comrades continued to arrive in scattered groups. I saw someone from the I Assault Unit, which had been sent to defend Udine.
I would love to know what happened there that day.
Colonel Bassi is said to have gone to High Command to ask General Montuori for headquarters for us.
The most important news of the day, however, is another, if it's true.
There is a rumour going around that our troops have crossed the Tagliamento, taught a lesson to the Germans and recaptured Udine. The enemy armies are supposedly fleeing to Cividale. Our fleet appears to have unloaded large contingents of men in Trieste. The city is supposed to have already fallen into our hands.
If it were only true!
This news goes from mouth to mouth, from dormitory to dormitory, from barracks to barracks. A new enthusiasm has spread not only among us Arditi, but also among the other soldiers.
Those cries calling for peace, revolution, Russia and even the Pope are no longer heard.
On the contrary, there is a will to avenge dead friends and erase the shame of this disgraceful retreat.

Chapter 10.III

Conegliano, Friday, 2 November 1917
Finally, a quiet day.
Unfortunately, the news spread yesterday afternoon by *Radiofante* was not true[265]. There has been no counterattack from our army. We have not taken back Udine, let alone Trieste.
On the contrary, the enemy continues to advance.
The morale of the troops, however, is quite high.
We left Sacile around noon and arrived in Conegliano at sunset.
They made us camp near the institute of oenology.
After so much suffering, we finally had a hot meal.
It is very cold, but the sky is starry and offers a good show, after so much horror.
I want to immediately transcribe what a sergeant from the 3rd company, commanded by Captain Pedercini, told us. He is one of the survivors of the I Assault Unit who fought in Udine. I crossed paths with him at dinner and asked him to come and tell us how things went.
Sitting around the fire, we were all ears.
The sergeant cleared his throat with a sip of cognac and then started his account. I'm transcribing it into Italian (he speaks mostly in Sicilian but tries to make himself understood).
I'll omit the word *"minchia"*, which he uses like punctuation.
«After the Colonel's speech, we started rushing toward Udine, even though many men had blisters on their feet[266]. We had few weapons, few cartridges and no machine guns. All that stuff was on the trucks we had loaded when we left Korada. We picked up some ammunition in a house in Cussignacco thanks to the chaplain of the "Taro" Brigade.»
«You met Don Carletti? What was he doing in Cussignacco?» I asked him.
I knew Don Carletti well when I was serving in the "Taro" Brigade.[267]

---

[265] *Radiofante, Radio Borraccia, Radio Gavetta, Radio Scarpa, Bollettino del Fante* were various ways of indicating unofficial news circulating among troops.
[266] In two days of walking, with no rations, they covered about 100 kilometres.
[267] Days before, the "Taro" Brigade had had to abandon its position at Costa Duole and progressively retreat so as not to be outflanked. After several defensive clashes between the Judrio and the Natisone, on 27 October it engaged in a harsh fight in Castel Madonna

«Someone called him Annibale. I don't know what he was doing there.»
«Don Annibale Carletti! It's really him! He is the chaplain of the 207th. He was awarded a gold medal on the Buole pass in May of Nineteen-sixteen. I was in that battle too. Go on.»
«Single-file, we walked towards Udine. It was raining. The ground was all mud. Along the way we collected some rifles and ammunition abandoned by all those escaping *"cagasotto"*[268]. We caught some of them running away from Udine, half drunk. We beat them up and sent them to Cussignacco with a small escort.
Civilians were leaving the city too, shouting "The Germans are coming! The Germans are coming!" at us.
We shouted back "The Arditi are coming! The Arditi are coming!".
Then Captain Radicati ordered us to split up into two columns.
I was in the column along the railway that goes to Pontebba.
We couldn't see the ones along the ring road because of the rain and fog.
I left the column and with a patrol unit went into the city to see what was happening. The streets were deserted. Houses and shops were closed.
Every now and then a truck drove by at full speed. One almost ran me down. There was a strange calm. Occasionally some shots could be heard.
In front of a hotel, in the middle of the road, we found a Bersagliere, lying dead in a pool of blood. A little farther on, near a school, was the body of a civilian. There were no "nails" to be seen.[269]
However, we could hear heavier rifle fire.
We went to Porta Pracchiuso, where our truck was to arrive with weapons, ammunition and machine guns.[270]

---

del Monte, where the commander of the 208th Regiment, colonel Amedeo Casini, fell on the field. It then turned back towards Udine, passing the San Gottardo bridge and took up positions on the left side of the Torre river in defense of the Remanzacco rolling road. On November 21 the Brigade was disbanded and on December 15 only the 207th Regiment was re-established. Along the Torre line, the remains of other Brigades were deployed to defend Udine and the withdrawal of the troops. To the left of the Udine-Cividale railway the VII Army Corps of General Bongiovanni: "Cavalleggeri di Saluzzo" and the Infantry Brigades "Messina", "Salerno", "Firenze", "Ferrara", the 14th and 20th Bersaglieri. To the right of the railway the XXVII Army Corps of General Badoglio: "Belluno", "Taranto", "Girgenti" and "Treviso".

[268] It is equivalent to "chickenshit".

[269] This is how the Germans were called for their strange helmet, the *Pickelhaube*, characterized by a long conical tip, i.e. the "nail". Introduced by the Prussians in 1842, it was progressively perfected (made lighter and with the possibility remove the nail before battle). It was used until 1915, when it was replaced by the *Stahlhelm*, less decorative but much more protective.

Instead, we found Bersaglieri cyclists from the 3rd Battalion.
We waited a while, but no trucks arrived. Captain Radicati was furious and pissed off. He ordered a couple of men to wait for the truck. Together with the Bersaglieri we headed out of town towards the Torre river. We didn't meet anyone until the railroad crossing, where we found a general with some officers and gunners who were setting up two field guns. The captain and other officers went to talk to them and to agree on what to do.
Suddenly we heard rifle shots and machine gun bursts in front of us. A patrol had found the *nails*. We got into combat order. We advanced to cover the turn of the road to Cividale in the direction of the bridge. The *nails* would surely be passing by there.
We of the 3rd company were on the right wing, the 1st covered the left side, the 2nd was in the centre. The 4th and the platoons of the II had our backs. We were walking in the countryside in the open. Sometimes in mud up to our calves. We went slowly because we could hardly see anything.
At some point someone saw something ahead in the fog. We threw ourselves on the ground, or rather in the water, but we were already soaked.
A German patrol!
We fired, we shot down some of them, the others ran away. We chased after them, but then they started shooting with their machine guns.
So we threw a few petards and they ran back. This happened again and again, until we got to a group of houses and a small church.»[271]
«Did you go to mass?» laughed a guy who had joined us to listen to the story. But there was nothing to joke about. In fact, I heard a thud, the sound of a mess tin falling, and I never saw him again. Later, I learned that *Pugnodiferro* had dealt with him.
«As we got closer, one machine gun started firing and then another, striking some of us. We threw ourselves down looking for some shelter. A tree, a wall, a mound of earth.
We sweated blood to flush out the Germans barricaded in the houses. Sometimes they strafed in front of us, sometimes on the side, sometimes behind us. Little by little, with patience, many of them had the displeasure of feeling the blades of our daggers. However, unfortunately, while we were decreasing in number and ammunition, they were increasing in number and in fire power.

---

[270] This was Porta Cividale, in the north-east area of Udine.
[271] This was certainly San Gottardo, a small suburb of Udine, near the bridge over the Torre river.

They came from every direction, like wasps, but instead of stingers they had light machine guns, like we had never seen before.[272]
They can be moved effortlessly by one man alone.
Each patrol had one or two.
Since the reinforcements we had been promised didn't arrive, we began to back away so as not to be surrounded. Still fighting, under a curtain of water and bullets, we retreated to the houses just in front of the railway line. Those bastards were firing explosive bullets.
The other companies had serious losses, too, with dead and wounded.
A bullet killed the colonel's adjutant, Lieutenant Bani, just as he was bringing him information from the city. Captain Boni, commander of the 4th company, died. Lieutenant Tuzi, commander of the 4th company of the II died. Lieutenants Muzio and Basilico were seriously wounded. I saw Lieutenant Aimè, commander of the flamethrower section, dead with a dagger still in his hand near two *nails* in a pool of blood.»
In mentioning our victims, the voice of this veteran of many battles cracked slightly with emotion. It took another long sip of cognac to get him back on track. We were all silent.
«Before he died, Captain Boni had a great satisfaction. With his men and the Bersaglieri he killed an important German general who was entering Udine by car. He thought that all Italians had bolted like hares ahead of his troops. He didn't know he was facing the Black Flames.»[273]
From all of us a chorus of "hurrà!" rose spontaneously in memory of Captain Boni and all those fallen in action.

---

[272] The *Leichte Maschinengewehre* was developed from the Maxim heavy machine gun. It weighed just under 20 kg. It used 100-shot belts and could shoot up to 500 rounds per minute with an effective range of up to 2 kilometres. Each company had six weapons.

[273] Many sources attribute to the Bersaglieri of the III cyclists, and in particular to Sergeant Giuseppe Morini, the deaths of the commander of the LI Army Corps, Lieutenant General Albert von Berrer (8 September 1857 - 28 October 1917), and an officer of his staff. Other sources mention the Arditi. It definitely was not the Carabinieri, as Achille Beltrame erroneously illustrated in the weekly magazine *"La Domenica del Corriere"*. The general was habitually at the head of his troops. Confident that the city had already been occupied by his Prussian Jägers that morning, he ventured too far with his car, ending up in the midst of the defenders near the San Gottardo bridge over the Torre river. His death was a serious loss to the German army. In Riga he distinguished himself with one of the most brilliant actions of 1917: a rapid, deep and enveloping manoeuvre of Russian positions. His place was taken by General Eberhard von Hofacker (25 June 1861 - 19 January 1928), whose son, Caesar (11 March 1896 - 20 December 1944), also a career soldier, participated in the attempt on Hitler's life on 20 July 1944.

«We resisted as long as possible, firing from the windows and from behind the garden walls, but cartridges and petards were getting scarce. It would have been hard to come out on top with only our daggers against their machine guns. Then we got the order to fall back to the ring road and to position ourselves along the moat.
Before the Germans arrived, Captain Pedercini ordered me to go into town with the lightly wounded to look for ammunition and reinforcements. I was also supposed to try and figure out where Lieutenant Benci's 1st company had gone. Its whereabouts were unknown.
We went back to Porta Pracchiuso, but the truck wasn't there yet. In my opinion, it had never left Zugliano. So, while the others scattered around the city looking for abandoned weapons and ammunition, I went with three men in search of the 1st company.
On the way we found the corpses of other civilians. From their hair and faces we could tell they were Germans. For sure they had mixed in with all the fleeing civilians. Some of our patrols had found them armed on the street that morning and had killed them. We also came across two Arditi on horseback. They had just shot two German cavalrymen, who had arrived in Piazza delle Erbe from who knows where. They told us that their comrades from the 1st company were at Porta Gemona north of the city. As we were setting off in that direction, we heard a motorcycle coming, accompanied by machine gun shots. We hid in a doorway. He was a German spearhead motorcyclist. He came ahead slowly, occasionally firing a volley. We waited for him to pass and then we fell on him with our daggers.»
The sergeant took the German's insignia, which he had kept as a trophy, out of his pocket.
«In addition to these, I also took his machine gun. Nice weapon.
We continued on to Porta Gemona, guided by the sound of shots. Finally, we found the company. They had constructed several lines of barricades across the street, using wagons and furniture from abandoned houses. We joined forces in defense. We fired the machine gun belts against their assault units, which were attempting to enter from Porta Gemona. When the ammo was finished, we attacked them with petards and daggers. It was a tough fight, but we cleared them out. After the attack, we returned to the city dragging our wounded. We had to leave the dead in the rain together with the enemy corpses.»
«Did you get that there?» I asked pointing to a deep and still-moist cut on his face.

«This is nothing. Look here...» he replied, lifting up his sweater with a slight grimace of pain. He had a blackish hole in his hip and a large hematoma on his chest.
«The collection continues under my breeches, but as we are among decent people I'd better not drop them here.»
We laughed, but we immediately got serious again as he went on with his dramatic story.
«If we had had their machine guns and a few battalions of support, no German would have entered Udine! Instead, we had few weapons and our flanks were exposed.
A runner, sent by Captain Radicati, asked for reinforcements to be sent to the ring road. Lieutenant Benci replied that he could not, since he needed every man to defend Porta Gemona. Disconsolate, the runner went back.
With my three men I stayed there to help.
Every once in a while, an enemy patrol tried to advance and sneak in around the houses, but we always beat them back. However, cartridges were getting short. Together with other injured men, I was sent to look for ammunition and reinforcements.
We found some cartridges, but no reinforcement at all.
While we were searching, we detoured to the main square because we heard fighting going on there. From afar we saw a platoon and a half of our men together with Lieutenant Crisanti. Some of them were attempting to break through the big iron gate leading up to the Castle. Before we could join that fight, we were surrounded by a platoon of *nails* with their rifles pointed at us. We were few and injured. If we hadn't raised our hands immediately they would have killed us on the spot.»
As he said those words the sergeant lowered his eyes as if he were ashamed of being still alive. He fortified himself with another sip of cognac and went on.
«We were already lined up and they were taking us somewhere when a group of Black Flames and Bersaglieri attacked and wiped out the escort, freeing us. Lieutenant Giudici of the IV Unit was there too. He had joined us that morning with fifty men of his company.
We took their rifles so we could keep on fighting on the streets, in the squares and in the houses. There was no longer a command. Someone said that Captain Radicati had fallen prisoner, mortally wounded. There wasn't much else to do now, except try to sell our *ghirba* as dearly as possible. We broke down the door of a grocery store to find something to eat. For some of us, that was the last meal.

A group of Germans passed by while we were eating. We dropped the food and jumped on them with our daggers. They were assault troops, too, and gave us a hard time. Two of our own were killed, but none of those *Stürmtruppen* survived.
We went back inside to finish eating, waiting for some other German to pass by. Then we went out looking for something to drink. We found a tavern with a broken door. Some Germans were inside, getting drunk. They were convinced that they had already conquered the city. We darted inside like lightning. None of them is ever going to tell about how he conquered Udine. We stocked up on drinks. This is the cognac I took in that tavern. Actually, it was...» and with one last long sip, the sergeant fully emptied his flask.
«Since it was getting dark and it was still raining, we split up into groups and took refuge in some abandoned houses. I don't remember the name of the street. For the Germans, it became the "street of death."
Everytime someone passed by, we burst out suddenly and without making a sound we sent him to hell with our daggers. Then we hid the bodies inside the houses. As more hours went by, the more inebriated they were and with their backpacks full of stuff stolen from the houses. Some of them managed to get away, but only because we were too exhausted and another tiring day was ahead of us.»[274]
I offered him some cognac to make him go on with his story.
«The very next morning we set off on the road leading to Codroipo. There was no one around, only corpses on the ground. We added more when we intercepted a German patrol which was coming in the opposite direction.

---

[274] In defense of Udine the Arditi lost 6 officers and over 400 soldiers, dead or wounded, out of a total of just over 1,000 men. Many others were forced to surrender due to lack of ammunition. The trucks carrying weapons never arrived and neither did the reinforcements promised by General Badoglio. Here is the list of the officers taken prisoners:
I Assault Unit - Captain Radicati, commander of the Unit, Lieutenant Giorgio Crisanti and second Lieutenant Giulio De Marchi (2nd company), second Lieutenant Ippolito Valentini (3rd company), Lieutenants Ugo Campanelli and Rodolfo Lionti and Cadet Giuseppe Bianchi (4th company);
II Assault Unit - Lieutenant Francesco Ferrero and second Lieutenant Giuseppe Diana (1st company), Lieutenant Giulio Celestini (2nd company), Lieutenant Renato Lalli and second Lieutenant Attilio Alemi (4th company).
These officers were transferred to Germany in cattle cars and interned for some months under appalling conditions in the Russian prisoner camp at Rasstatt. Subsequently they were sent to the Ellvangen camp in Württemberg, where some of them tried to escape numerous times, but without success.

We had turned into a large and very dangerous group, because we had nothing more to lose.
Another German patrol started following us. Sometimes we made the gesture of attacking them. They would run away and hide in a house or behind a cart or some tree. Then we would set off again and like mice they reappeared outside and started following us again.
With this back and forth we left Udine.[275]
We passed through a small village on fire.[276]
There were many fires here and there on the plain, storage deposits that our people had blown up. The hangars at the airport were also ablaze.[277]
The road was blocked by a column of military vehicles and wagons full of civilians, proceeding very slowly. The trucks were forced to drive behind ox-drawn carts. Along the roadside were overturned vehicles and the carcasses of dead animals. Some had been torn apart by people desperately looking for food. In the fields were campfires with people eating, sleeping, crying or yelling. At least it wasn't raining anymore. From time to time, however, it rained bullets from enemy planes attacking the column. Those bastards were killing poor civilians as well. Together with some cavalry, we scoured the countryside repelling the German vanguards.»
«We've seen this stuff too» someone said to put an end to the narration, convinced that there was nothing new to find out.
«Just a minute. You don't know what happened next. We arrived in Codroipo late in the evening. Many inhabitants had already left. The town had been ransacked by whoever had passed before us. We took refuge in abandoned houses. We lit a fire and ate what little was left. Then, dead tired, we fell asleep on the floor. In the morning someone woke me up by pulling on my arm. When I opened my eyes, I saw a corporal who made a sign to keep quiet and look around. I saw an incredible sight, something you'll never imagine...» the sergeant kept us all in suspense.

---

[275] The Germanic command took possession of the city in the early hours of October 29. After a few days the Austrians arrived and the city was divided into two sectors: the northern part to the Germans of von Below, the southern part to the Austro-Hungarians of von Batoki. It was the darkest period of the occupation. Requisitions were out of control, houses ransacked, citizens robbed and many women raped. A City Committee was set up to try to limit the abuses of the Austro-Germanic commands, which considered uninhabited houses as *res nullius* and therefore totally at the disposition of the occupiers.
[276] This was probably Pasian di Prato, the first town one encounters when leaving Udine in the direction of Codroipo.
[277] The airfield at Campoformido.

«There were Germans sleeping and snoring among us. They smelled of wine and alcohol. They had probably raided some farmhouses and then, blind drunk, they entered our house and in the dark mistook us for their comrades.»
«So what did you do?» asked *Trepugnali.*
«What would you have done?» replied the sergeant.
Trepugnali drew his finger across his neck.
«Good boy. That's just what we did!» confirmed the sergeant. «We found some others in houses nearby and gave them the same treatment.»
A few months ago, I would have been indignant at such an action.
Tonight, I felt nothing. I would have done the same, without thinking twice. I am in such despair about everything that's going on at the moment that my anger has turned to hate.
«Then what did you do?» urged *Trepugnali.*
«Then we had a good fight with the ones who were awake, but we showed them what a handful of Arditi from Sdricca is worth. Unfortunately, we lost more men and used up almost all our ammunition.
Then we headed for the bridges of La Delizia.[278]
There we gave support the defenders, helping a large mass of civilians and soldiers of the 3rd Army to cross over to the other bank of the Tagliamento.
The Germans, however, were stepping up their pressure. When we were already exhausted, the signal came to run over the bridge. As soon as we were across, I saw some Germans with machine guns attempting to cross over to where we were by mixing in with civilians and soldiers. A few moments later the engineers blew up all three bridges one after the other.
I saw men, objects and animals fly through the air and then fall into the water. It was a massacre, but at that point the Germans could no longer pass. The river was in flood and it was impossible to wade it or to use footbridges. While we were there, we heard that you guys were gathering in Spilimbergo and so we left.

---

[278] Three bridges connected Codroipo to Casarsa della Delizia: from north to south there were the highway bridge, the railway bridge and the military bridge. To prevent them from falling into the hands of the Germans, their demolition at 13.30 on 30 October sentenced tens of thousands of soldiers stranded on the left bank of the Tagliamento to capture. Later the allegedly untimely nature of the work of the engineers was widely discussed. However, both the parliamentary commission of inquiry into Caporetto as well as General Konrad Krafft von Dellmensingen (24 November 1862 - 21 February 1953), Chief of Staff of the 14th Austro-German Army, agreed on the appropriateness of the moment chosen for the destruction of the bridges.

In Casarsa we found a large number of stragglers and refugees who, like sheep, channelled themselves into the road to Pordenone.
We went to Spilimbergo, though.
We went twenty kilometres without seeing a living soul.
Only military trucks and a few field batteries passed, trying to avoid the grenades thrown from the other side of the Tagliamento.
At Spilimbergo we had the nasty surprise of not finding any of you.
Where the hell were you?
An artillery major told us that you had gone to Sacile. It meant going back and walking another 40 kilometres in the rain, which had started again.
The major, however, wouldn't let us leave. He needed men right away to stop the *nails* from crossing the river on foot. He was waiting for reinforcements, which were supposed to arrive soon.
So we had to get down into the trenches dug along the banks, together with a mishmash of territorial workers, sappers and gunners. But at least they were able to supply us with food, rifle rounds and hand grenades.
The Germans tried to cross by exploiting the little islands that had emerged despite the flood of the river. But every time we beat them back. Then finally an Infantry Battalion relieved us. We were happy to leave those muddy and flooded trenches.
We got to Pordenone late last night, some of us on foot and others, like me, in trucks. No civilians around. They were either shut up in their homes or at the station waiting for a train to escape. On the street there were only officer patrols with full powers. In recent days several stragglers have been executed without trial.[279]
Together with some of our officers and other wounded men I managed to find a seat on a train and so I arrived in Sacile yesterday around noon.
I was really happy to find you again.»
One by one, we all embraced him.
He is like a brother to us.

---

[279] General Andrea Graziani (15 July 1864 - 27 February 1931) stood apart for summary executions during the Caporetto defeat. Appointed general inspector of the evacuation movement during the retreat from the Isonzo to the Piave, he was tasked with restoring order among the stragglers by any means. He did so without scruple.
The "general of the firing squad" showed considerable ferocity, both before and after Caporetto, especially against Italian soldiers. He died in mysterious circumstances in 1931, falling from a moving train between Prato and Florence. He had become an important person in the fascist regime: lieutenant general of the Volunteer Militia for National Security (MVSN), a militarized civilian police force. The case was dismissed as an accidental death.

Chapter 11.III

Pieve di Soligo, Saturday, 3 November 1917

We are in a corner of paradise!

The horror of war seems far away, if it were not for those ugly mugs of the Arditi who have invaded this village.

In the mirror, I don't look so good myself.

In addition to the bruise from the punch, you can see in my face the stress and fatigue of ten days of forced marches and fights day and night, with little ammunition and little to eat.

Our uniforms are dirty and tattered, but now we have been able to wash and shave. At last! Tomorrow new uniforms, clean linen, weapons and ammunition should be arriving.

We left Conegliano at eight o'clock this morning. Nice day.

We passed through Susegana and Colfosco, before taking a road that goes up the hill. There was not a living soul.

Nice to see that the war has not arrived here.

Our column looked like a dark and sinister snake in the midst of a landscape made even better by the flaming colours of autumn.

The inhabitants of Pieve could hear the echo of our songs, before they saw us appear on the horizon. They all left their houses and welcomed us like heroes with smiles and handshakes. *O'pazzo* says that when they see us parading by in clean uniforms, they will give us hugs and maybe even kisses. I hope he is right. I've seen some beautiful girls in the village. But I don't think there are enough for everyone. There are too many of us.

Colonel Bassi passed among us to see how we are doing, physically and morally. When he passed near me, I felt a great charge of strength and energy. The Arditi of the Sdricca School would throw themselves into the fire for him. Meanwhile, we throw ourselves into the village!

It is Saturday evening.[280]

---

[280] While the Arditi of the 2nd Army were reorganizing in Pieve di Soligo, during the night between 2 and 3 November the enemy troops managed to force the front at Cornino, setting foot on the right bank of the Tagliamento. They then marched towards the Arzino torrent, forcing our troops to withdraw behind the Meduna torrent on the 4th. Italian artillery fire across the Tagliamento line could not prevent some enemy units across from Pinzano from reaching the right bank and starting to build bridges on the evening of the 3rd.

CHAPTER 12.III

Pieve di Soligo, Sunday, 4 November 1917

What a wild time last night!

The Soligo villagers will remember it for a long time.

All the taverns were packed and Arditi songs rang out in each of them.

There was even musical accompaniment. The villagers brought out their accordions, violins and double basses.

They invited us into their houses.

What a different atmosphere from the looted houses we've seen lately!

Fires were lit, tables were set, families were gathered round, and their faces were peaceful.

This morning, however, the atmosphere has changed.

Refugees from Conegliano, Sacile and many other towns have arrived in the village. They're all heading for the far side of the Piave.

They're saying that the Germans are coming. Some villagers from Pieve started packing. Most of them are in the square or on the street discussing what to do. They're asking us for information.

For now, we stay here.

At mass our chaplain, who celebrated together with the parish priest of Pieve, tried to reassure those present.

Many villagers have decided to postpone their departure for as long as we are there to defend them. In the meantime, they press small gifts and great kindnesses on us.

Trucks with clothing and weapons arrived in the afternoon. Instead of sweaters, they gave us grey-green shirts and long black ties. Now we feel better and ready to defend this territory. Especially now that we have heard that the High Command has ordered the army across the Piave![281]

P.S. Still no news of my family.

---

[281] At 10 in the morning, General Cadorna gave the retreat order to fall back to the Piave. Thus, the XII Carnic Corps and the rear of the 4th Army moving from Cadore remained cut off. According to some historians, the influx of troops and refugees would have been much more orderly and less disastrous if the order had been given a week earlier.

CHAPTER 13.III

Pieve di Soligo, Monday, 5 November 1917

Quiet day for us, but not for the villagers.

With so many refugees moving through, panic began to spread among the families and many decided to leave.

We, on the other hand, remain here. Pending new orders, we clean and polish our weapons, chat, play cards, smoke the last cigarettes.

Now that I have more time to write, I can relate two short stories that I heard recently.

More or less in the words of some comrades from the II Unit:

«While you of the VI were all snug in your beds, we were aboard the trucks on the night of the 25th. When we arrived in Cividale everything looked peaceful. The mayor had had posters put up to reassure people[282]. But how can you reassure people if they hear the roar of artillery approaching and see the Black Flames coming?

It means that all hell is about to break loose!

In fact, people were starting to pack up.

The first ones to leave were lucky because a flood of stragglers and desperate civilians started arriving. It was a solid column.

I have never seen such a thing.

Soldiers with neither arms nor insignia hollering: "The war is over! Long live peace! Let's go home!"

Soldiers yelling at us because we hadn't thrown our weapons away.

Soldiers storming grocery stores, taverns and restaurants looking for something to eat and drink.

Only the intervention of our officers prevented us from coming to blows with that scum.

The next day the same shameful show, if not worse.

Enemy planes were arriving in the city, dropping bombs. In the early afternoon we gathered in the square and then in parade formation, singing our hymns, we started walking towards Mount Korada.[283]

---

[282] The text of the manifesto was as follows: *"Citizens, the High Command assured me that Cividale is safe from any enemy attack. I call for you to remain calm and trust in our weapons. Cividale, 25 October 1917."*

[283] Mount Korada housed the command of the XXVII Army Corps of General Badoglio.

The march was difficult. The road was jammed with men, vehicles and animals and we were going in the opposite direction.
Some of the disbanded soldiers provoked and insulted us.
For a while, we took and stood it. Then we exploded. We threw ourselves like rams against a group of troublemakers. A furious brawl arose. Some of them had the unfortunate idea of pulling out their knives. So we pulled out our daggers. In a few seconds those pigs had their noses in the mud. I believe one of them was dead. If our lieutenant hadn't got there, gun in hand, surely we would have killed more of those cowards.»
«If Salvatore had been there, they would have all been goners for sure» intervened *Pugnodiferro*. We laughed and looked at *Cuteddu*, who however kept his face impassive as usual.
«Late that night we arrived on the slopes of the Korada. We camped outdoors until 5 in the morning waiting for new orders.
What do you think Badoglio's order was?
Go back!
Without having killed even one German?
You can imagine how mad we were.
With great disappointment, we went on to the barracks in Val Cusbana to await new orders, which arrived late in the morning.
Do you know what Badoglio's order was?
Go back even further! To Cussignacco!
There weren't enough trucks for all of us. So almost all the members of the unit and other wretches like us who hadn't found a place on the trucks walked fifty-eight kilometres in eight hours! In those conditions! Even worse, marching in the same direction as the rats who had thrown away their guns! We arrived in Cussignacco at nine in the evening with bleeding feet.»

A sergeant from the V Assault Unit told me this other story:
«There were ten of us, we had lost contact with the rest of the unit.
As we were wandering around near Pasian Schiavonesco[284], between Udine and Codroipo, we saw stray dogs around the corpses of some of our soldiers. We ran to chase them away with our bayonets. The dogs had begun to savage the bodies. One soldier's face was already all bitten up.
Poor fellow.

---

[284] Basagliapenta, a fraction of today's Basiliano, which until 1923 was called Pasian Schiavonesco. The denomination originated from a Slovenian presence (commonly called "schiavona" in Italian) in medieval times. In the nationalistic climate of the 1920s, it was preferable to cancel the original toponym.

We took their ammunition and then tried to bury them as well as we could.
As we continued on, we heard cries coming from a building.
We immediately ran to see.
It was a tavern.
There were Germans inside. About thirty of them.
They were drunk. They had tied up the innkeeper and were raping two girls. They were the innkeeper's daughters.
Daggers in hand, we entered in a fury.
We showed no mercy to any of those animals.
The girls were distraught at what they had gone through, but also at witnessing our massacre, I imagine.
The innkeeper offered us drinks and even wanted to cook something for us, but we convinced him to get out of there immediately.
He and his daughters followed us as far as Casarsa.»

CHAPTER 14.III

Pieve di Soligo, Tuesday, 6 November 1917

The long line of refugees continues without interruption.

At the same time, there are more and more families leaving Pieve in the direction of the Vidor bridge.[285]

It is sad to see these people going away.

But how can you blame them?

It looks like Pordenone has fallen and the Germans are entering Feltre.

On the walls of the village, the High Command has had posters affixed ordering all men between the ages of 15 and 60 to depart for the other side of the Piave.

We continue to stay here awaiting orders.

We have rested enough.

The men are itching to fight.

I still have no news of my family or of Noè.

P.S. In the evening, Colonel Bassi summoned the commanders of all six units. We have to be ready to go at any time.

We still don't know whether against the enemy or to cross the Piave.

---

[285] In the Middle Ages the strategic importance of Vidor as a transport hub and river port on the Piave led to the construction of a castle, no longer extant, and a Benedictine abbey, housing relics brought back from the Holy Land during the first crusade. For some centuries the abbey was a powerful institution and contributed to the land reclamation. In the thirteenth century, the Pio Ospedale di Santa Maria dei Battuti was founded with the aim of giving hospitality to the numerous wayfarers in transit through the territory.

Chapter 15.III

San Pietro di Feletto, Wednesday, 7 November 1917
We got the answer this morning.
We received an order from the 2nd Army Command: to impede and delay the advance of the enemy.[286]
We left at midday.
All the inhabitants left in the village were on their doorsteps and at their windows. They bid us farewell by waving handkerchiefs and wishing us a quick return.
The IV Unit, under the orders of Major Mannacio, went to Vidor, where our troops are setting up a bridgehead.
We and the other units headed for Conegliano, led by Colonel Bassi.
Once in Conegliano we received the order to deploy between the Piave and the Vittorio hills[287]. Our commanders were a little perplexed. A front of over fifteen kilometres and crossed by many roads is much too long to be defended by just over three thousand men. However, orders are orders.
We of the VI Unit have been assigned to San Pietro di Feletto.
My squad and I are occupying an outpost at villa De Bernardo.
In this area there are a lot of stately villas. I don't know what will happen to them if the Germans arrive. Another outpost is in Corbanese, a hamlet of Tarzo, where the V Unit is located.[288]

---

[286] The order of the commander of the 2nd Army, General Montuori, sent to Colonel Bassi, was as follows: *"9:30 a.m., November 7, 1917 - Enemy columns preceded by sizable patrols descending Piave routes between Cison di Valmarino and Corbanese - San Pietro di Feletto. Your Lordship must impede and delay enemy advances on the indicated front. An assault battalion must immediately be made available to Col. Brig. Coralli, Commander of the Vidor bridgehead. Assault troops at Vidor bridge must fall back to the right bank of the Piave. Point of muster: Onigo. Acknowledge receipt. Signed: General Montuori."*
[287] The town of Vittorio was officially born on September 27, 1866 with the union of the pre-existing municipalities of Ceneda and Serravalle. It took the name of "Vittorio" on 22 November in honour of Vittorio Emanuele II, the first King of Italy. In July 1923 the appellation "Veneto" was added at the same time as it officially received the title of city.
[288] The six assault units were positioned astride the routes leading to the Vidor bridge, used for the withdrawal of both the 4th Army and the left wing of the rear of the 2nd Army. The deployment from south to north was as follows: the II Unit of Captain Abbondanza presided over Pieve di Soligo with outposts in Refrontolo, the III of Captain Campo was in Soligo with outposts in Solighetto, the VI of Major Ambrogi was in Madonna di Loreto

Many dark clouds are gathering in the sky.[289]

with outposts at villa De Bernardo and Corbanese, the V of Captain Turotti controlled Lago and Tarzo with the 1st surviving company of the I Unit in Revine, commanded by Lieutenant Benci.

[289] On November 7, 1917, General Cadorna issued the following statement to the army: *"With unspeakable pain, for the supreme salvation of the army and the nation, we have had to abandon a piece of the sacred soil of the Homeland, bathed with blood glorified by the purest heroism of the soldiers of Italy. But this is not a time for regrets. It is time for duty, sacrifice, action. Nothing is lost if our spirit of retaliation is swift, if our will cannot be bent. Once before on the Trentino front, Italy was saved by the heroic defenders who upheld its name before the world and the enemy. Let today's defenders be austerely aware of the grave and glorious task entrusted to them, let every commander, every soldier know what his sacred duty is: to fight, to win, not to yield even one step. We are relentlessly determined: Italy's honour and life will be defended on new positions gained, from the Piave to the Stelvio. Let every warrior know the cry and command of the conscience of the Italian people: die, but never retreat!"*
Actually, Cadorna continued to give orders to withdraw.

Chapter 16.III

S. Maria di Feletto, Thursday, 8 November 1917

Today we fought with the Austro-Hungarian vanguard.

At dawn this morning we heard gunfire coming from the area guarded by the V Unit and by Benci's company.

We were instantly on the alert.

Shortly thereafter, we saw a patrol emerge onto the roadside.

They were not Germans, but Austrians.[290]

We mowed them down with our machine guns.

Others immediately took their places.

A very intense firefight followed. It was raining again, not much, but the raindrops got into our eyes and made it hard to aim.

One of the Arditi who had just arrived to help, was hit right in the eye. Really bad luck. He died soon after.

Hearing the gunfire, other men from our unit rushed to back us up.

The *Mucs* attacked us several times throughout the day, but this time we have machine guns too and were always able to beat them back.

The facade of the villa is now completely riddled with holes and many of the windows have been shattered.

No man on my squad was wounded or killed. They all fought valiantly.

There were several hubs of fighting, because we could hear firing both right and left of our position.

We had no reinforcements behind us, so when the enemy's pressure increased, slowly and constantly fighting, we moved back to the second line position: torrent Crevada - torrent Soligo.

At sunset we settled in Santa Maria di Feletto.

It's evening.

It's still raining, but calm seems to have returned, at least in our sector.

Gunshots can be heard from time to time.

They are warning shots rather than attack attempts.

We, though, are ready for any eventuality.[291]

---

[290] They were soldiers of the 50th Austro-Hungarian Division of the German general Hermann von Stein (13 September 1854 - 26 May 1927), part of the XIV Army under the command of General Otto von Below.

[291] General Cadorna had just released what was to be his last war bulletin:

"Yesterday the retrenchment of our line continued. The large units were able to move undisturbed. The cover troops, with numerous valiantly sustained clashes between the hills of Vittorio and the confluence of the Monticano in the Livenza rivers, delayed our foe's advance. Our airmen, overcoming fierce resistance from enemy planes, renewed the bombing of the opposing troops on the Tagliamento. 5 enemy planes were shot down."

The following day Cadorna was dismissed by the King, due to insistent requests both from the Allies and the new head of the Italian government, Vittorio Emanuele Orlando (18 May 1860 - 1 December 1952). The Duke of Aosta Emanuele Filiberto, commander of the 3rd Army and first cousin of the King, had been suggested in his place. Instead, whether for simple envy or acute foresight, Vittorio Emanuele III decided to entrust the High Command to a little-known Neapolitan general, Armando Diaz (5 December 1861 - 29 February 1928), the former commander of the XXIII Army Corps, part of the 3rd Army of the Duke of Aosta. He was joined by Generals Badoglio and Giardino as deputy Chiefs of Staff. After initially refusing, Cadorna accepted the position of Italian representative to the newly created inter-allied war council.

CHAPTER 17.III

Falzè di Piave, Friday, 9 November 1917
Cadorna has been sacked!
The news flew from mouth to mouth this morning.
The King has appointed General Diaz from the 3rd Army in his place.
O'pazzo is very happy.
«*Cù nu napulitan ch'cummann, vincimm sicur 'a guerr*» he said.[292]
I hope he is right.
«He can't do worse than Cadorna» said someone else.
I think he is right.
We didn't have much time to talk about this news and the appointment of generals Badoglio and Giardino as deputy chiefs of staff.
The look-out in the church bell tower was signalling the advance of enemy columns. Soon the usual patrols sniffing out the terrain turned up. Our orders were to wait until they entered the village and silently eliminate them.
My squad did its part too.
Cuteddu, *Trepugnali* and *Carestia* jumped simultaneously on three Austrians without giving them time to say a word. Then they dragged them inside a doorway so as not to leave any traces on the street.
Shortly thereafter, four more Austrians appeared. My men were ready to strike again, daggers in hand. This time it was my turn. I thought about my family and my brother Noè, missing who knows where, about my home in Dogna, about all my friends killed, about Friuli invaded by these barbarians.
I gripped the handle of my dagger firmly. The Austrians advanced carefully, pointing their rifles at windows and doors.
My heart was beating faster than usual.
A great big Austrian was guarding their rear, walking backwards. I had to take him out myself, facing him head-on. Despite the cold of that morning, I felt the sweat run down my back.
Suddenly someone in the village fired a shot and so those four condemned men turned on their heels and ran away. While everybody else was cursing in their dialects, I put my dagger back in its sheath.

---

[292]«With a Neapolitan in command, we will certainly win the war» translation from the Neapolitan dialect.

I didn't know whether to be sorry or relieved.
In any case, one day or the other I will have to do it, if I don't die first.
We saw no more patrols and calm reigned for about an hour.
At exactly 10 o'clock the attack began over the entire front.
This time the Austrians were backed up by artillery, which began shelling the village. Shortly thereafter our howitzers started to respond. We were in the middle of two fires.
I prayed that the house my squad and I were in would not be hit. A shell exploded in the street, shattering all the glass of the windows and breaking through the heavy wooden door. Air displacement caused the bodies of the three Austrians to be thrown against the wall at the bottom of the entrance. Fortunately, none of my men.
Other shells followed but thank goodness the house wasn't hit directly.
When the bombardment stopped, we heard the whistles of our officers.
We ran out and found a very different landscape in front of our eyes.
Rubble, stones and bricks cluttered the streets. Here and there were chasms opened by shells. Many homes had been hit and some were on fire.
The church and bell tower had also been damaged.
I was disturbed by the desperate yelps of a dog trapped inside a collapsed building. I saw some Arditi trying to dig a comrade out of the rubble.
I don't know if he was dead or wounded.
We all ran towards the access roads to the town. Usually the Infantry attacks as soon as the shelling stops. In fact, the *mucs* were already filtering through in some places. Combat went on street by street, house by house.
Together with another squad, we had to take out a *Schwarzlose*, which had been installed in the ruins of a stable and was spraying the road.
One Ardito lay dying on the ground, another one was dead for sure.
We threw smoke bombs to obstruct the machine gunner's view and so to get around it. One group went left, while we went right. I crawled through the rubble, then climbed onto a roof, followed by half of my men.
I was hoping to be able to hit the machine gun from above.
Unfortunately, the roof of had been damaged in the shelling and was unsafe. It couldn't hold us. We went back down. Behind the house were small gardens separated by low walls, enclosed at the bottom by another house.
We quickly climbed over all of them, until we reached the last house.
The door was not closed.
We entered silently, as the machine gun shots seemed very close.
I wanted to find a window overlooking the street to see how far we were from the *squarciaossa*.

As soon as we entered the kitchen, we found ourselves face to face with two Austrians. One of them had wounds in his legs and the other one was medicating him. On seeing us their eyes got wide and they immediately raised their hands in surrender.
There were four muskets and my revolver pointed at them.
«Bono taliano, bono taliano» said the one on his feet.
«*Talian soldier* good. *Talian General* shit» he added.
I gave him a nasty look and made a sign to keep quiet.
While *Bracciodiferro* disarmed them, we went to the two windows to see the situation. At that very moment, four or five petards rained down on the machine gun nest, followed by an attack by the other group. One of the servers, however, managed to escape their blades and was running away to the house opposite ours.
Like an arrow *O'pazzo* rushed out in pursuit.
Shortly after we heard a shot coming from that house.
I ran towards the entrance, revolver in hand, just as *O'pazzo* was exiting.
Looking me in the eyes, he said with a grimace: *«Puvariell, nù bastav 'na vit 'emmerd, pur 'na brutta morte tenev in sorte: 'stà c'à facc dint a litam.»*[293]
Meanwhile other men from the squad had turned the *Schwarzlose* around and were firing at the other enemy vanguards.
When the ammunition ran out, they would destroy it.
We couldn't take it with us.
«What do we do with the two prisoners?» *Carestia* asked me.
"We can't take them with us" I thought.
I interrogated them quickly to find out who was attacking us and with which forces. They were part of the 15th Mountain Brigade of General von Stein's 50th Division.[294]
There were many more of them.
We couldn't defend the village for much longer.
Outside the fire was increasing in intensity.
I had to decide what to do with the prisoners. We could neither take them with us nor did I feel like killing them right there in the kitchen, despite my anger. I don't know if I did the right thing.

---

[293] «Poor guy, as if his life of shit wasn't enough, fate had a bad death in store for him as well: he is now face down in manure» translation from the Neapolitan dialect.
[294] Lieutenant General Baron Hermann von Stein, artillery officer and Prussian war minister since October 1916, commanded the III Army Corps made up of Austro-German troops.

I shot the one who wasn't wounded point blank.
He fell to the ground like a sack of potatoes, screaming in pain and clutching his knee. For him, the war was over, at least for a while.
"The Austrian doctors will take care of him and maybe he won't be fighting against us anymore" I thought.
The other Austrian looked at me fearing that I would shoot him too. But he was already wounded and there was no need to waste another bullet.
Carestia nodded, approving my decision. He advised *Bracciodiferro*, who was rather surprised, not to say a word to *Cuteddu*: «He is capable of coming back here and slaughtering them both.»
We went out and headed toward the machine gun.
Cuteddu was firing the last bursts at the assailants, backed up by other Arditi armed with muskets. We started shooting too.
The enemy's pressure was becoming unsustainable, but providence brought two submachine guns to our rescue.[295]
We put the *Schwarzlose* out of action and, under cover of the two submachine guns, moved back into the village, positioning ourselves behind windows and among the heaps of rubble.
Then the submachine gunners followed us.
We waited for the first assault group to appear in our street.
Then, from the houses on the right we targeted the Austrians coming from the left side, and from the houses on the left the ones coming from the right side. We had to shoot with care as there was very little ammunition left.
Then *Mandulino* and another comrade, defying the hail of bullets, went outside to gather up rifles, ammunition and hand grenades from the Austrians who had fallen near our positions and distributed them.
From the racket that we could hear, it seemed that fighting was also raging in the other streets of the village. A second group attacked us, covered by two *Schwarzlose*, which were spraying the facades of the houses making it difficult for us to shoot from the windows. In the meantime, some attackers were throwing hand grenades through the ground-floor windows of the houses, followed by a group with flamethrowers to finish the job.
You could see they were experts.
I'm afraid they killed the Austrians that we had left, wounded, in that house.

---

[295] The Italian Villar Perosa is considered the first true submachine gun. It was designed as a portable double-barrel machine gun firing a 9mm round. It consisted of two independent coupled weapons, each with its own barrel, firing mechanism, and separate 25-round magazine.

The Arditi barricaded in the first houses in the street tried to fall back to the next ones, but as soon as they stepped outside, they were hit in full by the riflemen.
We tried to cover them by shooting from the windows and we may have hit some Austrians, but the fire of the machine guns didn't give us time to take good aim.
A grenade exploded inside the house defended by *Mandulino* and two other Arditi. When I saw a soldier with a flamethrower enter, my stomach tensed up.
Immediately afterwards there was a strong explosion. Huge tongues of fire spewed out of the door and windows, slamming into the Austrians nearby. One of the three Arditi had had the guts to blow up the server and the cylinder of inflammable liquid on his back.
Taking advantage of the thick black smoke and the moment of bewilderment among the enemy ranks, we ran out of the buildings to find some more defensible shelters.
We had to drag *O'pazzo* away by force. He was paralysed by *Mandulino's* death. Better to die from a bullet than burned alive.
We positioned ourselves behind a barricade erected from the rubble of a house. Some others dismantled a large door from its hinges to use as a shield. In front of us we saw a thick black cloud, while the flames burned the house where poor *Mandulino* was.
Lots of bullets were fired at random towards us. When we saw the outlines of the Austrians emerging from the smoke, we started shooting too, mowing them down. We wanted to leave them in the smoke as long as possible.
After we beat back a second attempt, a runner arrived with an order from Major Ambrogi. We were to abandon our position and fall back behind the Lierza torrent. There was a risk of being caught behind by some Austrian units, which had already crossed the Crevada, further south.
The whole VI was leaving the village.
It was just past noon.
The pistol squad remained on the spot. With bursts of gunfire, their purpose was to conceal our retreat, at least for a little while.[296]
We started running towards the other way out of the village, gathering up all the material possible to be able to prolong the defense.
Little by little, as the Arditi started arriving, I realized that several were missing.

---

[296] This squad consisted of six pairs: two of the pairs operated the two submachine guns, capable of 5,000 shots each, transported in 200 magazines by the other four pairs.

All in all, it had gone well, except for poor *Mandulino* and a few others. By blowing up that flamethrower they had allowed us to change positions and save our *ghirba*.

During the march we tried to comfort *O'pazzo*.

He was in tears and couldn't resign himself to the loss of his chum.

We crossed the Lierza without problems. It is a small torrent and even much enlarged by rain could hardly hinder the advance of the *mucs*.

We arranged ourselves along its course, trying to dig some holes with our shovels and prepare shelters. There were no sappers.

In the meantime, the last defenders of Santa Maria di Feletto arrived in dribs and drabs. Thank goodness, our pistol squadron is back safe and sound. We were all tense, waiting for the Austrians to arrive.

«This is not the way they taught us to fight at Sdricca. We were trained to attack, not to defend» complained *il Turco*, another sergeant from the VI Unit, when I offered him a cigarette. I agree with him.

An order from Colonel Bassi arrived before the Austrians did, however: all units were to withdraw even further and settle in defense of the area ahead of the Vidor bridgehead.

The II was located between Sernaglia and Moriago, the III between Moriago and Colbertaldo, the V in San Giovanni with the Benci company.

We of the VI arrived in Falzè di Piave towards dusk.

Here too, many villagers were leaving their homes, despite the reassurances of the parish priest.

From what I've seen in the last few days, if I were a villager, I would leave too, while I still can.

CHAPTER 18.III

Onigo, Saturday, 10 November 1917

Last night was fairly quiet, but we didn't sleep at all.

We were afraid of being attacked.

We fired a couple of shots at patrols checking out the terrain, but nothing more.

This morning we were ready to carry out a real attack, like yesterday in Santa Maria di Feletto.

Instead, we received the order to clear out, fall back to Vidor and cross the bridge over the Piave.

«*Sergente*, does that mean they don't need us anymore?» they asked me.

«It means that our Armies have now passed over to the right bank. So we no longer have to defend their retreat» I reassured my men.

Early in the morning we left in the direction of Vidor.

My squad was bringing up the rear.

We had to prevent attacks from behind, but also not to show the enemy that we were clearing out.

So we fired a few bursts with submachine guns and rifles, until we reached Sernaglia, where the II was deployed.

At that point they became our rear guard.

In Moriago we found the III Unit. After our passage and that of the II they would retreat too, acting as our rearguard.

Approaching Vidor, the major ordered us to sing our songs so that the Alpini, who were stationed outside the village, could recognize us.

From their trenches the Green Flames waved their hats to greet us.

We responded by unsheathing our daggers and singing even louder.

Still singing we marched through the village, hailed by the comrades of the IV, and then over the Piave bridge.

I was singing, but I had a lump in my throat, because I was going farther and farther away from home.

We set up headquarters in Onigo before noon.

Around 12.30, while the first squads of the II Unit were arriving, we heard the artillery concert begin firing around Vidor.

We could see the light streaks of the bullets and the columns of smoke.

The fighting lasted until evening.
Around eight o'clock we heard a loud roar.
The engineers had blown up the Vidor bridge.[297]

[297] That same day from his headquarters, King Vittorio Emanuele III sent the following proclamation to the Nation and the Army:
"Italians!
The enemy favoured by an extraordinary concurrence of circumstances was able to concentrate the whole of his efforts against us. The Austrian army, which our army had faced and defeated many times in thirty months of heroic struggle, has now received the aid, that they have long invoked and awaited, of numerous and fierce German troops. Our defense has had to fall back; and today the enemy invades and tramples that proud and glorious Venetian land from which the indomitable virtue of our fathers and the unwavering right of Italy had driven him back.
Italians!
Since proclaiming its unity and independence, the nation has never faced a more difficult test. But just as my Family and my people, merged in one spirit, have never wavered before danger, so too now do we face adversity with a virile and fearless soul. From this same necessity we will draw the virtue of equating our spirits to the greatness of events. Our citizens, of whom the Homeland had already asked renunciations, deprivations and pain, will respond to this new decisive appeal with an even more fervent impetus of faith and of sacrifice. Our soldiers, who already in many battles have measured themselves against the present invader, seizing his bulwarks and driving him away from our cities with their redeeming blood, will carry their tattered glorious flags forward again, side by side with our fraternally united Allies.
Italians, citizens and soldiers!
Be one sole army. Every cowardice is betrayal, every discord is betrayal, every recrimination is betrayal. Let this, my cry of unshakeable faith in the destinies of Italy, resound in the trenches as well as in the most remote part of the country; and let it be the cry of a people who fight and a people who labour. To the enemy, who relies even more on the dissolution of our spirits and our assembly than on his own military victory, we respond with one sole conscience, and with one sole voice: we all are ready to give everything for the victory and for the honour of Italy."
Unlike the King, the new Commander, General Armando Diaz, sent a laconic statement to his troops: *"I assume the position of Chief of Staff and I count on the faith and self-denial of everyone."*

Chapter 19.III

Onigo, Sunday 11, November 1917

Today we rested, but above all we licked our wounds.

Sadly, many Arditi are missing from the roll-call.

Toro, a sergeant from the IV Unit, told us what happened at Vidor.

«We arrived on the eighth. Some civilians were running away, but not many. There were Bersaglieri cyclists and lots of Alpini.[298]

They had to dig in outside the village, as far as Bigolino.[299]

Our orders were to defend Vidor and the bridge over the Piave.

The engineers had already mined it.

A colonel from the Alpini ordered us to occupy the trenches near the bridge. But they weren't trenches. They were only holes. There was only a bit of barbed wire. They told us to fortify them. With what? With spit and shit? There were better trenches on the other bank. They told us that we were supported by numerous cannons and howitzers: 102, 105, 149 and 205 located on the other side of the river near Cornuda.

So what the hell were we doing there?

In any case there were still lots of trucks and wagons crossing the bridge.

Major Mannacio set up his command post in a tavern opposite the bridge. We of the 3rd company positioned ourselves in the centre together with the 2nd, the 1st on the right wing and the 4th on the left. Towards evening, when it finally stopped raining, we lit fires in the trenches. They brought us something to eat and a few flasks of wine. At least that much. We could hardly go around looking for food in the houses. Most of the villagers hadn't left. Strange. Didn't they understand what kind of storm was about to break out?

The officers were almost all in the command post, that is, the tavern.

Lucky them! They probably had a good meal before the storm.

The night passed quietly. The next day we worked like sappers: we dug trenches, strung barbed wire and placed *chevaux-de-frise*.[300]

---

[298] They were Alpini of the 12th Group (Battalions "Val Pellice", "Pallanza", "Monte Granero") and of the 14th Group (Battalions "Courmayeur", "Moncenisio", "Val Varaita").

[299] It is a fraction of Valdobbiadene, just north of Vidor along the left bank of the Piave.

We also erected a big barricade in the village.
At least it wasn't raining and there was food to eat.
Before fleeing with his family, the innkeeper killed his pig to sell it to our command. We could hear the animal's squeals. We could also hear artillery fire in the distance, but for the moment no enemies.»
«Those were the shells falling on us over at Santa Maria di Feletto» I explained to *Toro*.
«It must have been pretty bad for you, then. After sunset, one of our patrols captured a German cyclist on the Valdobbiadene road. They made him sing even if he didn't know Italian. He said they were arriving in droves. Germans. In that case, we said, we'll cut off their moustaches tomorrow, too.
The night passed quietly, but we lit no fires in the trenches.
At least we ate.
The next morning, it was around 10, we heard rifle shots here and there along the whole line of defense. The Germans were trying to see if we were still there. From time to time they fired a machine gun too.»
«*Gera i alpini. Pecà che i sparava contro de nialtri...*» a corporal of the V Unit chimed in. «*Gera scuro, no i vedeva ben. Magari gera anca un fià imbriaghi. Gavevimo da drio i todeschi e davanti i alpini che i sparava. Gavemo sigà che gerimo taliani, ma i no sentiva o i no ne credeva. Cusì semo scampai più in su dopo Bigoino e gavemo traversà el fiume nuando. Bagnai fin su pei cavei!*»[301]
«These days I shoot first and then I look to see who it is!
Listen, that afternoon we saw a nice group of Alpini coming towards us, waving white handkerchiefs and making gestures we didn't understand» the sergeant said again. «Then a patrol went to get a closer look. They were Germans! They had disguised themselves as Alpini. Those bloody bastards! We had a close-quarter gun fight. They killed Lieutenant Murgia. Do you remember him? The guy from Sardinia...»
«I remember him» replied *Carestia,* for all of us.

---

[300] This was a medieval defensive anti-cavalry obstacle consisting of a portable frame covered with many protruding, long, iron or wooden spikes or spears, it could also be moved quickly to help block a breach in another barrier. During World War I, armies used *chevaux-de-frise* to temporarily plug gaps in barbed wire

[301] «It was the Alpini. Too bad they were shooting at us. It was dark, they couldn't see well. They may have also been a little drunk. We had Germans behind us and Alpini ahead, shooting at us. We shouted that we were Italian, but they either didn't hear us or didn't believe it. So we ran past Bigolino and swam across the river. We were wet from head to toe!» translation from the Venetian dialect.

«Before they shot him he killed two or three of them with his pistol, and the rest of them sold their *ghirba* at a high price too.»
«You should have done what we did» I said, turning to the corporal of the V. «So they could recognize us, we sang the Arditi hymn and nobody shot at us.»
«You were lucky. If it had been the *Caproni,* they would have shot at you all right!» an Ardito of the IV said to everyone's laughter.
«Yes, we saw you of the VI go by that morning...» *Toro* took up his story again «...and those of the II with Captain Abbondanza at the head. Then Colonel Bassi passed by with his staff. They went to the tavern to eat the pig. The morning was pretty peaceful for us. The Alpini, on the other hand, had a lot to do to repel the German vanguards.[302]
After noon the *crucchi* started with their artillery. Some shells fell on the village. They also shelled the other bank too. They wanted to prevent our engineers from mining the bridge, but they had already mined it. After a while our artillery began to shoot back. We were right in the middle. One of our 105 mm on the right bank was firing continuously, while all around us German shells exploded, trying to silence it. But it went on and on.
Then German machine guns joined the concert.
Quite a few. Bullets were whistling from all sides.
Last came the infantry assault. We pushed them back once, twice, three times. But the more we killed, the more they came. Everywhere.
We also counterattacked. Hand grenades and slashing daggers!
But they kept on coming. Those Germans are stubborn. They were determined to take the bridge at all costs. But nobody gets by us, at least as long as we have ammunition and sharp daggers.»
We all shook our heads in approval.
«Towards evening the clashes decreased somewhat and we received the order to withdraw. Before we could go, though, the Green Flames had to pass. When all the Alpini had crossed the bridge, we were left alone on the left bank. Luckily it was dark now. So the Germans didn't know that there were so few of us. Otherwise would have attacked us en masse. There were five hundred of us but we were shooting like five thousand. Our last cartridges.
It was all dark. The only light was that of the explosions of the shells behind us and the flares. It was enough to take aim.

---

[302] This was the 12th Silesian Division of the Stein group, a very strong unit that played a significant role in the breakthrough at Caporetto.

We cursed when our people on the other side turned on a spotlight to sweep the Piave. We needed the dark. The Germans attacked us again and once again we drove them back.
Then Major Mannacio decided that enough was enough.
We of the 3rd company were the last to cross the bridge.
Captain Manescalchi[303] wanted us to march in parade formation even if there were machine gun bullets whistling overhead. Once we were all on the other side, the engineers blew up the bridge.»[304]
«Tell us about Lieutenant Sistu» asked *Pugnodiferro*.
«That man is immortal» replied the sergeant immediately.
«A huge bomb fell on our trenches. The second lieutenant flew into the air and fell at least twenty paces further back, buried in earth and rubble. We thought he was dead.
Instead he leaped up, dirtied and bloodied and half scorched.
He carried on fighting as if nothing had happened.
"I'll never die" he was telling everyone.
I have never seen such a thing.
That guy is immortal, I tell you.»
«Not immortal. He is Sardinian» specified *Carestia*.

---

[303] In 1919 captain Alarico Manescalchi received the medal of the Military Order of Savoy, an honour intended to reward *"distinguished actions carried out in war by army units or by individual military members belonging to them, which have shown manifest proof of skill, sense of responsibility and valour"*.
[304] In the following days the 12th Silesian Division tried several times to cross the Piave in Vidor but was always repelled, suffering serious losses. Von Below then decided to open the way to Mount Tomba by using all available artillery against the hills between the Piave and Brenta rivers, that is between Valdobbiadene and Valstagna.

Chapter 20.III

Onigo, Thursday, 15 November 1917
Nothing important has happened these last few days.
At least for us, who are at rest.
All around, however, you can hear the sound of many ongoing fights.
Germans and Austrians try in every way to cross the Piave, but they have always been repelled.
By now we are well established.
Our six units are no longer part of the 2nd Army, which is in the process of reorganization by "the Butcher". He is now in better health.
We have been assigned to the IX Army Corps of the 4th Army.
In these days I have had time to put in order the notes I took during the withdrawal.
By now I've almost finished the second notebook.
Soon I'll have to find another one.
O'pazzo is now teaming up with *il Gat*.
He has not yet recovered from *Mandulino's* death.
As much as we try, we cannot distract him from his fixed idea.
He says he should have been by his side.
«You would have been killed too» we tell him.
He replies that none of us decides, only *"a fatalità"*.
I'm not too tranquil either, because I still have had no news of my family.
I am increasingly worried.

CHAPTER 21.III

Vettorazzi, Sunday, 18 November 1917

Yesterday we moved to this little village at the foot of the mountains.

We are in the service of the 18th Division, which with the 17th has the task of guarding the front between Mount Tomba and Vidor.[305]

It is a very solid line of defense.

The 4th Army troops are well trained for mountain fighting.

In addition, their morale is high, given that they weren't severely tested during the breakthrough of the front.

For days the artillery has been thundering.

One continuous rumble.

We can hear fighting in the mountains around here.

Today we saw several wounded men carried down.[306]

Many planes fly overhead.

If we see a black cross under the wings, we shoot at it with our muskets.

Some planes are British.

They're out to destroy the scouts on the balloons.[307]

It's starting to feel like winter.

---

[305] Those two divisions linked the defensive organization established along the Piave to the one that was being established on the Monte Grappa massif. From 18 to 30 November the Arditi were used as a precaution to guard the line of maximum resistance between Vettorazzi and Castelli.

[306] From November 13, the second Battle of the Melette, the high and bare mountain hills in the northern part of the Asiago plateau was underway. The line had to be maintained at all costs to prevent the Austro-Hungarians from descending on Bassano and the Venetian plain and thus attacking the Italian troops deployed in defense of the Piave from behind. The imperials were led by the commander of the Tyrolean Army Group, Field Marshal Franz Conrad von Hötzendorf (11 November 1852 - 25 August 1925).

[307] The Austro-Germans had placed numerous tethered balloons along the Piave river.

CHAPTER 22.III

Vettorazzi, Friday, 23 November 1917
Today the mail sack arrived.
We hadn't seen it in far too long. There was a lot of excitement in camp.
After so much suffering and so much fighting, everyone felt the need to have some news from their families.
I saw the faces of my comrades light up as the postman delivered letters and postcards. I envied them. I was hoping there was something for me too. But I was afraid that there would be nothing.
My heart was beating faster, even more than in combat.
Then suddenly I heard my name called. It was the voice of the postman.
He was holding a postcard for me.
It was my sister Margherita's writing! There were only a few words: *"We've left. Like mother wanted. An affectionate hug from all of us"*.
A few signatures below and at the top a date: October 21, 1917.
A few days before the breakthrough and our retreat!
I was greatly relieved. My mother must have heard or dreamed something and decided to pack up and leave Dogna.[308]
Just in time!
Now I wish I knew where they are.
I hope some other postcards will arrive in the next few days.
I still don't know anything about Noè.

P.S. Fighting is still continuing on the Asiago plateau.
Yesterday morning the III Assault Unit was bloodied in a fight on Mount Monfenera but stopped a new attack.
We are always ready to intervene if the line is breached.
Whatever the cost, the *mucs* must not get down to the plain.

---

[308] The Canal del Ferro was occupied by the Austro-Hungarians of the group commanded by the Austrian general Alfred Krauss (26 April 1862 - 29 September 1938). On 29 October the garrison of Chiusa Forte surrendered to the 30th Feldjäger Battalion of the 59th Alpine Division.

Chapter 23.III

Vettorazzi, Thursday, 29 November 1917

The French troops of the XXXI Army Corps arrived to relieve the IX Army Corps and therefore us as well. In the next few days we will go to the province of Vicenza, to a quieter area than this.

Was it really necessary to call on the French for help?

When we crossed paths, they looked down on us with a hint of contempt. I don't know where their sense of superiority comes from. As far as I know, they haven't won the war on the western front. Maybe they're still reliving Napoleon's conquests, but they forget that in the end he was defeated.

«They're looking down their noses at us. And look at their moustaches» noted *Carestia.*

Their moustaches are long and hang downwards, giving their faces an expression of annoyance and disgust.

We don't understand what they're saying, but we have heard the word "macaroni" several times.

Some of us joked saying: «I wish they'd fill our mess tins with macaroni...»

Some others, though, got offended and would have liked to pick a fight just to make it clear who we Arditi are.

«Let them make the acquaintance of the Germans in the mountains and when they return we'll see if they are still so full of themselves.»

I ordered *Biunnu* to keep an eye on *Cuteddu* at all times, so that he won't get into trouble with the French. He assured me that he would, unless something happened in the latrines, because he doesn't follow him there.

«I hope that at least when their breeches are around their ankles down in a latrine, they do not feel superior and provoke us» I replied.

Chapter 24.III

Vettorazzi, Saturday, 1st December 1917
Today I turned twenty-one. For over two years I have been at war.
I received a gift from my men: a new notebook.
By now I was writing smaller and smaller in the few pages left.
Even I was having trouble reading the last things I wrote.
«Where did you find it?» I asked.
«*Mezzomago* found it. He knows people in high places...» *Carestia* told me with a wink.
«Where did you steal it?» I asked *Mezzomago*.
«I didn't steal it. I just used some magic on a quartermaster.»
«Do you write about us in those notebooks too?» intervened *Trepugnali*.
«Among other things...» I replied.
«*Ü dé s'pöderà lèsel chèl lìber?*»[309] jumped up *il Gat*.
«Bèrghem, first you have to learn how to read» *Mezzomago* replied, tapping his knuckles on his head. «*Te ghe da stödià!*»[310]
Everyone laughed.
«*Mé lèse mia. Mé scólte adóma chi professùr intregòcc compàgn de té.*»[311]
«At the end of the war I will read you something» I said to cut it short.
«...to those of us still alive» added *Carestia* with his usual concreteness.
Il Gat echoed him: «*Sperém che 'l sergènt a l'gh'àbie de scrìv amò mia tate pàgine.*»[312]
I gave him a dirty look and so did everyone else.
«*Ölìe dì che sta guèra la ède la fi impó a la svèlta.*»[313]
«Ah, that's better. I was going to beat you up, *bischero*[314]» *Pugnodiferro* said to him, brandishing his huge hands.
I offered drinks to everyone.

---

309 «Can we read your book someday?» translation from the Bergamo dialect.
310 «You have to study.»
311 «I don't read. I listen to fake professors like you.»
312 «Let's hope the sergeant has only a few more pages to write.»
313 «I only wanted to say that I hope this war ends soon.»
314 It means fool or stupid in the Tuscan dialect.

CHAPTER 25.III

Cartigliano, Tuesday, 4 December 1917
Yesterday we left Vettorazzi.
They made us take the long road that passes through Farra, Fonte and then Bassano del Grappa, where we stopped for the night.
Today we arrived here in Cartigliano, north of Vicenza.
We camped near the Brenta river.
It's cold and it's very humid. To the ones who complain I say just remember about the heat we suffered last summer on the Bainsizza plateau, for those who were there like me.
You always suffer, but the cold is better than the heat.
Last night I went to Bassano with some men from my squad.
The streets were crowded with soldiers and the taverns even more.
Somehow, we managed to get into a tavern near the bridge.
There was a great deal of confusion amid the thick cigarette smoke.
The confusion was even greater around one of the tables.
I went to take a look and saw *Bracciodiferro*.
He was challenging an Alpino in his specialty: arm wrestling.
Pugnodiferro acted as referee together with another Alpino.
Soldiers from all units were shouting. There were French soldiers, too.
The Alpino was physically robust. He looked about to burst out of his uniform. His face was all sweaty. *Bracciodiferro* was also concentrated on his efforts, but he seemed to be suffering less. Then I saw his face swell up and change expression. That was it for his opponent. He was forced to bend his arm down until the back of his hand hit the table.
A roar broke out, screams of joy mixed with swearing in all dialects.
Reluctantly, the Alpino handed over some coins to *Bracciodiferro*, who immediately pocketed them. Many other coins were changing pockets around that table.
Bracciodiferro looked around to see if anyone else wanted to challenge him. Almost immediately, a great big Frenchman with very long and sloping beard and moustache came forward. He was a *chasseur*.[315]

---

[315] The *chasseurs à pied* were the light infantrymen of the French Imperial army. They were armed like their counterparts in the regular line infantry (fusilier) battalions but were trained to excel in marksmanship and in executing manoeuvres at high speed.

He sat down in front of *Bracciodiferro* and put a pile of coins on the table. *Bracciodiferro* counted them and put the same number of coins beside his. He accepted the challenge.

The Frenchman straightened his moustache and then pulled up his sleeves. His arms were huge. He probably wanted to impress his opponent.

All around the table the French and the Italians were trying to understand each other by gestures to fix the bets.

I don't like to bet, but this time I too wagered with a Frenchman who was close to me.

The two challengers crossed their hands with a snap and remained fixed in that position for several minutes. They weren't moving, but you could see how much strength they were exerting. Even so, the Frenchman was smoking a cigarette and by moving his lips passed it from one side of his mouth to the other. In answer, *Bracciodiferro* began to whistle the Arditi hymn.

It was funny to see those two giants, rigid in their position, surrounded by a wall of soldiers who were freaking out and screaming at the top of their lungs. The two referees were also immobile, a Frenchman and *Pugnodiferro*, who monitored the elbows of the contenders, whose left hands were open and flat on the table.

I was watching *Bracciodiferro's* face. I was waiting for it to swell before the final effort, which always led to victory. The wait lasted a few minutes. Then finally his strange expression appeared. The Frenchman's arm began to bend more and more as he gnawed on what was left of the cigarette.

The background noise became deafening.

The back of his right hand slowly approached the table.

Usually the opponents of *Bracciodiferro* give up with a crash.

The Frenchman, on the other hand, resisted indefinitely.

Indeed, after spitting out the butt, he slowly began to recover.

For the first time I saw *Bracciodiferro* worried. His face swelled even more to resist the opponent's comeback and end the game. All to no avail as he still resisted. The soldiers all around were now shouting their cheers directly into the ears of the two challengers.

Driven by those screams, the Frenchman recovered even more, returning his arm almost to the starting position.

Then, I don't know how, with a sudden twist he managed to bend the arm of our comrade. But it looked to me as if he had moved his elbow and even raised it a little off the table, which is against the rules.

For that reason, *Bracciodiferro* let go, so he told us later.

The chasseur raised his arms to heaven in victory and so did his referee.

Pugnodiferro, though, waved his arms in a negative sign and *Bracciodiferro* yelled something bad at his challenger.
When the Frenchman tried to gather the coins on the table, *Bracciodiferro* threw a direct punch, smashing his nose.
An indescribable brawl immediately broke out, first around the table and then throughout the tavern. I don't know what happened to the coins, which fell to the ground when the table was overturned.
We gave as good as we got.
Until someone shouted that the Carabinieri were coming.
So, in order not to make matters worse, we stopped fighting and we all ran away in a crazy stampede, the French, too. In our escape we ran right over some of the *Caproni* and took the opportunity to give them several kicks and a few slaps.
«*Belìn*, that shitty Frenchman raised his elbow» repeated *Bracciodiferro* several times, as we were leaving Bassano.
«*Tè gh'ìet de storzìghel prima 'l brass, o ciavado!*»[316] *il Gat* answered him every time.
«Let's hope we don't get into trouble with the *Caproni*» was the fixed thought of *Carestia.*
«What happened to the money that was on the table?» I asked at some point.
«*Belìn*, I lost my money too!» *Bracciodiferro* exclaimed, who only then remembered it.
There has been no inquiry into the brawl or perhaps they weren't able to identify us.
The next morning, we left Bassano del Grappa, some of us with a black eye, but particularly happy to have shown the French that it doesn't pay to be haughty with the Arditi.

---

[316] «You should have bent his arm right away, you big dummy!» translation from the Bergamo dialect.

CHAPTER 26.III

Cartigliano, Thursday, 6 December 1917
Yesterday was a beautiful sunny day.
Today the sky is overcast, but for me it's as if the sun were out.
The mail brought me two pieces of good news.
The first one is a postcard from Margherita.
She wrote to me that the family has settled in Florence and that my father is with them. Everybody is fine.
The other is a letter from my brother Noè. At long last!
"Caro fradi,[317]
solo ora son buono a scriverti. Io stò bene come spero di te, non ostante tutto quello che ha suceduto. A fin otubar me la soi vioduda bruta quando che i mucs han atacat. Par fortuna son stato vivo e senze ferites. Penso che la nestra casa cumò a è ocupata dai mucs e anche tutto il pais. La nostra familia a è partida qualchi dì prima de la gran ritirata par andar a Treviso. Non son buono a dirti dove son cumò. Se tu hai notizie ti prego di dirmele. Scrivimi anche come stai tu. Il mio Battaglione Gemona è stato sciolto e cumò son nel Battaglione Mercantour. [318]
Ti abbraccio, tuo fradi Noè."

---

[317] The letter is written in a mixture of Italian and the Friulan dialect.
Translation: *"Dear brother, only now can I write to you. I am well as I hope you are, despite all that has happened. At the end of October, I did fear the worst when the Austrians attacked. Fortunately, I am alive and unhurt. I believe that our house is now occupied by the Austrians as is the whole village. A few days before the great retreat, our family left for Treviso. I can't tell you where it is now. If you have any news, please give it to me. Also write and tell me how you are. My Battalion was dissolved and now I am in the Mercantour Battalion. I embrace you, your brother Noè."*
[318] At 3 a.m. on 27 October the commander of the XII Army Corps stationed in Tolmezzo, General Giulio Cesare Tassoni (27 February 1859 - 10 October 1942), received the executive order to retreat. The troops had to quickly abandon their positions to avoid encirclement by the Austro-Germans, who were invading the Friuli plain. As on the rest of the Julian-Carnic front, the troops garrisoned in Val Dogna, including the "Gemona" Alpine Battalion, were surprised by the breakthrough between Plezzo and Tolmino. A few days after the end of the retreat, on 18 November, the "Gemona" was dissolved and the veterans aggregated to the "Monte Mercantour" Battalion. In two and a half years of war the Battalion had lost 636 men, of whom 115 dead and 63 missing.

He hasn't yet learned to write in good Italian.
He'd rather fish in the Fella than study.
But thank heavens, he's fine.
I replied immediately.
"Dear brother,
I was very relieved to receive your letter and hear that you are well.
It doesn't matter about the house.
Lord willing, sooner or later we will drive out those brigands.
The important thing is to be alive and healthy. We have lived through terrible days. For me today is a beautiful day, however, because I've received news from both you and our family. Margherita wrote me. They are not in Treviso. They got all the way to Florence with our wagon! Our father and many refugees from the Canal del Ferro and Carnia are also with them.
So they feel less homesick.
As for me, I'm fine and I have no wounds. I have fought and will continue to do so as long as the Lord gives me strength. I hope you will do the same.
Mandi, your brother Pietro."

Just yesterday the remains of our six units were disbanded. From over 5,000 who we were at Sdricca, there are a little over 1,700 of us left. They have regrouped and rebuilt us into two units of three companies each and assigned us to the 1st Army.[319]
The I Unit is commanded by Major Ambrogi.
My squad and I have joined the II Unit, under Captain Abbondanza.
There is a rumour going around that Lieutenant Colonel Bassi will be promoted but sent away to command an Infantry Regiment.

---

[319] The decision to keep the assault units alive was hardly a foregone conclusion. Among the military leaders some doubts had surfaced about the advisability of continuing the experience. Their high performance before Caporetto and during the retreat was acknowledged by all. Nonetheless, called into question were the absorption of the most valuable elements from the Infantry and the other branches, as well as their discipline in the rear lines, anything but conformant to the dominant military mentality. In a memo to the High Command, the Ordination and Mobilization Office emphasized that these units could produce excellent results, if well employed, dismissing the most serious accusations as rumours (looting and theft during the retreat by Arditi of the 2nd Army). It also recommended strict discipline with the use of vigorous officers, the removal of the most turbulent individuals and the possible dissolution of the units, if the acts of indiscipline were frequent and of a collective nature. On January 8, 1918, the High Command established a unique numbering system for the 21 existing or planned assault units, instead of the autonomous one within each Army. The numbers went from I to XIII, XVI and XVIII, and from XIX to XXIV.

The news from my family and Noè has cheered me up.
Our army has recovered and is stopping the enemy advance.[320]
There are French and English troops at our side now, with lots of guns and planes. All this makes me think that the worst is over and that this tragic autumn is about to end.

[320] Actually, in the third phase of the battle of the Melette (3-5 December), the Italian troops, in spite of having blocked the imperial advance, were forced to withdraw their defensive line to the south-eastern edge of the Asiago plateau. The defense had been desperate. The Italians lost 700 officers and 18,000 soldiers. The Austro-Hungarian command itself recognized the tenacity and fury with which the Alpini and Bersaglieri had fought.

CHAPTER 27.III

Debba, Wednesday, 12 December 1917
From Cartigliano we have moved thirty kilometres further south.
We passed through Vicenza. The city is full of soldiers coming and going. We saw French soldiers preparing trenches outside the city, as if waiting for an attack. We are quartered in Debba, at the foot of the Berici Hills.
It has been raining for a few days.

Debba, Saturday, 15 December 1917
Debba is a small town on the main road.
There is not even a square. The *"Bar della mano amica"* has become our mess. The I Assault Unit is located about a kilometre away in Lòngara.
It's a slightly larger village with a square. The command and officers' mess have been installed in a beautiful villa in the hills.[321]
I don't know how long we will stay here. There is no real training ground, nor the "dummy hill". On the other hand, however, we are very close to Vicenza, where we can do some friendly raiding.

Debba, Monday, 17 December 1917
It's snowing. In a few hours the landscape has become different and far more beautiful. For a while, fresh snow will cover the colours of war.
I don't envy the soldiers who are up in the mountains, though.
Who knows how much snow and how much cold?
There has been intense artillery fire over the past few days.
On the contrary, today everything is quiet.

Debba, Friday, 21 December 1917
Yesterday General Clerici reviewed our two units.[322]
He thought he would find a bunch of unruly and lazy soldiers, instead we surprised him with a perfect drill.
At the end he gave a speech of about half an hour in which he praised us several times. I remember well these words: «Arditi of the Black Flames, your superb reputation precedes you: a reputation of being such unsurpassed warriors that no enemy can resist.»

---

[321] The monumental Villa Papadopoli.
[322] He was Chief of Staff of the 1st Army.

If he really thinks so, why are we here sitting on our hands?
Up there our comrades are fighting, while we are waging war on fleas.
For some days we have been singing a new verse to our song:
Gli Arditi prima stavano a Sdricca di Manzano
ed ora stanno a Debba, di faccia all'Altipiano.[323]

At the end of his speech, the general invited us to praise the sovereign. «Long live the King!» we cried. But immediately afterwards with greater force our seventeen hundred voices roared: «Long live Colonel Bassi!»

Debba, Tuesday, December 25, 1917
It's Christmas. It is a cold and foggy day.
During mass the artillery was still thundering.
On the Asiago plateau they forgot what day it is today.
We are lucky to be here. I feel sorry for the soldiers up there.[324]
It's a sad Christmas.
We have been far away from our families for far too long.
We are also sad because it is Colonel Bassi's last day with us.
He has been sent to command the 76th Regiment of the "Napoli" Brigade.[325]

---

323 *"The Arditi were once at Sdricca di Manzano, and now they're in Debba, facing the plateau"* translation from Italian.

324 The imperials had decided to launch a decisive attack to break through the line of the plateau and spread out through the plains. The commanders had promised the troops not only Christmas mass in the Basilica of San Marco in Venice, but also Venetian women and plunder from the rich warehouses of the Royal Army. The attack began on December 22nd with intense shelling. Over the next three days the clashes were very violent with continuous attacks and counterattacks. Calm only returned on the evening of December 25th. The Austro-Hungarians had conquered Monte Val Bella, Col del Rosso and Col d'Echele. However, once again they had failed to break through the line, thanks to the heroic defense of Arditi (XVI and XXIV Units), Bersaglieri (5th Regiment) and Infantrymen (Brigades "Regina", "Toscana" and "Sassari" in particular).

325 The removal of the Arditi founder was presented as a normal career progression. As a matter of fact, it was the consequence of a clear divergence of views with Badoglio on the use of assault troops. In particular Bassi was against the establishment of an assault Army Corps. The veterans of the Sdricca School, especially some of the officers, did not welcome his transfer nor even the reorganization of the units, in which they saw the intent to attenuate their special characteristics in order to bring them more into line with normal infantry regiments. In April 1918, Lieutenant Colonel Giuseppe Bassi was sent with Italian troops to France. From 15 to 19 July he took part in the defense of the Ardre Valley. On July 22-23, he was granted the honour of leading the counter-offensive at the head of a special column made up of Italian and French troops. He exceeded his targets, penetrating over five kilometres into German defenses and capturing prisoners, machine guns and pieces of artillery. For these actions he received the Military Order of Savoy and the Le-

How can he command infantrymen after he has led the Black Flames?

Vittarolo di Lusiana, Thursday, 27 December 1917
We moved again.
Now we are at the Plateau Troops Command School.
We are just south of Asiago.
It means that soon we will spring into action.
There are many barracks and a shooting range.
Today is sunny.
Despite the good weather there is a pause in the fighting on the plateau.

---

gion of Honour Command for merits of war. In September-October 1918 he took part in the battle of Chemin des Dames with the Italian II Army Corps, entering Belgium among the first. After the armistice of 11 November, he returned to Italy and was promoted to colonel. In June 1920 he was sent to Valona in Albania in command of an assault group, which victoriously defended the honour of Italy. At the end of August, he landed in Trieste with his troops and was assigned to the Army opposing the Fiume rebellion which was led by d'Annunzio and supported by many of his own Arditi. Once the rebellion was suppressed, Colonel Bassi was appointed commander of the 7th Infantry Regiment stationed in Milan.

Chapter 28.III

Vittarolo di Lusiana, Monday, 31 December 1917

In recent days the weather has been fine.

That's why the fighting has picked up again more violently than ever.

At night the moon lights up the mountains as if it were day.

Spotlights are not needed.

It seems that the French troops have won a great victory on Mount Tomba yesterday[326]. Who knows if there were any of the ones we got into fights with in Bassano?

We heard that last weekend enemy planes bombed Treviso, Castelfranco and Padua, where the High Command is now installed.

At this time last year I was in Dogna with my family.

I wonder if I will ever see my mother, father and brothers again.

Who knows if we'll ever be able to get back to Dogna?

I am hoping both for God's help and for good luck.[327]

---

[326] This was the first combat sustained by French troops on the Grappa. The Italian and French artillery barrage began on the morning of the 30th and intensified in the early afternoon. At 4:00 p.m. the 47th French Division started the attack. In spite of a limited number of losses, it managed to knock out over 2,000 opponents among those killed, wounded or captured.

[327] On November 29, Archduke Eugene of Habsburg (21 May 1863 - 30 December 1954) officially requested an end to the offensive. The Austro-Hungarian High Commander had agreed but insisted on beefing up the defensive line of the Grappa area. He rightly believed that he would not be able to maintain the ridge of Monte Tomba, as long as the mountains remained in Italian hands. This determined all subsequent operations in December. In parallel, the German command left the administration of Friuli to its Austrian ally and withdrew its troops from the Italian front. Despite the regulatory bodies, there was a flourishing black market in all the lacking goods: cloth, soap, silk and more. Degeneration was rampant in many of the Austro-Hungarian units in the Isonzo armies. The rear line was teeming with looters and deserters, sometimes banded together in real gangs. Farmers were harassed and some were even murdered. Forceful intervention was necessary to maintain order. In any case, everywhere in Friuli the army dedicated itself to confiscating all available copper utensils, cauldrons, pans, brasses and bells. There was great need of those metals to be used in the manufacture of crowns for artillery shells.

CHAPTER 29.III

Reading this part of the diary was much more difficult than the one before. In some places the handwriting is almost indecipherable, both for the irregular strokes and for the presence of numerous corrections and many words discoloured by water.
For this reason too, these pages seem to me to be even more fraught with the weight of the dramatic events following the breach of the front in Plezzo and Tolmin.
Caporetto was a dramatic entry in the long list of tragic events reaching back over more than two years. It was a tragedy even more painful for the Friulan soldiers like my grandfather: seeing their land invaded, imagining their own houses sacked, having no news of the fate of their families.
Added to this was what they had seen with their own eyes along the roads of Friuli.
I can only try to imagine my grandfather's emotional state and the thoughts that must have tormented him.
I have read some pages over and over.
I could almost feel the humidity of the persistent and torrential rains of those days. I could almost see the bruised and cloudy sky of Friuli, the murky and swift waters of the Tagliamento river, all elements of a scenario that rendered the exodus of the population even more painful and sad, the retreat of the soldiers even more bleak and bitter. For a few moments it seemed to me that I could feel quite clearly the dizziness that one feels on the brink of a disaster of colossal proportions.
According to Cadorna, in those October days, over a million soldiers, of whom 350,000 were disbanded, and 400,000 civilians trudged along the inadequate network of roads leading to the bridges over the Tagliamento. The only railway line, Udine-Pordenone-Treviso, was overwhelmed and later unusable due to the Austro-German advance.
With the withdrawal of the front from the Isonzo to the Piave, enemy troops occupied the entire provinces of Udine and Belluno and partially those of Treviso, Venice and Vicenza. It was a territory of about 14,000 square kilometres, populated by 1,152,503 inhabitants, according to the 1911 census. Nearly half of them decided to leave their homes voluntarily in order to save themselves.

The number of refugees, estimated by two special censuses, fluctuated between 515,000 and 630,000, although some scholars believe these figures to be approximate by default. In any case, most of them were from Friuli. Many of my ancestors were also among these refugees.

I had never studied the episode of Caporetto in depth.
So, before starting to read the diary, I decided to read up on it. I discovered that of all the events in the Great War it is the issue that has been most widely written about in Italy, from 1918 on. There is the testimony of those who actually trod those muddy roads, both from the vanquished and the victors; there are the memoirs of the generals; there are the documents of the Commission of Inquiry; there are historical studies and even some novels.
Over the years, conflicting explanations have alternated and accumulated, some patently false, some deliberately incomplete as to the causes of that defeat and who was responsible for it.
Personally, I believe that the main fault is attributable to the High Command, in other words, Cadorna, and to the generals of the 2nd Army.
A Commission of Inquiry was set up in 1918 to investigate the causes of the defeat at Caporetto and ascertain if there had been a "soldiers' strike" modelled on the Russian revolution that year, as some have maliciously speculated. After interrogating more than a thousand witnesses among whom generals, superior and junior officers, NCOs and privates, in the summer of 1919 the Commission delivered its Report[328]*, concluding that our Armies had not been adequately prepared for the enemy offensive, even though it had been discovered in advance, despite attempts to disguise it.*
Cadorna had given little credence to the offensive, while Capello had done little to counter it. In addition, there were the errors of the generals: failure to command and incompetent behaviour on the field. In particular Badoglio, who badly managed his 700 pieces of artillery precisely at the most crucial moment of the attack: the lack of counterbattery and enfilade fire allowed the enemy to infiltrate our lines almost undisturbed. For this reason, many modern historians point to him as one of the main culprits of the disaster.
In the Report, however, his faults were greatly smoothed over, since in the meantime he had become one of the architects of victory, as Deputy Chief of Staff.

[328] The official Report on Caporetto only became public in 1967.

After the war Badoglio had a brilliant military and political career. On the contrary, Capello, although he too adhered to fascism, soon fell out of favour for his affiliation to Freemasonry.
The faults of Cadorna and Capello, however, were not only limited to drawing up an inadequate defense against the Austro-German attack plan. Their guilt began in the period before Caporetto.
On one hand they were accused of having deeply undermined the Royal Italian Army's morale with a discipline as rigid as it was obtuse; on the other of having sent a great number of soldiers to the slaughter in a systematic, inhuman, ineffective way. Over two years of unnecessary carnage.
At the same time, historians believe that, paradoxically, without Caporetto's drama there would have been no subsequent Italian victory nor the consequent conclusion of the entire conflict.
In any case Caporetto, like Waterloo, will always be synonymous with a sensational defeat. Official data list 10,000 dead, 30,000 wounded and approximately 300,000 prisoners, to which must be added the loss of over 3,000 pieces of artillery, over 1,700 howitzers, 3,000 machine guns and 300 thousand rifles, not to mention the enormous quantities of fuel, supplies and war material (ammunition, vehicles, trucks, etc.), either lost or destroyed during the retreat.
Unlike Waterloo, however, a few days after the defeat what some have called the "miracle of Caporetto" took place.
A defeated army and a prostrate nation awoke as if from a bad dream and, instead of collapsing definitively, found the moral and material strength to resist indefinitely on the Piave line and then to counterattack victoriously.

At this point I was ready to continue reading the diary and anxious to find echoes of great history in the little history of my grandfather.

4th Part

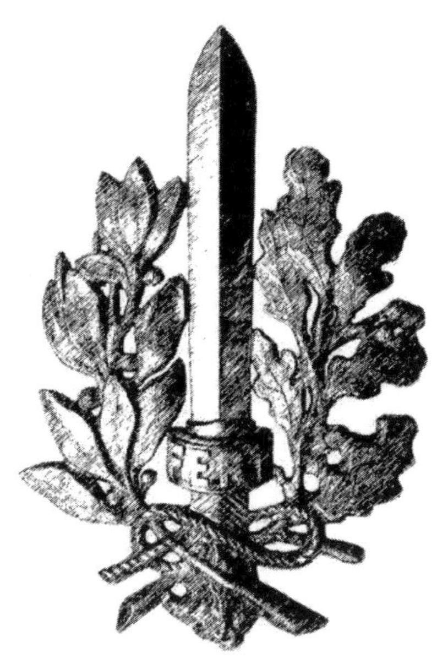

GREYGREEN REDEMPTION

Chapter 1.IV

Vittarolo di Lusiana, Tuesday, 1st January 1918
Last night enemy planes bombed Vicenza.
There have been some deaths.
Thus began 1918.

Vittarolo di Lusiana, Friday, 4 January 1918
The good weather continues.
The sky is blue and the sun is shining.
There is snow, but it feels like spring.
For a few days now we've been getting our mail on time.
I have already received a letter and postcard from my family.
They are all well. As soon as they give me my winter leave, I will go and visit them in Florence. I've never been there.
Pugnodiferro says it is "pretty".

Before I leave, however, there is to be an operation
Radiogavetta says it will be a big deal and we must win at all costs.
It would be the first one since last fall's retreat. This is why the High Command has decided to throw the best army units into the mix.
Besides us there should be some regiments of Bersaglieri, the "Sassari" and "Liguria" Brigades, some Alpine battalions and a lot of artillery.
«With the Sassari we will win for sure» says *Carestia*, who hopes to see his old comrades again and fight alongside them. In that Brigade all the soldiers come from Sardinia, apart from the officers.
«*Se cumbattimm che Bersaglieri è meglio assaj*»[329] responds *O'pazzo* every time; he's hoping to meet some ex-comrades, too.
The rest of us, me included, just hope that our soldiers will be courageous.

Vittarolo di Lusiana, Sunday, 6 January 1918
We had a Friulan riunion last night on the eve of Epiphany.
The sky was clear and starry.
We lit a *pignarûl* to remember our traditions.

---

[329] «It's a lot better if we fight together with the Bersaglieri» translation from the Neapolitan dialect.

Smoke and sparks always blew east, towards Friuli.
It means good luck for the months to come.
We gave each other great slaps on the back and hugs.
I don't know if it was the smoke or the cold, but it seemed to me that almost everyone's eyes were a bit teary.
Around the fire we began to discuss the future, with a crescendo of voice and purpose, as the cognac in the bottle decreased.
«*No viod l'ore di parâ vie i mucs di cjase.*»[330]
«*I vin di comencjâ a parâju vie di ca. E dopo i vin di côriji daûr a pidadis in tal cûl ch'a scjàmpin fin a Viene.*»[331]
«*Ce ditu? Pidadis in tal cûl? I vin di copâju ducj, ch'a no tornin pui chei mucs e chei slavats a robâ in ta nestre tiere.*»[332]
«*Tâs, tâs. No vin di fermâsi. I vin di rivâ fin a Viene. Ch'a provin ancje lôr ce ch'a vul dî scjampâ a rote di mul e vêi il forest in cjase.*»[333]

«What the hell are you yelling about?» intervened at some point a corporal walking by. He had not noticed that in addition to me there was also another sergeant, nicknamed *Peç*, a Friulan from Gemona.
«*Cjapinlu chel osteon!*»[334] shouted *Peç*.
The corporal understood that he was getting into trouble and started to slink away. We all got up abruptly, and chasing after him, caught him like a hare and buried him in the snow.
As he was attempting to re-emerge, *Peç* screamed at him: «*I no tu âs di interompi furlans e cjargnei cuand ch'a cjacarin di roubes series. Âtu capît, macaronat?*»[335]
I don't know what he understood, but he had the good sense not to reply.
So we dug him out of the snow and took him with us to drink cognac to warm up.
«*Minchione*[336]» I said to him, «we're your brothers. Happy Epiphany.»

---

[330] «I can't wait to kick those Austrians out of our home» translation from the Friulan language.
[331] «We'll start by sending them away from here. Then we'll run after them and kick them in the butt until we reach Vienna» translation from the Friulan language.
[332] «What? Kick their butts? We have to kill them all, so that neither Austrians nor Slavs can ever come back to steal in our land.»
[333] "Hush, hush. We mustn't stop. We have to get to Vienna. Let them see what it feels like to have to run away and have foreign people at home.»
[334] «Let's get that bastard!»
[335] «You mustn't interrupt Friulans and Carnians when they are talking about serious things. You understand, dozy *maccarone*?»
[336] It is the equivalent of "twat" in the Sicilian dialect.

CHAPTER 2.IV

Vittarolo di Lusiana, Sunday, 13 January 1918

Despite the cold and snow, we have resumed our training exercises.

As closely as possible we have tried to reconstruct the Sdricca training fields. Every day we shoot, throw petards, stab bales of compressed hay, run, jump over barriers, simulate attacks.

Many exercises are performed under fire from machine guns and artillery.

Unfortunately, at the end of our daily efforts we are not welcomed by the beautiful taverns of Manzano and its pretty girls.

We are isolated in this small village populated by four souls.

At most, we go down to Lusiana or extend the journey as far as Santa Caterina. Even there, however, many civilians have already left.

We smoke, chat, play cards, winning and losing some money from each other.

The comrades do not want *Mezzomago* at any table, because they are afraid that he will use his tricks to win. On the other hand, he is in great demand to perform his magic around the barracks. He manages to do it even without the finger he lost in Pinzano.

Bracciodiferro also wanders around the barracks, hoping to challenge the most muscular, but having already beaten everyone, now no one dares to face him.

In one of the barracks the command has made books and newspapers available. They call it the "Soldier's House".[337]

However, the soldiers prefer to attend the cooperative canteen and the barracks where they have set up a boxing ring and every evening there are fight challenges between some of the Arditi.

---

[337] The so-called "soldier's houses at the front" appeared in the autumn of 1916 on the initiative of Don Minozzi in order to make the lives of soldiers less bleak. They were small chapels, built from wooden boards, made into rooms for reading books, playing musical instruments, holding lectures. In 1916 there were a few dozen. By May of 1917 there were 100 of them (25 with cinemas). In November they grew to around 200, for an army of over 2 million men. When Cadorna was accused of neglecting the propaganda among the troops, he mentioned only this initiative in his defense. He did authorise it but gave it no significant financial support. Activities for the moral support of the troops and propaganda were actually only developed after Caporetto, with the advent of the new High Command.

One evening, two Bersaglieri from the 5th Regiment accompanied by numerous comrades came to throw down the gauntlet. They had a lot of guts. The first one went down almost immediately. The other stuck it out longer, but in the end he too was knocked down by our boxer. Their comrades lost their bets and we "fleeced" them out of a pile of *schèi*.[338]
Never bet against the Arditi!
To kill time in moments of rest, some comrades enjoy building common objects using shell cases, forcing crowns, grenade splinters and other war material.
I have seen letter openers, inkwells, rings, chains and even a lighter.
Another very frequent activity is that of playing jokes on the newcomers.
Ice-water buckets, push-ups on the latrine, snow down their backs, in their underwear, in their shoes, in their beds.
If they try to fight back, we start the *"cappotta"*.[339]
In addition, we don't spare them petards between their legs or knife tossing. They're lucky there's no Captain Racchi's "Swing."
It is hard for them, but at least the food is abundant and the barracks are heated. In the trenches they were certainly worse off.[340]

---

338 "Money" in the Venetian dialect. It derives from the inscription *scheid.munz*, abbreviation of *Scheidemünze*, or "divisional currency", which was stamped on the Austrian coins circulating at the time of the Lombard-Veneto kingdom (1815-1866).

339 The victim was wrapped in a blanket and then received a volley of slaps and punches.

340 General Diaz was much more attentive to the needs of the soldiers than General Cadorna, who had embodied the rigid Piedmontese military tradition all too well. Diaz worked to significantly improve the living conditions of his troops. Rations were always to arrive hot and on time, mail had to arrive punctually, clothing and linen had to be adequate. The duty shifts had to be respected: 5 days in the trenches, 5 in the first reserve line, 10 in the immediate reserves line, 20 in the rest quarters. Discipline was always present, but numerous leisure activities were allowed. In addition to the 15-day winter leave, an additional 10-day leave was introduced. Free life insurance of 500 lire for the enlisted men and 1,000 lire for the NCOs was stipulated. Promises were made (then not kept) to give land to the peasants at the end of the conflict. It is no coincidence that the new commander of the Highland Troops, General Gaetano Zoppi (1850-1948), on January 11, 1918 sent the following circular to all the dependent generals: *"There can be no certainty of leading combat troops to victory, unless their spirits are prepared to win it. The faith of the leaders must be passed on to their men, who must read in their eyes the assurance of gaining the upper hand over the enemy. Among the main duties of Commanders is to carry out this preparation of the soldiers' spirit; neglecting it is a sign of ineptitude to command. [...] Let us remember that we command men and not things."*

Chapter 3.IV

Vittarolo di Lusiana, Sunday, 20 January 1918
Today I received a postcard from Noè.
He says he's fine and hopes to see me during his winter leave.
I also hope to see him, because it will mean that I won't have lost my ID in the operation now under preparation.
Just yesterday we learned that we will have to take Monte Val Bella again.
After the artillery opens gaps in the barbed wire, we will have to storm the defensive lines and open the way for the Bersaglieri of the 5th Regiment.
The I Unit will have to do the same in Col del Rosso and Col d'Echele.
They will be reinforced by the "Sassari" infantrymen.
O'pazzo is satisfied.
«*E bersaglieri so' na garanzia. Stat tranquilli.*»
Then he tried to cheer up *Carestia*: «*Guagliò aier sera t'allucevano e'rient e mo' teni na faccia e nu muort? E bersaglieri nun sarann pugili bùoni, ma so' ottimi combattenti. Sta tranquillo.*»[341]

On Friday evening there was a bout between our boxers and those of the "Sassari" who came from their camp at Fontanelle.
Our Italo-American champion won the first match, albeit with some difficulties.
The second match was very hard-fought and frankly I can't say who deserved the victory most. The referees were also undecided. Perhaps not to disappoint our guests, who fought heroically on the Karst and recently on the Asiago plateau, they eventually awarded the victory to the Sardinian guy. This sparked the enthusiasm of the "Sassari" infantrymen and the protests of us Arditi, especially of all those who had placed bets.
Luckily it didn't end in a fight.
In practice, those who had won their bets at the first match had to return the money to the Sardinians. Me too.
In the third and last match, the boxers were two little guys.

[341] «Kid, last night your teeth were shining and now you have a droopy face. Bersaglieri may not be good boxers, but they are great fighters. Don't worry» translation from the Neapolitan dialect.

Extremely fast. Hard to count the amount of punches landed in just a few minutes, but neither of them gave in. However, during his last onslaught the Sardinian managed to plant the right *"castagna"*.[342]
Our boxer fell to his knees and was unable to get up in time.
Blood was spurting from his eyebrow.
The infantrymen of the "Sassari" exploded with joy carrying their little boxer in triumph. We had to console ours and pay the winnings to Sassari and to *Carestia,* too.
He had always bet against our three boxers!
You can tell that the bond with his fellow soldiers has remained very strong.
«Caresti', ti si fatto l'argià stasera» O'pazzo told him *«e mo' e offrì a bevr a tutta a squadra.»*[343]
He gladly paid for everybody's drinks.

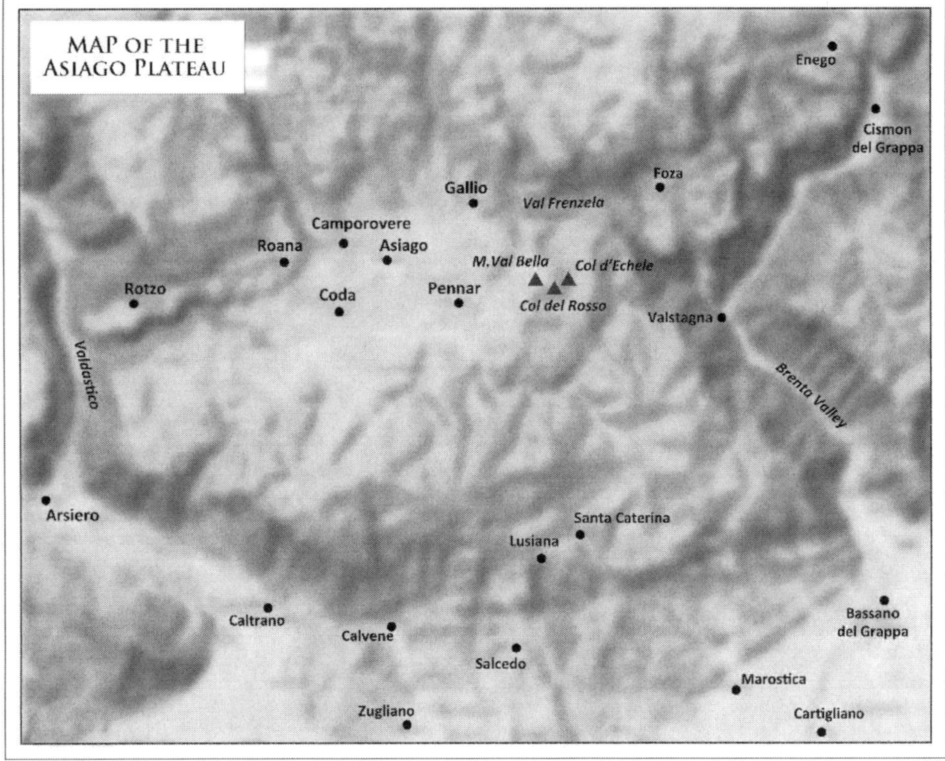

342 The equivalent of a "knockout punch".
343 «*Carestia*, you made money tonight so now you have to offer the whole squad a drink» translation from the Neapolitan dialect.

CHAPTER 4.IV

Vittarolo di Lusiana, Saturday, 26 January 1918
There is a lot of activity in our camp.
The order has arrived to get ready. We leave tonight.
«At last!» many say.
We are sick of waiting.
Those who return will go on winter leave.
Today our ration was more abundant than usual and this is a sure sign that the operation will start soon.
They gave us white coats to put over our uniforms to blend in with the snow. We have painted our helmets white.
The first to wear a white coat and helmet was *Biunnu*.
«You look like a snowman» *Mezzomago* said, to everyone's laughter.
«*Sugnu vistutu comu 'n pupo di neve, ma sugnu armatu comu 'n sarracinu*»[344] he replied, waving his bayonet in the air.
«I can give you a nice brushstroke of white on your face and moustaches too, if you want, so the *tognìt* won't see you at all in the snow» added *Pugnodiferro* jokingly.
Everyone's spirits seem high to me.
In the meantime, some of us are carefully checking their muskets, some sharpening their daggers, some smoking one cigarette after the other, some putting their things in order in the barracks.
Then there is the usual exchange of letters to be sent to the families of those who unfortunately will have to *leave their shoes in the sun*.[345]
I also exchanged letters with my squad.
I hope I can tear them to pieces after this action.
I wrote a letter to my family and that of some comrades, but I said nothing about the danger we are about to face.
We of the II Unit will have to take Monte Val Bella, together with the Bersaglieri of the 5th Regiment.
The I Unit was assigned the conquest of the two nearby hills, Col del Rosso and Col d'Echele, with the help of the "Sassari" Brigade.[346]

---

[344] «I'm dressed like a snowman, but I'm armed like a medieval knight» translation from the Sicilian dialect.
[345] It was a way of saying "to die".

Carestia and *O'pazzo* keep on debating the courage of their ex-comrades. *Carestia* prefers the support of *sos Dimonios*[347] because, according to him, they are second in value only to the Arditi.
O'pazzo tries to convince him that the Bersaglieri are the best, always after the Arditi, of course.

---

[346] At the end of the Christmas battle, on the evening of December 25, the commander of the 1st Army, General Pecori Giraldi (18 May 1856 - 15 February 1941), entrusted the Highland Troop Command to General Gaetano Zoppi, soliciting him to promptly counter-attack to regain possession of the strongholds just lost. On January 3, Zoppi summoned the commander of the XXII Corps, general Arcangelo Scotti, and the commander of the 33rd Division, general Carlo Sanna, announcing that he wanted to recapture Monte Val Bella (1,314 m.), Col del Rosso (1,281 m.), Col d'Echele (1,107 m.), Casara Melaghetto and Pizzo Razea. In addition to the tactical need to give more breath to the defensive line of the plateau, this offensive was also supposed to raise the morale of the troops and transmit a signal of renewed energy and efficiency by the Italian army to its allies. The responsibility for the operation, strictly classified in order not to alert the enemy, was entrusted to General Sanna. The preparation of the attack was very accurate. Many logistical problems due to climatic and environmental difficulties were solved. Many surveys were made to study the terrain and the enemy lines. For the first time an effort was made to co-ordinate the different branches that would participate in the action and to involve the officers up to company command. Great attention was also paid to the morale of the troops, as we can infer from the words of General Zoppi: *"Our troops have repeatedly given proof of valour and daring when prepared for battle with care by their Leaders: any failures are largely due to the inadequacy of this very important command action. [...] On your responsability, Honourable Commanders of the dependent Units, is the constant vigilance which ensures that the spirit of the troops is prepared intensely, continually, for victory: give it all your energies vitalized by the love of the Homeland, in this solemn moment of its history, in which its future will be decided".*
[347] "The Devils" in the Sardinian language. The Austro-Hungarians were very impressed by the ardent warriors of the "Sassari" Brigade when on the Karst in November 1915 it was able to conquer the trenches of the "Frasche" and "Razzi". From then on, even in official Austrian documents they were referred to as "die Rote Teufel", or the Red Devils, for the colour of their red collar stripes (in the rain the white half became reddish). In the spring 1916 the Duke of Aosta also called them "The Devils Brigade". *Dimonios* is also the title of their hymn, sung in Sardinian.

CHAPTER 5.IV

Cima Echar, Sunday, 27 January 1918, 4:00 p.m.
Last night around 7:00 p.m. we marched off.
Our spirits were high, but we were ordered not to make our usual noise and forbidden to throw petards.
Few civilians, women, old people and children waved goodbye to us.
The I Unit left shortly after.
We tramped for several hours in the snow.
The road was illuminated by the moon.
Around midnight we arrived at the Osteria del Puffele, where we picked up a good supply of petards, cartridges and cognac.
We met the infantrymen of the "Sassari".
Carestia and other Sardinians from our unit managed to greet their old comrades.
«So, did you say goodbye to all of them?» I asked him, as we resumed our march towards the Costalunga entrenchment.
«Some of them. By now there are a lot I don't know. New they are. Born in '99. They're going to get a nice baptism of fire.»
«My brother was also born in '99. But he already got baptized last fall in the Carnia zone.»
«An attack baptism is better than an escape baptism. Too bad that Sassari is not in our column» concluded *Carestia.*
"A nice baptism indeed" I thought. "Let's hope we can celebrate at the end of the battle."
A few hours later we arrived at the barracks of Cima Echar and immediately went to *feed the fleas.*[348]

The attack is scheduled for tomorrow morning.
It's supposed to be a beautiful, sunny day.
After rations, again very plentiful, we lined up in a square around our officers. Our commander, Captain Abbondanza, gave a short speech.
Here are his words.

---

[348] It means "to go to sleep" in the jargon of the Italian soldiers during WW1.

«Arditi di Sdricca! We have proved ourselves on many battlefields, from Mount San Gabriele to the Piave river. Italy expects from us another victory to be inscribed forever in history. Tomorrow we shall give it!»[349]
A roar went up from our ranks.
Then someone started to sing two new verses just composed:

Di bianco ci han vestiti,
ma siam le Fiamme Nere dei battaglioni Arditi.
Di prendere il Val Bella c'è stato comandato,
doman sicur Vittoria ci avrà incoronato.[350]

In chorus we all continued:

Bombe a man e colpi di pugnal!
Se non ci conoscete, guardateci dai passi,
siam gli Arditissimi del colonnello Bassi!
Bombe a man e colpi di pugnal!

After falling out, we met many Bersaglieri, who looked at us partly with admiration and partly with surprise at our boldness.
Pugnodiferro addressed a group of them: «Hey! *Chicchiricchì!* Stay behind us tomorrow. Don't think about those chickens. If we come back down alive I'll teach you how to catch 'em, pluck 'em and cook 'em.»
The Bersaglieri surely thought he was talking about girls, because they didn't know he was a butcher in civilian life.
Our company commanders talked us through the attack once again.
Two columns will attack the Val Bella stronghold on the right and on the left in an enveloping manoeuvre in order to make it fall from the rear.
My company will open the way for the left column, supported by the Bersaglieri of the 14th Battalion.
The command was given to a "plumed" major.
The other company will conduct the right column, followed by the Bersaglieri of the 24th Battalion.

---

[349] On January 27, General Gaetano Zoppi sent the following telegram to the commanders of the units involved in the operation: *"This operation, although not extensive, is of the utmost importance especially for obvious moral reasons. From here, once an unsurpassed barrier to the invader has been established, the germ of our vindication must take root. Both Army and Country are looking to us. Likewise, our allies, who have already conquered their laurels on our land, are looking to us. We must show ourselves their equal."*
[350] *They have dressed us all in white, but we are the Black Flames of the Arditi battalions. We are ordered to take Val Bella, surely Victory will crown us tomorrow.*

The central column is made up of another company of ours and the 46th Bersaglieri Battalion. It will enter into action when the conquest is completed, to clean up and occupy the stronghold in a stable way.
We don't understand why all the commands were given to the officers of the Bersaglieri.[351]
Some people are saying that after the victory they will be able to *far la maffia*.[352]
Since noon our artillery has been firing on the left side of Mount Val Bella in an area different from our real target. The aim is to make the *magnapapate* believe that our attack will come there.[353]

5:00 p.m.
A new order has just arrived.
Tonight we will have to move to Costalunga. We will spend the night in a cave halfway between our lines and the Austrian ones.
The attack is scheduled for tomorrow at 7:30 a.m.
May the Lord protect me this time too.

---

351 The left-hand column was commanded by Major Borghesio, the right-hand by Captain Marconi, the central one by Major Besozzi.
352 In the jargon of the trenches it means "preening".
353 At 12 o'clock the pseudo-preparation firing started, aimed at the trenches of Zocchi-Stellar and Bertigo. The objective was to divert attention from the true target of the offensive. The shelling had positive effects between Bertigo and Ronco di Carbon, a tiny inhabited area at the foot of Mount Sisemol (1,242 m.), opening up gaps for the secondary operation carried out by the Bersaglieri (20th Regiment) and by the Arditi (IV Unit, 3rd company) of Captain Ruggero Micheloni.

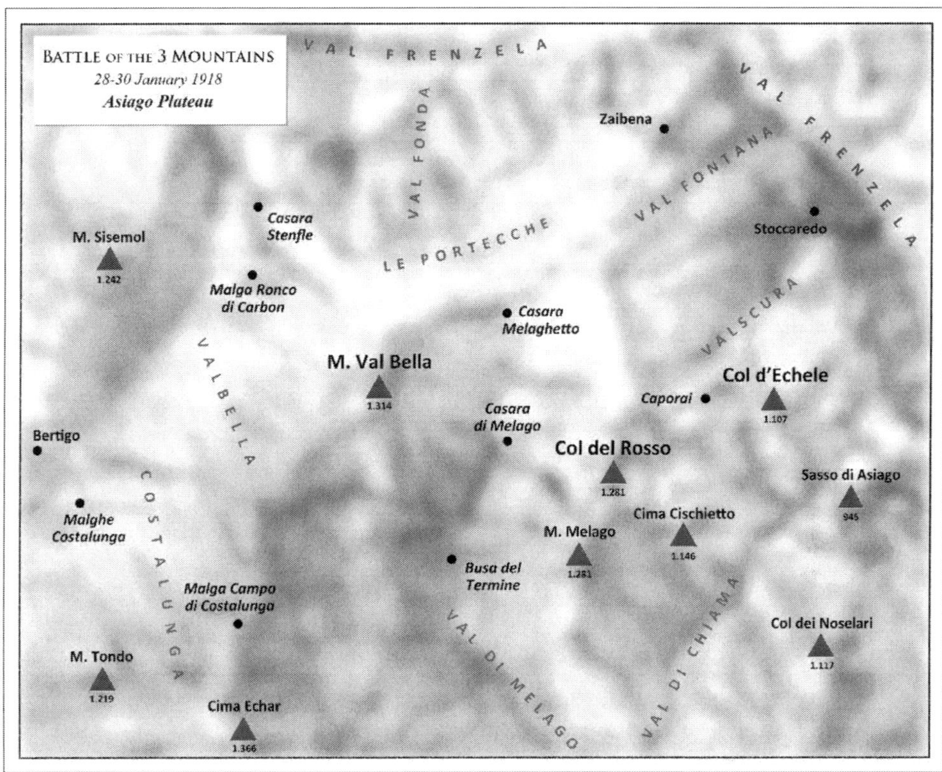

CHAPTER 6.IV

Vittarolo di Lusiana, Tuesday 29 January 1918
My ghirba is still in one piece, but...
Things didn't go the way they were supposed to.
Biunnu and *Cuteddu* are missing. I'm afraid they are dead.
O'pazzo is seriously wounded.
Carestia, *il Gat*, *Bracciodiferro* and *Pugnodiferro* are injured too.
We have had a lot of losses.
We didn't take Mount Val Bella.
Today other units will make another attempt.
I don't feel like writing anything else.

CHAPTER 7.IV

Vittarolo di Lusiana, Sunday, 3 February 1918

Almost a week has gone by since our operation on Mount Val Bella and now, with a clear mind, I can try and describe what happened.

On the morning of the 28th, we left the cave where we had spent the night under cover of darkness.

We assembled in a hollow at the foot of Val Bella ready for the assault.

At 6.30 our guns began to fire gas shells on their rearguard and then explosive shells on the strongholds of Val Bella, Col del Rosso and Col d'Echele and on the breaches where we were supposed to pass. It was a sunny day and the artillery observers could adjust their aim well.[354]

Above us a lot of Caproni flew over, going to bomb the Austrian lines.[355]

As soon as the artillery barrage moved forward, our company commander, captain Ugo Milone, gave the attack signal. We jumped towards the gaps which the shells had opened in the barbed wire.

We swooped down on the Austrian front line and swept the defenders away with petards and daggers.

On my right was *Pugnodiferro*. I saw him use his weapon in a terrifying way in a hand-to-hand combat with two mucs, who did not want to surrender. I heard the sound of their jaws being broken by his brass knuckles and then I saw the effect on those disfigured faces.

We all seemed possessed by a fierce anger, which we vented against that first group of defenders. I suppose it was the anger accumulated during that long and painful retreat from Friuli.

The *mucs* understood that and surrendered.

I am afraid, though, that some of my comrades did not stop immediately.

---

[354] The artillery deployed a large number of pieces, about 500, in relation to the limited width of the front (3 kilometres). At 6:30 a.m. gas firing started on Val Frenzela, on Stenfle and Val Kamant to prevent the arrival of reserves in support of the defenders of the three mountains. At 7:30 destructive shelling began on the strongholds and the gaps through which the attacking troops had to pass. The shelling lasted until 9:30. The results were generally positive, except on Mount Val Bella, where the imperials had found shelter in the numerous caves and tunnels previously excavated by the Italians.

[355] These were three-engine biplanes and triplanes produced by the brothers Gianni and Federico Caproni in Vizzola Ticino and Taliedo. They were the bombers most widely used by the Royal Army during the Great War.

When the Bersaglieri arrived, we stormed the second enemy line.
Here the reception was worse, because they started shooting at us as soon as we arrived. Some of us fell, but by now we were like a runaway train and they could no longer stop us.
When we jumped into the trenches the hand-to-hand was of a ferocity that I had never seen before. I believe I saved the life of more than one comrade and I believe that more than one comrade saved mine. In that confusion, anything could happen, even taking a shot or a bomb from a friend. In any case, thanks to our strength and continuous training, we emerged victorious from that deadly fight.
By the time the Bersaglieri arrived, we had already done the job and were gathering the enemy weapons and prisoners to send behind our lines.
Our white coats were all torn and dirty with mud and blood.
Carestia was bleeding from one shoulder. He hadn't been able to avoid a bayonet thrust. With great difficulty we convinced him to go back together with *il Gat*, who had taken some bomb splinters in his legs. I saw them go away holding each other up. *Carestia* was silent while *il Gat* was cursing in his dialect with every step.
I had no wounds apart from a few scratches and bruises. But my left ankle hurt like the devil. I sprained it during the scuffle. I was limping.
Reluctantly I remained among those in charge of manning the trench.
The rest of the company set off to storm the third enemy line, followed by the Bersaglieri of the 14th Battalion.
I had lost sight of Captain Milone. Later I found out that he had been hit and carried back to the cave from where we had started which was being used as a dressing station. He died in the arms of the medical officer, second lieutenant Novena. Poor captain. I will always remember him with pleasure.
Unfortunately, his death and that of many other Arditi and Bersaglieri was not crowned with victory.
All because of a red flare!
There was an agreement with the artillery on the colour of the flares.
The black smoke meant a request to move the barrage deeper into Val Frenzela. The blue smoke was deceptive, only indicating precise times.
The yellow signalled a partial failure and requested an immediate resumption of the barrage. The silver-rain flare indicated an urgent need of reinforcements. Finally, the red flare indicated that they were to stop firing on the stronghold, because our central column was breaking into the peak of Val Bella.

Well, my comrades were just beginning the attack on the third enemy line near the Stenfle wood when a red flare rose from Val Bella and the gunners immediately stopped bombing. But that flare had been thrown by the *mucs*! We do not know whether it was the work of a traitor or if, instead, it was a signal for their artillery.
The consequences for us were very serious. The *mucs* took advantage of this to emerge from their burrows dug into the rock and attack our column, trying to get around it and encircle it. As if that were not enough, on the left side we were targeted by machine guns from Mount Sisemol and by embedded rifles and artillery.
From the trench where I was, I realized that things were getting worse.
Confirmation came when the first wounded Bersaglieri began to return.
«Major Borghesio is dead!» they said, with tears in their eyes. He was the commander of the left column.
«Captain Buttà of the second company took over the command, but the attack is going horribly wrong!»
«The artillery stopped shooting too early on the target and the *tognìt* are coming out like ants from all over the mountain!»
«Platoons of Hungarians emerged from Ronco di Carbon and took us on the left!»
«Where are the Arditi?» I screamed into the face of a wounded Bersagliere.
«I don't know, Sergeant, they were ahead of us...»
I don't think I ever swore so much in my whole life.
I sent two comrades to see what was going on.
I wanted to go too, but I couldn't put any weight on my foot.
In the meantime, the Austrian artillery fire had increased and some shells were falling on the line we had conquered. A shell slaughtered a group of wounded men who were being treated.
I saw another group of Bersaglieri come running. Among them there were also some Arditi. No one from my squad.
«We are getting slaughtered out there!» one said to me. «They're shooting at us from all sides! It's suicide!»
«Why are you here and not back there fighting?» I yelled belligerently.
«They were surrounding us, sergeant. We had nothing more to lose and so we threw ourselves at a group of Austrians and we broke through. Many of our guys are either prisoners or dead by now» he replied.
His face was desperate.
A shell loaded with steel bullets exploded near us and that Ardito took two shrapnels in his body. A Bersagliere died on impact.

I assembled all the able-bodied men present in the trench and told them to go immediately in support of our comrades to avoid the humiliation of their being taken prisoner. The Arditi and Bersaglieri jumped out without making a fuss. In the meantime, a sergeant major of the Bersaglieri had sent some runners to our rear lines to communicate the situation and get new orders. Our telephone lines were unfortunately interrupted.
Shots of all kinds of weapons could be heard coming from the Stenfle ridge. As we fought in the snow, an air battle raged in the sky.
Suddenly an Austrian patrol appeared before us. They wanted to retake the trench. We mowed them all down with their own machine guns. The fact that they had arrived back where we were was a very bad signal.
Weapons in hand we were all tense, ready to shoot anyone who approached. We were fighting for our lives. If we had been attacked by a company, I don't know how long we could have resisted or how we could have lasted in hand-to-hand combat. Most of the men left in the trenches were wounded or were no longer at full strength.
I don't know how long we waited with fingers on the trigger.
It seemed like a very long time to me.
«They're coming!» someone shouted.
We aimed at an indefinite point in front of us.
"It's the end" I thought.
Instinctively I checked to see that my amulet was still in my pocket.
Many times I had asked myself how I would die. I had never imagined it could happen in the snow on a beautiful sunny day. I consoled myself with the thought that some money would come to my family now that I had taken out insurance. If I had died last year, they would have received only my death certificate and maybe my belongings.
«They're ours!» the same guy yelled, lowering his binoculars.
A great sigh of relief spread through the trench. It seemed to me that for a moment that sigh was louder than the sound of weapons. Someone blessed the Lord, someone cursed, someone coughed, everyone lit a cigarette.
We saw a group of Bersaglieri and Arditi run towards us.
Some of them were limping. In their midst I recognized the shapes of *Mezzomago*, *Bracciodiferro*, *Trepugnali, Pugnodiferro* and the two Arditi that I had sent out on reconnaissance.
When they arrived I asked about *Biunnu* and *Cuteddu*.
«I don't know where they are...» *Mezzomago* replied «...in all that confusion we split up into lots of small groups.»

«The last time I saw *Cuteddu*, he was in a shell hole, sheltering himself from machine gun shots. He was with some Bersaglieri» added *Bracciodiferro*, while being treated by *Trepugnali*. He was bleeding from one arm.

Pugnodiferro's face was a mask of dried blood.

«It's only a scratch. A sliver just grazed me. A few centimetres to the right, and I would have had my belly in the sun.»

«*Biunnu*?» I asked. Nobody answered.

«*Biunnu*?» I asked again.

«We don't know what happened to him, *Sergente*» *Mezzomago* replied.

«At one point, there were lots of shells raining down on us. Everyone was looking for shelter. Ever since then we lost sight of him.»

«But why the hell did our artillery stop firing on their lines?» *Bracciodiferro* broke in angrily. «The *magnasego* were able to crawl out of all their holes safely and counterattack us from all sides. This mountain is like swiss cheese, full of galleries and caves!»

«And with this sunny day the visibility is perfect. When I get back, I'll kill those artillery observers!» *Pugnodiferro* exploded.

The sound of a whistle interrupted us.

«Go! Go! Quick! Back to the starting line!» a Bersaglieri lieutenant shouted to everyone. The order had come to fall back.

The attack was suspended. The attack had failed.

I made the return trip by hopping on one leg. My ankle was very swollen.

We made a stop at the cave. We were looking for *O'pazzo*.

The cave echoed with moans and screams. It was full of wounded. Unfortunately, some of them had red cards[356]. Others were already dead.

There was a strong smell of medicine and blood. The earth was soaked with blood. A horrible sight: a pile of arms and legs thrown in one corner. The doctors had amputated them.

We found *O'pazzo*, just as two stretcher bearers were taking him to the field hospital. Fortunately, he had a green card. The doctors had bandaged his chest wound. He saw us and smiled.

«*Cose e' pazz*»[357] I read on his lips. I squeezed his hand.

«*Sergè, dicci a Miezzumago de fa' na magia, de famme guarì...*»[358] he managed to say, while we followed him out.

---

[356] Near the front lines, the doctors gave first aid to the wounded. Those with the red cards were judged incurable and non-transportable.

[357] «It's crazy» translation from the Neapolitan dialect.

[358] «Sergeant, tell *Miezzumago* do some magic and make me better…»

«You're lucky, my friend. Now you'll go back to Naples» *Trepugnali* said to comfort him.
«*Nun voglio tornà a casa, guagliù, voglio restà cun vuie...*»[359] these were the last words we heard him say before the stretcher bearers took him away.
Together with the other survivors, we went back to where we had started from that morning. *Trepugnali* acted as my crutch. Together with us there were *Carestia* and *il Gat*, both bandaged.
On the way back our already low mood worsened when we learned that the right column hadn't had better luck either. They too had suffered serious losses. Captain Abbondanza was among the wounded.
Once back at Cima Echar, the wounded were carried farther on to Osteria del Puffele. All the men still in one piece remained. In the afternoon, a further attack was planned with the central column, which had not gone into action.
We separated from *Trepugnali*, *Mezzomago* and *Pugnodiferro*, who, despite his head wound, insisted on staying.
Meanwhile, our artillery had resumed shelling Mount Val Bella.
Better news arrived from the I Assault Unit. Together with the "Sassari" Brigade they had succeeded in taking Col del Rosso and Col d'Echele and now they were fending off the furious counterattacks of the *mucs*.[360]
The second attack on the Mount Val Bella was launched around 4:30 p.m. when the light was already fading. The command had reinforced our troops (II Assault Unit and 46th Bersaglieri) with a company from the IV Assault Unit and a Battalion from the "Liguria" Brigade. Unfortunately, this attempt also broke down under enemy fire. Two hours later, the command suspended the attack. Thank goodness the three guys from my squad made it through with no serious damage.
While we were licking our wounds in the rear, we saw many wounded comrades from the I Unit and infantrymen from the "Sassari" pass by.
Carestia had tears in his eyes when he found out that his countryman, second lieutenant Nino Sistu, had died that morning. Always at the head of his platoon he had collapsed after his fourth wound. After what had happened to him in Vidor a lot of people thought he was immortal.

---

[359] «I don't want to go home, guys, I want to stay with you…»
[360] Despite Italian efforts to keep the operation on the "Three Mountains" secret, the Austro-Hungarians had found out about it. Skeptical at first, they became convinced after a series of clues and warning signs. They thereby decided to replace the exhausted troops on the line with fresh and combative units.

Almost all the officers of the I Unit were wounded, including its valiant commander, Major Ambrogi, ex-commander of my VI Unit at Sdricca.[361]
At least they can say they have achieved their objectives.
They captured thousands of rifles, one hundred machine guns, some trench mortars and over two thousand five hundred prisoners, including a colonel and all his officers. It was Lieutenant Alecci who caught them. Finally, two Arditi managed to shoot down a plane, which was flying low.
That same evening of the 28th they took us back to Vittarolo.
On the 29th Mount Val Bella was attacked again. This time there were no erroneous flares and the *mucs* were driven out by the Arditi, Units IV and XVI, by the Bersaglieri, 5th and 14th Regiments, and by the infantrymen of the "Bisagno" Brigade.[362]
Afterwards they had to defend the three strongholds from continuous counterattacks, with the support of the XXIV Assault Unit and the infantrymen of the "Liguria" Brigade.
In memory of this operation, I want to transcribe a portion of the order of the day released by the 33rd Division Command.
In the name of Italy, you swore to win and you have won.
In the name of Italy, with a proud and emotional heart, I thank each of you, I who was fortunate enough to command you.
Throughout the fluctuations of the struggle I followed you, hour by hour, with trepidation, but without a shadow of a doubt. As long as the fate of the battle was in your very firm hands, I was sure of success.
I know well how much it has cost. I am well aware of the heroism of the living and the dead, the zeal of the leaders and that of the wingmen, the mutual assistance that all the armed forces lent each other in the worst hours, the tireless fervour of those behind the fighters who supplied those services which in battle constitute a valuable auxiliary weapon.
There can be no gradation of heroism among you.
[...]
In this most bitter season, after a long period of struggle without joy, against an enemy to whom the excellence of the positions held, the mirage of the near plain, so sweet and rich, the pride of recent victories which he

---

361 All the commanders of the three companies were wounded: Captain Benci (1st company), Captain Càffaro (2nd company), Captain Manescalchi (3rd company), and also Lieutenants Bravi, Carpinelli, Mozzoni and Cao, commander of the Bettica section.

362 At 12.32 on 29 January, Colonel Castelli, commander of the 209th Regiment of the "Bisagno" Brigade, announced that Mount Val Bella was finally occupied. He later complained, with good reason, that he was not mentioned in the bulletin of the day, despite having played a decisive role in the success of the operation.

foolishly attributed to his own weapons, multiplying his offensive spirit and certainty of victory, you have re-established the great tradition of Italian offensives that, inch by inch, have dislodged the enemy from his formidable bulwarks.
Alongside the undaunted Italian defenders of Grappa, alongside the heroic French conquerors of Mount Tomba, today you take a radiant place acknowledged by all of Italy and specially acknowledged by our superior allied commands.
All of Italy thrills with enthusiasm and joy.
Italy sees in you combatants that neither the fiercest barbaric phalanges nor the most entrenched fortifications may halt when faith is in your hearts and the will to win the only measure of the danger to be faced.
Under these auspices, spring appears in this hard-fought circle of mountains, not as a season of dark anxiety or of turbid doubt, but as a season of florid promises for the final recovery.
Glory to all of you who sealed this augury with your heroic devotion.
Infantrymen of the Sassari Brigades (151-152), Liguria (157-158), Bisagno (209-210); Bersaglieri of the IV Brigade (Regiments 14-20) and of the 5th Regiment; Arditi of the I, II, IV, XVI, XXIV Assault Units; Alpini of the Bassano Battalion; Artillerymen of the Central and Eastern Complex; Bombardiers of the 53rd Group; Machine gunners of the Divisional Group; Soldiers of Military Engineering (VII Battalion)!
for all of you and in your name, commanders and soldiers, I know I can promise, as I promise, to the Homeland that when the time of new trials comes for Italy, from well-deserved rest, you will spring indomitable.
Long live Italy!
signed Lieutenant General Sanna [363]

I guess I haven't forgotten anything.
Here at the camp it is sad to see so many vacant beds and half-empty dormitories. Many fellow soldiers are hospitalized, buried in war cemeteries or still missing.[364]

---

[363] General Carlo Sanna (3 January 1859 - 17 July 1928) took part in many battles and victories on the Karst, in particular the conquest of the Selz hill, considered impregnable. During the Caporetto retreat, always in command of the 33rd Division, he covered the Italian withdrawal, ordering the destruction of the Pinzano bridge over the Tagliamento.
[364] "The Battle of the Three Mountains", as it was later called, cost the Italians 45 officers dead, 185 wounded and 38 missing, 15 of whom were captured; 534 soldiers died, 3,162 were wounded and 1,286 missing, of whom approximately 600 were captured. Imperial casualties are unknown.

CHAPTER 8.IV

Vittarolo di Lusiana, Monday, 11 February 1918

The cover of yesterday's issue of «La Domenica del Corriere» was dedicated to us.[365]

The illustration shows a group of Arditi, led by Lieutenant Alecci, bursting into a refuge on Mount Val Bella and capturing an Austrian colonel and all his officers.

«It doesn't look like the lieutenant at all» said *Pugnodiferro*, as he carefully examined the newspaper. «If I were him I would go and protest, also because they coloured his flames crimson instead of black.»

«The artist didn't have his photograph» said *Mezzomago*.

«If they put me on the cover, I'm going to Milan to have my portrait drawn by that artist, even with my head all bandaged, like now. And the flames have to be black!» replied *Pugnodiferro*.

Even if the illustration does not resemble Lieutenant Alecci and does not have the right colour flames, we are deservedly satisfied since the Commander of the 33rd Division has completely forgotten about us.

On February 3 he organized a military parade in Vicenza.

He had the "Sassari" march with their wounded at its head.

But we were the ones at the head of the attack columns on 28 and 29!

We weren't very happy that they didn't invite us.

"There can be no gradation of heroisms among you."

So General Sanna wrote in his order of the day.

And instead…

Carestia pointed out to us that the general is Sardinian.

«Then he should have had you and the other Sardinians from the Black Flames march too!» *Mezzomago* replied.

«They did not forget to invite us. They didn't want us there!» I said.

«The proof is that a few days later they honoured the Bersaglieri. Then on February 7 they sent the "Sassarini" to parade in front of General Diaz!» [366]

---

[365] The colour plates of *"La Domenica del Corriere"* showed the Italians the main events of the war. Thanks to an innate imagination, combined with rigorous realism, the author, Vicenza-born Achille Beltrame, managed to effectively represent places and characters, which he had never seen in person and without ever moving from Milan.

«They're afraid of us, *Sergente*» said *Trepugnali*.
«In fact, you'll be facing twenty years in jail if you get out alive» *Mezzomago* replied.
«*Chèsto l' völ dì èss invidiùs, ve l' dighe mé*» added *il Gat*.
«*I gh'à pura che m' ghe pórte vià i fómne.*»[367]
«Fear and envy. Who knows what will become of us at the end of the war?» I thought out loud.
«*Quando la fenirà sta guèra i ghe darà 'l congé e m' turnerà a cà a laurà la tèra*»[368] said *il Gat*.
«Go work your land and fatten up your cows. Then I'll take care of skinning and cutting them up» said *Pugnodiferro*.
«I meant to say what will become of us Arditi» I specified.

---

[366] In three years of war it had never happened that the troops were paraded in triumph through the streets of a city centre amid the jubilation of the population. This was so exceptional that the *"Gazzettino"*, the main newspaper of the region Veneto, published the event on its front page. On 3 February, the commander of the 1st Army, General Pecori Giraldi, welcomed the "Sassari". On the 7th the Chief of Staff, General Armando Diaz, attended the parade. In in his brief speech he said: *"You do not know, and perhaps you will never know, what you have done for Italy."*

[367] «This means they're envious, I tell you. They are afraid that we will take their women away» translation from the Bergamo dialect.

[368] «When this war ends, they will discharge us and I'll go home to work the land.»

CHAPTER 9.IV

Vittarolo di Lusiana, Thursday, 14 February 1918
This morning a miracle took place!
The door to our barrack opened and *Cuteddu* appeared!
We were all speechless for a few seconds.
«Salvatore, is that you?» someone managed to say.
He nodded slightly. That was the signal to gather around him, hug him and squeeze his hands, one of which was bandaged. He stood there almost impassively. His face was even more hollow than usual.
However, despite the severity of his features, I seemed to glimpse a bit of joy in him to be here with us again.
«Where the hell have you been?» *Pugnodiferro* came out point-blank.
«Are you okay, Salvatore?» I asked him.
He shook his head in the affirmative as he sat down on a cot with difficulty. We and all the others in the barrack gathered around him waiting for him to say something.
His black eyes fixed us one by one.
«*Biunnu muriu*»[369] he hissed, clenching his jaws.
«*A m' pensàa che te födèsset crepàt pò a' té*»[370] *il Gat* replied.
«*'un sugno muorto. Ora aiu a vindicari macari a iddu.*»[371]
Trepugnali asked the questions we all wanted to ask him:
«What happened to you in that shell hole? Where have you been till now?»
With patience, little by little, we managed to elicit his words and reconstruct the events.
While he was taking cover from artillery fire in the shell hole with the Bersaglieri, a very large shell arrived. He only remembers a deafening noise and then nothing more. When he woke up it was already dark, but he couldn't move. His arms and legs were paralyzed. He felt a great weight on top of him. He didn't know if he was alive or dead. The "ta-pum" sound of Austrian rifles convinced him that he was still on this earth, buried among the corpses of men who had been with him in that hole. He couldn't tell if he was wounded.

---

369 «Biunnu is dead» translation from the Sicilian dialect.
370 «We thought you had kicked the bucket too» translation from the Bergamo dialect.
371 «I am not dead. Now I have to avenge him too» translation from the Sicilian dialect.

Slowly he tried to create spaces in the mass of bodies, dirt, snow, stones and to move his hands, arms and legs. This was also difficult because he could no longer feel the fingers of his left hand.
After much effort he managed to slide out of that grave.
His chest was hurting badly. He couldn't tell, though, if he had been hit.
His uniform was completely encrusted with frozen blood.
He didn't know what time it was, only that it was dark and cold.
Inch by inch he crawled over to a big rock. To protect himself from the cold, he removed the greatcoat from the body of an enemy and used it as a blanket. Luckily, he had a flask of cognac and some chocolate with him. He fell asleep not knowing whether he would wake up the next day.
He was awakened instead by our artillery, in preparation for the second attack on Mount Val Bella. Fortunately, the barrage did not strike the ground where he was hidden.
When he saw our troops chasing the Austrians, he got up and made himself known by waving a white handkerchief. His luck held a second time, because none of the Arditi from the 2nd company of the IV, shot at him, even though it might have been one of the enemy's usual vile tricks. Sometimes the *mucs* pretend to surrender. As we get closer, other ones pop out from behind them shooting at us and throwing hand grenades.
They accompanied him to the rear lines with an advanced case of frostbite in his feet and hands and then to a field hospital. No gunshot wounds, but some broken ribs and he is deaf in one ear. Today they sent him back to our unit.
He told us he saw *Biunnu* hit in full by a shell.
There was nothing of him left to send to his family.
A great sadness had fallen on us at the thought of *Biunnu*.
Then *Cuteddu* asked us a question: «*Unne sta 'u napuletano?*»[372]
«He's the smartest of us all» I replied. «He's having fun with the Red Cross nurses at the Verona hospital.»
«He got a ball in his chest» said *Carestia*.
Cuteddu surprised us with a wry comment, which we would never have expected from him: «*S'u pigghiava n'anticchia cchiù vasciu, avia picca rifari u gallettu chi fimmine.*»[373]
Life goes on.

---

[372] «Where is the Neapolitan?»

[373] «If he had been hit a little further down, he wouldn't playing the cockerel with women.»

CHAPTER 10.IV

Vittarolo di Lusiana, Friday, 15 February 1918
Tomorrow we set off for our winter leave.
Fifteen days of rest after much fatigue.
I haven't seen my family in over a year.
A lot of things have happened in these thirteen months!
The Battle of Bainsizza, the Arditi School in Sdricca, our retreat over the Piave river, the fight on Mount Val Bella.
I thank heavens and my mother's amulet that things have always gone well for me.
But for how long?
The war will not be over for a long time.
Meanwhile I will enjoy my leave.
But my heart aches at the thought of not being able to go back to my own home.
Who knows how badly those barbarians have treated it?
Instead of going east, I will have to take the troop train along with the men going south. Luckily, I will get off in Florence. I do not envy those who have to go even further south, especially the Venetians and the Friulans whose families are refugees in Campania, Puglia, Calabria and, even worse, in Sicily. It is a very long journey.
We were told that we must relinquish all our weapons before leaving.
New regulations.
That's all right for petards and muskets, but none of us intends to leave his dagger behind. It's like a brother.
I hope I won't meet many *imboscati* in Florence, because I would certainly be tempted to use it.

CHAPTER 11.IV

On the troop train to Florence, Saturday, 16 February 1918

Stopover in Bologna.

There were many people on the platform waiting for the train to arrive.

Some soldiers got off, but the train is still crowded.

Whole cars are occupied by the Arditi of the I, II, IV, XVI and XXIV Units, all veterans of the recent battle.

We sang our entire repertoire.

If there had been any petards, they would have surely been thrown.

During the journey two *Caproni* opened the door of our compartment to check documents. When they saw us they immediately did an about-face.

We yelled all kinds of insults, but it could have gone much worse for them.

In my carriage there were some Black Flames of the I Unit.

They told me what happened in Col del Rosso.

They attacked about half an hour after we did. So they could see the beginning of our right column's attack on Mount Val Bella.

After getting through the gaps in the barbed wire, their 2nd company headed straight for Casara Melaghetto, while the 3rd company went up the western slopes of Col del Rosso.

«Their front line was still dazed from the shelling. We overwhelmed them and took them prisoners» said a corporal of the 2nd company. «The trouble came later, when their artillery, but also ours, rained shells on our heads! We lost quite a few men. Captain Càffaro climbed a tree and began shaking the red disc to signal our observers to lengthen their aim.

We went forward in that hell all the same. We went through a small wood. Some trees were burning. In that wood, many *tognìt* had flattened themselves into holes and were shooting at us. We flushed them out one at a time. Some surrendered, others were killed on the spot. In the fight our captain was shot in the arm. Austrians who had surrendered carried him back to our lines. We kept going, led by Lieutenant Bertoni. The Sardinians had the guts to come after us. Even though their commander was already knocked out. They weren't shouting "Avanti Savoia!", but "Avanti Sardegna!". Many of them were born in '99. [374]

---

[374] It was the 2nd Battalion of the 151st Regiment.

The worst of it was when we arrived near Casara Melaghetto. There were many machine gun nests. They were firing at us from some positions on the Mount Val Bella too.»
«At least you were on the flat ground. We had to attack the trenches by running uphill in the midst of machine gun fire and shelling, including our own. May God strike them dead!» a sergeant from the 3rd company intervened. «The snow was all stained with blood. That blood gave us even more energy, though. Throwing petards, we managed to enter the trenches and here we put our daggers to work. In one trench we came face to face with *Stürmtruppen*. "We couldn't wait to see you" we yelled at them. It was a fight to the death. One of them almost gouged out my eye. But I stuck my dagger in his throat first while we were rolling on the ground. I don't know about you, but in moments like those I feel an enormous strength...
We were howling like wolves. In another trench there was a group of Romanians. As soon as they saw us, they raised their hands. At one point we were attacked on the right side, which had remained unguarded. Luckily, the submachine gun section intervened and sprayed them pretty good.»
The sergeant took a little red horn from his pocket and kissed it. It is his amulet.
«Not to brag, Sergeant, but that day I killed more with my dagger. Look here at the notches on the handle» the corporal of the 2nd entered the conversation.
«Very good, corporal, but one *Stürmtruppen* is worth ten of yours!» the sergeant replied, frowning.
«What happened next?» I asked to interrupt the macabre contest.
«We split up into two groups...» the corporal tried to continue, but a nasty look from the sergeant immediately silenced him.
«We kept climbing. We left the task of cleaning up the trenches to our Sassari chums»[375] continued the sergeant. «The artillery continued to target us. Both explosive and shrapnel shells. One of the countless splinters, which were whining close to us, pierced Captain Manescalchi's helmet. He continued to lead the attack as if nothing had happened, but blood started dripping from his head leaving a red trail behind. After a while he collapsed and we sent him back down. We continued the climb to attack the ridge line. There was a lot of resistance. There were many *"squarciaossa"*. At one point the *magnasego* emerged from their trenches yelling "hurrà! hurrà!" and they counterattacked us with their bayonets.

[375] It was the 3rd Battalion of the 151st Regiment.

That was their biggest mistake.
In close combat they can hope for a lucky hit, but otherwise there is no comparison. We know how to dodge their lunges and stick our daggers in their side or neck. And if you have too many in front of you, throw a petard in the middle, jump on 'em and kill'em one by one. Often it works. I have to say that in that fray the Sassari seemed to me to be doing very well.
Even the young recruits are far from being *piscialettos*.[376]
Seeing that things were going badly for them, the *tognìt* turned on their heels and ran back to their trenches, but they did not have time to rally, because we were already on them. So they ran toward the other side of the mountain. We shot many of them as they ran away. Finally, we were at the top of Col del Rosso. It must have been eleven o'clock.
Meanwhile shells were criss-crossing over our heads; ours on the way to their rear line at Stoccaredo, Zaibena and Sorgente and theirs heading to our lines. Dammit! More than one shell fell on us!
We realized that the mountaintop was not yet completely cleaned out. They were still shooting at us from some trenches up ahead. A bullet hit Lieutenant Carpinelli, who had taken command of the company, in the hand. He bandaged it and then led the assault. Another ball hit him in the chest. He had to stop. Others were hit, but our charge didn't halt. Our machine gunners sprayed the trenches, until we were a few metres away. At that point we threw petards and threw ourselves at them. We liquidated the ones who resisted, the others raised their hands and we went them back to the starting line right away. Meanwhile, the sappers had come to turn the trenches and the Sassarini to occupy them.»
«Tell me about Lieutenant Alecci.»
«Alecci? Alecci made a great catch. He had gone with his men to patrol the area. And there he found an entire regimental command holed up in a cave. A *fifàus*. We saw that Colonel pass by with all his medals and the train of his officers. We jeered at him.
Around 2:00 p.m. their artillery began to shell heavily on the positions we had conquered. Lord, strike them all dead!
When they started to lengthen their shots, we understood that they wanted to counterattack with their Infantry. Let them come, we said.
The machine guns, ours and theirs, were already all aimed. Lieutenant Bravi was leading them. Did you hear that later he was wounded in the lower belly?

---

376 A term indicating people without experience. There was a song that said: *"To piss us off, Cadorna sent us the class of '98, still pissing their beds."*

They must have heard us because they did come, and lots of them. *Stürmtruppen*. They emerged from everywhere, from the rocks, from the shrubbery, from the paths. This time we did the target shooting for quite a while. Until the "Fix bayonets" order rang out. We put our bayonets in place and charged, hurling our last petards.

What a fight! Violent, very violent.

The only *tognìt* who did not surrender were on the ground either dead or wounded. A couple of them, however, ran away. They chased them as far as Stoccaredo, already destroyed by our bombing, almost to Zaibena. But then the patrols had to return due to the critical situation at Mount Val Bella. By the way what happened to you that day?»

«Excuse me, but I hadn't finished my story...» the corporal intervened, before I could answer the sergeant's question.

The nasty look, which we both shot him, shut him up once again.

«On board! The train is leaving!» the conductor started yelling.

We all got back on board at the sound of the stationmaster's whistle.

While our train rattled towards Florence, I explained in detail how things had gone, or rather, how they hadn't gone there on Mount Val Bella.

CHAPTER 12.IV

Florence, Sunday, 17 February 1918
Nobody was waiting for me in Florence.
I hadn't written that I be arriving. I wanted surprise my family.
Instead, the surprise was on me. And more than one.
After saying goodbye to my fellow soldiers who got off in Florence, I went to look for the house where my family is staying.
It was not difficult to find it since it is close to the station.
It is a large apartment building for railway workers.
In the courtyard and on the street there were many children playing despite the cold. They were speaking in Friulan.
When they saw me arrive, they ran away to hide, all except the three older ones, who came close to stare.
They were thin and poorly dressed.
«*Di dunà seiso?*»[377] I asked.
«*Tumieç*»[378] replied the boy who looked like the leader of the gang.
«*Ancje iò*»[379] added another.
«*E tu di dunà setu?*» I asked the third. «*Âtu pierdût la lenghe?*»[380]
«*Iò sei di Sclûse*»[381] he replied, looking down at the ground.
«*Sacrabold! No ti ài mai viodût a Sclûse. Di ce famee setu?*»[382]
«*Iò sei fì dal Miro, ma cumò gno pari al è in vuere in tai alpins.*»[383]
«*Dunà ch'a son in cheste cjase chei di Dogne?*»[384] I asked him.
I assumed that everyone knew each other among refugees.
«*A son su al tierç plan.*»[385]
«*Bon. Cjape chi e mangje cun la mularie.*»[386]
I left them sharing a chocolate bar and raced up to the third floor.

---

377 «Where are you from» translation from the Friulan language.
378 «Tolmezzo.»
379 «Me too.»
380 «And where are you from? Have you lost your tongue?»
381 «I am from Chiusa Forte.»
382 «Good heavens! I have never seen you in Chiusa Forte. What family are you from?»
383 «I am the son of Miro, but now my father is at war in the Alpini.»
384 «Where are the ones from Dogna staying in this house?»
385 «They are up on the third floor.»
386 «Good. Take this and eat it with the other children.»

I knocked on one of the two doors on the landing.
«*Cui isal?*»[387]
I recognized my sister Margherita's voice.
«*I' sei il plevan. Ch'a mi viergj la puarte, siore*»[388] I replied, to tease.
I was happy to see them again.
When the door opened, I saw my sister's face light up.
However, I had a bad feeling.
«*Benedet il Signôr! Al è rivât Pieri, gno fradi, vignêit a viodi*»[389] she began to shout, almost crying, and threw her arms around my neck.
As I entered, I realized that it was almost as cold as outside in the flat.
In the darkness of the corridor I saw a woman come out of a room with one child in her arms and another one attached to her skirt. I did not know her.
My sister Attilia came out of another room and ran to meet me.
«*Dunà ch'a son ducj?*»[390] I asked.
«*Lusiute e Matiuti son malats, biadins. No sintitu rucâ? Mame a è lade a fâ la spese. Mabile a è a lavorâ e i fantats son atôr*»[391] so Attilia gave me the picture of the situation, while dragging me into the room from she had just left. That room was a bivouac!
The floor was covered with mattresses, blankets, sheets, a few pillows, boxes and suitcases, scattered clothes.
Under a pile of blankets were little Lucia and Mattia, both with colds and sickly-looking. They barely greeted me.
My sisters didn't look so good either.
«*Seiso ducj in chest canìz?*»[392] I asked fearing the answer.
They nodded their heads with a resigned expression.
«*E che femine cui puès cui isale?*»[393] I continued.
My sisters explained the situation to me. The whole building had been made available to refugees with two or even three families housed in each flat. In the other room of this flat there is a family from Collina.
Eight people in my family and six other people in such a small space!
I will have to find another place to sleep.
But that's not the worst.

---

[387] «Who is it?» translation from the Friulan language.
[388] «I'm the parish priest. Open the door for me, Signora.»
[389] «Lord be blessed! Pietro, our brother, has arrived. Come and see.»
[390] «Where are all the others?»
[391] «*Lusiute and Matiuti* are sick, poor things. Can't you hear them coughing? Mum went shopping. Amabile is at work and the kids are around somewhere.»
[392] «Are you all living in this messy room?»
[393] «And who is the woman with the children?»

The rooms are not heated.
The kitchen is shared and the fire is only used for cooking, what little they manage to put together.
The allowance which my family receives is just 5 lire a day. Food is scarce due to the war and prices have increased very steeply. With that money they can buy very little. Some savings come from my father.
I've always sent money, too. I don't know about Noè.
Living in the city costs much more than in Dogna, where we had our vegetable garden and animals.
Fortunately, Amabile has managed to find a job and bring home some money. Our mother is not shopping; she is queuing for the ration of bread, rice, cornmeal and perhaps milk.
They took me to see the kitchen. Small. They have to take turns.
My eyes fell on a shelf. I saw a tin can, which, unfortunately, I know well.
It is the "Torrigiani" sauce. Our military cooks always put it on pasta or overcooked rice. Disgusting. Among us soldiers we often guess which ingredients they throw in to make it so disgusting.
«*Dipo, mangjaso ancje vou che ròibate?*»[394] I asked in amazement.
Margherita's answer surprised me even more:
«*Ce po. A lu puarte Mabile ch'a lavore là.*»[395]
Unbelievable! My sister works at the Torrigiani plant in Sesto Fiorentino! She works in the factory that produces one of the things most detested by us soldiers. I better not tell anyone.
Today there were lots of surprises and each one worse than the other.
They introduced me to the other family. They speak a slightly different Friulan than ours. All the words end with "o" even if they are feminine, but we understand each other.
«*Ancjo il gno omp al è in vuero*» Signora Angela said to me, «*ma al è un grum di timp ch'al no mando uno cartulino o uno lètaro. Jo soi preocupado. Jo o voi ogni dì in te glisio a preâ par lui.*»[396]
«*Ch'a no steti a preocupâsi. Forsit il so omp al scriv alc ch'a no plâs a la censure e las sôs lètares a no pàssin.*»[397]
After trying to reassure the woman, I asked Attilia to accompany me to the ration point. I wanted to surprise our mother.

---

394 «Tell me, do you eat that junk too?» translation from the Friulan language.
395 «Sure. Amabile brings it. She works there.»
396 «My husband is also at war, but he hasn't sent a postcard or letter for a long time. I'm worried. I go to church every day to pray for him.»
397 «Don't worry. Probably your husband writes things that don't pass the censors and so they block his letters.»

As we were walking along, she noticed that I was limping a little.
«*Ce âtu, Pieri? A mi par che tu clopis.*»[398]
«*O ài chjapât une stuarte gjuand di balòn*»[399] I lied to her.
«*Veiso timp di gjuâ di balòn?*»[400] she asked me, surprised.
«*Cepo, no traìn migo ogni dì*»[401] I replied.
At the ration point there was a long line of people.
While we were looking for our mother, someone started to protest because we were not queuing. As I turned around to see who it was, he immediately stopped yelling. Nevertheless, I heard the words "Arditi", "dangerous" and "dagger" whispered among the people.
We continued the search until we found her.
I went to stand by her side in silence. She slowly turned her head.
«*Ioi! Ce fâtu chi? Metiti in code ancje tu, si tu vûs vêi la ròibe*»[402] she said seriously.
I would have liked to embrace her, but I didn't, because I know she wouldn't have appreciated it on the street in the presence of strangers.
She went on: «*Si no tu âs la tesare, alore no stâ chi. Va a bevi alc e spietimi a cjase.*»[403]
«*Bon. Mandi mame, si viodin daurman*»[404] I whispered in her ear, taking leave.
As we retraced our steps, I again heard the words "Arditi", "dangerous" and "dagger", but also the word "Austrians" whispered among the people.
I asked Attilia why she or Margherita don't go to queue instead of our mother.
«*A vûl lâ iei. A è di bande insisti*»[405] she replied. I know very well that when our mother decides to do something it's useless to object.
«*Âtu sintût ce che nus àn dit?*»[406] Attilia asked me.

---

[398] «What's wrong, Pietro? You seem to be limping» translation from the Friulan language.
[399] «I turned my ankle playing football.»
[400] «You have time to play football?»
[401] «Of course, we don't shoot every day.»
[402] «What are you doing here? If you want to get food you have to queue like everyone else.»
[403] «If you don't have a ration card, then don't stay here. Go have a drink and wait for me at home.»
[404] «All right. Bye, mom, see you soon.»
[405] «She wants to go. It is useless to insist.»
[406] «Did you hear what they said?»

«Arditi, dangerous, dagger and Austrians. They're right. We Arditi are dangerous with our daggers for the Austrians» I replied with a smile on my lips.
«Chjale che su disin a nou chi sin todescs!»[407]
«Ce disino? Chi sin todescs? Nou?»[408]
I could not believe it.
«Par lôr ducj i profugos a son todescs, ancje chei ch'a vegnin di Trevîs e di Vigneisie.»[409]
I could hardly believe such an absurdity.
«A dìsin ancje ch'a è colpe nestre par la vuere e parcè ch'al è pouc di mangjâ.»[410]
My surprise turned to anger. The blood rushed to my head.
I remember that my hand instinctively searching for my dagger.
Luckily, I had left it in my backpack.
«Cui ch'al dîs chestis monadis?»[411]
«Ducj!»[412]
I was furious.
My family had to flee from their home, I have risked my life many times for these people. And they think that my family and I are Austrians?
It makes me furious even now to think about it.
Attilia took me by the arm and tried to calm me down, but she failed.
Nobody can calm my anger.
«Sumo, Pieri, anin a cjase a viodi si son rivâs i fantats.»[413]
In order not to think about what she had just told me, I tried to concentrate on a small problem, that of where to sleep: *«Prime o ài di cirî un puest par durmî cheste gnot. Cognostu qualchidun ch'al fite une cjamare ca atôr?»*[414]
Attilia took me to a guest house near their home.
«Nine lire a night» said the landlord. «But since you're a soldier, I'll let you pay seven lire and fifty cents.»
I know I was rude, but I could not help saying nastily: «Do you know how much the army pays me a day to defend your room and your ass? One lira

---

407 «Look, they say we're Austrians» translation from the Friulan language.
408 «What are they saying? That we are Austrians? Us?»
409 «For them all refugees are Austrians, even those who come from Treviso and Venice.»
410 «They also say that we are to blame for the war and for the scarcity of food.»
411 «Who says this nonsense?»
412 «Everybody!»
413 «Come on, Pietro, let's go home and see if the boys have arrived.»
414 «First I have to find a place to sleep tonight. Do you know someone who rents rooms around here?»

and eighty-nine cents! *Camorrista*! Crook! You should be ashamed of exploiting our misfortune!»
«*Brut slavrât! Brut slambèrc!*»[415] Attilia doubled the dose before we left, even if that filthy individual could not understand her words.
After walking around for a long time, we found an old woman who rented me a shabby room for four lire.
Tomorrow I will go and find a place in one of the barracks. I know there are many in Florence.
When we got home, our mother had already returned.
I was finally able to hug her.
«*Ce bere chi tu as. An rot las fuarfis? Tu sês avonde ben*»[416] she said, looking me up and down.
«*No pos dî il stes di vou*»[417] I replied frankly.
«*Ce vino di fâ? Mangjâ a l'è pouc par ducj e di gracie ch'a nu su àn dât cheste cjamare.*»[418]
As we were talking about the situation, loud noises could be heard in the corridor. Agostino and Girardo were returning home. As soon as they saw me, they were speechless. I didn't have time to say: «*Veiso pierdût la lenghe?*»[419] before they were all over me already and full of questions.
«*Dunà âtu il curtìs di Ardît?*»[420]
«*Tros mucs âtu copât?*»[421]
«*Âtu cjapât une medae d'aur?*»[422]
They have grown taller, but they are thinner, too. I calmed them with a few pats on their heads. Their heads are shaved and their clothes are ragged. Both have bruises and scratches on their faces.
«*Ce veiso fat ai cjavei?*»[423]
«*Avevin cjapât i pedoi*»[424] replied Attilia for them.
«*E ce veiso fat in ta muse? Su a sgrifignât un gjàt?*»[425]

---

[415] «You pig! You slime!» translation from the Friulan language.
[416] «What a mop. Did the scissors break? Anyway, you look pretty good.»
[417] «I can't say the same about you.»
[418] «What can we do? there is little for everybody to eat and thank heavens they gave us this room.»
[419] «Have you lost your tongue?»
[420] «Where's your Ardito knife?»
[421] «How many Austrians did you kill?»
[422] «Did you get a gold medal?»
[423] «What have you done to your hair?»
[424] «They had lice.»
[425] «And what did you do to your face? Did a cat scratch you?»

Agostino replied: «*Che altre dì i vin begherât cui fruts di cà. A nus disevin chi sin todescs...*»[426]
«*Canàes! A mi somee che li veis cjapades. Cjale ce carùmbules e ce sgarazàdes!*»[427]
«*Cjapades, ma ancje dades di buines.*»[428]
«*O ài rot un dint a un di lôr, un palòt*» Girardo whispered proudly, «*ma no stâ dîlu a mame.*»[429]
«*Une dì o che altre scugnarìn lâ a cjatâiu in presòn*»[430] sighed Margherita, looking at them sideways.
As they loudly protested their right to defend themselves from the slander of being German, I heard Lusiute's voice come out of a pile of blankets: «*Cuand tornino a cjase, Pieri?*»[431]
I wish I knew.
I sat down beside her and tried to give her some hope: «*Chest an di sigûr, stelòn. Tu intant viôd di guarî*» and also a little satisfaction: «*Ce biele fantate che tu ses deventade.*»[432]
She is not even nine years old.
«*E iò?*» asked Matiuti, who is the same age.
«*Fati viodi. Ioi! Ancje tu tu ses deventât un biel fantat.*»[433]
Then I made everyone happy by pulling sticks of chocolate, bread, biscuits and tins of meat out of my backpack.
While we ate, they told me about the vicissitudes of their journey by cart from Dogna to Florence and the problems they found down here. My mother and father thought that as refugees they would have been better off in Florence, since all the administrative offices of the Friulan municipalities have moved here. Instead, the treatment is not good. Committees and patronages make lots of promises, but few facts. People are hostile. There is little work. It is a miracle that Amabile found a paying job. Too bad she works in that dump.

---

426 «The other day we had a scuffle with the guys here. They said we are Germans...» translation from the Friulan language.
427 «Scoundrels! It seems to me that you took a beating. Look at those lumps and scratches!»
428 «We gave as good as we took.»
429 «I broke a tooth of one of them, an incisor, but don't tell mom» translation from the Friulan language.
430 «Someday we we'll be going to visit them in prison.»
431 «When are we going home, Pietro?»
432 «This year for sure, lovey. Meanwhile, you try to get better. What a beautiful girl you have become.»
433 «Let's see. You too have become a handsome boy.»

Given the situation, my father returned to Switzerland to work. At least he sends some money. If it is so bad here in Florence, I dare not imagine what the situation of those poor refugees in the south is like.
For my part, I told them everything I could say to a mother and siblings.
I talked a lot about the Sdricca School and little about the war, even if Agostino and Girardo wanted to know more.
When Amabile returned from work we played a joke on her. Everyone played dumb. Quietly, I got behind her. Then everyone started staring at her, eyes wide and open-mouthed.
She looked at them in amazement.
As soon as she turned around and saw me, she gave a shriek of fright, amid general laughter.
«*Rochel! Vustu fâmi murî di spavent?*»[434]
«*E tu? Vustu fâmi murî cun che ròibate che tu metis in tal sugo?*»[435] I replied, referring to the "Torrigiani" sauce.
We should use it to poison the Austrians!
«*Iò? Chjale che iò tai carotis e speli cartufulis dute il dì.*»[436]
I realized that she was giving off the same smell as the sauce.
While she was eating, I had to tell my story again, adding some new details, since everyone was still there to listen. Then she told me about her job, underpaid, and what she sees in that factory.
If I had doubts before about that sauce, I now have certainties.
Before I left them to go to bed, my mother nodded to Agostino, who brought me a suitcase and said: «*Al è alc par te.*»[437]
Everyone was watching me. When I opened the suitcase, I felt my heart fill with joy. I almost fainted. I couldn't have had a better surprise: there were all my books by Salgari and Verne! I thanked everyone for the efforts they had made to bring those books to safety.
«*Crodevi che i mucs ju vessin usâts par impiâ il fûc o netâsi il...*»[438] I stopped concluding the sentence just in time. Despite everything, I was in a house and not in a barracks.
«*Al è ancjemò alc*»[439] said my mother.
From under an old blanket Margherita pulled out an accordion.
It was the sergeant's!

---

[434] «Stupid! Do you want make me die of fright?» transl. from the Friulan language.
[435] «And you? Do you want to make me die from all the junk you put in that sauce?»
[436] «Me? Look, I cut carrots and peel potatoes all day long.»
[437] «Here's something for you.»
[438] «I thought the Austrians would have used them to light the fire or wipe their...»
[439] «There is something else.»

Now I'm in this rented room.

Shabby. Cold. But at least there is an oil lamp and so I was able to write down all the events of today.

The surprise of the books and accordion was beautiful.

The family's conditions, however, are a bad surprise, one which I wasn't expecting.

The worst part is that I don't know how to help them.

Chapter 13.IV

Florence, Thursday, 21 February 1918
I solved the problem of the night.
I looked in on every barracks in Florence, until I found a bed to sleep in.
At least I won't get fleeced by those greedy landlord bastards.
These days I always accompany my mother and sisters when they leave the house. So, when they see my black flames, ignorant people avoid insulting them. I also accompany my brothers to school. Their Florentine peers have stopped calling them Austrians. I hope it will last even when I am no longer with them.
Today I went to the station. *Pugnodiferro* was supposed to arrive. He lives just outside Florence. When he got off the troop train, he was very happy to see me. On the sleeve of his tunic he wears the badge for war wounds and on his right temple a clearly visible scar. No less visible is the dagger he carries in his belt, even if it is forbidden on leave.
«So, *Sergente*, do you like Florence?» he asked me immediately.
«I like Florence, but I don't like a lot of the Florentines.»
«Come on, why? A few are *grulli*[440], but the others aren't bad.»
I explained to him the unfortunate situation of the refugees, who, as *O'pazzo* would say, find themselves *"cornuti e mazziati"*.[441]
«*Sergente*, tell me who these people are and I'll smash their faces.»
«There are many of them, too many. You would break your hands.»
«*Imboscati*? I'd be happier to break their noses.»
«No. I've seen lots of them around, but it's not them. These are women, children, old folks.»
«I can't believe it. The people of Florence are nice.»
«Maybe they were nice before the war. Now they are nasty and ignorant.»
While we were talking, just outside the station we were stopped by two *Caproni*. They wanted to check our documents. I handed them mine.
Pugnodiferro, on the other hand, let his document drop to the ground.
«Pick it up, private, and show it to me» one of them said.
«I am wounded. I can't bend over. Don't you see the badge on my arm, Mister Carabiniere?» he replied with artificial courtesy.

---

[440] Typical Florentine word for idiot.
[441] The English equivalent is "insulted and injured".

«Then ask your partner to help you, private.»
«He is a sergeant. I am a private. I can't give him orders.»
At which the other Carabiniere bent down and picked up the document. He studied it carefully, hoping that some stamps were missing, but it was all in order, so he reluctantly handed it back to him. It wasn't over yet.
«Private, you know you can't go around wearing that dagger?» the first *Caprone* started up again.
«The dagger is part of the Ardito's uniform, Mister Carabiniere.»
«Hand it over, please.»
From his expression, I realized that *Pugnodiferro* was about to attack.
«Give it to me, private» insisted the other.
«You'll have to take it by force if you can» he replied, ceasing to be polite and squeezing the handle. I intervened before the two Carabinieri could lay hands on their muskets. I don't know how *Pugnodiferro* would have reacted. Reluctantly, I ordered him to give me the dagger.
«As long as there is a war on, we can only use it against the *magnasego*» I told him.
Somehow, I convinced him to give it to me, but he first wanted to wrap it in a handkerchief. The *Caproni* were not worthy to touch it.
They will return it to him at his leave's end.
When they left, we went into a nearby tavern to have a glass of red wine.
«*Che bischeri*![442] They took my dagger, but they left me this, which is much more dangerous» he said, putting his brass knuckles on the table.
«Just as I imagined» I replied, as I opened my tunic to show him my dagger.
He grinned. «And did you imagine these?» he asked, pulling two petards out of his pocket and laying them on the table. I started laughing.
«No, not those. What are you doing with them in Florence?»
«There are nasty people around, *Sergente*. You never know» he replied with a wink. We spent an hour talking. He updated me on the news from the base. Our units are being rebuilt after the fighting in late January. New Arditi are being recruited. On our return we will have to train them as well as we were trained in Sdricca.
«Isn't anybody waiting for you at home?» I said to him at some point.
«I wrote that I was coming, but not when. I want it to be a nice surprise.»
«I also wanted to make a surprise, but the surprises were on me. I hope you have better luck.»
We agreed to meet again in a couple of days.

---

[442] Typical Florentine word for foolish.

CHAPTER 14.IV

Florence, Monday, 25 February 1918
The days go by fast.
Yesterday was a beautiful day. I was a guest at *Pugnodiferro's* house.
He wanted to introduce me to his family. Despite the shortage of food, his mother made an excellent lunch. I hadn't eaten so well in a long time.
There was a lot of meat. They have a butcher shop and so they manage to have things that we can only dream of.
When it was time to say goodbye, they gave me a bag with meat, eggs and even milk.
I wanted to pay for them, but there was no way.
«It is for your family...» *Pugnodiferro's* father told me «... and also to apologize for the not-so-warm welcome to Florence.»
I almost had tears in my eyes as I thanked them for such generosity.
I hope to be able to pay them back one day.
«All right. When I come to visit your homeland, after you have kicked out the *Austrelli*» he promised me.
The joy of that day was transferred to my family's house when I opened the package and they saw all those good things to eat.
At dinner my mother insisted on sharing the food with the family who lives in the other room. She is a saint.

Chapter 15.IV

Florence, Thursday, 28 February 1918

These days I am rearranging everything that I have written down up till now. There are already lots of pages. And to think that I only started to distract myself from thinking about an attack.

In the early days it was hard for me to write. Now it's much easier.

I wish I could write like Salgari and Verne, but I do what I can.

Their stories are fantasies. Mine are true!

It has a certain effect on me to reread what I wrote after the Bainsizza fight and see the nervous and tattered pages written during the retreat on the Piave.

They remind me of the fear I felt, for my fate and that of my family, and the pain for the loss of so many comrades, especially those from my squad: *il Vólp*, *Mandulino* and *Biunnu*.

But they also remind me of some good things, such as the Sdricca period, the friendship and courage of many friends.

A lot of things have stuck with me and maybe they will remain forever, but many others I had almost forgotten.

Sometimes I wonder what I will do with these notebooks if I get out of the war alive.

I do not know.

Maybe I will make copies to give to my comrades, who have lived through these struggles with me, if we get together after the war.

Or I'll put them in a box to reread when I'm old, if I want to.

I do not know.

Meanwhile, I have to get out of it alive.

CHAPTER 16.IV

Florence, Friday, 1st March 1918
Yesterday we caused a big fracas. But I'd do it again.
We taught them a good lesson. They deserved it!
The past few days I have often met up with *Pugnodiferro*. We stroll around showing off our black flames. He is introducing me to this city, especially the taverns.
As far as the brothels are concerned, on the other hand, I'd rather not visit there. I have seen how miserable the guys are with the "pallida".
I don't think it's worth ruining your life for a few minutes of pleasure.
On the contrary, some guys go with infected prostitutes on purpose to get sick and avoid being called up or to get away from the front.
Pugnodiferro thinks differently and justifies himself thus:
«What if a shrapnel or a dum-dum bullet takes my nads away? Then I couldn't fuck anymore!»
He is right. We have seen many soldiers hit below the belt. Some died from loss of blood. But I am sure I won't lose my attributes.
With us on our tours of the city, there were almost always two of his friends, an Ardito from the XVI Unit, who also fought on Mount Val Bella, called *Tromba* (for the noises he makes in the latrine!), and *Periscopio*, a tall, thin corporal from the "Siena" Brigade, which fought first on the Karst in the Selo-Komarje area and later during the retreat on the Piave.
Since my leave is about to end, yesterday *Pugnodiferro* wanted to take me to see Florence from above. In fact, the view of the city from Piazzale Michelangelo is magnificent. There were low grey clouds, but for a few moments some rays of the sun shone through.
They looked like the beams of searchlights when they scour the mountains and rivers at night to expose troop movements.
Those beams are often a prelude to artillery or machine gun fire.
Instead, yesterday's rays were peaceful and made the Cathedral of Santa Maria del Fiore even more beautiful.
Last Sunday I went in with my mother and sisters. They were enchanted at all those altars, the crucifixes, the paintings and the dome. I admired the work of the bricklayers.
In our small church of Dogna everybody prays.

Here, instead, you get distracted.
We villagers are not used to all this magnitude and all this wealth.
On the way back, the three Florentines were arguing about which season in Florence is the most beautiful. Even though they were speaking in dialect, I understood everything, since their dialect is identical to Italian. They just have a strange way of pronouncing the letter c.
Everything was relaxed.
By chance, we met a group of workers who had just come out of a nearby workshop. They were all young men more or less our age. They were wearing the tricolour band on their arms.
Even in Florence there are many *imboscati* who avoid the front but make much more money than those who risk their lives in the trenches or attacks. It bothers us to see them, almost like the Carabinieri. Nevertheless, we see so many of them everywhere that we've got used to them and don't bother giving them a second look.
Yesterday, however, one of us did look at them and realized that some of them were mocking us. I don't know if they realized who we were. The sun was setting and it was getting dark. The days are still short.
«O look there! Those shitty *Cyclamen* are laughing at us» said *Tromba*.
It was true. I saw them too.
«Let's giv'em a nice coat of white paint!» proposed *Periscope*.
Pugnodiferro did not have to hear it twice. He had already taken off at full speed with us right behind.
«No blades, though!» I ordered, while I was running awkwardly.
My ankle still hurts.
Seeing us running towards them, some of them ran away, but others stayed their ground, ready to fight.
Pugnodiferro and *Tromba* immediately knocked out their opponents with well-placed punches and were already facing two more. *Periscopio* mowed his opponent down and was rolling on the ground holding him tight.
I found myself fighting two of them. One was bigger than me. I dodged a blow from the smaller one, dumped him on the ground and gave him a knee in the mouth. It made an awful sound.
He was out of the fight. The big guy, instead of punching me, pulled out a hammer and started wielding it.
That meant the fight was no longer fair and so I pulled out my dagger and showed it to him.
«If you use your hammer, I'll use this. I'm warning you» I said fiercely.
He didn't have time to decide what to do.

Pugnodiferro grabbed his arm from behind and I think he broke it, judging by the howls.
All the other *imboscati* were already lying on the ground, bruised and in pain.
«*Bischeri! Si c'avete tanta voglia di menà le mani venite al fronte invece di nasconde' 'l culo nel Lungarno! Vi s'insegna noi a menarle bene ai crucchi*»[443] *Pugnodiferro* shouted at all of them.
On our way back he said to me: «*Sergente*, didn't you say no blades?»
«I said it to you» I replied, tapping him on the shoulder.
When we went into a tavern for a drink, *Periscopio* was all excited at the fight. We much less so. In fact, we immediately changed the subject.
It seems that Russia will be signing a peace treaty with the central empires a few days from now.

P.S. When I got home this morning Margherita noticed a small tear in my trousers right at the knee with a blood spot around it.
«*Ce âtu fat tai bregòns?*»[444] she asked me.
«*Nue, nue. Mi sei inciopedât iar sere e o sei golât par tiere.*»[445]
«*Biadìn. Ti setu fat tant mâl? Setu scartufulât?*»[446]
«*No jo no*» I said sincerely. «*Sta cuiete.*»[447]
«*Gjavju chi ti ju lavi e ti ju infleci. No tu voràs migo tornâ su cui bregòns sbusâts? Ce ch'a disaressin i tiei soldâts?*»[448]
So I spent all morning at home in my underwear.
I had a bruise on my knee. Shaped like teeth.

---

443 «You pricks! If you really want to fight, come to the front instead of hiding your asses in the Lungarno! We will teach you how to fight against the Austrians.»
444 «What did you do to your trousers?» translation from the Friulan language.
445 «Nothing, nothing. I stumbled yesterday evening and fell down.»
446 «You poor thing. Did you hurt yourself ? Did you scrape your knee?»
447 «No, I didn't. Don't worry.»
448 «Take them off, so I can wash and patch them. You don't want to go back to the front with holes in your trousers? What would the soldiers on your squad say?»

CHAPTER 17.IV

Florence, Saturday, 2 March 1918
Today my leave ended, fifteen days without hearing even one gunshot.
Peace has a strange effect.
But it was not a good off-duty period like last year's in Dogna, even if then the windows were rattling continuously due to the blows of our 305.
My family is in a bad way. There are eight of them in a room, which cannot be heated with a fire. They have to share the kitchen, even if there is not much to cook. In fact, they've all lost weight. The other refugees are in the same conditions, if not worse. Fortunately, having left home before the disaster, my parents managed to bring something from home: pillows, mattresses, sheets and blankets, spare clothes, plates and cutlery.
There are people who escaped with only the clothes on their backs.
If only the local people understood the situation and helped them out.
Instead, the Florentines detest refugees. They believe that the war and the lack of food are their fault.
Tonight we had a good meal with the family.
Pugnodiferro brought me another bag full of food.
This time, however, I paid for it, even if he didn't want me to.
After dinner I said goodbye to everyone one by one.
I told the two children to be good and to be patient, because soon we will return to Dogna.
I told Agostino and Girardo to keep their noses clean and not to mess around too much with the Florentine boys.
I told my sisters to help our mother or, at least, try to do it.
I told my mom to hold fast and not to worry about me. After two years on the front I now know how to stay alive.
«*Atu ancjemò il grop?*»[449] she asked me.
«*I lu ài simpri in ta sachete*»[450] I replied, patting the pocket of my trousers.
It is always with me.
«*Viôd di no pierdilu.*»[451]

---

[449] «Do you still have the amulet?» translation from the Friulan language.
[450] «I always have it in my pocket.»
[451] «Try not to lose it.»

«*I lu ten da cont miôr da la sclope*»[452] I said with a smile.
«*Bon. Tu varâs bisugne di lui.*»[453]
This sentence chilled my blood and wiped the smile off my face.
I gathered my courage and with a bit of fear asked her the question, which I had wanted to ask for a long time: «*Mame, ditu che i tornarai?*»[454]
She took my hands in hers.
She raised her eyes to heaven and then, staring at me intensely, said:
«*Al sarà ce ch'al Signôr vorà. Tu preilu simpri e no stâ pierdi il grop, ch'al è benedet.*»[455]

P.S. I brought with me the book "The two tigers" by Salgari.
I hope the Italian tiger will soon defeat the Austro-Hungarian tiger.

---

[452] «I am more careful of it than my rifle» translation from the Friulan language.
[453] «Good. You will need it.»
[454] «Mom, do you think I'll come back?»
[455] «It will be whatever the Lord wants. Pray to him always and don't lose the amulet, which is blessed.»

Chapter 18.IV

Florence-Vicenza, Sunday, 3 March 1918
I'm on the troop train for Vicenza.
In the carriages occupied by us Arditi, we are all singing and drinking.
When we got on, our comrades welcomed us with shouts of joy, hugs and water balloons. As soon as the train started moving an explosion of "hurràs!" shook the railway station.
Infantrymen carriages are not so cheerful.
Just outside Florence I discovered that *Pugnodiferro* was on the train too.
«What are you doing here? Didn't you have some more days of leave?» I asked him.
«I couldn't sit on my hands at home anymore, *Sergente*. It bothered me to see so many *imboscati* around the city and not to be able to beat them all up. I got my dagger back from the Carabinieri and I left. For sure, I only gave up a couple days' leave» he said.
I got tired after all, too.
But I wasn't at my own home and I didn't have so much food available!
Anyway, as long as he was happy...
I heard some terrible things from some comrades from Veneto and Friuli whose families have taken refuge in the south of Italy.
The situation is far worse than in Florence. There is so much misery.
There is almost nothing to eat.
As if that were not enough, some areas are infested with malaria.
There have been deaths.
To make matters worse, there is also a language problem: the refugees do not understand a word of the dialects spoken down there. I know the problem well, because I too experienced it at the beginning with many of my comrades from the "Taro" Brigade.
The people from the south resent the refugees too and do nothing to help them. Even down there the charities or aid societies do little or nothing.
This is worrying and upsetting.

Chapter 19.IV

Debba, Sunday, 10 March 1918
From Vittarolo we descended to the plain and moved back to Debba south of Vicenza. We are now part of the XXII Army Corps of the 6th Army.
We are all together again: *Bracciodiferro*, *Carestia*, *Cuteddu*, *Mezzomago*, *Pugnodiferro* and *Trepugnali*.
Only *O'pazzo* is missing, since he is still recovering.
Carestia has been promoted to sergeant.
Bracciodiferro and *Pugnodiferro* have been promoted to corporal major and *Cuteddu* to corporal. It impresses me and makes proud to see them with the black "moustache" on their sleeves. No promotions for *Trepugnali* and *Mezzomago*, though, because of their troubles with Military Justice.
Everyone's morale is high.
We have a lot to do because many recruits have come to be "weaned".
At night there are many raids.
During the day there are numerous training exercises to keep us in shape and to teach our tactics. It's a shame not to have a training field similar to that of Sdricca. There is not even Racchi's "Swing" for us to have fun with the recruits.
In the evening we occasionally go to Lòngara to visit the friends from the I Unit. Sometimes they come to see us at the "Bar della mano amica".
At times we go to Vicenza, even if headquarters would like us to be incarcerated here, as if we were dangerous patients to keep in quarantine.
Indeed, we are dangerous, but we would be even more dangerous if they locked us up in a cage.
We say *"me ne frego"* and go anyway.[456]

---

[456] The expression "me ne frego", equivalent to "I don't care", but much stronger, became famous thanks to Gabriele d'Annunzio. It appeared for the first time in the posters dropped on Trieste by the Carnaro aviators. It seems that this motto was taken from a speech that took place on June 15, 1918 in Giavera del Montello during the battle of the Solstice, when Major Freguglia ordered Captain Zaninelli and his company to attack an Austrian stronghold in Casa Bianca. Freguglia added that it was a suicide mission, but that it had to be accomplished at any cost. Zaninelli looked at Freguglia and replied: «*Commander Sir, I don't care (me ne frego), I'll do what I have to do for the king and for my Country*». He put on his best uniform and went to die. Casa Bianca is now called Casa Zaninelli in his honour.

For now, the Carabinieri don't give us trouble and always open the gates to us at the barrier posts around Vicenza.
As we approach them, we sing a new rhyme:

Non far lo spiritoso, real carabiniere
ma lascia il passo libero a queste Fiamme Nere.[457]

A corporal and a sergeant always come with us on liberty.
They arrived in early February from the 71st Infantry Regiment.
The corporal is from Novara. We've nicknamed him *Canarino*, because he sings very well. We wanted to give the sergeant the name of *Vero*, because before the war he was a glassmaker in Murano, an island near Venice.[458]
In the end, however, we decided to call him *Faro*, because of his eyes which look like the headlights of a truck.
«Have you really been in the war zone since May '15?» we all ask him in turn. Without waiting for the answer everyone jokes about the colour of his eyes with phrases like:
«How come you're still alive? With those eyes of yours, snipers should have shot you at least a hundred times in the trenches.»
«If we go with you on night patrol, we don't need the spotlights.»
«Why the Arditi? You should be in the spotlight section!»
He laughs at these jokes and his light eyes shine even more. He can play wind instruments. After all, as a civilian he used to blow glass. He played in his regiment's band. He makes a nice duo with *Canarino*.

On March 3, Russia signed an armistice and left the conflict.[459]
This isn't good news.
Now the Germans can move their troops from the eastern to the western front and the Austrians to our front.
We expect a great offensive. The *mucs* will soon want to cross the Piave to get to Venice, Verona and Milan.

---

[457] *Don't get smart, royal Carabiniere, let these Black Flames through.*
[458] "Vero" means glass in the Venetian dialect.
[459] On March 3, 1918 the peace treaty was signed at Brest-Litovsk in Belarus. The conditions imposed by Germany were very harsh. In addition to paying an indemnity of around 6 billion DM, Russia had to surrender a vast territory. Finland, Belarus, the Ukraine and the future Baltic states thus entered the German sphere of influence, Bessarabia was annexed to Romania and portions of the Transcaucasian region went to the Ottoman Empire.

CHAPTER 20.IV

Debba, Sunday, 24 March 1918
Today is Palm Sunday.
The chaplain celebrated a high mass at the camp.
The command has had postcards printed with the names and dates of the battles fought by our unit:
Bainsizza level 800 - September 29, 1917
Kal plateau level 814 - October 8, 1917
Conca di Plezzo - October 13, 1917
Moriago-Mosnigo - November 10, 1917
Mount Val Bella - January 28, 1918

I sent one to my family and one to Noè.
I believe that more dates will have to be added soon.
From the newspapers we learned that on March 21 the Germans unleashed a major offensive on the western front and are advancing victoriously.[460]
Here, however, the *mucs* are quiet, but we are sure that they are planning something.

---

[460] On March 21, General Erich Ludendorff (9 April 1865 - 20 December 1937), the true grey eminence of the German High Command, launched the great offensive, which was supposed to make Germany win the war. His troops attacked British positions on the Somme, causing them to collapse and rapidly advanced to their rear lines. The results achieved were impressive compared to the outcome of other battles on the western front: the Germans captured 90,000 prisoners and 1,300 cannons, inflicted 212,000 Anglo-French casualties, destroying the entire British 5th Army. All this cost him 239,000 dead and wounded among officers and soldiers, with some Divisions reduced to half their strength and many companies with only forty or fifty surviving men.

Chapter 21.IV

Debba, Sunday March 31, 1918
Today is Easter. In Dogna after mass it was tradition to go to the square with hard-boiled eggs in your pocket.
My mom used to boil them with spinach to colour them green, with onion skins to make them red, with blueberries to make them blue.
All of us were in the square. We placed an egg on the ground against the wall of a house. In turn, everyone took aim at the egg and threw his coin.
If you managed to plant your coin in the egg, you won it. In the end we went off to eat all those half-destroyed eggs at the "Al Pastore" tavern, near the church.
Today the chaplain celebrated another high mass at the camp.
Someone grumbled: "Fewer masses and more attacks!"
Instead of fighting, we will soon be busy pulling up stakes and moving a few kilometres from here to San Pietro d'Intrigogna.

San Pietro d'Intrigogna, Sunday, 7 April 1918
We have moved to this village.
We liked Debba better.

San Pietro d'Intrigogna, Sunday, 21 April 1918
Nothing new to note in these weeks.
Usual life, usual drills, usual rambles to Vicenza.
The *mucs* are still quiet.
The *crucchi*, however, continue advancing on the western front.[461]
The other day we discussed what we will do after the war.
«Me sirche söbet öna fómna in paìs, bèla o bröta me 'nterèssa mia, l'è assé che la respire e che la sées zùena. La spuse söbet. Pò m' trà 'nsèma öna quach is-cècc issé i me öta a laurà 'n di cap»[462] said *il Gat*.

---

[461] In an attempt to replicate his initial success, General Ludendorff launched a series of attacks in various parts of the front. In April the Germans broke through the lines held by the British and Portuguese near Ypres.
[462] «I will look for a woman from my town right away, beautiful or ugly, it doesn't matter, as long as she is breathing and is young. I'll marry her at once. We'll have some children, so they help me work in the fields» translation from the Bergamo dialect.

«Will you marry her even if she has moustaches?» *Mezzomago* asked him.
«Al fósch de nòcc a s' ghe éd negóta.»[463]
«Ma ti i senti, ciò! Baucco!»[464] *Faro* pointed out to him.
We all laughed, even *il Gat*.
«At the end of the war I'll go back to my shop and butcher animals» exclaimed *Pugnodiferro*.
«Then you'll keep doing what you're doing now» said *Carestia*, making us all laugh again.
«I'll stay in the Arditi» said *Trepugnali*.
«That's better than twenty years in jail with criminals, who don't let you sleep at night» said *Pugnodiferro*.
«No. Look, *Pugno*, I would stay anyway. This is a job too.»
«Ma va in mona, Pugnal, 'casso ti disi? No se un lavoro questo! No se vita questa!»[465] intervened *Faro*.
«How can you go back to blowing glass, every day, every month, every year, as if nothing had happened after all we've been through?»
«Varda, mi go meio soffiar el vero che copar cristiani»[466] replied *Faro*.
«Our minds will forget» I added. «Even if it seems difficult, we will go back to normal lives and little by little we will forget, as if it were a bad dream.»
«That's why the sergeant writes in his notebook, in order not to forget everything» said *Pugnodiferro*.
Cuteddu listened at our chatter, looking at us as if we were imbeciles.

---

463 «At night in the dark you don't see anything » translation from the Bergamo dialect.
464 «But you can feel them. Pumpkin head!» translation from the Venetian dialect.
465 «Get lost, Pugnal! What the hell are you saying? This is not a job! This is not life!»
466 «Look, I prefer blowing glass to killing Christians.»

Chapter 22.IV

San Pietro d'Intrigogna, Sunday, 28 April 1918

The 2nd company is preparing for an operation in the mountains.

They will attempt the *coup-de-main* that a Platoon of the I Assault Unit tried and failed on 16 April.[467]

The 1st company and mine did more training at the shooting range. There have been some wounded, including an experienced aide-de-battle.[468]

We call him the *Argentine* because he comes from over there. A fragment of petard almost took his eye out. He had already been hit by a splinter in his eyebrow and a bullet in his leg during the fight on Mount Val Bella.

San Pietro d'Intrigogna, Sunday, 5 May 1918

The men of the 2nd company have returned to camp.

They are all unharmed, but quiet and disappointed: the action has failed again. We gathered around them to find out how it went.

This is the story that *Mitraglia*, another aide-de-battle, told us, interspersed with one curse after another in his Piacenza dialect.[469]

«We are Arditi, not spiders! They wanted us to take positions on a high, sheer, rock wall. They call it the "Pyramid". And they showed it to us at the last moment, on the morning of the 29th! Captain Calabrese decided to attack on both sides: I with twenty men on the right, Lieutenant Zardi with another twenty men on the left.

---

[467] On the night between 15 and 16 April the 1st platoon of the 2nd company of the I Unit, led by Captain Mereu, attempted to occupy an Austro-Hungarian position on a cliff south-east of Mount Spitz, at the confluence between the Val Gadena and the Val Brenta. The failure was due to difficulties of the terrain and the lack of specific training for mountain operations. The plan, however, was not shelved. The new attempt was drawn up with great precision on April 29 by the commander of the "Regina" Brigade, Colonel Brigadier Biancardi. The action was entrusted to around seventy men taken from the 2nd company of the II Assault Unit, led by captain Calabrese.

[468] To replace the many second lieutenants, who had either died or been injured in combat, the High Command created a new rank: the aide-de-battle, drawing from the sergeants who had distinguished themselves for courage and valour. The aide-de-battle became the highest rank among non-commissioned officers and could command a platoon.

[469] Most likely this was Osvaldo Fabbricatore, awarded a silver medal for the fighting in June 1918 in Zenson and Fossalta, where he was killed.

There were four patrols of reinforcements, three with flamethrowers and one with a submachine gun. There was also a platoon of regimental Arditi of the 10th Infantry.
In order to have complete freedom of movement, we only had a dagger, a musket with ten magazines, eight petards and a gas mask. We left haversacks, blankets and ammo pouches in our lines in Valstagna. We set off at around three in the morning. It was pouring down rain. Even better.
The rain hid the sound of our footsteps. However, to make sure, we even wrapped up our feet. As soon as we arrived, we immediately realized that it was impossible to climb those rocks. Smooth, slippery and without foot or handholds. Holy cow! While I was deciding what to do, doesn't the moon come out too? This is bad, I thought. Sure enough, shortly afterwards a patrol of *tognìt* came up the side. There must have been thirty of them. As soon as they saw us, they started shooting at us with their Steyr rifles[470] and throwing hand grenades. One man was wounded by a fragment. We replied in kind, but then we turned around before they could start shooting at us from above. The surprise was gone to hell.»
«Who got hit with the fragments?» *Trepugnali* asked.
«*Il Rosso*. Nothing serious.»
«What about the left column?» I asked.
«They too found themselves faced by a sheer wall of rock about twenty metres high. While they were searching for a way to climb, the *tognìt* started throwing flares. They had spotted them. So the lieutenant decided to retreat too. We were all pissed at how things had gone.»
«Did you try again?» I asked.
«Yes, the big boss of the 10th Infantry wanted to try again. If we couldn't capture it, then it had to be destroyed. I spent the whole day studying the terrain on May 1st. Holy cow! We left at 11 with three ten-man patrols. The group on the right was commanded by Lieutenant Consolini. When they got to the base of the "Pyramid", the *tognìt* were well awake and they were peppered with hand grenades. Lieutenant Zardi's squad was in the middle. He started shooting at the enemy position. Instead, I tried to get around the cliff from the left. I wanted to attack them from behind, but even there they were careful and they immediately responded to the fire. We couldn't get close enough to roast them with the flamethrowers. We tried all night, but there was nothing to do.

---

470 The Steyr-Mannlicher M1895 was the rifle designed by Ferdinand Ritter von Mannlicher and supplied to the Austro-Hungarian army.

We hit some of them, but the rest of them kept shooting like crazy. At dawn we decided to go back. If they want to destroy that position, they have to either send the Alpini or shell it.»
«Holy cow!» echoed *Pugnodiferro*. «I'd already written "Pyramid" on the postcard of the XXII, which I wanted to send to my father...»
«*Ma và in mona, và! Bischero!*» replied the aide-de-battle.

Chapter 23.IV

Marsan, Friday, 10 May 1918
Last Wednesday we moved again.
Now we are in a village near Marostica.
The I Assault Unit is with us there too.

Marsan, Sunday, 19 May 1918
I am starting to write again.
I have been very ill, so ill that last week I had to report sick. As soon as the medical officer saw me, he immediately gave me a certificate for the hospital. There were three other fellow soldiers with the same illness.
They call it the "three-day fever".
Three days? No way!
I was sick for a week.
My fever was so high that the doctor asked me if I wanted to blow up the thermometer. My face turned purple. I had aches in my eyes, ears and back. All my bones hurt. I was sweating day and night. But the worst was the headache. I felt like I had guns firing from one side of my cranium to the other.
I am better, but the headache has not yet passed.[471]

---

[471] From the symptoms and the name, it was the fever then called "Spagnola". Contagion occurred through coughs or sneezes. The first wave swept through Italy between April and May and did not present the virulence and danger of the second wave which reappeared in the autumn and continued into 1919. The latter was characterized by serious lung complications, which often caused deterioration and sudden death. It is estimated that the worldwide pandemic caused between 20 and 100 million victims, many more than the entire war. With over 375,000 deaths, Italy was second in Europe only to Russia, which had 450,000. In order not to demoralize the nation, the Italian government forbade talking about this epidemic, banished obituaries, tolling of bells, processions and funerals. As they were not subject to censorship, the first to mention it were the Spanish newspapers in February 1918: *"A strange form of epidemic disease has appeared in Madrid. The epidemic is of a benign nature, not having resulted in fatal cases."* Actually, before the infection hit Madrid, around 1,100 American soldiers had been bedridden in Fort Riley, Texas. Nevertheless, with all due respect for the Iberians, the name of the disease, spread by the press, has gone down in history as the "Spanish flu".

Marsan, Monday, 20 May 1918
Today was dedicated to changing the numbers on our caps and shoulder boards. We have changed our name! From now on the glorious II Assault Unit has become the XXII, the same number as the Army Corps.
We are a bit sorry, but the High Command has decided thus.
The I Unit changed its name too. From today it is numbered XX.
Pugnodiferro complained: «*Avevo già scritto 'na cartolina del II che volevo manda' alla mi' mamma...*»[472]
«*Zonta na XX e và in mona, và!*»[473] suggested *Faro*, laughing.

We were pleased with the gold medal of military valour awarded to one of our former comrades at Sdricca, Lieutenant Sabatini.[474]
In December he went to Santa Caterina di Schio to form the new III Assault Unit belonging to the 1st Army. On 13 May he performed a great exploit on Mount Corno. With four other Arditi he conquered the fortified peak of the mountain and captured many prisoners, 2 cannons, 4 machine guns, war material. Colonel Bassi will certainly be proud of him.

P.S. Old *Spuafogo* has returned to us with his flamethrowers.[475]

---

472 «I had already written a postcard of the II, that I wanted to send to my mom...» translation from the Tuscan dialect.

473 «Add a XX and go to hell!» translation from the Venetian dialect.

474 Carlo Sabatini, born in 1891 in Alessandria and called to arms in 1915. He fought on the Sabotino in the 34th Infantry Regiment and in August 1916 participated in the conquest of Gorizia with the 11th Infantry as second lieutenant. Wounded in the arm, he was awarded a silver medal. He had already returned to the front in October with the rank of lieutenant. He then fought on the Karst ("Brescia" Brigade) and on the Bainsizza plateau ("Puglie" Brigade), in command of a machine-gun section. A volunteer at the Sdricca School, he commanded the 1st company of the IV Assault Unit. He led the 3rd company of the III until 29 November 1918, when he transferred to the XIII, destined for Libya.
This is the motivation for the Gold Medal of Military Valour: *"Always first to rise to the challenge, the true personification of the highest military virtues, with a marked spirit of self-sacrifice and magnificent daring, with a prodigious climb, prime example to the four Arditi who followed him, he was able, under the vigilant eyes of Austrian lookouts, to boldly swoop down on the opposing garrison and engage them in a violent close-quarter battle. None of the enemies was saved, most were killed and fell off the cliff. He captured six of them, including the commanding officer of the garrison. After being joined by a strong group of his fellows, he firmly established himself on the position. Monte Corno di Vallarsa, 13 May 1918."* For that same action a silver medal was awarded to sergeant Giovanni Degli Esposti, to the soldiers Torri, Brancato and Cataldo.

475 With the reorganization of May 1918, each assault unit was assigned three flamethrower sections equal to 18 weapons, 6 per company.

Chapter 24.IV

Marsan, Monday, 27 May 1918
Something very big is about to happen.
Our officers seem more excited than usual.
We see planes flying over our field all the time.
Radiogavetta says that the *mucs* are about to attack.
Meanwhile, yesterday the Arditi of the XXIII Assault Unit carried out an important operation at Capo Sile. They captured 7 officers, over 400 soldiers, 4 trench mortars, 10 machine guns and plenty of ammunition.[476]

---

[476] Alone or with the help of other troops, in May the Arditi pulled off several surprise attacks in various areas of the front: on 18 at Ca' Tasson north of Grappa, on 19 at Capo Sile (XXIII Unit), on 20 at Stoccareddo (XIII), on 21 on Spinoncia (XXX), on 23 at Cima d'Oro near Salò (XIV) and at Zugna Torta (XXIX), where Lieutenant Sante Dorigo earned a gold medal and the Unit a bronze medal. On 25-26 at Cima Zigolon, Cima Presena and Passo del Monticello (III), on 26 again at Capo Sile (XXIII), with the help of artillery and some flamethrower sections. In this action the courage of the assailants was personified in Lieutenant Leopoldo Pellas, who was awarded a gold medal with the following motivation: *"From a profound consciousness of duty, from a strong spirit of revenge against the enemy who had killed his brother captain of the grenadiers, he attacked among the first, although wounded, pursuing his opponent and continuing with brilliant valour in this bold and successful action, successively attacking three lines, inflicting heavy casualties on the enemy and taking prisoners. Upon reaching the target, with admirable tenacity he continued his forward attack; surrounded by his foes, he refused to surrender and defended himself with extraordinary constancy and magnificent heroism to the death, establishing himself in the admiration of the enemy himself, who two days later, by means of a message launched from an aircraft, announced that they had buried with full military honours the brave fallen one. Capo Sile, 26 May 1918."*
The success of all these actions once again demonstrated the effectiveness of the Arditi and the renewed fighting spirit of the Royal Army. The highly decorated Lieutenant of the 11th Assault Unit, Alessandro Tandura, also took part in the action at Capo Sile. Shortly thereafter he became famous for the first parachute jump (at the time called "the silk umbrella") behind enemy lines. Although he had never launched nor flown before then, on the rainy night between 8 and 9 August he boarded a Savoia-Pomilio SP4 twin-engine driven by the Canadian ace pilot, Captain William Barker, and was parachuted into the Vittorio Veneto area, his birthplace, *"to collect data and information on the movements, deployments, intentions of the enemy"*. Twice arrested and twice he escaped and in three months sent valuable information, gathered missing troops and led them against the enemy at the time of the Italian offensive in October. He was decorated in the field with a Gold Medal of Military Valour, an addition to his numerous other honours.

CHAPTER 25.IV

Limena, Sunday, 9 June 1918
Yesterday we transferred to Limena.
We are part of the 3rd Assault Group of Division "A", together with the Units VIII and XXX.[477]
Colonel Trivulzio commands us. I learned that he is from Udine.[478]
They told us that we must always be on the alert and ready to get in trucks and leave for combat.
It is now certain that the *mucs* are about to attack.[479]
This afternoon *Mezzomago* said some weird things. He asked us to bury him, if he is killed in the next fight. He doesn't want to end up like some of the dead, whom he once saw in a ditch, all black, swollen and with faces full of worms. We all promised each other and then we drank to our health, touching our flames and our "attributes".

---

[477] On 10 June the High Command ordered the establishment of the Army Assault Corps, made up of the following units:
Special Division "A" (General Ottavio Zoppi)
1st Group - Assault Units V, X and XX, commanded by Colonel Grillo
2nd Group - Assault Units XII, XIII and XIV, commanded by Colonel Raggio
3rd Group - Assault Units VIII, XXII and XXX, commanded by Colonel Trivulzio
Czeco-Slovak Division (General Andrea Graziani)
1st Brigade - Regiments 31st and 32nd, commanded by Colonel Brigadier De Vita
2nd Brigade - Regiments 33rd and 34th, commanded by Colonel Brigadier Sapienza
The High Command entrusted the command to General Saverio Grazioli (18 December 1869 - 20 February 1951), who established his headquarters in Montegalda.
To replace the nine assault units subtracted from the Army Corps, the High Command wanted to establish newly created units with the previous numeral increased by 50 or L, in Roman numbers. Many of these units, however, never became operational and their personnel merged into the reserve units of the Assault Army Corps.
[478] In 1921 Colonel Carlo Trivulzio, as a substitute member, was part of the commission charged with designating the "Unknown Soldier" to become the symbol of all the soldiers killed and missing during war.
[479] Despite attempts at camouflage, the great Austro-Hungarian offensive was well known to the High Command. In addition to the information obtained from deserters, much news arrived from carrier pigeons launched by spies infiltrated in the occupied territories. Since August among those spies were Max di Montegnacco, lieutenant in the Arditi, and Count Arbeno d'Attimis (1895-1981), lieutenant in the cavalry, who organized the Udine insurrection in early November 1918.

Chapter 26.IV

Limena, Wednesday, 12 June 1918

Yesterday we gathered in Ronchi di Campanile together with the other eight units of the "A" Division: V, X, XX, XII, XIII, XIV, VIII and XXX. General Grazioli, commander of the Assault Army Corps, reviewed us.

The sight of such a mass of Arditi gave me great confidence in the victory.

There is an innovation in our troop uniform. For a few days now, instead of their caps all privates have been wearing a fez like that of the Bersaglieri, but black in colour, including the bow.

NCO's and officers have kept the old cap.[480]

In our Army Corps there is a Division of Czecho-Slovaks.

They previously fought alongside the *mucs*. Now they are on our side.

«*Xe da fidarse?*» *Faro* asked, while we were eating our rations.

«As strong as we are, certainly they aren't» replied *Carestia* whose expression denoted his disgust at the Torrigiani sauce, «but I'm sure that they'll fight to the death. If the *tognìt* take them, they'll hang them as traitors.»[481]

«They are better than Romanians and Poles» said *Trepugnali*. «They are all little runts. The toughest are the Hungarians.»

«Have you ever met Bosnians? The toughest of all they are. They know how to handle their knives well, too» said *Carestia*.

Cutèddu raised his eyes from the mess tin. When the talk is about knives, he always pricks up his ears.

«I really hope I'll get to meet them. So they'll learn to wet themselves too as soon as they see us!» concluded *Pugnodiferro*.

---

480 The standard headgear of the privates was the model 1915 kepì, called *scodellino*, i.e. the little bowl. Officers and non-commissioned officers wore the 1907 cap.

481 The Czecho-Slovak Division was made up of former prisoners of war willing to fight for the Allies and the independence of their country.

CHAPTER 27.IV

Limena, Thursday, 13 June 1918
Today is the feast day of Saint Anthony of Padua.
I have asked him to protect me in the days to come.
I've also tied my amulet into my pocket to prevent it from falling out.
In the camp we are preparing for the upcoming fight.
Muskets are oiled and daggers are sharpened.
Morale is very high.
We sing a lot.
The food is abundant and the drink too.
Some guys have already started asking me to write letters to send to their families if they should lose their "dog tags".
The mail continues to function regularly.
The other day we got a postcard from *O'pazzo*.
He writes he is fine and that he will be back with us soon.
«*Iddu è fuodde*»[482] commented *Cuteddu*, as he trimmed his moustaches with his dagger.

P.S. Tomorrow at Orgiano the King will review the four Czecho-Slovak regiments.

482 «He is crazy» translation from the Sicilian dialect.

CHAPTER 28.IV

Limena, Saturday, 15 June 1918
The hurricane has broken out.
Yesterday before midnight.
The artillery began its deafening concert.
The *mucs* have launched their offensive.[483]
We are ready.
"A Noi!" [484]

---

[483] The Germans pressed for this offensive in support of their attack on the western front. William II, Emperor of Germany and King of Prussia, and the German High Command were very irritated by the so-called "Sisto case". In April 1918 a leak had revealed the attempts of Emperor Charles I of Austria to arrive at negotiations for a fair and reasonable peace, taking additional advantage of the diplomatic channel offered him by his brother-in-law, Sisto of Borbone-Parma, brother of his wife Zita and officer in the Belgian army. Charles denied the evidence but had to yield both to the Germans and to his High Command, who opposed peace. The offensive was prepared with great care and scope by the Austro-Hungarians, employing over sixty Divisions. The morale of the army still seemed high as did confidence in the success of the action, despite the fact that the country was at the end of its tether and on the brink of starvation. The strategic aim was to reach the Po Valley to take possession of Italian stockpiles, to force the enemy into an armistice and to release forces to concentrate later on the western front.
The plan included a diversionary attack on the Tonale Pass, called Lawine (avalanche) operation, ahead of one from the Asiago plateau towards Vicenza by Conrad's 10th and 11th Armies (the Radetzky operation) and another one across the Piave in the direction of Treviso by Boroević's 5th and 6th Army (Albrecht operation). These two probes were to constitute the arms of a pincer to close in the Padua area.

[484] The war-cry "A Noi!", meaning "To Us!", was introduced on February 14, 1918 by Major Luigi Freguglia, commander of the V Assault Unit (XXVII from May 20). It replaced the war-cry "hurrà!", commonly used when presenting arms. Later, Captain Anchise Pomponi suggested replacing the traditional "present-arms" with this gesture: the right hand brandishing the dagger and then suddenly lifting it up. This variant was proposed in April to the then commander of the 2nd Army, Lieutenant General Giuseppe Pennella, who sent it to the High Command, along with other aspects of the organization of the Assault Units. In support of the proposal, the General Pennella wrote in his own hand: *"I witnessed rehearsals of this movement. It is impressive and expressive, as well as beautiful."* The variant was approved with some reluctance (*"The Arditi are already too... Arditi"* noted Badoglio, deputy chief of staff) and quickly spread among all assault units.

Limena, Sunday, 16 June 1918
The artillery duel continues uninterrupted.
So many guns are firing from one side to the other that individual shots can no longer be distinguished.[485]
All sorts of news arrive.
The *mucs* are attacking from the mountains to the plain.
It seems that they have emerged in Val Brenta and are threatening Bassano.
It's said they have crossed the Piave in several places.
It's said that Treviso and Montebelluna are about to fall.
Other rumours say that our army is beating them back.
On the road we see trucks, wagons, motorcycles, troops and cars full of senior officers passing continuously.
The air is full of dust.
On the sides of the road there are at least 600 trucks parked, ready to transport our Division wherever it's needed.
At 10 a.m. the officers of all the Assault Units were summoned by General Zoppi to the church of Rubano.
Later the commander of our 3rd company, Captain Adelchi Turotti[486], told us that everything is going well and that the Homeland expects a lot from us.
Today or tomorrow we will leave, we don't know yet where.
We are already in battle gear, armed to the teeth.
In the meantime, we sing.
We have already exchanged letters for our families.

---

[485] The Italian High Command knew the enemy's plans in advance, including the date and time of the attack, to the extent that in the area around Mount Grappa and the Asiago plateau the tactic of "anticipated counterpreparation" (prearranged fire against an enemy that is preparing for attack) was implemented, in particular by the artillery of the 6th Army, commanded by General Roberto Segre. Immediately after midnight the artillery of the Royal Army began firing for almost five consecutive hours thousands of large-calibre shells, so many that the Alpini, who were climbing Mount Grappa, saw the entire front lit up like daylight as far as the Adriatic Sea.

[486] He was the oldest officer in the XXII Assault Unit. Previously he had commanded the 3rd Battalion of the 77th Regiment, "Toscana" Brigade. He was seriously wounded on 7 August 1916 on the Sabotino during the defense of the recently conquered San Mauro ridge (the capture of Gorizia). For his part in this action he was awarded a bronze medal, to which was later added a silver medal for the battles on Mount Val Bella, during which he was wounded again.

We waited anxiously all day for our marching orders.
Finally, at 9:00 p.m. a phonogram arrived:
"The Assault Division must move to the 3rd Army front to cooperate in the defense of the Piave river".
We will leave at 1:30 a.m. in the direction of Roncade.[487]
About time!

---

[487] Shortly before departure, General Grazioli communicated the so-called Decalogue of Ardito to his Assault Units.

1. Ardito! Your name means courage, force and loyalty; your mission is victory, at all costs. Be proud to show the whole world that no one can resist the Italian soldier. Think of the treasures you are defending with your valour: the freedom of your families, the beauty of your country, the wealth of your nation. This will give you invincible strength.

2. In winning, numbers and weapons do not count: above all else are discipline and daring. Discipline expresses beauty and sublime moral force; Daring is the severe and firm will to impose your superiority on the enemy anytime, anywhere.

3. Victory lies beyond the last enemy trench, to the rear; to reach it, use violence and cleverness, and do not worry if during the assault some of the enemy remain beyond your reach. If the enemy outflanks you, hold your nerve, outflank him in turn.

4. Always try to realise what is happening on the battlefield, and rush to help comrades in danger. When you feel the situation faltering, throw yourself forward and forward again.

5. When attacking, use your hand grenades and dagger, the true weapons of every Ardito. When defending the terrain, you have won, use your rifle and your machine gun. Protect your machine guns if you want them protect you. Cover the noise of the advancing enemy horde with the song of your machine guns. At that song you'll see the horde melt away and the enemy will fall like wheat to the scythe.

6. If you reach the enemy's rear lines, sow terror and disorder there; in this case one courageous man counts for a hundred men, an Italian Ardito counts for a thousand enemy soldiers.

7. The terror that you instil in the adversary is your most powerful weapon: keep your fame alive. Be ruthless when the enemy is on his feet, be benevolent with him when he is down.

8. If you are wounded or missing, your debt of honour is to let your unit know where you are and to try and reach your comrades at all costs.

9. Do not aspire to any prize other than the smiles of the beautiful Italian women whom you defend with your courage. They will cover you with flowers and bestow kisses on your audacious forehead when you return victorious, proud of your manly strength, beloved son of the greatest Italy.

10. Run into battle! You are the most brilliant expression of the genius of our own people. The entire Country is following like a shining path your heroic race to the attack!

CHAPTER 29.IV

Grancona, Sunday, 23 June 1918

I have saved my *ghirba* once again, but we've been through an ordeal and not everyone survived it, unfortunately.

Bracciodiferro is dead. It seems so incredible to me that one small lead ball could have crushed such a big and strong man.

We will no longer hear *Canarino's* warbling. He too was killed by the fragments of a shell. *Mitraglia* also died.

Mezzomago was taken prisoner. He was with *Trepugnali* and other Arditi at the command post with Captain Abbondanza and Captain Turotti.

They too have been captured.

When we returned to the farmhouse, we found the bodies of Lieutenant Frichetti, aide-de-battle Fabbri and three other Arditi, but the two captains, *Mezzomago* and the others were no longer there and are still missing at roll-call. *Trepugnali* was also captured, but then managed to escape and told us what happened.

Pugnodiferro and *Carestia* are wounded. *Cuteddu*, *il Gat*, *Faro* and I got away with a few scratches and a few lumps.

On the night of 17 June, we climbed onto the trucks amidst shouts and songs. No rifle shots or throwing petards. Those were reserved for the *mucs*. Our column of trucks travelled until dawn.

We arrived in Roncade around nine in the morning.

There was a lot of confusion in the village. Ambulances loaded with wounded were arriving from the front lines and fresh troops were marching away in the opposite direction.

A few kilometres away was one of the hottest areas on the front.

The day before the command had thrown into the fray our XXIII Assault Unit and the "Sassari" and "Bisagno" Brigades. They had taken and lost Fossalta, Capo d'Argine and Gorgazzo several times.

We waited for new orders all morning.

We could feel the battle raging all around us and we saw many planes flying over us. The men were edgy and tired of sitting on their hands, waiting.

In the afternoon our unit was ordered to head towards Fossalta to block an infiltration. The 1st and 2nd company went forward in formation, while we followed about a kilometre behind, together with the command.

As we marched, a runner sent by the captain of the 1st company arrived. He told us that General Latini, commander of the 25th Division had requested a sudden change of direction. The general himself had taken command of the two companies and was heading towards San Pietro Novello to block some large enemy units infiltrated behind our troops, which were deployed to defend the line along a canal, called Palumbo. The terrain in this area is very insidious. Flat and free of hills, furrowed by ditches full of water, canals both wide and narrow, tracks and roads, with dense vegetation formed by vines, trees, hedges and fields of wheat and corn.
Shortly after we set off on the road to Villa Premuda an Austrian plane targeted our column. We threw ourselves to the sides of the road to shelter behind the trees from the machine gun fire.
The plane turned around and then came back after us. Someone tried to shoot it with his musket, but with no luck. Then it left. We saw that one of our planes was chasing it. They fought further on, but we didn't see how it ended. Meanwhile the sky was getting darker. Black clouds drifted over from the Piave. We got back on the road.
We hadn't travelled even one kilometre when we heard a great uproar of rifles and machine guns start up right in front of us. Our comrades had come into contact with the *mucs*. At this Captain Abbondanza ordered us to rush over to the right to cover the flank of the two companies.
We crossed a cornfield and passed over some ditches, until we too collided with the *mucs*. With my platoon I had to clean out a grove of trees.
Our energies redoubled when we realized we were fighting Hungarians.
Two years ago on the San Michele the Honvéd killed our infantrymen stunned by gas with blows of their iron clubs. We still remember it well.
The flamethrowers created a barrage of fire. Then, when they stopped, we launched ourselves into the grove from all directions. Blind fury was our guide. The combat was extremely violent. They didn't hold back either.
Better not to describe what happened in that grove.
I will always remember the bestial scream of my men at the end with daggers raised and the smell of blood and burning. There were no prisoners.
No Hungarian surrendered. Some had died with their club in hand.
I took a club. It was fearsome: the upper part is iron and bristling with spikes. I planted it in the trunk of a tree, which it pierced like butter.
«Look at this» said *Trepugnali*, showing me a double-bladed axe.
Most of us were more interested in taking possession of their Kiraly cigarettes. In that fight we sustained three dead and eight wounded, one of whom died later. He was one of the new draftees. Poor kid, he hadn't been able to avoid a bayonet blow to the stomach.

We took weapons and ammunition from the dead and went on past the grove in a rush, alternating running with sheltering on the ground.
Until we met a couple of machine guns, which began targeting us.
We threw up a smokescreen with petards. In the meantime, four teams surrounded and silenced them. The servers of one of the two machine guns surrendered. They weren't Hungarians, so we took them prisoners.
Bracciodiferro hoisted a machine gun onto his shoulder and had the prisoners carry tripods and ammunition. He wanted to use it against the *mucs*.
Unfortunately, it was a mistake. Shortly afterwards, a rifle shot fired from a bush hit him square in the forehead.
If he had been advancing in a crouch like the others, he certainly wouldn't have been shot. Our flamethrowers set fire to the bush and sniper.
I immediately ran to see how *Bracciodiferro* was. He had died instantly.
Pugnodiferro yelled out a series of unrepeatable blasphemies.
The prisoners were afraid of being executed. I had them taken away.
I had tears in my eyes. I had in my own pocket the letter that *Bracciodiferro* had written to his family in case of death.
We couldn't stay there. We had to go on. We went on.
There was another gunfight.
We took twenty prisoners without suffering losses.
Another enemy patrol preferred to run away as soon as they saw us.
The other platoons had also come up against enemies hidden in the ditches and flattened behind the hedges.
Towards evening we arrived at the Palumbo ditch line.
On the right we met up with the XXV Assault Unit and on the left with our two companies. It was raining and really humid.
That day our unit had captured about five hundred prisoners and fifteen machine guns, recaptured five 75 mm pieces of our artillery and released a hundred of our soldiers.
The most important thing was to have fought off the *mucs* beyond the Palumbo ditch. I felt satisfaction, but also a great sorrow for *Bracciodiferro* and the other men lost in the fight in the grove.
During the night my company left control of the ditch line to the 1st and 2nd company.
We moved back about two hundred metres near a half-ruined house, where the command of the unit was installed.[488]

---

488 This was Casa De Mollo in a central position with respect to the two companies in the first line. Units of the 70th Infantry Regiment, "Ancona" Brigade, took positions on the left and a Battalion of cycling Bersaglieri on the right.

Faro has been promoted to sergeant major.
His pay has doubled from 1 to 2 lire.
«As soon as we get back to the field you have to "wet your new insigna"» I congratulated him, patting him on the back.
«*Speremo de tornar indrìo in pìe e non sbusài*»[489] he replied.
For us the night passed quietly.
Those on the front lines, however, had to repel many attacks.
The following morning, Captain Abbondanza went to Division command for instructions. The order was to push the *mucs* back to the other side of the Piave. The action was to begin at 5:00 p.m. with the help of two other units, including the XIV.
Despite the pain and fever, having dislocated his wrist in a car accident the previous day, the captain remained at his command post.
Around 2:00 p.m. there was a very violent attack in the area where the XIV Unit was lining up. Their commander, Major Ambrogetti, sent a request for help to our command. Captain Turotti ordered us to go to the rescue. He remained where he was with Captain Abbondanza and about twenty men, including cyclists, signalmen and runners. Among the latter were *Trepugnali* and *Mezzomago*.
«They attacked us a few minutes after you left» *Trepugnali* told us.
«Unfortunately, there was only one window to shoot from to repel the attack. So they were able to approach and surround us. They threw a hailstorm of hand grenades at us. Our ammunition was scarce so we couldn't reply in kind. When they ordered us to surrender, we answered with some Thévenots. Luckily, they didn't have flamethrowers or they would have roasted us all. The aide-de-battle and two others tried to escape to call you but he was killed at the door. Then a hand grenade came in through the window and slaughtered about half of us. Soon after they broke into the house. There was a lot of uproar. Poor second lieutenant Frichetti was shot dead. Captains Abbondanza and Turotti seriously wounded. *Mezzomago*'s legs were full of fragments. We defended ourselves for a while but, as things were looking pretty bad, we decided it was better to give up. They were Hungarians. An assault unit.»
«Those bastards!» someone hissed.
«They disarmed us and kicked us out. They lined us up against the wall of the house, intending to shoot us all with the machine gun. Luckily an Austrian officer intervened and saved our lives.

[489] «Let's hope to get back still standing and not full of holes» translation from the Venetian dialect.

Reluctantly and violently they pushed us towards the Palumbo ditch, beating us with their whips. Four of them escorted us, while all the others continued on to San Pietro Novello.
I had no wounds and apart from the daze of the explosions I was fine.
I studied the situation. Little by little I sidled up to one of the escorts.
Three of my daggers had been taken away, but not the fourth, the thin one I always have in my sleeve. I planted it in his heart and threw myself into a cornfield. The others shot at me, but they didn't catch me, because I was well hidden among the plants. I ran at breakneck speed to shake off one of them, who had decided to recapture me. I stayed hidden until I saw soldiers of XIV and then I jumped out. I warned their commander of what had happened and came looking until I found you. Thank heavens.»
We embraced *Trepugnali*, very moved by what had happened.
In one fell swoop we had lost our two commanders and *Mezzomago*, not to mention our dead.
Now the command of the XXII has been taken over by Captain Seraglia.
Previously he commanded a reserve group of the XII Unit. When he learned that our unit was without guidance, he rushed over on his own initiative to reorganize us.
For our part, we reinforced the XIV Unit, repelling the attack on the left, which was intense. While we were attempting a counterattack, a shell exploded near *Canarino*. The fragments hit and killed him.
I saw *Faro's* eyes: they were full of anger and tears.
Around 7:00 p.m. we returned to the command post and found the remains of the fight. Shortly after the other two companies arrived and Captain Seraglia lined up us in a defensive position.
Later, in the dark, we tried to take back the lost ground.
Little by little, we flushed all the enemy groups out and threw them back to the other side of the Palumbo ditch.
During this action *Carestia* saved my *ghirba* but took a bullet in his thigh.
As we walked side by side I slipped backwards. The ground was slippery from the rain. While on the ground, I saw an enemy emerge from behind a tree and aim his rifle at me.
Instinctively I shouted: «*Trai! Trai!*»
Carestia and the *muc* both fired at the same time.
I saw the *muc* fly backwards and heard a thud near me.
It was my comrade.
«All right, *Sergente*. Did I get him?» he asked me from the ground.
«Yes, you got him. I owe you my life. Are you wounded?»
«Yes, *Sergente*. The *tognìt* stung my thigh.»

As I was taking him back to the dressing post near the Command, *Carestia* asked me: «What were you yelling at me before?»
«I was shouting: Shoot! Shoot! ...in Friulan.»
«Next time yell *Tìra! Tìra!* ...in Sardinian.»
That evening we recaptured the line on the Palumbo ditch and took sixty more prisoners.
The night and morning of the 19th passed fairly quietly.
At around 1:00 p.m. the enemy artillery began shelling the line on our left.
After twenty minutes there was an Infantry attack.
Once again a breach was opened up in our left side.
And so, to avoid being encircled, we moved back in good order to the Fornaci-Fossalta road.
Here we found Colonel Raggio, who lined us up to cover the road.[490]
With a patrol I went as far as San Pietro Novello, where we made a big catch. At the entrance to the village we recovered two of our 210mm guns and captured the *mucs* that were guarding them.[491]
That day I too was promoted to sergeant major.
Faro immediately came to congratulate me and pat me on the back:
«Ciò beo, adesso ti ga da paghar da bevar anca ti.»[492]
«Willingly, *vecjo*. We must drink to the memory of *Bracciodiferro* and *Canarino* and to the health of *Mezzomago* and our commanders.»
«Speremo che i ghe daga da magnar...»[493]
Towards evening we received the order to leave the area and go to Casale sul Sile. For us the battle was over.[494]
We spent the whole 20th of June outdoors near the San Michele del Quarto railway station with the rest of the Assault Division. As always, after an action, we asked about the fate of friends in the other units. We learned of the death of both Captain Giulia, commander of the V, and of Captain Enrico Benci of the XX. He was called *the Grenadier* for his stature and

---

490 He commanded the 2nd Assault Group of the "A" Division.
491 Shortly before the VII Lancieri di Milano (Milan Lancers), commanded by General Count Gino Augusti, had repelled the advance of the enemy troops infiltrated beyond the Piave lines. While outnumbered in men and weapons, they fought, on foot as well, hand-to-hand with bayonets, inflicting a decisive defeat in the struggle. The event would go down in history as the "Charge of San Pietro Novello".
492 «Dude, now you have to buy the drinks too» translation from the Venetian dialect.
493 «Let's hope they feed them.»
494 In the three days of combat the XXII Assault Unit captured over 700 prisoners, 21 machine guns, a bomb launcher and recovered 10 of our 75mm guns and 2 of our 210mm guns. Out of a force of about 600 men, 8 officers were lost (2 dead, 4 wounded and 2 captured) and 143 soldiers (16 dead, 74 wounded and 53 missing).

strength. He took part at all the main battles of the I Assault Unit of Sdricca. It is a serious loss. On the 21st we took the train to Lonigo.
On the 22nd we continued on foot to the Grancona area.
During the march the troops sang at the top of their lungs. We had received good news. The *mucs* were no longer advancing and their walkways were destroyed by our artillery and by the fury of the Piave in flood.
Their great offensive was about to turn into a great defeat.[495]

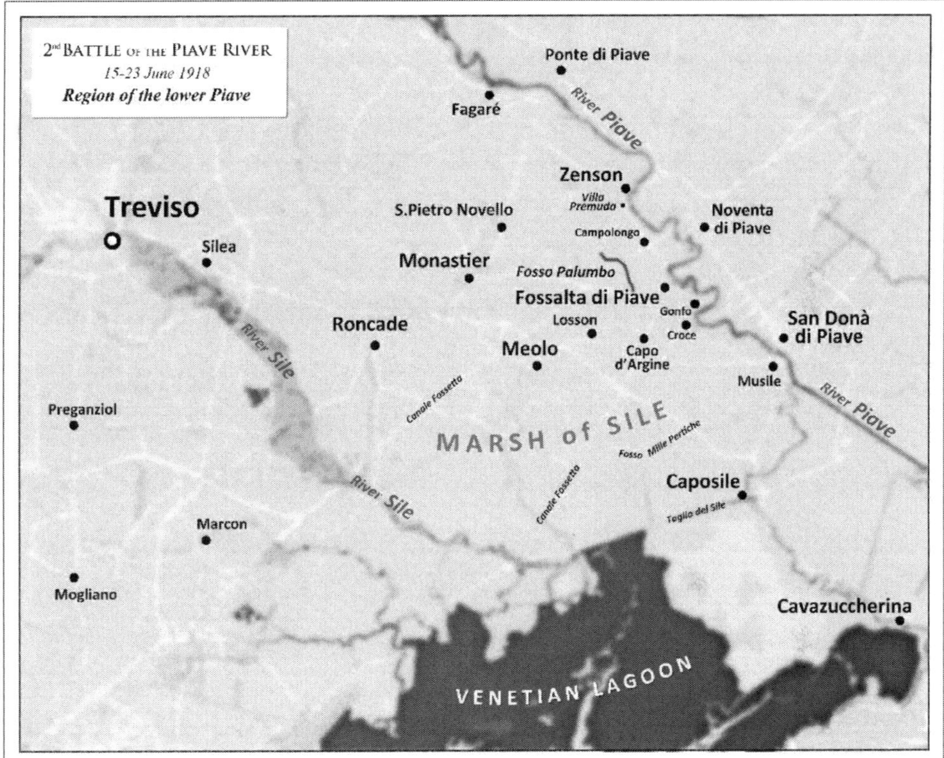

[495] In the face of the failures on Mount Grappa, General Boroević had already on the morning of 19 June proposed withdrawing to the left bank of the Piave to Emperor Charles. At 7:16 p.m. of the following day the decision was taken: general retreat at night, but with no conspicuous pull backs in order not to tip off the Italians. On the night of the 21st, the retraction of artillery, trucking, field hospitals and wounded began beyond the Piave and on the night of the 22nd, that of supplies, artillery and uncommitted reserves. Only minimal troops remained in line to deceive the Italians. On the night of the 23rd the definitive retreat was carried out, hampered by the Italian artillery and made even more tragic by the flood of the Piave. Already in the evening war bulletin of the 23rd, General Diaz announced to the country the victorious outcome of the battle of arrest: *"From Montello to the sea, the enemy, defeated and pursued by our valiant troops, crosses in disorder to the other side of the Piave"*. After the beating at Caporetto, the Royal Army had been able to recover and drive back the powerful Austro-Hungarian army.

CHAPTER 30.IV

Grancona, Tuesday, 25 June 1918

All the newspapers are giving news of our great victory.

The offensive has been blocked.

The *mucs* have been driven back to the left bank of the Piave.[496]

Now calm reigns along the river and also in the mountains.

Our Division was mentioned in the war bulletin of 19 June.

Unfortunately, we heard bad news about Major Francesco Baracca.[497]

He was shot down on the Montello that same day. He was our ace of aviation. He won over thirty dogfights.

We are very sorry.

Replacing Captain Turotti in command of our company is Lieutenant Filippo Meloni. *Carestia* is very proud, since he is a fellow Sardinian.

Grancona, Saturday, 29 June 1918

Today in Villa Orgiano his majesty the King Vittorio Emanuele III and the Chief-of-Staff, General Diaz, reviewed our Assault Division.[498]

I saw them go by. The King is really small in stature.

---

[496] In citing the heroic behaviour of the Army of Grappa, the High Command wrote in the war bulletin of June 18, 1918: *"Each soldier, defending Mount Grappa, felt that every handbreadth of the mountain was sacred to the Homeland!"*

Shining testimony to this are the 640 medals of Military Valour awarded for that battle, 486 of which to privates. The sensational defeat suffered by the Austro-Hungarian army on the Piave caused a moral collapse in their ranks, who lost confidence in the victory.

[497] Major Francesco Baracca (9 May 1888 - 19 June 1918) shot down 34 planes in 63 fights before being himself shot down on the Montello near Nervesa. It is not clear whether he was hit by an Austro-Hungarian plane or ground shots. His body was found four days later near the wreckage of his aircraft with a bullet wound to his right temple. As a tribute to the cavalry, the branch from which he came, he had a prancing horse painted on the left side of his aircraft. In 1923 Baracca's mother authorized Enzo Ferrari to use this emblem on the cars he piloted for the Alfa Romeo team, and subsequently on the cars of the company which he founded after the Second World War.

[498] On June 28, the "A" Division was renamed 1st Assault Division. The day before the 2nd Assault Division had been founded, under General Ernesto De Marchi. The 1st Division relinquished Units V, XIV and XXX, replaced by Battalions I, VII and IX of the 1st Bersaglieri Regiment. Colonel Roberto Bertolotti, former commander of the 1st Bersaglieri Regiment, took the place of Colonel Trivulzio at the 3rd Assault Group.

General Diaz has a resolute air but looks kind-hearted.
They gave out many awards.
Captain Benci received the Silver Medal of Military Valour in memory.
From what I have seen over the last few days almost everyone should have been rewarded.
«Among Infantrymen a Black Flame shines more brightly and immediately merits a medal of valour» I explained during a discussion between us after the ceremony. «In the midst of Black Flames, however, his light fades because we are all brilliant. It is hard to choose, when everyone is brave.»
«*Par ciapar un bronsin nialtri gavemo da far l'imposibie...*»[499] grumbled *Faro*.
«… or lose our *ghirba*» suggested *Carestia*.
«*No, grasie. Tegneve el bronsin!*»[500]

---

499 «To get a bronze medal we have to do the impossible...» translation from the Venetian dialect.
500 «No thanks. Keep your bronze medal!»

Chapter 31.IV

The second battle of the Piave or "Battle of the Solstice", as Gabriele d'Annunzio[501] *named it, was of much greater proportions and intensity than can be imagined from the pages of my grandfather's diary.*
Among the dead, wounded, missing and prisoners, the Austro-Hungarians lost almost 150,000 men and the Italians around 90,000 (6,110 dead, 27,660 wounded and 51,860 missing).
The Arditi wrote epic pages in the various theatres of war.
The IX Unit of Major Giovanni Messe became legendary, conquering in a few days as many as four vital strongholds on Mount Grappa (Col Fagheron on June 15, Col Fenilon and Col Moschin on June 16, Asolone on June 24).[502]
On the Montello the XXVII Unit led by Major Luigi Freguglia brought glory to itself in numerous engagements.[503]

In demonstration of how arduous was the task of the Assault Units in that battle, the statistics on the losses suffered by the various branches speak for themselves.

---

[501] Gabriele d'Annunzio (12 March 1863 - 1st March 1938), writer, poet, playwright, patriot, aviator, soldier, war hero, politician, journalist, for many decades was one of the most prominent and influential personalities in Italian literature and political life.
[502] Major Giovanni Messe (10 December 1883 - 18 December 1968) was awarded the Military Order of Savoy and his unit received the silver medal with this motivation:
"For unstoppable, audacious impetus, in one sole bound he reached bloodily formidable positions." After taking Mount Asolone the commander of the IX Army Corps, General Emilio De Bono, wrote of the Arditi: *"Likewise in yesterday's offensive action they showed unparalleled aggressive spirit, valour, determination, fortitude. If you fight like they do you perforce must win. I am sure that the other infantry regiments of the Army Corps will know how to emulate them."*
In the June fighting, the IX Assault Unit lost 19 officers and 305 soldiers, including the highly decorated standard-bearer Ciro Scianna, to whom the king awarded the Gold Medal of Military Valour.
[503] The XXVII alone was able to halt the enemy advance and regain part of the lost ground. Thanks to this Unit's bloody reconquest of an important stronghold called "White House", the whole line of resistance reverted into Italian hands, and could then be used by the troops for the counterattack. Among other actions of those days, the capture of the commander of the 132nd Brigade Honvéd, General Enrico Bolzano von Kronstadt is noteworthy. The Unit had 3 officers killed and 9 wounded, 55 Arditi killed and 101 wounded.

The Arditi lost 20% of their strength; the Infantry 16%; the Bombers 7%; the Bersaglieri 6%; the autonomous machine gunners 5%; the Engineers and the Field Artillery 2%; the Field heavy artillery 1.7%; the Siege artillery1.5%; the Mountain artillery 0.7%.
The Assault Division with its nine units achieved several tactical victories, but for various organizational reasons it did not become the vanguard of the counter-offensive, as had been planned by the commands.
It suffered severe losses: 1,200 killed and wounded and more than 350 missing out of an organic force of 5,000 men.
It was necessary to remove it from the front to rest and regroup.

By pure chance, I discovered that in those days the future Nobel Prize winner for literature Ernest Hemingway, aged eighteen, was located in the Fossalta area. He had volunteered with the United States Red Cross and served as an ambulance driver.
He was awarded a silver medal for having rescued many wounded soldiers, even though he himself had been hit by bomb fragments and a machine gun bullet. From that experience and his subsequent hospitalization in a Milanese clinic he drew inspiration for his famous novel "Farewell to Arms".
Who knows if my grandfather met him in Fossalta?
Hemingway surely came into contact with the Arditi and was inspired by them, so much so that he wrote the short novel "The Disappearance of Pickles McCarty".
It tells the story of an Italo-American boxer who has mysteriously disappeared from the ring, just as he was about to become world champion, and has clandestinely returned to Italy to join the Arditi. The story was written in 1919 during Hemingway's Michigan summer vacation.
Numerous historical facts are recognizable in the story:

- *the conquest of Mount Corno (13 May 1918)*
- *an Arditi counterattack in Fossalta di Piave (late afternoon of 17 June 1918)*
- *an Austrian shelling of Col Campeggia and the breakthrough of the Austrians on the Strada Cadorna in Ponte San Lorenzo and at the Osteria alla Cibara (morning of June 15, 1918)*
- *a battle at Col Spiazzoli, north-east of Ponte San Lorenzo (early afternoon of June 15)*
- *the epic action of the Arditi when they broke through on the Asolone and in one swift bound pushed as far ahead as Col della Berretta and Col Bonato (morning of 25 October).*

Reading this part of the diary I discovered so many things, things that I could never have found in books.
It is very different seeing the great battles through the eyes of those who fought them on the field risking their lives.
Even though I was already familiar with the trajectory of the great story, every page of this little story was a surprise and revealed to me many facts, facts which no one knew anymore or had ever known.
At every turn of the page I had the sensation of discovering a mysterious and unexplored world, like when you pick up a stone to find a teeming ant-hill underneath; a world that can sometimes be unpleasant and dangerous, as when under the stone is a spitting viper. Some pages, in fact, revealed events that were anything but pleasant for me, especially when they concerned my family.

Ever since the fifth grade, I knew that Italy had won the last battle and that this victory had made a decisive contribution to the conclusion of the First World War.
I was anxious to discover what my grandfather and his unit had contributed to that great battle.
Among the things that grandfather left behind is a typed sheet with the list of places where he fought.
Among these is the name of a village that I had never heard of before: Moriago.

5th Part

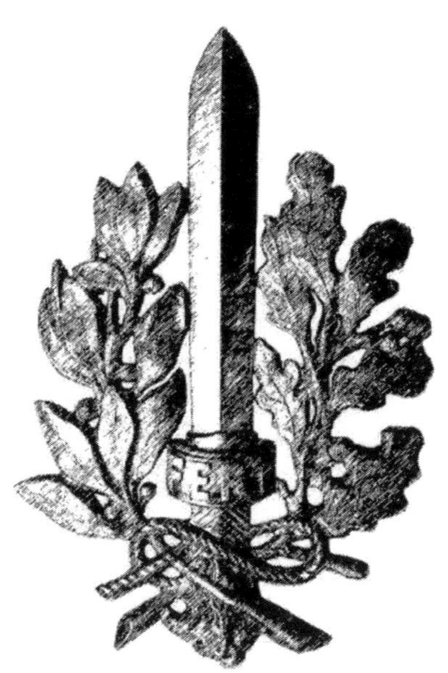

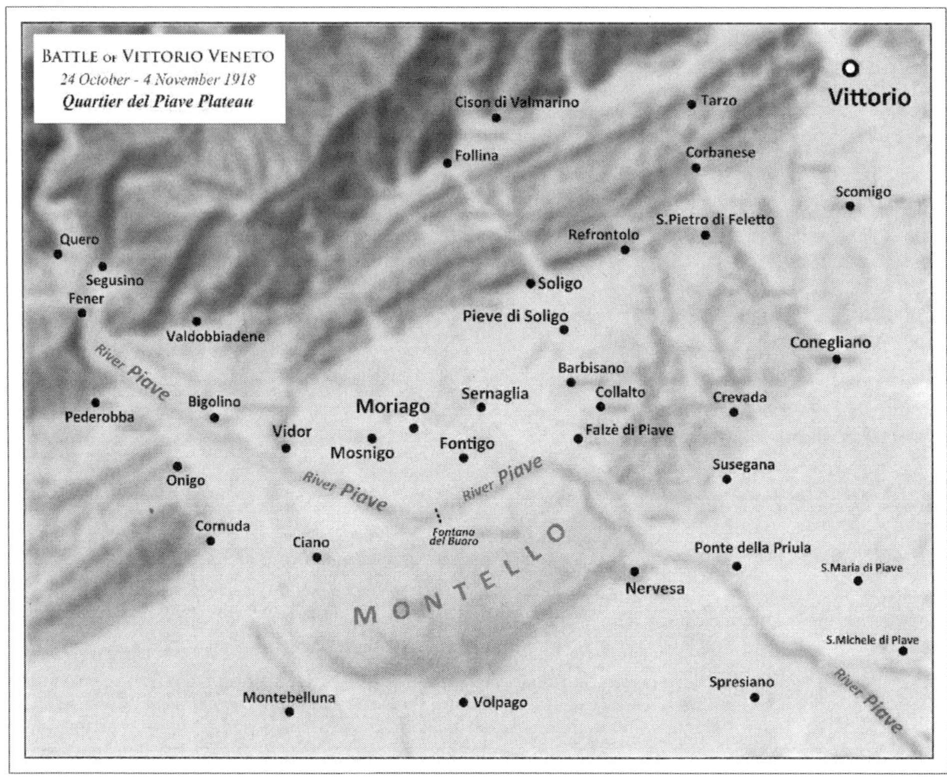

CHAPTER 1.V

San Germano dei Berici, Sunday, 7 July 1918
I got a postcard from Noè.
He is recovering.
He was wounded during the June fighting.
He told me he's fine.
I'll go and visit him.
I haven't seen him since I joined the army.
Over two and a half years have gone by.

Chapter 2.V

San Germano dei Berici, Monday, 8 July 1918
Good news. Today *O'pazzo* is back.
We made a big fuss over him, laughing and joking around.
He wanted to show us the scar on his chest.
«Six months for that little scratch? Look here» *Carestia* took off his shirt and trousers to show his numerous wounds, imitated by *il Gat*, *Pugnodiferro*, *Trepugnali* and *Faro*, who, however, has no wounds.
At that moment, *Lu-Lupo*, our company's new aide-de-battle, entered the barracks.
Everyone awkwardly stood to attention half-naked, but with chins held exaggeratedly high and proud faces, while he shouted: «What are you doing? A str-str-striptease? You fi-fi-filthy guys!»
«No, sir, aide-de-de-ba-ba-battle» replied *Pugnodiferro*, making fun of him.
«Tw-tw-twenty push-ups ri-ri-ri-right away!»
«To o-o-o-orders» replied *Pugnodiferro*, starting the exercise. «O-o-one, tw-tw-two, thr-thr-three, fo-fo-four, fi-fi-five...»
«Too ea-ea-easy like that, a-a-asshole!» screamed *Lu-Lupo* in his ear, climbing on *Pugnodiferro's* back with his boots.
Pugnodiferro kept on doing the exercise without a word.
At the eighteenth push-up *O'pazzo* also got on his back.
«*Si' diventato forte, guagliò!*»[504]
At this point *Pugnodiferro* collapsed.
Then *Lu-Lupo* sat on his head and began to slap him, while everyone clapped in time.
When he got up, with a red face, he hugged *Lu-Lupo* and congratulated him on his promotion.
We have fought many battles together.

---

[504] «You've gotten strong, boy!» translation from the Neapolitan dialect.

CHAPTER 3.V

San Germano dei Berici, Thursday, 11 July 1918
We have just gotten back from two days of training in Monte della Torre with the other troops of the 3rd Group: VIII Assault Unit and IX Bersaglieri Battalion. We repeated the same exercise several times: the conquest of a line of entrenchments and then reorganising it in defense.
It was very hot, not only for the sun and the humidity, but also because machine gun bullets and artillery shells were whining over our heads.
We veterans of Sdricca are used to it, because this was the daily bread at the school. The new draftees and the Bersaglieri, however, were having a pretty hard time. I had to yell at them a lot, telling them to keep down and keep moving ahead. They did as I ordered and nobody was hurt.

That evening around the fire we started singing a new song, which recalls the great victory of last June.
It is so beautiful and full of pride that we sang it many times, accompanied by the roll of a drum and the trumpet played by *Faro*.
These are the words: [505]

---

[505] *The Piave murmured calm and placid at the passing of the first infantrymen on May the 24th;*
The army was marching to the frontier, to make a barrier against the enemy!
In silence they passed by that night, they had to go forward in silence!
Audible, meanwhile, from the beloved banks, was the hushed and gentle exultation of the waves.
It was a sweet and propitious omen. The Piave murmured: "the foreigner shall not pass!"
But on a sad night the word betrayal was spoken, and the Piave heard the anger and dismay.
Ah, how many people did the river see arriving, leaving their homes; for the shame of Caporetto.
Refugees everywhere, from the distant mountains, came to crowd its bridges.
From the violated banks could be heard, hushed and sad, the murmur of the waves.
Like a sob in that black autumn. The Piave murmured: "the foreigner returns!"
The enemy returned in pride and hunger, wanting to feed all his desires,
He saw the fertile plain from on high: he wanted to devour and revel as before!
No! Said the Piave, No! Said the soldiers, never again will the enemy take a step forward!
The Piave swelled its banks! Like soldiers battling the waves...
Red with the blood of the haughty enemy, the Piave ordered: "Turn back, foreigner!"
Back went the enemy, to Trieste, to Trento and victory spread her wings to the wind!
Sacred was the ancient pact and in the ranks could be seen Oberdan, Sauro and Battisti resurrected!
Italian valour shattered the gallows and the arms of the Hangman at last!
The Alps secured, its banks liberated ...the Piave fell silent, its waves appeased.
And in the Homeland, the grim Empire defeated, Peace found neither the oppressed, nor foreigners!

Il Piave mormorava
calmo e placido al passaggio
dei primi fanti il 24 maggio;
l'esercito marciava
per raggiunger la frontiera
per far contro il nemico una barriera...
Muti passaron quella notte i fanti,
tacere bisognava, e andare avanti!
S'udiva, intanto, dalle amate sponde
sommesso e lieve il tripudiar dell'onde.
Era un presagio dolce e lusinghiero
Il Piave mormorò:
"Non passa lo straniero!"

Ma in una notte trista
si parlò di tradimento
e il Piave udiva l'ira e lo sgomento...
Ahi, quanta gente ha vista
venir giù, lasciare il tetto
per l'onta consumata a Caporetto!
Profughi ovunque! Dai lontani monti
venivano a gremir tutti i suoi ponti.
S'udiva, allor, dalle violate sponde,
sommesso e triste il mormorar de l'onde:
come un singhiozzo in quell'autunno nero,
il Piave mormorò:
"Ritorna lo straniero!"

E ritornò il nemico
per l'orgoglio e per la fame:
volea sfogare tutte le sue brame...
Vedeva il piano aprico,
di lassù: voleva ancora
sfamarsi e tripudiare come allora...
No! Disse il Piave. No! Dissero i fanti,
mai più il nemico faccia un passo avanti...
Si vide il Piave rigonfiar le sponde!
E come i fanti combattevan le onde...
Rosso del sangue del nemico altero,
il Piave comandò:
"Indietro, va', straniero!"

Indietreggiò il nemico
fino a Trieste e fino a Trento...
e la vittoria sciolse le ali al vento!
Fu sacro il patto antico:
tra le schiere, furon visti risorgere
Oberdan, Sauro, Battisti...
Infranse, alfin, l'italico valore
le forche e l'armi dell'Impiccatore!
Sicure l'Alpi, libere le sponde...
E tacque il Piave, si placaron le onde...
Sul patrio suolo, vinti i torvi Imperi,
la Pace non trovò,
né oppressi, né stranieri!

«*L'ha scritta nu napulitano*» boasts *O'pazzo*.[506]
«*Alura, ést che te sìet a Napoli, te pödìet dìga che l' metès dét pò ach i Ardicc in chèsta cansù e mia dóma i Fancc*»[507] *il Gat* always replies.
«Let's put them in» *Pugnodiferro* proposed enthusiastically. «Listen here: *Il Piave mormorava calmo e placido al passaggio dei primi Arditi il 24 maggio.*»[508]
«The Arditi weren't born yet on May 24» I reminded him.
«They were born on July 29th, 1917!» said *Carestia*.

---

[506] *La Leggenda del Piave (The Legend of Piave)* was written and set to music by Giovanni Ermete Gaeta (5 May 1884 - 24 June 1961) in Naples on the wave of enthusiasm for the victorious battle in June. In order to popularize his song among the troops,.Gaeta asked for leave from the post office where he worked, but it was not granted. So he asked a friend to replace him and, armed with a mandolin, he took a train to the front. With the help of the singer Raffaele Gattordo, aka Enrico Demma, he played and promoted his song among the soldiers under the pseudonym of E. A. Mario. Its success was immediate and the song spread quickly everywhere, lending pride and morale to the army. General Diaz himself sent Gaeta a telegram, acknowledging how much his song was benefiting the national recovery: *"Your song The Legend of Piave at the front is more effective than a general!"*. The song was published on 20 September 1918, always under the pseudonym of E. A. Mario. During the post-war period, it served to idealize the Great War and make people forget the atrocities, the suffering and the deaths that had characterized it. Gaeta received numerous honours for his song, also from the king, who wanted to meet him personally. Equipped with a great poetic and musical talent, in spite of working all his life at the post office which now was proud of him, he wrote over 2,000 songs, interpreted by both Neapolitan singers and tenors. His most famous songs are *Le Rose rosse*, *Vipera*, *Santa Lucia luntana*, *Balocchi e Profumi*, *Tammurriata nera*.

[507] «So, when you were in Naples, you could have told him to put the Arditi in his song and not just infantrymen» translation from the Bergamo dialect.

[508] *The Piave murmured calm and placid at the passing of the first Arditi on May the 24th.*

«In a few days it will be a year» added *Trepugnali*.
«Then let's put this way. Listen: *No! Disse il Piave. No! Dissero gli Arditi, mai più il nemico faccia un passo avanti...*»[509]
«It does not rhyme with *avanti...* » objected *Carestia* correctly.
«*Lassa sta', Pugn'eferr. Tu nun si nu poeta, tu si nu chianchiere*»[510] *O'pazzo* pointed out.

---

509 *No, said the Piave, no, said the Arditi, never again will the enemy take a step forward!*
510 «Forget it. You are not a poet, you are a butcher» transl. from the Neapolitan dialect.

Chapter 4.V

San Germano dei Berici, Sunday, 14 July 1918
Today I went to visit Noè at the convalescent home.
I found him playing cards with other wounded guys.
None of them stood up to greet me. They had lost their legs.
Noè, however, got up and ran to hug me, happy to see me.
«*Cemût ese, fradi? Pulît?*»[511]
«*Iò sei pulît e tu? Ce âtu fat?*»[512]
«*Schegjis di bombe in tun braç. A mi dûl ancje mò. E no sint pui nue in tune vorele.*»[513]
"*Can da l'ostie! Al no si è fat nue, ma al vai il muart*"[514] I thought.
With similar wounds an Ardito would have already returned to his unit.
«*O ài ancje un palmon malementri*» he said, coughing. «*O podevi lâ cun Diu scjafoiât.*»[515]
Between bouts of coughing, he told me all his adventures, first in Val Dogna, then during the retreat and finally in the June fight, when during a shelling he was injured and poisoned by the gas launched by the *mucs*.
I listened to him attentively, but it all seemed like nothing in comparison to what we had gone through.
«*E tu, Pieri, ce âtu fat cun chês flamis neris?*»[516]
«*O ài fat trop e nue. O ài fat nome ce chi vevi di fâ.*»[517]
«*Alc tu às di vei fat si tu sês sergjent majôr. Sumo contimi.*»[518]
At that precise moment I realized that I had no desire to tell anything to anybody. Only the Arditi, the infantrymen of the "Sassari" and the "Bisagno", and the 14th Bersaglieri could understand what I had done.
Noè took me around the convalescent home, introducing me to his Alpine friends, who had all kinds of wounds.

---

511 «What's up brother? Everything good?» translation from the Friulan language.
512 «I'm fine and you? What happened to you?»
513 «Shell fragments in one arm. It still hurts. And I am deaf in one ear.»
514 "You rascal! That's nothing and yet you are complaining!"
515 «I also have a damaged lung. I could have died of suffocation.»
516 «And you, Pietro, what have you done with those black flames?»
517 «I've done many things and nothing. I only did what I had to do.»
518 «You must have done something if you have become a sergeant major. Come on, tell me.»

Some of them had their faces all bandaged, certainly disfigured by some splinter.
Then there were those who had lost an eye or, worse, both.
Many were without hands or arms.
In one of the pavilions were those who had had one or, even worse, both legs amputated. Noè also introduced me to some Red Cross nurses.
Seeing my uniform, one of them told me that in another pavilion there were some Arditi who had been wounded on Mount Grappa.
«*Cuant tu tornis in ta tô compagnie?*»[519] I asked Noè point-blank.
«*Iò speri di no tornâ pui. Iò sei invalid di vuere, satu. A mi daran la pension.*»[520]
At that precise moment I pitied my brother. There was nothing to be done. With a stroke of luck, he had found the "smart" wound and the way to get out of the war entirely, albeit with a damaged lung.
It's clear that things have changed.
Last year with Cadorna and Capello guys with wounds like his would have been sent back immediately to fight even if they were still bleeding.
I told him I had to get back to my unit.
I said goodbye and took my leave.
Before going, however, I went to look for the pavilion the Red Cross nurse had told me about. There were Arditi from the IX Assault Unit, with serious wounds inflicted in the fighting on the Mount Grappa.
We talked at length.
Some of them could not hold back their tears.
They knew they could never go back to their units to fight again.
For them the war was over and yet they were crying.

---

519 «When do you plan to return to your company?»
520 «I hope I never have to go back. I'm a war invalid, you know. They will give me a pension.»

CHAPTER 5.V

San Germano dei Berici, Tuesday, 16 July 1918
The Division Command is looking for volunteers who know how to swim well. They want to set up a team of swimmers to cross the Piave at night without being seen by the *mucs*.[521]
Some men from my company went to the selections.
They will be tested by swimming in the Bacchiglione.
I asked *Faro* why he didn't try out, since he is from Murano.
«*Mi no so bon nuàr!*»[522] he replied, raising his bright eyes to heaven.
«The *tognìt* would see him im-im-immediately, *con quei oci che el ga!*»[523] ironized *Lu-Lupo*.
How strange.
Even if I come from the mountains, I get by fine in the water.
He comes from the seaside, but he cannot swim at all.
«*Mi so bon sonar e lavorar el vero. L'acqua se bagnada!*»[524]

The newspapers say there has been a major German offensive on the Marna, but the French are resisting with the help of the British and now also with the help of the Americans.[525]

San Germano dei Berici, Sunday, 21 July 1918
Training. Always training.
All possible methods of opening gaps in barbed wire with pliers, Ravelli bombs and the shooting of Stokes at close range are being studied.[526]

---

[521] After the battle in June, General Zoppi (16 January 1870 - 17 March 1962) entrusted Captain Remo Pontecorvo with the task of selecting and training a special unit of swimmers for special missions on the other side of the Piave. Out of over 400 volunteers, only 82 passed the tests of skill and endurance in the waters of the Bacchiglione, Brenta and Sile rivers. Due to their way of slithering into the river and then swimming silently with only their nostrils above the water, these raiders were called "Caimani del Piave". They wore only swimming trunks and helmets, but were equipped with a dagger, musket and the inevitable petards.
[522] «I can't swim!» translation from the Venetian dialect.
[523] «The Austrians would spot him immediately, with those eyes of his!»
[524] «I know how to play music and work glass. Water is wet!»
[525] Nearly one million American soldiers had arrived in France.

We practice climbing over the wire with walkways and trellises.
We've also experimented with portable spotlights to blind the enemy in the attack area.
While we train, on our front there is nothing new.
Radiofante says the High Command is preparing a big offensive for the spring of next year. We will cross the Piave and push the *mucs* back beyond the Isonzo.
On the western front, however, the fighting continues.
The newspapers say that our allies are counterattacking on the Marne.[527]
If they ever defeat Germany, we are all convinced that the *mucs* would instantly deflate like potato sacks.
But defeating the Germans is not an easy task.

P.S. The "three-day fever" broke out again in the village.
Civilians are said to have died. Some fellow soldiers have fallen ill too.

---

[526] The bomb launcher created in 1915 by Englishman Sir Wilfred Stokes was the forerunner of modern mortars. The Royal Army received Stokes from the United Kingdom as a portion of the supplies furnished by the Allies to replace materials lost during the Caporetto retreat. Each Infantry Battalion included a platoon with 4 mortars. The team assigned to the piece was made up of a graduated foreman, a loading soldier, two bomb-handers and two assistants. For shoulder transport, the weapon could be broken down into three parts: the barrel (19.5 kg), the base plate (12.7 kg) and the bipod (16.7 kg).
[527] When the German offensive push was exhausted, the Allies, under the unified command of the French general Ferdinand Foch (2 October 1851 - 20 March 1929), took the initiative with a series of attacks with limited objectives, but in rapid succession to subject Ludendorff's troops to constant pressure. In addition to their superior numbers, they were able to take advantage of the increased availability of tanks and planes.

CHAPTER 6.V

San Germano dei Berici, Monday, 29 July 1918

Today we had a party.

Exactly one year has passed since the birth of the Assault Units.

On July 29 of last year the 1st company of the I Unit performed a training exercise on the "dummy hill" of the School of Sdricca. The king, the duke of Aosta and Generals Cadorna and Capello were full of praise.

Few men from that glorious unit are still here with us.

Many died in defense of Udine. Others, including Captain Radicati, have been taken prisoner by the *mucs*.

«Who knows if Abbondanza, Turotti and *Mezzomago* are in the same prison camp as Captain Radicati?» asked *Trepugnali*.

«Who knows if they're still alive?» I replied. «If the *tognìt* have little to eat, the prisoners risk starvation.»

«*A l'ghe pènsa Mès-mago coi sò magée a troàga ergóta de mangià per töcc i presunér*»[528] said *il Gat*.

«No way! *Chillu è nu miezzu mago, mica nostro signore Gesù Cristo c'à moltiplic e pan e pisc e cagne l'acqua c'ò vin!*»[529] *O'pazzo* cut him short.

For the very occasion of today's party, the silver pin of our unit arrived.

It depicts an Ardito jumping from the trench with a dagger in one hand and a petard in the other.

"Sii fulmin del ciel, bufera e flagel" is written alongside.[530]

Above there is the date of birth of the II Unit: 1-IX-1917.

We pinned it on our ties.

A bronze medal has also arrived with an engraved list of the unit's victories: Bainsizza q.800, Kal plateau, Conca di Plezzo, Moriago-Mosnigo, Mount Val Bella, Zenzon, Fossalta di Piave.

On the front side there is a winged woman with the inscription "A noi!".

---

[528] «With his magic *Mezzomago* will take care of finding something to eat for all the prisoners» translation from the Bergamo dialect.

[529] «He is only half a magician, not our Lord Jesus Christ who multiplies the loaves and fishes and transforms water into wine» translation from the Neapolitan dialect.

[530] *"May thou be lighting bolt, storm and scourge"* translation from Italian.

Around the edge is the motto *"Si fractus illabatur orbis impavidum ferient ruinae"*.[531]
«*Cose e pazz'. Na scritta in tedesco…*»[532] commented *O'pazzo*, shaking his head.
«*Ma 'n che manéra, porsèl de chèl diaól, i à scrìcc in todèsch? Cósa cassaso ölel dì?*»[533] *il Gat* asked me.
«It isn't German, you blockhead! It's Latin. But I don't know what it means» I replied to both.
«*Latino? Allora, guagliù, o saccio io cosa vuol di'.*»[534]
«Watch out, *guagliò*, that if you come up with more bullshit like you did with FERT, I'll make another hole in your body and send you back to *Napule*» threatened him *Pugnodiferro.*
«*Vabbuo'. Allora non v'ò dico e mo tengo per me. Ce voglio stà a prossima battaglia e mettere n'atu nome dinta a medaglia.*»[535]

---

[531] *"Even if the world fell to pieces, I would let its rubble strike me, unafraid"* translation from Latin (Horace, Odi, book III, n.3). It indicates a tenacious man, of solid principles, who does not yield to difficulties and obstacles.
[532] «That's crazy. An inscription in German…» translation from the Neapolitan dialect.
[533] «Why the hell did they write in German? What the heck does it mean?» translation from the Bergamo dialect.
[534] «Latin? In that case, guys, I know what it means» translation from the Neapolitan dialect.
[535] «All right. So I won't tell you, I'll keep it to myself. I want to be there at the next battle and add another victory to the medal» translation from the Neapolitan dialect.

CHAPTER 7.V

San Germano dei Berici, Wednesday, 7 August 1918
Last night I had a strange dream.
I dreamed that the war was over and that I was walking in Val Dogna with a little boy by my side. But I don't know who he was.
He did not look like any of my brothers.

San Germano dei Berici, Sunday, 11 August 1918
On Friday we performed a major training exercise between Villa del Ferro and Orgiano.
There were divisional machine guns and mountain artillery as well.
We were supposed to conquer land infested with machine gun nests.
The newspapers write that the Allies are continuing to advance.
They have thrown back the Germans by almost fifty kilometres![536]
Here, however, we only talk about a few raids and d'Annunzio's great exploit. The other day with a squadron of SVA he flew over Vienna and launched thousands of leaflets.[537]
«*A l'gh'ìa de bötà zó di bómbe, chèl là, mia di tochelì de carta!*»[538] commented *il Gat*.

I transcribe the text.

VIENNESE!
Learn about the Italians.
We are flying over Vienna; we could drop tons of bombs. All we are dropping on you is a greeting in three colours: the three colours of liberty.

[536] On 8 August, a second offensive began in front of Amiens, led by Franco-British troops supported by 600 tanks and 800 planes: the allied success was such that General Ludendorff defined that day *"the blackest for the German army"*. On August 15, the action continued with a vigorous counterattack on the Somme by British and Americans.
[537] On the morning of 9 August, eight of the eleven Ansaldo SVA (reconnaissance and bombing biplanes) reached Vienna from Padua, dropping 50,000 copies of a leaflet written by d'Annunzio in Italian (impossible to translate into German) and 350,000 copies of another leaflet written in German by Ugo Ojetti, journalist and war volunteer. Militarily irrelevant, the raid resonated worldwide and widely impressed the population of Vienna.
[538] «He should have thrown bombs, not pieces of paper!» translation from the Bergamo dialect.

We Italians do not wage war on children, on old people, on women.
We are waging war on your government, the enemy of national liberty, on your blind, stubborn, cruel government that is able to give you neither peace nor bread and feeds you on hatred and illusions.

VIENNESE!
They say you are intelligent.
Then why are you wearing the uniform of Prussia?
By now, you see, the whole world has turned against you.
You want to continue the war? Continue it; it's your suicide.
What do you hope for?
The decisive victory that the Prussian generals promised you?
Their decisive victory is like the bread of Ukraine: You die waiting for it.

PEOPLE OF VIENNA, think of your own fates. Wake up!
LONG LIVE LIBERTY!
LONG LIVE ITALY!
LONG LIVE THE ENTENTE!

San Germano dei Berici, Wednesday, 21 August 1918
It feels like a vacation.
This morning King Vittorio Emanuele came to visit us in Granze delle Frassinelle and gave captain Seraglia the flag of the XXII Assault Unit.
Carestia, *Trepugnali*, *O'pazzo* and many other comrades, however, were not in line with us. They are sick with the "Spanish flu", as they are calling that raging fever.
It seems that it is spreading throughout Italy and also among the *mucs*.
It seems that many people succumb instead of getting better after three days.[539] I hope I won't get it again.

San Germano dei Berici, Tuesday, 27 August 1918
Yesterday we did a grand-scale exercise between Brenta and Bacchiglione.
The whole 1st Assault Division was involved.
We were divided into two rival groups and we fought hard.
A couple of soldiers were wounded.

---

[539] Myxovirus A, responsible for the pandemic of 1918-19, was isolated only in 1933. Medical treatment was very primitive and often ridiculous, so much so that some scathingly defined the therapy adopted in Italy: *"four quinine tablets and some straw to die on"*. Many clinicians lashed out against the abuse of a new drug, useful in lowering fever, but guilty of favouring pulmonary and cardiac complications: its name was Aspirin.

San Germano dei Berici, Thursday, 29 August 1918
Today is a bad day.
O'pazzo didn't make it. He is dead. It was the "Spanish flu"!
«He had lung complications» said the medical officer.
We are all really sad.
If he had stayed home in Naples, it might not have happened.
Who knows? It is all fatality, he would say.
We will miss his chatter and his cheer very much.
In this war, many have died not only on the battlefield, but also from illness. Fortunately, *Carestia* and *Trepugnali* have recovered.
Yesterday *Pugnodiferro* got sick. We're hoping for the best.

San Germano dei Berici, Monday, 9 September 1918
Today *Faro* had to buy everyone a drink, including *Pugnodiferro*, who has recovered. On Tuesday he turned 24.
He has been in the army since July 1914.
Before joining the Arditi he was in the 71st Infantry.
We also celebrated the defeat of the Germans on September 2nd.[540]
It seems that the *crucchi* are no longer invincible.
We remembered with sorrow all the comrades we have lost on the way: *O'pazzo*, *Mandulino*, *Biunnu*, *Bracciodiferro*, *Canarino*, *il Vòlp*, Nino Sistu, Captain Benci and many others.
We drank to the health of those who are prisoners of the *mucs*, such as *Mezzomago*, captains Turotti, Abbondanza, Radicati and many others.
If they get a penny for each of our blessings and for each toast to their health, they will come home fat and well fed at the end of the war.
Lately, 5 officers and 40 soldiers from the XII have joined our unit to complete our staff.
Our vacation is about to end. A rumour is going around that at the end of September the command wants us to take a fifteen-day tour of duty in the trenches on Montello. The men are starting to grumble.
They want to get their hands on the *tognìt* and not on the lice and mice that infest the trenches.
We are all very pissed off. Hopefully it's not true.

---

[540] An Anglo-Canadian attack, preceded by a tremendous bombing (one million shells) and supported by tanks, broke through the Hindenburg line (Siegfried Stellung for the Germans), among the last and strongest Germanic defensive positions, east of Arras. In the afternoon Ludendorff ordered a new general retreat to the Hindenburg line, south of the Somme. Kaiser Wilhelm complaining to his staff went so far as to say: *«The war is lost.»*

San Germano dei Berici, Thursday, 12 September 1918
The order has arrived to abandon these quarters.
We have to transfer to San Giorgio delle Pertiche in the province of Padua.
We are going farther away from Montello.
So maybe the story of the tour of duty in the trenches isn't true.

San Giorgio delle Pertiche, Sunday, 15 September 1918
We moved here in three stages. About fifty kilometres on foot.
Where are our trucks?
When we took off our boots, we stank up the entire camp.

San Giorgio delle Pertiche, Wednesday, 18 September 1918
Radiofante says that the 2nd Assault Division has taken over the line from the 15th Infantry Brigade in the Grappa sector.
So the story of duty in the trenches is true.
We are afraid we'll soon have to do it, too.
Before it was too late, I went with *Faro* and *Lu-Lupo* to a photographer's studio in Camposanpiero to have a picture taken together: the two sergeants and the aide-de-battle of the 3rd company of the XXII.
We had to wait a long time. There was a long queue of officers and soldiers. Of course, the captains went before the lieutenants, the lieutenants before the officer aspirants, the aspirants before the NCO's and privates.
I wanted to protest, but *Faro* blocked me, telling me not to.
«*No sta far cagnara che senò no femo ła foto.*»[541]
That photographer is making money thanks to the war.
I don't know how many cigarettes we smoked before our turn came.
We finally entered the room. On one side there was the camera on a tripod, on the other a black backdrop, a carpet and a chair.
The photographer made *Lu-Lupo* sit, as he was the highest in rank, and positioned us behind him, as if we were his bodyguards.
For the occasion, *Lu-Lupo* and I wore the XXII silver pin on our ties.
Faro had forgotten it at the camp.
The photographer told us not to move, not to speak and not to raise our cigarettes to our mouths. He slipped under a black cloth behind the camera.
He fiddled around a little and then counted to three.
On three we were dazzled by a flash of light.
«Done. Next!»

[541] «Don't make a fuss, because otherwise we won't get the picture» translation from the Venetian dialect.

CHAPTER 8.V

San Giorgio delle Pertiche, Thursday, 26 September 1918
The order we all feared has come.
Our Division will have to relieve the 57th Infantry in the Montello trenches.
The Division has been assigned to the 22nd Army Corps.

P.S. We have collected our photograph. We look pretty good.
We kidded *Lu-Lupo* for his boots. An aide-de-battle shouldn't have such muddy boots.

Salvatronda, Friday, 27 September 1918
For the moment, we of the 3rd Assault Group have been side-lined in Salvatronda, near Castelfranco Veneto, on the road to Treviso.
While waiting for new orders, we play cards and football.
We also entertain ourselves by looking at the drawings in the newspapers circulating among the troops. They make fun of the Austrians, the Germans, the Turks and the Bulgarians, but also the Italian *imboscati*.[542]
Even when I was in the Infantry it was said that the army is divided into four categories: *Fessi* are those, like me and my comrades, who fight in the front line; *Fissi* are those with permanent positions in the Division, Army Corps and Army commands[543]; *Italians* are the ones who stay in the rear; *Italianissimi* are those who stay comfortable and safe in the cities, even farther away than the rear.

---

[542] The trench newspapers began to spread after Caporetto and with the establishment of the so-called Service P, patriotic propaganda service, on February 1, 1918. A few days later another circular was issued authorising both the dissemination of political newspapers, subject to the review and approval of articles, and the publication of trench newspapers. *"Definitively approved is the compilation of satirical-humorous army magazines, to be distributed among the troops as widely as possible, and to which, as is already in practice, soldiers will be allowed to contribute. Similar newspapers may also be compiled by smaller units (using their own resources) under the supervision of the Information Offices"*. The best known trench newspapers were La Tradotta, La Giberna, Sempre Avanti, La Ghirba, La Trincea, Il Razzo, L'Astico, Il Montello, La Baionetta. Drawings and cartoons were granted more space than written texts, since many soldiers were illiterate. The editorial staff of these newspapers, fortnightly or monthly, saw the contribution of personalities of the calibre of Carrà, De Chirico, Jahier, Malaparte, Sironi, Soffici and Ungaretti.
[543] *Fessi* is the equivalent of stupid or fool. *Fissi* is the equivalent of steady or fixed.

In those newspapers there are also pages that don't make you laugh at all, if one is able to read. They report how things are going in the occupied territories. There is much misery and hunger due to looting, stealing, requisitions, confiscations, taxes, fires and devastations.
When I read these things, I think of my poor home.
Luckily my family escaped in time. In Florence things are not so great for them, but if they had stayed in Dogna it would have been worse.
The leaflets, which enemy planes occasionally launch on our camps, say that the people remaining are content, because there is a lot to eat and they get along well with the *mucs*, who are good and kind.
We don't believe these lies, because we know those scoundrels well, especially the Bosnians and Hungarians.[544]
In fact, our daily newspapers say that in the occupied territories there is a lot of violence against the civilians, rape, murderers, hangings and deportations.

Caonada, Saturday, 28 September 1918
We have reached the foot of Montello. We're waiting on the sides of the Montebelluna-Selva road. Tomorrow we will relieve the infantrymen of the 57th. I dare not imagine what sewers those trenches must be.

Caonada, Sunday, 29 September 1918
Happy. All of us. An unhoped-for order has arrived. We no longer have to relieve the 57th Infantry. We're going back! We like this type of retreat. We greeted the counterorder with many bursts of "hurrà!".
There is another piece of good news.
Last Friday Bulgaria asked for an armistice.[545]

Vedelago, Monday, 30 September 1918
Our units are scattered between Vedelago and Castelfranco Veneto.
We are awaiting new orders.

---

544 Romanian prisoners said that during the invasion of Veneto, the Hungarians' behaviour had been savage. While the Bohemians and Poles simply got drunk, the Hungarians sacked houses and taverns, also using violence against women.
545 The armistice was signed on that Sunday. Bulgaria was forced to immediately evacuate the territories it occupied in Greece and Serbia, demobilize its army, turn over weapons, ammunition, vehicles and horses to the Allies, return military equipment stolen from the Greek IV Army Corps during the occupation of Eastern Macedonia and open its borders to allied military operations. A month later, on October 30, Turkey also signed the armistice.

Vedelago, Monday, 7 October 1918
We were looking forward to new orders.
Finally, yesterday they arrived. We moved toward the front again.
We camped on the road to Istrana.
Today it rained all the livelong day.

Vedelago, Tuesday, 15 October 1918
Yesterday major Raffaele Di Orazio took over command of the unit, while captain Alberto Seraglia passed to second-in-command.
Right away he took all the officers to the Montello in order to study the terrain beyond the river. Sooner or later we will have to cross it.
Meanwhile, the rumour has spread that Germany has asked France for an armistice.
«*Sperém che la sées issé, che se la guèra la fenéss a m'turna töcc a la nòsta cà*»[546] commented *il Gat*.
We looked at him sideways.
«We have to win the war and maybe go as far as Vienna» *Trepugnali* said.
It was everyone's thought.
«*Tripögnài, tè te dìghet issé perché quando la guèra la fenéss te gh'è de 'ndà 'n galéra*»[547] replied *il Gat*.
«I'd rather go to jail than listen to the French taking our piss. We have to beat the *tognìt* ourselves and avenge last year's retreat» replied harshly *Trepugnali*.
«*A mé me 'nterèssa adóma che la guèra la ghe 'n dàghe ü tài e i la piènte lé öna ólta buna*»[548] were the last words of *il Gat* before being grabbed and roughed up. I let them do it.
The rain has turned the earth back to mud.

Vedelago, Sunday, 20 October 1918
Something big is about to happen.
We are seeing major movements.
Troops, trucks and carriages pass by on the road, raising a great deal of dust. Many Italian and English planes speed across the sky.
The weather stays fine.
Another clear proof that something is about to happen is the poster they've stuck up all over our camp. It was issued by the P Service. [549]

---

546 «I hope so, because if the war ends, we all go home» transl. from the Bergamo dialect.
547 «Trepugnali, you're saying that because when the war ends you'll have to go to jail.»
548 «I just want the war to end and the fighting stop once and for all.»

I copied the text.

ASSAULT BATTALIONS!
Black flames! Red flames!
The greatest flame is the love of your homeland blazing in your soul which, more and more each day, leads you to epic unforgettable struggles and to sublime tests of selflessness and sacrifice.
You have long since surpassed the name ARDITI, which accompanied your baptism on the battlefield, since from your boldness of the first hour you have ascended with a leap to HEROISM.
Thinking of you, Italy is moved and exalted!
Hearts as steady as your fists, minds as cold as your daggers, souls as ardent as the flames of bombs, you are running, running, on the path to GLORY!
Break through their hordes, defeat the knaves, burn the filthy rags they wear, plunge your dagger into the hearts of the unhappy ones who have violated the sacred soil of Italy, pillaged our possessions, raped our women, terrified our children and lashed their tender flesh!
A tooth for a tooth and an eye for an eye!
Only blood will wash away the offense, only flame will purify the blame.
Forward, forward with iron and with fire!
ITALY IS LOOKING TO YOU!

A big group of Arditi had gathered in front of the poster.
Cuteddu was there, too.
He asked me what it said.
«It says we have to take the *tognìt* out» I explained.
He shrugged.
He knew that already.

[549] This was the name of the propaganda, assistance and surveillance service, established by the High Command with the circular of 9 January 1918: *"A genuine service of information on troop morale, also employing specially chosen officers and trustees of sure faith and proven seriousness who should be sought, with no a priori prejudices, in every field, as well as appropriately exploiting the results of epistolary censorship"*. This service was intended to improve the moral and material conditions of the soldiers and of the civilians in territories controlled by the armies. It was mainly entrusted to complement officers, who carried out intellectual activities in civil life (among them were Piero Calamandrei, Giuseppe Lombardo Radice, Giuseppe Prezzolini, Ardengo Soffici and Gioacchino Volpe). According to a disclosure of the 1st Army, the name of P Service was chosen to avoid talking about propaganda and propagandists the closer they came to the troop units themselves.

Vedelago, Monday, 21 October 1918
Radiofante says that tomorrow or the day after our Army Corps will have to approach the Piave. So much for France's victory!
We are confident that next spring's great offensive is about to begin.
Now!

P.S. Last Friday our Division was assigned to Gen. Caviglia's 8th Army.[550]

Vedelago, Tuesday, 22 October 1918
The command has ordered us to be ready to go.
Even today the sky is blue and the sun is shining.
These are perfect conditions for an attack.

6:00 p.m.
The trumpet sounds the "fall in".
Here we go!

---

[550] Enrico Caviglia (4 May 1862 - 22 March 1945) was one of the most bright, educated and talented generals of the Royal Army. In August 1917 he wrote a memorandum to General Cadorna: *"V.E. will agree that the tactic used across the entire front where we are engaged is to launch the infantry attack after two hours of artillery bombing. However, this practice does not take into account the operational needs that vary greatly from sector to sector. Why only two hours? Why not half an hour, or ten hours? Note that we are rarely in a position to evaluate the effectiveness of the shelling. Have breaches in the barbed wire been opened? Have the machine guns been taken out? Have the countless trench mortars hidden in caves been silenced? [...] Still, as V.E. is certainly aware, countless times, if not the totality of the times, even in the face of evident ineffectiveness, in terms of the length of preparation, we continue creating new ones with no variations in an insult to reality, military art and human respect for the suffering and the value of our soldiers. Any madman knows how to kill people."*
Esteemed by the Allies, respected by the enemy, appreciated by his soldiers, he used to study in detail the situation in the field and not behind his desk. Victorious on the Bainsizza plateau at the helm of the 24th Army Corps, fundamental at Caporetto in protecting the retreat of the 3rd Army, whose capture would have led to the collapse of the army and the probable defeat of Italy, the true architect of success in the final battle in command of the 8th Army. In 1919 he was appointed Senator of the Realm and for a few months held the position of Minister of War. In December 1920 it fell to him to repress the Fiume Exploit during the so-called "Bloody Christmas", alienating many sympathies. His moral intransigence, combined with a decided capacity for analysis, sometimes bordering on foresight, led him to not join the Fascist movement, which he criticised openly. Although appointed Marshal of Italy in 1926 and Knight of the Supreme Order of the Santissima Annunziata in 1930, despite not infrequent consultations with the King and Mussolini, he was always set aside in favour of Badoglio, whose actions he stigmatized throughout his life, in particular the inglorious "escape" at Caporetto.

Chapter 9.V

Casa Antiga di Collalto, Tuesday, 29 October 1918
I came out of it alive and unscathed this time too. Thank heavens.
We are spending the night here.
From this hill you can see the plain lit up by many fires.
Right now, I don't feel like writing about what's happened these past few days.
I am exhausted, but happy, because the *mucs* are retreating.

Casa Mongesa, Wednesday, 30 October 1918
From Collalto we continued our march to Pieve di Soligo, Refrontolo, San Pietro di Feletto. We reversed the direction of the route we had travelled during our retreat last October.
Now we rejoiced to see the signs of their retreat: wrecked guns, piles of ammunition and abandoned wagons, kitchens and barracks demolished, sand-bag walls flattened.
The landscape has been completely devastated by our artillery fire. Mortar shells have gouged holes three metres deep and at least five wide.
Buildings are razed to the ground.
Corpses are scattered everywhere, some horribly mangled.
I'll never forget one body with its head detached but still wearing a helmet.
Lots of mules and horses slaughtered by shells.
Thousands of flies are already attacking the corpses of men and animals.
The ground is littered with many unexploded shells, especially mortar.
It will take a lot of work to clean everything up.
We marched on, dodging the dead, rubble and craters on the road, collecting guns, bayonets, rifles and other enemy material to keep as a memento of these days.
We were all singing at the top of our lungs.
We sang because we were happy to be alive in the midst of this carnage.
We ran into General Zoppi on horseback.
He greeted us shouting: «Viva gli Arditi!»[551]

551 «Long live the Arditi!» translation from Italian.

Even more heart-warming was the greeting of the first civilians, whom we met on the road to Vittorio.
Old men waved their hands, as if to bless us.
Women waved their handkerchiefs and threw kisses at us.
Children ran alongside our columns.
They were happy to see and touch us.
They were even happier when we gave them pieces of bread.
They were hungry, thin, dirty and dressed in rags. I felt bad for them.
The leaflets that the *mucs* had launched on our lines said that in the occupied territories people were doing well. Seeing those children, we had the confirmation that it was all false!
Who knows how people have suffered this year?
Outside some of the houses, colourful blankets and rags waved to form the tricolour of our national flag. Almost all homes have no doors or windows. Some have no roof. The *mucs* dismantled everything to use the wood.
Even the iron gates have been taken away.
We continued to march singing without ceasing the Arditi hymn and the "Canzone del Piave".
We sang even louder every time we came across columns of prisoners.
We sought their eyes to look at them with contempt, but their eyes were always cast down.
We met some Italian soldiers who had escaped from prison camps, dirty and undernourished. To them as well we gave bread, biscuits and cigarettes.
They thanked us with tears in their eyes.

Now we are waiting at Casa Mongesa, along the Conegliano-Manzana road. The VIII is in Bagnolo and the IX Bersaglieri is at the Casa Olivo.

Colonel Bertolotti has returned after his illness and has taken over command of the 3rd Group.[552]

---

[552] On October 30, the 1st Division returned to the Assault Army Corps, which in the final battle had 18 officers and 318 men killed, 56 missing and more than 980 wounded, capturing 8,000 prisoners, 68 guns and 223 machine guns. The XXII Assault Unit ended the battle with a force of 21 officers and 514 soldiers, divided between the command, the three rifle companies, the machine gun company, the flamethrower section, the Stokes bomb launcher section, and the baggage train. It counted over 40 dead, including complementary lieutenant Luigi Bevacqua from Pinerolo, and 130 wounded, including two officers.

Casa Mongesa, Thursday, 31 October 1918
The enemy is on the run and our army is chasing it, gradually liberating the occupied territories as we go.[553]
Our army must forge ahead as far as possible before the High Command of the *mucs* asks to surrender. I would like to be among those troops, too.
«It's too e-e-easy now» says *Lu-Lupo*.
«*No xe roba par nialtri*»[554] confirms *Faro*.
«It's true. It isn't for us Arditi to chase after the fools who're running away. It is a pity, though, that we're losing the opportunity to meet the girls in the liberated villages» points out *Pugnodiferro* a bit disappointedly.

Casa Mongesa, Friday, 1st November 1918
The news is getting better and better.
The front is moving rapidly to the north and to the east.
Enthusiasm is growing more and more among the men.
In the afternoon *Cuteddu* came to me and took me aside. After moving away from the group, he stopped and started looking around. Nobody was watching us.
Then he pulled out a package from under his tunic.
«*Ogni prumissa debbito è. Tenisse, Seggente*»[555] he said, staring into my eyes.
There was something soft and light in the package.
I unwrapped it with curiosity. It was a *coppola*![556]
I looked at *Cuteddu* questioningly.
«*Era ri me frati Pietro.*»
«Thanks, Salvatore, but...»
«*U tinisse vossia, Seggente. Aviti u stissu nomi.*»[557]
He shook my hand tightly and went away. It was the most beautiful and unexpected gift I have ever received. I am still moved by his gesture.

---

[553] On 31 October Feltre and Sacile were liberated, while the previous day Vittorio and San Donà di Piave were freed. On 31 October, the Italian High Command issued the first general directive for the pursuit of the enemy, indicating specific objectives for each Army and urging advances along the entire front to gain as much ground as possible in the short time left before the armistice. The 7th, 1st and 4th Armies were to occupy the salient of Trentino, while 8th, 10th and 3rd were to occupy the Venetian plain and then resolutely advance towards the Tagliamento and the Isonzo, preceded by cavalry.
[554]«This isn't for us» translation from the Venetian dialect.
[555]«Every promise is due. Take it, Sergente» translation from the Sicilian dialect.
[556]A traditional kind of flat cap typically worn in Sicily, Calabria and Sardinia.
[557]«It belonged to my brother Pietro. You keep it, Sergente. You have the same name.»

Casa Mongesa, Saturday, 2 November 1918
More news of victory keeps arriving.[558]
Yesterday our troops invaded the plateau of the seven municipalities and then freed Belluno.
In Friuli they have reached the Livenza river.
It seems that the *mucs* have requested an armistice, but our High Command wants an unconditional surrender.
«*Scoltime, par mi prima de firmar un toco de carta, gavemo da rivar fin Viena. Magari anca fin Budapest*»[559] says *Faro* firmly.
Pugnodiferro is even more extreme: «Right to the Kaiser's house we have to arrive!»
«Quite right! I want to ki-ki-kick the Ka-ka-kaiser in the butt!»
«With your muddy boots?» I asked *Lu-Lupo*.
«Of course. In fact, I'll muddy them up even more!» he replied without stuttering.
We applauded him for a long time.

---

[558] On all fronts the Austro-Hungarian troops were on the run, more or less in disorder.
On November 1st, 1918, General Diaz had issued the following proclamation, which was launched from planes to the populations of the lands still occupied:
"Brothers of Italy! The Italian army advances victoriously to free you once and for all. The enemy is in rout and, fleeing from your loyal, glorious cities, announces our arrival, our victory. He leaves behind tens of thousands of prisoners, hundreds of guns and all his ambitions. The oath of our heroes has been fulfilled; through the strength of arms and justice the prophecy of our martyrs has come true; freedom is risen, in the name of Rome, from the holy tombs of our dead. After a century of war, of hopes and anxieties, the whole country reunites around its king.
Brothers! Be as calm and steadfast in joy as you were in pain, be the incorruptible custodians of the purest human civilization that has ever seen the light of the world. Do not forget the iniquities and wiles of the conquered enemy but reject his sad example of cruelty and violence. From today the Italian army is your army. Help it to restore order for the good of all, as many of you, from Cesare Battisti to Nazario Sauro, have done to help it achieve this victory."
While Emperor Charles of Austria and his military leaders were attempting in vain to make the terms of armistice less onerous, on November 2 Italian and Anglo-French troops occupied various locations, including Rovereto.
[559] «Listen to me, before we sign a piece of paper, we have to get as far as Vienna. Maybe even Budapest» translation from the Venetian dialect.

CHAPTER 10.V

Casa Mongesa, Sunday, 3 November 1918

Now that things have calmed down a bit, I will try and describe the action which kept us busy between 26 and 28 October.

On the 23rd we first moved to Volpago and then in the evening we camped on the Montello, straddling the road number 12. We camouflaged the tents with branches so they wouldn't be visible to Austrian aviators.

The IX Bersaglieri had moved to road 11 and the VIII Unit east of road 10.

The command of the 3rd Group, based at the Osteria dei Faveri, had been entrusted to Major Nunziante, commander of the VIII, since Colonel Bertolotti had suddenly fallen ill.

The major summoned all the officers to convey the objectives.

Subsequently, Lieutenant Meloni told us that the 8th Army had the task of separating the enemy armies deployed in the mountains from those in the plains and then quickly heading to Vittorio. We and the other units of the 1st Assault Division were to act as the vanguard of the Army.

So our job was crucial to the outcome of the battle.

In particular, four units had to capture the Roggia dei Mulini[560] and then the line of villages (Mosnigo, Moriago, Fontigo, Sernaglia, Falzè), seizing the enemy artillery between the line and the Piave river.

The other units of the Division, divided into two columns, after conquering Falzè, were to cross the Soligo and attack the hills of Collalto-Colle di Guardia, together with the forces of the VIII Army Corps.

These were the objectives entrusted to our XXII Assault Unit:

- cross the river by boat the night on the 25th
- eliminate surveillance on the other side to enable the engineers to build a pontoon bridge at Fontana del Buoro
- clean out the Roggia dei Mulini entrenchments
- silence the artillery in the area
- conquer Moriago.

[560] This was a canal that received water from the Piave downstream from the Abbey of Vidor and carried it to Moriago, where it fed a series of mills and forges and then flowed back to the Piave. The Austrians had dried up the canal by obstructing the outlet upstream and turned it into a front-line trench.

Once again Moriago was the destiny of our unit.[561]
The II had already fought there during the retreat.
IX Bersaglieri and VIII were to cross two bridges further east and then conquer Fontigo and Sernaglia respectively.[562]
Two companies from the XII Unit, led by captain Alarico Manescalchi, were to reinforce our three attack columns.
«All clear?» asked Lieutenant Meloni.
Then, without a pause, he shouted: «A chi la vittoria?» [563]
«A Noi!» we replied as one man.
«*Gera ora. No ghe la fasevo altro de spetar. Speremo che sia dele bele barche. Non voria mai cascar in acqua*»[564] *Faro* confessed to me, as we went to communicate the objectives to our squads.
He was more afraid of water than shells and rifle bullets.
I too was tired of waiting and so were our men, who greeted the news of the impending action with enthusiastic shouts.

---

[561] In mid-December 1917 the Austrians had evicted the inhabitants of Moriago, sending them to Tarzo, a village near Vittorio. According to the testimony of Don Angelo Frare, forced to act as the mayor of Mosnigo from 10 November, in Tarzo there were over two thousand people evicted from the villages of Segusino, Valdobbiadene, San Pietro, Santo Stefano, Guia, Bigolino, Vidor, Colbertaldo, Mosnigo, Moriago, Col San Martino and Pieve di Soligo. From Don Angelo's diary: *"Religious care and material labor for the distribution of food were shared with the local Archpriest, we always helped each other out and agreed on the requests to put to the Command. The parish priest of the refugees, aided on one hand by the refugees themselves and on the other by the local parish priest, was assisted by the best people of the town. My position was very difficult. I had to defend the refugees both from the enemy and from the inhabitants; I was often caught between the hammer and the anvil."*

[562] In the sector of the 8th Army, 8 bridges were planned, flanked by 11 walkways:
- sector of the XXVII Army Corps (General Antonino Di Giorgio):
bridge A at Abbazia, in front of Vidor (by the 25th bridge-builders company);
- sector of the XXII Army Corps (General Giuseppe Vaccari):
bridge B, at Fontana del Buoro (5th company), intended for the XXII Assault Unit;
bridge C, at Casa de Faveri (16th company), intended for the IX Bersaglieri;
bridge D, at Casa Biadene (4th company), intended for the VIII Assault Unit;
bridge E, in front of Falzè di Piave (27th company);
- sector of the VIII Army Corps (General Asclepia Gandolfo):
bridge F, at Nervesa (12th company);
bridge G, at Casa Pastrolin (7th company);
bridge H, at the station of Susegana (29th company).

[563] «Who will win?» translation from Italian.

[564] «Finally. I couldn't stand to wait any longer. Let's hope the boats are good. I wouldn't ever want to fall into the water» translation from the Venetian dialect.

The rest of the day passed quietly. Nice weather. Many planes in flight. Just a few artillery shots from time to time.
During the night we were awakened by an uproar.
Leaving the tent, we saw intense flashes from the Grappa sector, accompanied by the continuous roar of the artillery.
«They're not joking up there» said *Carestia.*
Hell seemed to have broken out. Where we were, though, all was calm.
You could only see the beams of the floodlights, searching through the night.

Montello, Thursday, 24 October 1918
The morning was dark and cloudy with heavy gusts of rain.
On the Grappa sector the fight had not stopped.
We started getting ready, checking our weapons, stocking up on ammunition and provisions, exchanging the usual letters and dismantling the tents.
In the afternoon, with much cursing, we had to reassemble them, since the action had been postponed.
The river was too swollen from the rain that had fallen in the mountains and therefore we had to wait for a better time before building the bridges and crossing over.
It would have been nice to start avenging Caporetto today.
Exactly one year ago the enemy offensive began with all its tragic consequences for us and for the population of the occupied territories.
In the mountains, the artillery concert continued non-stop all day.
«*Ma un si doveva attacca' noialtri*?»[565] *Pugnodiferro* kept asking everyone.
«It's a diversion. So the enemy converges there and we break through here» *Carestia* was trying to explain to him, drawing lines in the mud with his stick.
«The important thing is that the *tognìt* don't all run up to the mountains. I want to get my hands on some of them as soon as we cross the river.»
«We find them, you'll see. They are not so weak» *Trepugnali* reassured him.
It rained all night. Judging from the flashes, thunder, beams of light and coloured flairs, the fighting in the mountain area doesn't seem to have diminished in intensity.
I fell asleep with that rumble in my ears and woke up with the same rumble. Outside, however, the sky was blue and the dawn announced the sun.

[565] «But weren't we supposed to attack?» translation from the Tuscan dialect.

Montello, Friday, 25 October 1918
Good news came from Mount Grappa during the day.
It said that the 4th Army had launched an attack in force, with the support of the 6th, that our troops had conquered the Pertica, the Solarolo, the Prassolan, taking over two thousand prisoners, that the French had conquered the Asolone, that the left wing of the 12th Army had gone on the offensive too, conquering important positions. The morale of the men was higher and higher and they couldn't wait to get into action.
Pugnodiferro went around the camp saying to everyone: «Are we going to let the French boast about the victory in our country? Are we going to let guys from the other armies boast that they have defeated the *tognìt*?»
I saw *Cuteddu* sharpen his dagger and knife for hours on end.
«Look, if you keep doing that, all you'll have left is the handle» I said jokingly. He stopped for a moment, scowled at me and then resumed with even more energy.
Carestia has been sharpening his dagger and switchblade knife as well.
Trepugnali was desperate for a third dagger.
It made me feel positive to go around the camp seeing all those men busily preparing their weapons. It wasn't necessary to encourage them.
Rather, you had to keep them in check, so they didn't make too much noise. How different was their spirit, compared to that of the infantrymen of the "Taro" Brigade before a fight.
A sergeant from the engineers brought some bad news. The current of the Piave was too strong and did not yet allow them to build the bridges. He explained that when the speed of the water is greater than 2.5 metres per second, the anchors do not hold, they plough the gravelly bottom and the boat pontoons break up. According to the latest measurement, the water speed was over three metres per second. We still had to wait!
Towards evening, we went together with the officers to see the point where the crossing is to take place. It's called Fontana del Buoro. There is a grotto from which water gushes, pouring directly into the Piave.
The river was brown, like the Fella when it is in flood.
The little islands and banks of gravel were submerged by the water, which was rushing swiftly.
The other bank is flat and devoid of cover. They call it the "green island", but it is not an island. [566]

[566] It is a strip of land in the municipality of Moriago which stretches out towards the banks of the Piave in the so-called "grave". Before the evacuation of the population it had been divided into 16 garden lots and rented to as many families of the village.

Instead our bank is heavily forested and therefore perfect for hiding boats and material to build the bridge.
I saw *Faro* talking to some bridge-builders from the 5th company.
«*Ghe go dito che ghe pago da bevar a tuti, basta che no me fa cascar in acqua*»[567] he confessed to me, as we returned to the camp.
«Simply put, you'll let them drink if they don't let you drink.»
«*Ma mi ghe pago da bevar vin!*»[568]
We had another quiet night.
A few machine-gun bursts, a few howitzer shots, but nothing more.
Instead, the noise of the battle on the Grappa still came through loud and clear.
Flashes from the guns fire and explosions made it possible to distinguish the outlines of the mountains.[569]

---

567 «I told them that I'll buy everyone drinks, just as long as they don't drop me in the water» translation from the Venetian dialect.
568 «But I'm paying for wine!»
569 The Italian military and industrial apparatus produced its maximum effort in 1918. For the October offensive, the deployment of artillery in the service of the six Armies was impressive: 1,487 batteries, of which 462 heavy (1,852 guns), 263 heavy field (1,044 guns), 586 small calibre (2,344 guns), 166 trench mortars. About six million rounds were made available to the artillerymen.

CHAPTER 11.V

Montello, Saturday, 26 October 1918

In the morning we were put on standby alert for the evening.

We inspected the river again. It looked like it was still in flood.

The command, however, had decided that the action should be carried out that same night. At least it wasn't raining.

The day was spent with the usual preparations.

Our line continued to be quiet.

The *mucs* didn't seem to have noticed the massing of troops and our preparations. If any of their planes attempted to fly over the Montello, they were immediately scared off by our fighter aircrafts.

Abundant rations were distributed, with liqueurs and cigarettes.

The morale of the troops was still very high, even if the news from the Grappa sector was not so good. The resistance our Armies were finding was much more stubborn than expected. Mountain peaks were conquered and lost in continuation, with serious casualties on both sides.

«We will break through the fr-fr-front» *Lu-Lupo* said to all, accompanying his prediction with big slaps on the back.

In the afternoon the "fall in" was sounded.

Major Di Orazio reviewed the unit. Then he gave a very short speech.

«Arditi of the XXII Assault Unit, all of Italy is looking at us. I have only one thing to say to you: be worthy of honour!»

Those were the same words that Colonel Bassi used.

We unsheathed our daggers, without the usual shout. Our cry could have crossed the Piave and awakened the *mucs*.

Silently, one after the other, we lined up and started the approach march to Fontana del Buoro.

Meanwhile the sky was clouding over again.

By around 7:00 p.m. all the trenches on the right bank of the river and the woods behind them were filled with Black Flames. Infantrymen from the "Cuneo" Brigade of the XXVII Army Corps were gathering behind us.

I was among those who had to be ferried to the other side by boat to form the first bridgehead, together with many men from the XII and the engineers. Our task was to protect the bridge-builders and open breaches in the first line of barbed wire.

With me were all the survivors from my squad at Sdricca: *Carestia*, *Cuteddu*, *il Gat*, *Pugnodiferro* and *Trepugnali*.
Luckily for him, *Faro* was not with my group. He was to cross the river on the pontoon bridge together with the rest of the XXII.
«*Se vedemo de là, fradeo*»[570] he said, giving me a hug.
I returned the hug: «*Mandi, fradi.*»[571]
Lieutenant Meloni was also ready to board the boats. Together with some other men he was supposed to string up the telephone line.
«*Buena suerte*» the *Argentine* wished me, giving me a pat of encouragement. He is a courageous and experienced aide-de-battle, with us since the fight on Val Bella last January. He too was to have been among the first to cross the Piave.
Shortly before embarking, *Cuteddu* approached me and to my surprise he said to me: «*S'iddu a scampamu macari stavota, ci fazzu un rialu, signo' Seggente.*»[572]
«Thanks, Salvatore. Let us be worthy of honour» I replied.
He shook my hand and went back to his place.
Even before getting into the boat, we were already all wet.
It had started to rain heavily.
Our artillery fired a few shots here and there, as in the previous days, so as to not tip off the *mucs*, who were aiming the beams of their reflectors at our rear, now deserted.
At 8:00 p.m. the order to board the boats arrived. Even though the boats were piloted by experienced soldiers, ferrymen before the war, the crossing was not easy. The current was very strong. The boats struggled to advance and were pushed downstream.
Our blood froze when one of the first boats capsized and we saw the men being dragged away by the current.
Falling into that water, cold and fast, loaded down with bombs and ammunition meant drowning for sure.
When our turn came, I recommended my soul to the Lord and squeezed tightly the amulet I had in my pocket.
Arditi and bridge-builders pushed our boat into the water.
The ferrymen began immediately to point their long oars and to curse.
We curled up in the bottom.

---

[570] «See you on the other side, brother» translation from the Venetian dialect.
[571] «Goodbye, brother» translation from the Friulan language.
[572] «If we get out alive this time too, I'll give you a present, Sergeant sir» translation from the Sicilian dialect.

I confess that I closed my eyes and prayed that everything would turn out all right.

More than once it seemed to me that the boat was capsizing and every time I got ready to rid myself instantly of all the weights I was wearing.

That crossing felt endless.

When I finally felt the bottom of the boat rasping on the bank, I raised my head and sighed with relief.

«Go! Go! Go!» the ferrymen shouted.

We did so very willingly, jumping out quickly.

The sound of the waves and the gusts of rain covered the sound of our landing. Setting foot on that bank was a great thrill for me.

And so, I believe, for the others.

I felt that perhaps it was the beginning of our revenge.

The bridge-builders began their work immediately.

We, armed with pliers, went to cut the first barbed wire. Then we split into various groups to clear the area of sentries. Our orders were to act in absolute silence. Only daggers had to work.

My group took care of the area on the right.

We crawled through the grass and the puddles for many minutes, until we saw a small light come on and off. In front of us was a dilapidated farmhouse. Another small light appeared and then immediately disappeared. Someone had lit a cigarette. There were two of them. They were in the back under an awning to shelter from the rain.

While we were trying to figure out if there were any more, we heard coughing somewhere else. So there were at least three. We waited again, until we were sure that there were only three of them. At that moment it was pouring and the night was very dark. Crawling we surrounded the hut.

Two men got ready to pounce on each of the *mucs*.

One had to throw him to the ground, the other to stab him to death.

We had attacked that way many times, even in the dark.

We could not fail. We did not fail. At my signal, a knock from the gun barrel on the helmet, the men jumped on their targets and eliminated them.

We lit a match to see what unit they were from.

Hungarians. Hussars on foot.[573]

I left four men among the rubble and, with the others, continued patrolling along the shore, always in a crawl.

---

[573] Depending on their recruitment area, cavalry soldiers were assigned to the Hussars (Hungary), the Dragoons (Austria), the Uhlans (Galicia, Bohemia, Croatia). The defensive line attacked by the XXII Assault Unit was manned by Hussars of the 11th Division.

Every now and then our lines fired few shells toward their rear and every now and then they fired back. Isolated shots.
Quite different from the drumming of artillery on the mountains, which we could hear in the distance.
After half an hour we detected another location.
We waited a long time to figure out how many enemies there were.
They seemed like a lot. At least a dozen. As we were getting ready to attack, all hell broke loose.
Their artillery began to hammer the river in various points, including the one from which we had arrived. Their searchlights must have picked up one of our pontoons. Their sentries went on high alert. With all that noise, however, it was no longer necessary to do things in silence.
We peppered them with petards and went on the attack.
They only had time to get off a few shots.
There were eleven of them. They were Hussars too. There was also a lieutenant. There was a machine gun. It was just after 11:00 in the night.
I sent two men to warn the other four and above all to check the situation at the landing point.
Had they gotten the pontoon bridge up?
How many had already crossed over before the *mucs* targeted it?
Without the rest of the unit, the operation could not be completed.
In the meantime, we turned the trench inside out, repositioned the machine gun and *Trepugnali* added a Hussar dagger to his collection.
Our artillery was still strangely silent, while theirs seemed to be operating along the entire course of the river from north to south, guided by the beams of the spotlights. The sky was illuminated by coloured signal flares.
After a while I heard shouting on my left: «Who goes there?»
«Black flames!»
They were ours.
«Eighth Unit!»
"What was the VIII doing here?" we wondered.
«We crossed over your bridge» said a sergeant, «ours wasn't ready yet.»
They hurried away in the direction of Sernaglia.
After a while I heard shouting again on the left: «Who goes there?»
«Bersaglieri! Ninth Battalion!"
"What are they doing here?" we wondered.
«We used your bridge» said a corporal major, «they hadn't even started on ours yet.»
They hurried away in the direction of Fontigo.

«Who goes there?» I heard again.
"Who the hell is it now?" we wondered.
«Black fl-fl-flames!»
It was *Lu-Lupo*.
They were our comrades. Third company.
Before the *mucs* opened fire the whole 3rd Group had crossed over.
Blessed be our bridge-builders.[574]
Our second company had lined up on the left of the bridge, with the first in the middle together with some platoons from the XII Unit.
Distributed among the various companies were the flamethrowers, Stokes bomb-launchers and machine gunners.
We also had a mountain battery available.
At that point I started feeling better.
«*Benedeti quei fioi. Gavarò da pagarghe da bevar a tuti.*»[575]
It was the voice of *Faro*.
«But how… if you're all wet?» I said, wringing out his sleeve.
«*Va in mona ti e 'sta acqua del casso*»[576] he replied.

---

[574] At 11:00 p.m. Major Nunziante ordered the VIII Assault Unit and the IX Bersaglieri to use the B bridge of Fontana del Buoro, the only one of the three bridges destined for the 3rd Group to have been completed by the tireless and brave bridge-builders led by captain Gambizza. Further downstream captain Mezzani's engineers, at the price of great sacrifices, had managed to throw up bridge E in front of Falzè. A first group of about 150 Arditi from the LXXII Assault Unit had already crossed to the left bank of the Piave, when the Austrian artillery destroyed the bridge, killing many men. Although isolated from the rest of their unit, those Arditi fought valiantly until the 29th, when they managed to rejoin their comrades, who had crossed on the Fontana del Buoro bridge. On the morning of the 28th the LXXII commander, Captain Ettore Marchand, was torn apart by a large-calibre shell. His remains were mercifully collected and placed in a galvanized box in a war cemetery along the Piave.

[575] «Blessed be those boys. I'll have to buy everyone a drink» translation from the Venetian dialect.

[576] «Go to hell, you and all this crappy water.»

CHAPTER 12.V

Moriago, Sunday, 27 October 1918
At around midnight our artillery began to hammer the "Mulini" defensive line facing us, but also the lines further back in order to hit their batteries and their command centres.
We were under the arching of hundreds of shells, criss-crossing in the sky in a rain that showed no sign of diminishing.
Around 00:30 a.m. we saw a continuous glow coming from the Fontigo area. What remained of the village was probably on fire.
We waited for over two hours for our shells to prepare the ground and shatter their lines of defense.
Around 2:30 a.m. we moved in and reached a position just before the area where the shells were falling. The ground shook with every explosion, like an earthquake. Stones, dirt and twigs rained down on us.
When the command "Fix bayonets!" arrived, we knew that the time to attack had come. We were waiting for our artillery fire to lengthen a bit and for the two words which would cause us to jump up and attack, as if driven by a powerful spring.
Shortly thereafter those two words rang out across our line.
«A Noi!» the officers shouted.
«A Noi!» we replied, starting the assault.
We started running in the dark, pierced by the glare of explosions and coloured flares.
Everyone ran towards his fate.
Within minutes, everyone would find out what fate had in store for him.
We ran, avoiding the holes, dodging the iron stakes of the torn barbed wire, jumping over the skeins of barbed wire entangled with the Friesian horses shattered by shells.
We ran at least a hundred metres before the defenders who had survived the shelling began to react. I heard the hiss of many bullets and I saw some of our soldiers fall. But that didn't stop us.
We first threw petards, then attacked hand-to-hand, with bayonets or with daggers. In that furious fray I seemed to see *Cuteddu* smiling for the first time.

Some machine-gun nests came to life and started singing.
Our flamethrowers promptly silenced them.
I heard the servers scream as they burned.
An awful sight.
The ground was completely churned up by the shelling and you had to be careful where you put your feet. Furthermore, mortal danger could emerge from every shell hole, every ditch, every pile of rubble. Little by little we conquered all the entrenchment and took the first prisoners.
They too were Hussars.
We had reached the "Mulini line".
As we were reassembling our ranks to proceed toward Moriago, their artillery began to target us. A shell exploded right in the middle of a group of prisoners, causing a massacre.
We immediately started moving north again.
Scattered groups of defenders hidden in the ditches or shell holes peppered us with rifle and machine-gun bullets. Patiently, one by one, we flushed them all out.
In front of a dense thicket, a sudden barrage of fire forced us to stop.
That's where poor *Trepugnali* was shot, as I later discovered.
May God have mercy on his soul.
To overcome resistance, we hit the thicket with our Stokes and the concentrated fire of six flamethrowers.
Despite the rain, trees and bushes started to burn, so our machine guns were able to see where the Hussars were positioned and annihilate them.
More than one of them was burned to death. Some of the survivors fled to the rear, others came out with their hands up.
Forward, forward, always forward, overwhelming every defense, every time losing friends along the way.
Around 4:00 in the morning we arrived in the vicinity of Moriago.
It was still raining and the fog had risen.
Our artillery kept on shelling, not only the village, but also the area in front of it. We launched flares to ask to lengthen their aim. They must not have seen them, as shells kept bursting in front of us.
To avoid being hit by our artillery, we went back to the "Mulini line".
It was there that I learned of *Trepugnali's* fate.
We went back to the grove. It was still burning.
Thanks to the glow we found *Trepugnali's* body.
He was lying on his back. I knelt down to hear if he was still breathing.
He was dead. A machine-gun burst had caught him right in the chest.

«The only good thing is that he won't have to serve the 20 years in prison that they sentenced him to» said *Carestia*.
He too, like me, had tears in his eyes.
I slung him over my shoulder and carried him to the trenches.
We had promised to bury with dignity those of us who were killed.
Other dead and the wounded were being gathered up.
«He had a premonition» *Pugnodiferro* confided to me, he too with tears in his eyes.
Cuteddu sat down next to *Trepugnali's* body and stayed there for hours.
While awaiting the order to attack Moriago, we received good news from the other units. The IX Bersaglieri had seized Fontigo at 4:30 a.m. and the Black Flames of the VIII had conquered Sernaglia around 6:30.
We also learned that the *mucs* had managed to strike our bridge, but that the bridge-builders had reactivated it, allowing various infantry brigades to cross over.[577]
While we were eating our rations came Major Nunziante's order to move forward by 10:00 a.m. and attack Moriago at 10:30 with the help of men from both the XII Unit and the "Mantova" Brigade.
It was 9:00 in the morning. The rain had finally stopped tormenting us.
The artilleries continued their violent duelling and every now and then a few shots fell near me.
Just before we started off, bad news arrived: our bridge had been destroyed again, as well as all the others. We were isolated.
«No hot chow this morning» someone joked.
«We'll have coffee in Moriago» replied *Pugnodiferro*.
«You can have the *tognìt's* coffee. It's bloody awful!» they replied.
«I'll look for a general. I'll get rid of him and drink his coffee. At least that should taste good» replied *Pugnodiferro*, who always wants to have the last word.

---

[577] On the evening of the 27th, only 19 battalions had arrived in what the military authorities had called "Sernaglia plain". In addition to the "Cuneo" and "Mantova" Brigades, which were backup to the XXII Unit, the "Piemonte" and the "Porto Maurizio" of the 60th Division and two battalions of the "Messina" had crossed. The support of the artillery located on Montello was substantial, but supplies were lacking as the bridges had been severed. Although the Royal Army and the Allies had formed two other bridgeheads, one further north near Valdobbiadene and one further south near the Grave di Papadopoli and the plain of Cimadolmo, the Austrian commands did not consider the situation serious. Loss of land was minimal, and they were relying on the arrival of reserves. The counterattack was scheduled for the morning of the 28th. General Boroević, however, was forced to report to his High Command in Baden that Hungarian troops, especially in the 5th Army, were mutinying anew.

After checking our weapons and stocking up on hand grenades, including those of the enemy, we headed back to Moriago.
I remember that it was foggy and humid. Our uniforms were wet. My teeth were chattering from the cold. The cognac had not been able to warm me.
I checked to see if my amulet was still in my trouser pocket. It was there.
We passed through the burnt thicket from last night.
It was still smouldering. With the embers we lit our cigarettes. On the ground there were the corpses of many Hussars. Some were charred.
Every now and then we heard the crackle of a *Schwarzlose*, then the familiar sound of our petards, and then silence once again. The *mucs* were starting to emerge from Moriago. We had to be very careful. Every ditch and every bush could hide a hazard.
We started to move forward. We were lucky. We found no obstacles on our path. We came close to the village while our shells continued the demolition work. Crawling on the ground, each of us took a position inside one of the large shell holes.
All the survivors of my squad at Sdricca were in there with me.
I looked at their faces one by one, hoping to see them alive in Moriago.
No one spoke. No one wanted to talk anymore. It was time to act.
I looked at my watch. There were a few minutes left till 10:30.
At 10:31 we were already on the assault, defying the fire of the defenders.
The crossfire of our machine guns covered us as we ran screaming towards the rubble of the first houses in the village.
The machine guns of the *mucs*, on the other hand, tried to shoot us down.
I was running in zigzags a little to the right and a little to the left, but I well knew that in all that confusion the difference between life and death is only a matter of centimetres. The trenches and the barbed wire around the village had been devastated by our large-calibre mortars and so we were able to overwhelm the defenders.
I fired all the rounds of my revolver in close combat.
We passed over the line leaving a trail of dead and wounded behind.
Head-on, we attacked the next line, that of the houses.
Behind us we could feel the mass of the Infantry coming.
A field gun had started firing at us at zero height.
We ran towards it from two different directions. The gunner had to decide which of the two groups to shoot. He knew, however, that he would not have had time to reload, aim and fire on the other group.
I saw the cannon's mouth swing towards us.
He had made his choice.

«Down! Down!» I screamed, throwing myself into a hole at the very moment I heard the thunder and felt the air displacement from the cannon shot. I don't know how I was reminded of what Captain Racchi had told me when I had challenged "the Swing": «Never take a risk if you haven't got at least one escape plan in mind.»
I had just done it, instinctively, like the other time. When I lifted my head, the other group led by *Faro* was already jumping on the gunners.
I looked around. The others had thrown themselves into the holes too, and everyone's skin was safe.
The fighting was moving toward the interior of the village, where every dilapidated house had become a bunker, a cave, a shelter for armed men and machine guns, to be conquered with patience and cunning.
The scenario was appalling. Everywhere corpses and bits of human and animal flesh. A sickening stench. The central square was devastated. The bell tower was partially destroyed.
Spuafogo and his men looked like devils from hell. With their jets of blazing liquid they set fire to every dangerous corner, from which every now and then a man would run out, enveloped in flames, to be shot down by riflemen out of compassion.
Does it make sense to describe everything that happened in that village?
After almost three years of war, you know that the slightest distraction or the smallest hesitation can cost your *ghirba*.
You know that if the enemy does not surrender immediately, he must be eliminated. You know that even if he surrenders, you have to be careful that it is not a trap, as has often happened.
After over an hour of bitter fighting house by house, we liberated what was left of Moriago.[578]
We captured numerous prisoners, all Hungarians, lots of weapons, some cannons and several carthorses which had miraculously survived the shelling.

---

[578] The first Ardito to enter Moriago was a soldier from the XXII Assault Unit (2nd company). Enrico Barbi, born in 1896 in Gubbio, received the Bronze Medal of Military Valour with the following motivation: *"First to enter Moriago, he attacked an enemy centre with bombs, destroying it and capturing prisoners. On successive occasions he demonstrated courage and disregard for danger. Moriago, 27-28 October 1918".*
Among the first to enter Moriago were also men from the XII Unit, led by Corporal Elia Da Rios, later awarded a Bronze Medal of Military Valour. *"He demonstrated truly commendable courage and calm in combat. Example and spur to his companions, he distinguished himself in the attack on the village of Moriago, and then in a risky patrol service for which he had offered himself as a volunteer. Moriago, 29 October 1918".*

From the prisoners we knew that the bulk of the troops were positioned back in the hills, with the *Stürmtruppen* remaining on the plain.
In the meantime, the fog had lifted, making way for a beautiful blue sky.
Our heliographer[579] communicated the outcome of the assault to the Division command, but for safety's sake, the same message was sent both with a pigeon and with a swimmer. I saw him leave with only a pair of shorts and his helmet on.
Carestia, *Cuteddu* and *Pugnodiferro* were fine, apart from a few scratches and bumps. So too *Faro* and *Lu-Lupo*. *Il Gat*, however, had taken a bullet in his foot. He limped around cursing.
Unfortunately, we learned of the *Argentine's* death.[580]
"*Mala suerte*" I thought with great displeasure.
There is also an officer, Lieutenant Bevacqua, among the dead. He was only eighteen years old. He was born in '99.[581]
The infantrymen of the "Mantova" had also arrived in the village.
«*Tè, te ghe tróvet el cafè del generàl?*»[582] one of them asked *Pugnodiferro*.
«No, he ran away with the coffee as soon as he saw our Black Flames» he said, displaying his flames.
While the infantrymen remained in the village, we went forward to a stream, the Rosper, where we captured other prisoners. From there we saw that our artillery was shooting at the surrounding hills.
An order from the Major called us back to village.
We were not to go any further so as not to create a void behind us.
The bridges were still unusable. Just as soon as the engineers repaired them, the enemy artillery managed to destroy them.
We were still isolated from the rest of the army and had to prepare to repel an inevitable counterattack.

---

579 The heliograph was an optical communications tool widely used by armies. Morse code messages were transmitted using flashes of light, solar or artificial, reflected by a mirror.

580 This was almost certainly the aide-de-battle Pietro Secco. Born in Argentina in 1892, he was originally from Seren del Grappa, near Feltre. Returning to Italy in 1912 for his military service, he was detained because of the outbreak of the war. Before joining the II Assault Unit as a sergeant major (15 January 1918), he had served in the 77th Infantry Regiment. In 1917 he had earned a Silver Medal of Military Valour in a fight on the Karst. In 1920 he was awarded another Silver Medal to the memory for the events of Moriago.

581 Lieutenant Luigi Bevacqua, of Pinerolo, in 1920 earned a Silver Medal to the memory, which was added to the Bronze Medal awarded to him in 1919 for actions carried out during the arrest battle on the Piave in June 1918, with the rank of second lieutenant of the XXII Unit.

582 «Hey you, did you find the general's coffee?» translation from the Lombard dialect.

We worked all day preparing the defense. Several of our SVA biplanes threw down cases of food, ammunition and even blankets in the fields.
In the late afternoon we buried *Trepugnali* in the village graveyard.
It had been shelled too. The walls were torn apart and many tombs were blown up, scattering fragments of marble, wood and bones all around.
While soldiers were burying the dead, some Arditi were resting on the tombstones that remained intact.
Our Command had also been installed inside the cemetery.
There were so many holes in the ground that we didn't have to dig. We chose a pit, laid *Trepugnali's* body in it and filled it with earth. We planted an iron cross, found nearby, and engraved his name on it with the tip of one of his daggers. We gave his throwing knife, which he kept in his sleeve, to *Cuteddu*. We were silent for a long time in front of his grave.
On leaving the graveyard, we recovered two cases of food just dropped from one of our planes. Life went on.
Wrapped in a blanket, I rested a couple of hours in a half-destroyed barn. The straw was not too dirty and fairly dry. *Carestia* woke me up. We had to get ready. A long night of vigilance and certainly of fighting awaited us.
The whole 3rd company was positioned to guard the east of the village. We settled down behind the rubble of what had once been a very large house. *Carestia* and *Cuteddu* had to move the remains of two enemies torn apart by a shell. We had a nice supply of petards, cartridges and cigarettes.
There was hardly any "petrol", unfortunately.
Don Carmelo, our military chaplain, came by. As a joke among us we call him "Don Cammello", because he comes from Sicily. He's gutsy, though. He stays in the front line with the soldiers. He has already earned a silver and a bronze medal. He encouraged us to defend the positions we had won and to fight with serenity because "God is with us!".
Our enemies, too, are convinced that God is with them. The *crucchi* even have "*Gott mit uns*" engraved on the buckles of their belts.[583] Perhaps at that very same moment the *mucs*' chaplain was also inciting them against us to take back their lost positions. Yet we have the same God.
«In the next few hours, will the Lord listen more to the *tognìt* or to us?» I asked *Carestia*.
«A Noi!» he replied, unsheathing his dagger.

---

583 "God with us". It was originally the motto of the Teutonic Knights, a monastic, military and hospital order founded in the Holy Land during the Third Crusade (1189-1192) by Germans from Bremen and Lübeck to assist pilgrims from Germany. The motto was later adopted by the kings of Prussia and then by the German emperors.

CHAPTER 13.V

Moriago, Monday, 28 October 1918
It was a very rough night.
The artillery never stopped thundering.
After midnight a great uproar of rifle-fire, machine gun fire and petards broke out on the other side of the village. Shortly afterwards the *mucs* attacked on our side, throwing lots of hand grenades.
Even if we were shooting blindly in the dark, we created such a wall of bullets that their shouts of "hurrà!" soon turned into a chorus of howls of pain.
The barrels of our machine guns and rifles were red-hot.
After about an hour they attempted a fresh assault, which we quashed in the same way, shooting with their weapons, too.
We only had a few casualties.
«We are Black Flames! Forget it! *Schwarzen Flammen! Verstehst du*?»[584] some of us yelled at the attackers.
In response, they fired a machine-gun burst and then shouted something I didn't understand. Maybe it was Hungarian.
That night they attempted two more assaults, which we repelled.
At the first light of dawn we saw the ground before us strewn with dead and wounded. Many of them were moaning and asking for help. My eyes were burning. I had a headache and a dry throat. I'd lost count of the cigarettes smoked that night.
We saw a soldier who was moving his bowels in a corner of our wall. We had sunk to the level of animals. We threw curses and stones at him, as if he were doing the worst thing in the world in the midst of that carnage. He ran away with his trousers down to find another place.
As the sun rose, their artillery began to target us again in preparation for another infantry counterattack. We didn't move from our spot. As poor *Biunnu* had said, if a shell is destined to hit you, there is no point in hiding. That shell did not hit us and when the infantrymen attacked, we threw them back again, using the flamethrower as well, just to make it clear that they would never get by on our side.

---

[584] «Black Flames! Do you understand?» translation from German.

After this attack, I went back into the village to get news.
The bridges were either destroyed or under artillery fire and so we were still cut off. The situation was starting to get alarming. Even the officers seemed very nervous.
Enemy planes flew over occasionally to check our positions and drop some bombs, but they were immediately chased away by ours. I saw one of their planes crash behind the hills.
In the middle of the morning I was ordered to go to the fields between Moriago and Fontigo with other men from the XXII, the XII and the "Mantova" Brigade armed with several machine guns.
The major feared that the *mucs* would try to sneak in between the two villages to then attack us from behind. At the same time patrols of the IX Bersaglieri were leaving from Fontigo. The major had it right.
Less than an hour after we had positioned ourselves at the edges of a country road, we saw an enemy patrol advancing, taking advantage of the cover of trees and bushes. We let them proceed to the last man, then we started mowing them down with our machine guns. They responded to our fire.
When the Bersaglieri came up behind them, we held them in a vice-like grip until they decided to surrender.
A small group of Arditi escorted them to the riverbed, where it had been decided to assemble all the prisoners.
We stayed in the fields to avoid further infiltrations.
There were rifle-shots, machine gun bursts, petards and hand grenade explosions everywhere on the plain.
The Bersaglieri told us that they had taken Fontigo at dawn on the 27th with the help of some comrades from the XX, the glorious unit that just a year ago had sacrificed itself in defense of Udine. They too had had to fight house by house against the Hungarian Hussars and *Stürmtruppen*.
Now Fontigo is defended by the Infantrymen of the 29th Regiment, "Pisa" Brigade.
A plane with a black cross flew over, without strafing us. We aimed a couple of musket shots at him. Shortly thereafter, however, a heavy rain of *shrapnels* began to pour down on us.
The pilot had reported our position to the artillery.
We ran out of that place, which had no shelters big enough, and headed for the "Mills line". Only a few of us were wounded, although not seriously.
On the way to the area where we had fought the first night, an Ardito ran towards us with bad news. A group of prisoners had picked up some weapons lying on the ground and rebelled, shooting some of our guards.

We rushed over there to nip the revolt in the bud.
They had barricaded themselves in the rubble of a small group of houses and in an entrenched line dug all around it.
They welcomed us with a hailstorm of bullets.
«Let'em use up all their ammo and then we'll move in for a hand-to-hand fight» proposed *Pugnodiferro*, fondling his brass knuckles.
«We can't stay here all day waiting for their convenience» I said.
We had enough petards for an assault.
We approached in a "stop and go" way, throwing ourselves each time into one of the many shell holes in the ground. There was a machine gun lurking behind a wall, which was quite bothersome. If it didn't jam or run out of rounds, sooner or later it would have killed somebody.
A sniper would have been helpful in shooting the machine gunner.
I asked for a '91 to try the shot.
I told *Pugnodiferro* and *Cuteddu* to make another rush and I would shoot the machine gunner. The shot was not easy, also because I wasn't familiar with that shotgun. I made a notch at the top of the pit to rest the rifle barrel. Then I fired a test shot to see if it had gone where I wanted. I thought it had. I told the men to get ready and I aimed at the point where the machine gunner's helmet was supposed to appear.
My blow should have pierced it.
While I was taking aim carefully with my finger already on the trigger, the wall crumbled to pieces and both the machine gun and the gunner flew into the air. One of our mountain guns had intervened.
«Nice shot, Sergente» *Pugnodiferro* said, patting me on the back and going on the attack. *Cuteddu* was already running ahead.
I emptied the entire magazine against other rebels and then joined the fray.
But when I got there it was too late. It was almost over.
Cuteddu would have liked to kill the ones who had surrendered in time to escape the daggers, while *Pugnodiferro* wanted to break at least one of their arms to render them harmless.
Instead, we just took off their belts, suspenders and buttons. So they could only use their hands to keep their breeches from falling off.
In the early afternoon we returned to the fields where we had intercepted the enemy patrol, with no unwelcome encounters.
We lay in wait for the arrival of some other band.
But nobody came. On the contrary, it seemed to us that the shots were decreasing and growing more distant.

We waited until sunset, when a runner informed us that we were to go back to the "Mills line", where the whole 3rd Group was gathering.
Here we took stock of the dead and wounded.
The capture and defense of Moriago had cost us many of both.[585]
However, there was a lot of enthusiasm among the troops.
There was a rumour that the *mucs* were surrendering.[586]
We said goodbye to the comrades of the XII Unit.
They had to go back to the 2nd Group.
The night passed quietly.
Finally, we could sleep.[587]

---

585 Between 26 and 28 October, the 3rd Assault Group, reinforced by two companies of the XII Unit, counted 11 dead, 13 wounded, 1 missing among the officers and 38 dead, 448 wounded, 143 missing among the troops. Almost all the missing soldiers went unaccounted for on the first night of battle: many of them disappeared during the contrasted operations for crossing the river. The percentage of wounded was very high, a good number of them with light wounds, which did not require evacuation to health facilities.
Moriago received the gold medal for civil merit and changed its name to Moriago della Battaglia on August 1st, 1962 (decree of the President of the Italian Republic).
The area where the 3rd Group landed and had the first clashes, originally called "Green Island", took on the name of "Island of the Dead" after the war. A memorial stone placed there in the 1920s commemorates the soldiers who fell in those days.
586 The dangerous stalemate that arose on the morning of the 28th, with troops blocked on the Grappa sector and the Piave river, was resolved with a "brilliant decision" by General Caviglia. As early as the evening of the 27th he ordered the XVIII Army Corps, in reserve, to cross the river at the Grave di Papadopoli (Salettuol bridge) and to go on towards Nervesa in order to widen the bridgehead of the 10th Army and open the way for the VIII Corps with whom to continue towards Conegliano and Vittorio. Likewise encouraged by Caviglia's vibrant order of the day issued at 2 pm, the "Como", "Bisagno" and "Sassari" Brigades raced to achieve their goals. It was a decisive move and the beginning of the end for the Austro-Hungarians.
587 On the night of the 29th the crossing of the Piave by the 8th Army came to an end in front of Nervesa and Ponte della Priula. The ratio of power passed in favour of the Allies: on one hand the Austrian reserves were too far away to intervene, and on the other some regiments began refusing to march towards the front line and fight. That same night General Giuseppe Vaccari (2 February 1866 - 6 September 1937), former commander of the "Barletta" Brigade and then Chief of Staff of the 3rd Army, brought all the officers of the command of his XXII Army Corps to the left bank. His aim was to dispel any hesitation at a time when the fate of the battle was still uncertain. *"Wings to wings. Crises can only be resolved on the far side of the Piave! Firm and iron will, unyielding energy, will aid us to overcome the difficulties and pursue the enemy relentlessly"* was his incitement to the officers. Highly decorated, in 1921 he became Chief of Staff of the Royal Army, taking over from Pietro Badoglio, remaining in office until 1923. Senator of the kingdom from 1926, he was awarded the title of count in 1936.

CHAPTER 14.V

Piana della Sernaglia, Tuesday, 29 October 1918
Around 4:00 in the morning we set off in the direction of Fontigo.
We passed through the Manente Mill, where the command of the XXII Army Corps was installed. We saw General Vaccari giving orders.
With the rest of the 3rd Group we took up positions along the course of the Raboso stream, near Sernaglia.
We were at the disposal of the Division command, ready to intervene in support of the 1st and 2nd Groups, which were advancing towards Soligo and beyond. But there was no need.
In the early afternoon the order came to move toward Collalto.
We marched along singing.
Good news kept arriving. There was a rumour that the *mucs* were on the run with our troops in pursuit.[588]
Confirmation arrived when one of our planes threw down thousands of white cards to us.
It was a phonogram signed by General Caviglia to our Army Corps.
I transcribed it:
Enemy withdrawing from the region around Vittorio - stop - Accelerate march to prevent him from escaping and thus avenge Caporetto.

---

588 Seeing that the allied troops continued to advance despite a strenuous defense, many Austro-Hungarian units began to refuse to fight and to fall back into disorder. At 2:30 p.m. on the 29th General Boroević informed his High Command that, since he could no longer rely even on the units considered to be the most disciplined, he had ordered the evacuation of the whole first defensive position. Meanwhile, Italian planes strafed the columns of a demoralized and retreating enemy, bombing the rows of wagons and vehicles and the reserve-collecting centres, creating further panic. Rather than organizing a counterattack, the Austrian commanders were forced to coordinate the movement of the troops, which were mutinying more and more and looting the deposits. In the evening Boroević proposed to his High Command to progressively remove troops from the occupied territories to prevent the defeat from turning into a rout. At 10:30 p.m. he received approval together with an appeal to calm the troops and make them fight at least till the following week in order to avoid the danger of an unconditional peace. In parallel, Emperor Charles authorized General Weber von Webenau to take the first steps toward obtaining an armistice.

CHAPTER 15.V

Casa Mongesa, Monday 4 November 1918

Yesterday our troops liberated Udine and the Black Flames of the XXIX entered Trento with the Cavalry and the Alpini.[589]

Without a shot, Bersaglieri and Fanti landed in Trieste.[590]

The *mucs* have signed the surrender!

At 3:00 p.m. the ceasefire will begin.[591]

---

[589] They were the cavalrymen of the "Alessandria" Regiment and the Alpini of the IV Group. Later the troops of the "Pistoia" Brigade also arrived

[590] Beginning with October 30, the city had risen. A public safety committee had declared *"the forfeiture of Austria from the possession of Italian Adriatic lands"*. The Austro-Hungarian Empire had accepted these decisions and the following day the Habsburg representatives and the 3,000 garrison soldiers left. The Italian troops who arrived in the city on November 3 met with no resistance. Under the command of General Carlo Petitti di Roreto, the units of the "Arezzo" Brigade and of the II Bersaglieri Brigade, transported on ships escorted by seven destroyers, disembarked on the San Carlo pier at 4:20 p.m., to be greeted festively by the Italian population.

[591] Austria-Hungary had sued for surrender on 29 October. On 30 at Villa Giusti, the Austrian commission took note of the conditions of the armistice, without, however, assuming responsibility for accepting them. They tried to buy time, telling the Italian High Command that they had to wait for further instructions from their authorities. At the same time, the Italian army continued chasing the enemy in retreat. The morning of November 3 arrived with no decision having been made by the imperials, while men continued to die at the front. At that point Diaz warned that if the armistice was not signed by midnight, the ongoing negotiations would be cancelled. This peremptory ultimatum helped to break the deadlock. At 3:00 p.m. a phonogram from the Austrian Chief of Staff, Arturo von Arz, arrived at Villa Giusti, saying that the clauses fixed by Italy and its allies were accepted without conditions. The ceasefire was to go into effect at 3:00 p.m. the following day. Due to inaccuracies in the transmission of the surrender communication, however, many Austrian commands confused the time of the armistice signing with that of the cessation of hostilities and invited their soldiers to lay down their arms several hours in advance. The Italian High Command, instead, well mindful of this, gave the order to continue the offensive until the last minute so as to occupy as much territory and capture as many prisoners and material as possible in the last, fast, rush. Thus, ironically, soldiers continued to die until a few moments before the stroke of 3:00 p.m. on November 4. The last to die was an eighteen-year-old second lieutenant from Cagliari, Alberto Riva Villasanta, cut down by one of the last machine gun bursts, while he was chasing the enemy in retreat, under the command of the regimental "Crimson Flames" of the VIII Bersaglieri. The Gold Medal of Military Valour was awarded to his memory with the following motivation:

The news spread like wildfire through our camp.
Trumpet blasts, drum rolls, and bass-drum beats can be heard.
All the men are cheering, firing musket shots and throwing petards right and left. Waving flags, various groups go from tent to tent to spread the news and their ranks grow larger and larger. *Pugnodiferro*, *Carestia*, *il Gat* and *Cuteddu* broke into my tent along with another ten comrades. They dragged me out and started throwing me in the air among bursts of "hurrà!". Then, singing and shouting, we all went to get *Faro* to give him the same treatment.
His men were already making him fly, while he yelled: «*Fioi, mi no so bon svołàr. Ciapeme! Ciapeme!*»[592]
We took over. It was a race to see who could throw him higher.
At the end of the "service" he hugged us all.
His eyes shone more than ever with tears. Then, drying them, he shouted: «*Fioi, andemo a ciapar Lu-Lupo!*»[593]. We started running.
In the meantime, a group of *Arditissimi* had stormed the quartermasters, who immediately surrendered, handing over bread and bars of chocolate, but above all barrels of cognac and wine.
The euphoria is general.

3:00 p.m.
The "fall in" was called.
In a few hours we had guzzled everything in sight, one round after another, one song after another. Lots of soldiers can no longer stand upright. If we were attacked right now, we wouldn't be able to fight as we know how.

Still a teenager he volunteered for war, taking on the greatest risks. Arditi commander in a Bersaglieri Regiment, he was the bravest of the brave. First to ask for the honour of the most dangerous exploits, he often anticipated an order with its execution and, in his unit, tempered by many an ordeal, he was ever an example of sublime heroism. With ardent faith in victory, in the days leading up to the offensive of vindication, he managed to infuse his men with the fighting strength and energy, which was then consecrated on the field in a magnificent contest of heroic daring. In the crossing of the Piave and Livenza rivers, thrown back with unstoppable ardour by violent counterattacks, always first among the first, great in his sublime fury, he was able, with bold firmness, to lead his troops in various overwhelming assaults, routing the enemy everywhere. Only a few moments before the cessation of hostilities, breaking through the desperate opposing defenses in a supreme attack, he fell gloriously on the field, a magnificent example of sacrifice for the greatness of the Homeland.
Piave-Livenza-Tagliamento, 27 October - 4 November 1918.

[592] «Guys, I can't fly. Catch me! Catch me!» translation from the Venetian dialect.

[593] «Guys, let's go and get *Lu-Lupo*!»

Somehow or other we lined up around the officers.
Our commander, Major Di Orazio, climbed up on a table and armed with a megaphone spoke: «Arditi of the XXII Assault Unit, in this battle, too, you have covered yourselves with glory!»
A great roar rose up from our ranks.
«The Flag of the 3rd Group, Assault Units XXII and VIII, IX Bersaglieri Battalion, will be awarded the Silver Medal for Military Valour!»
Another roar. Many fezs and caps have flown into the sky.
«I have the honour of reading you the motivation for the Silver Medal to our Group: *By boldly launching itself on the left bank of the Piave, it overwhelmed its formidable defenses, pushing on as far as the opposing artillery which it conquered after a bloody fight. Although isolated, it resisted fierce and repeated counterattacks. Resuming the advance, it rushed towards its goals, devising, with magnificent daring, the ultimate and definitive phases of the manoeuvre. Piave, October 1918.*»
Another long roar rose up from our ranks.
«Arditi of the XXII Assault Unit, thanks also to your courage, the battle has been won!»
«To whom the victory?» someone shouted.
The loudest «A Noi!», I have ever heard rang out, accompanied by the sound of daggers being drawn and pointed skyward.
«Arditi of the XXII Assault Unit, I have another important announcement to give you.»
For a moment, silence, filled with hope, fell on the field.
My heart inebriated with happiness, I waited for the Major to articulate the words as simple as they were extraordinary, of which I had dreamed so many times.
«The war is over!» [594]

---

594 On the evening of November 4, the Italian High Command sent the world the last war bulletin, prepared by the head of the press office, General Domenico Siciliani:
"The war against Austria-Hungary, which the Italian army, inferior in number and equipment, began on 24 May 1915 under the leadership of His Majesty and supreme leader the King and conducted with unwavering faith and tenacious bravery without rest for 41 months, is won. The gigantic battle, which opened on the 24th of last October and in which fifty-one Italian divisions, three British, two French, one Czechoslovak and a US regiment joined against seventy-three Austrian divisions, is over. The lightning-fast and most audacious advance of the XXIX Army Corps on Trento, blocking the retreat of the enemy armies from Trentino, as they were overwhelmed in the west by the troops of the VII Army and in the east by those of the I, VI, and the IV armies, led to the utter collapse of the enemy front. From the Brenta to the Torre, the enemy in flight was pushed ever further back by the irresistible onslaught of the XII, VIII, X Armies and the cavalry divisions.

In the plains, His Royal Highness the Duke of Aosta is advancing at the head of his undefeated III Army, eager to return to those previously successfully conquered positions, which were never lost. The Austro-Hungarian Army is crushed: it suffered terrible losses in the dogged resistance of the early days, and during the pursuit lost an enormous quantity of materials of every kind as well as almost all its stockpiles and supply depots. The Austro-Hungarian Army has so far left about 300,000 prisoners of war in our hands along with several entire officer corps and at least 5,000 pieces of heavy artillery."

At the bottom of the original printed message, General Armando Diaz, added the following sentence in his own hand: *"The remnants of what was one of the world's most powerful armies are returning in hopelessness and chaos up the valleys from which they had descended with boastful confidence. Chief of Staff of the Army, General Diaz."*

The fundamental role of the October battle on the fate of the entire world conflict, so far as accelerating its conclusion, was underlined by General Ludendorff: *"In Vittorio Veneto Austria did not lose a battle; it lost the war and itself, dragging Germany down with it as well. Without the destructive battle of Vittorio Veneto, we could have continued our desperate resistance"*. In the ten days of battle, the Royal Army suffered almost 37,000 casualties (5,652 dead, 26,541 wounded and 4,305 missing), many fewer than in Cadorna's bloody battles of the Isonzo. The Austro-Hungarian army lost between 30,000 and 90,000 men, depending on the source, and lost 428,000 prisoners, including 24 generals. Huge was the Italian war booty in terms of artillery pieces, machine guns and other materials.

Emperor Charles I of Habsburg abdicated on November 11, after a fruitless attempt to transform the empire into a federal state. Yugoslavia, Hungary, Czechoslovakia and Poland were born from its ruins. A republic was proclaimed in Austria on 12 November and on 16 in Hungary. In Germany, due to the army revolt and the collapse of the country, overwhelmed by many revolutionary ferments, Kaiser Wilhelm II was forced to leave the throne on 10 November and flee to the Netherlands. He formally abdicated on 28 November. On 11 November, Germany signed the armistice. The First World War was over.

Those two gunshots in Sarajevo on June 28, 1914 not only cost the lives of Archduke Francesco Ferdinando of Habsburg-Este and his wife, but of over 9.7 million soldiers, added to which were 21 million wounded. Germany and Russia had over 2 million killed, France 1.4 million, Austria-Hungary 1.1 million, The United Kingdom and its colonies 890 thousand, the Ottoman Empire 770 thousand, Serbia 370 thousand, Romania 250 thousand and The United States 116 thousand. Italy sustained 650,000 deaths (of which 57,000 prisoners of war) and over 1.2 million wounded among the military, out of a total of 5.6 million men mobilized. On Italian soil 1,024 English, 480 French, 336 Czechoslovakians and one American died. Even the European population was not spared: about 950,000 civilians were killed directly by military operations and almost 5.9 million perished from collateral causes, in particular famine and food shortages, diseases and epidemics and lastly also from the racial persecutions that broke out during the conflict. The Paris Conference, which began in mid-January 1919, was convened to establish the conditions for peace. With great difficulty, various treaties were signed: Versailles with Germany (28 June 1919), Saint-Germain with Austria (10 September 1919), Neuilly with Bulgaria (27 November 1919), Trianon with Hungary (4 June 1920) and Sèvres with Turkey (10 August 1920). The treaty of Versailles, which imposed harsh conditions on Germany, is considered by historians to be the spark that later set off the Second World War.

CHAPTER 16.V

It was by chance that my grandfather started writing.
He only did it to relieve the tension before an attack, one of the many he had to make.
From that moment on, he continued to write, narrating his war efforts, his relationships with comrades and his family.
At first in a very simple form, but later in a richer and more articulated way, as if it were an adventure novel.
As soon as the war ended, however, he decided to stop.
He wrote nothing more.
Nor did he ever want to talk about the war.
However, what he did succeed in documenting between December 1916 and November 1918 represents for me something unique, devastating but epic, tragic but remarkable.
I don't know why he wanted to pass these memories on to me.
He decided to do so when I was still a little boy.
I like to imagine that he had a flash of clairvoyance, a bit like his mother, my great-grandmother. He sensed, or perhaps only hoped, that I would make good use of it a hundred years after the events narrated.

After the armistice and the end of the war, grandfather remained in the military until 23 December 1920.
What did he do in those two years?
What happened to his comrades?
I couldn't stop now.
I wanted to know.
I searched in libraries and bookstores, finding old books written during and after the war by the ones who had fought and new books written on the wave of a renewed interest in the events of a century ago.
I also searched the web and social media, where I was lucky enough to encounter other Arditi fans, who provided me with valuable information, drawn from books that were almost impossible to find.
I was thus able to reconstruct the movements and actions of the XXII Assault Unit.

Year 1918

After the armistice, the XXII Assault Unit was engaged in training exercises aimed at integrating the reserves, 5 officers and 286 enlisted men who arrived on November 6, 1918.
It also handled arrangements for its quarters, transferred on November 15 to Scomigo and San Pietro di Scomigo, less than ten kilometres from Vittorio (the name "Veneto", already in use after the battle, became official only in July 1923).
That same November 15, Lieutenant Colonel Raffaele Repetto took over the command of the 3rd Assault Group and in December the commander of the XXII Unit, Major Raffaele Di Orazio, was replaced by the Major Tommaso Aiello.
In the meantime, the High Command decided to deploy the entire 1st Assault Division in Libya, to regain control of Tripolitania, at that time largely in the hands of the rebels.

Year 1919

At the beginning of January, the 3rd Group (VIII and XXII Assault Units, IX Battalion Bersaglieri) began moving toward Venice, where it was to board ship for Tripoli.
Leaving the Conegliano area for that of Treviso, the XXII camped in Santandrà, while the VIII and IX went to Paderno.
At the end of the month the transfer to the province of Venice went ahead, with the XXII located in Martellago, the VIII in Peseggia and the IX in Scorzè. Departures to Libya followed in succession over the course of a month, starting in mid-February. The 3rd Group was the last to leave.
On 19 March the XXII embarked together with the group command on the steamer "Umbria", which sailed the following day in the direction of the intermediate port of Gallipoli (Puglia region).
The navigation, already difficult because of rough seas, was marred by an accident connected to the conflict. At 9:20 p.m. the steamer hit a loose mine and the explosion caused a breach in the hull and the flooding of the hold. The ship was about to capsize from the general panic on board and the big waves. Prompt intervention by the officers and the disciplined behaviour of the Black Flames, who arranged themselves so as to balance the weight of the water on board, prevented the serious accident from turning into a tragedy.

In addition to 2 dead and 18 injured, 83 men disappeared into the sea, either washed away by water from the breach or, having jumped overboard after the explosion, overwhelmed by the waves on the lifeboats. 47 missing soldiers were from the XXII Assault Unit.
From the historical diary of the 3rd Group: "The steamer continues at full speed changing course, heading towards Mola di Bari and then towards Bari no need for assistance. During the journey, the wounded will be treated and those who may still be in the flooded hold will be rescued".
On 23 March the XXII left Bari by train to Taranto and the following day boarded the steamer "Taormina".
I assume that the facts narrated by my grandfather happened in Bari or Taranto: the hasty escape from a pub, chased by the family of the owners, who didn't appreciate the compliments that an Ardito had given to the girl behind the counter.
Together with the story of the naval accident and the rescue of his friend from Murano, this is the only episode that grandfather ever related about his five years of military service.
They left on the 26th and reached Tripoli on the 28th.
On 30 March General Zoppi, on a visit to the troops, gave the XXII Assault Unit the appellation of "Serenissimo" (the most serene) for their behaviour during the naval accident.
The XXII reached the rest of the Group at the oasis of Gurgi, west of Tripoli and south of the track for Zanzur.
Although it began with bellicose intentions, the mission ended up being a long vacation. Once the operation against Misrata to liberate the Italian prisoners was cancelled, there were no clashes with the Arab armed gangs. The units dedicated themselves to acclimatization marches in the desert, carrying out fire drills and road works.
Following the agreement reached with the rebel leaders, the planned service duty at the Fonduk-el-Toghar outpost was also suspended from 23 May as part of the easing of the military apparatus in Tripolitania.
Return operations began on June 9th.
The XXII was the last unit to leave, on June 30, aboard the steamship "Ferdinando Palasciano", together with the command and part of the IX.
On July 3 the Arditi and Bersaglieri landed in Taranto.
The following day, aboard four railway trains, they were transferred to Emilia to carry out public security services.
The XXII was based in Luzzara, where it remained from 7 to 20 July.
Here it had to fight a flu epidemic, which affected many of its men.
We don't know if it was the "Spanish flu".

Due to growing tensions with the new Kingdom of Serbs, Croats and Slovenes, but also to avoid possible internal clashes with the rapidly expanding socialist forces, the 1st Assault Division was sent back to the eastern border under the XXVIII Army Corps.
On 22 July they arrived at the Longatico station in western Slovenia.
The 3rd Group moved to the Postojna area (XXII in Grascè), where it remained until 29 August, when it was temporarily withdrawn to the Karst, west of Trieste, with the three units distributed in Come (VIII), Cobinaglava (XXII) and Goriansko (IX Bersaglieri).
On 9 September they were moved to the armistice line again.
Partly by train and partly on foot they travelled to the end of the Carnaro Gulf. Command and the XXII settled in Castua.
Tension was greatly heightened by the situation in Fiume (currently Rijeka in Croatia), where the population's strong sentiment of Italianess had not found satisfaction in the decisions made by the Allies at the Versailles peace conference. On September 12, 1919 Gabriele d'Annunzio entered Fiume to annex the city to the Kingdom of Italy.
He was followed by the commander of the 3rd Group, Lieutenant Colonel Repetto, a large part of the VIII Unit (250 Arditi and numerous officers including Major Nunziante, Captain Sessa, Lieutenants Machinè, Tuttoilmondo, Cornaglia, Menicucci, Cipri, Spada, Narbona), a company of the XIII Unit led by Lieutenant Ettore Frignani, the entire 2nd company of the XXII Unit, with its commander Captain Umberto Sbacchi and Lieutenants Anelli, Bellia, Bonanni, Carpinelli, De Marchi, Donati, Mazzoni, Tonacci.
The other two companies of the XXII continued their service in the outposts, even though Colonel Repetto on the armistice line had invited the commander of the 3rd company to defect and follow him. If he had done so, my grandpa would have found himself participating in the Fiume exploit.
What remained of the 3rd Group was first transferred by truck to Vippacco (20 September) and then to Manzano (6 October), the new headquarters of the command and of the Bersaglieri Battalion. The XXII was settled in Schompass and the reconstituted VIII in Prebacina.
In order to avoid any more defections to Fiume (as many Arditi of the XII Unit under the command of Captain Pietro Tongiorgi had done on 24 October), the 3rd Group was moved farther away from the border before the end of 1919. The command was established in Mariano del Friuli and the XXII located in Moraro.

Year 1920

The XXII Unit survived the dissolution of the 1st Assault Division.
After welcoming into its ranks officials and enlisted men from the disbanded XIII, together with the X and XX Units it formed the new 1st Assault Group (10 January), then called the Assault Regiment (14 January).
Headquartered in Palmanova under the orders of Lieutenant Colonel Alberto Amante, between February 17 and March 17, the XXII once again guarded a section of the armistice line, relieving the 25th Infantry Regiment.
At the end of March, the Assault Regiment moved to the Trieste area with a view to its future departure for Albania.
The plan was for it to reinforce the Italian garrison in Valona, surrounded by rebel tribes, supported by the government of Tirana, with a framework of Turkish officers and equipped with French weapons and ammunition.[595]
The heated political climate in Italy and the strong opposition of the socialist forces to the military commitment in Albania resulted in rail strikes, protest demonstrations and calls to insubordination.
On 11 June, the day before their departure, many Arditi of the X Unit participated in uniform in peace marches, which, however, ended in gunfights on the streets of Trieste and an attempt to storm the Rozol barracks, where the units were housed.
The XXII 3rd company, my grandfather's, was positioned to watch over the surrounding wall and the entrance. Several times rifle skirmishes took place between the Arditi on guard and the column of armed civilians, who once again tried to storm the barracks.
The following day the embarkation took place in a highly charged atmosphere, forcing the steamship "Pietro Calvi" to sail away quickly, leaving several bags, six carts and numerous cases of ammunition on the pier.

[595] According to the Treaty of London (April 26, 1915), a secret treaty between the Triple Entente and the Kingdom of Italy, the latter was to have obtained full sovereignty over Valona, the island of Saseno and "a territory sufficiently broad to ensure the defense of these points". The rest of Albania was destined for the establishment of an autonomous neutral state, but under an Italian protectorate. This agreement, however, was only binding for the French Republic, the United Kingdom and the Russian Empire, but not for the United States. With the Treaty of Tirana (July 20, 1920) and the subsequent treaty of friendship with the Albanians (August 2, 1920), Italy recognized the independence and full sovereignty of the Albanian state and Italian troops left the country. This treaty also sanctioned the Italian withdrawal from Valona, while maintaining authority over the small island of Saseno, to guarantee Italian military control over the Otranto canal.

Apparently only 400 men from the two units were brought on board, prodded by the Carabinieri.[596]
The assault regiment sent to Albania consisted of the following units:
XXII (Major Marchi), XX (Major Carissimo), X (Major Priore) and IX (Lieutenant Colonel Messe, then repatriated due to illness and replaced by Domenico Mondelli, of the same rank). [597]
The IX had been reconstituted in April.
Unlike the trip to Libya, the mission in Albania was characterized by bloody fighting and the scourge of malaria.
On 19 and 20 June there was fighting near the entrenched camp of Valona, with 15 men killed and 87 wounded.
On 21 June the command was entrusted to Colonel Giuseppe Bassi, who took over from General De Gaspari.
On 23 July there was more hard fighting between Mount Longia and Mount Messovum, reconquered by the Black Flames of the IX and XX, at the price of 12 dead and 38 wounded.

---

[596] The Trieste episode was not the only one. On June 26 in Ancona, the Bersaglieri, 11th Regiment, refused to board ship for Albania, barricading themselves in their barracks and shooting at the Carabinieri. The officers' intervention brought calm, but the order of departure was revoked. On June 30, the infantrymen of the "Como" Brigade occupied the railway station of Cervignano, in fear of being transferred to Trieste and then to Albania. On the same day in Brindisi a group of Arditi rebelled against the embarkation and clashed with the Carabinieri, assaulting their barracks (one dead and twenty wounded). They also fired at the steamer, with their commander and fellow soldiers already on board, to prevent its departure.

[597] Domenico Mondelli (30 June 1886 - 13 December 1974) was one of the most interesting and eclectic figures of the Royal Army. A career soldier, at the outbreak of the war he was one of the first aviators, thanks to the license obtained in February 1914. He carried out reconnaissance, earning a Bronze Medal, and then bombing missions, at the command of a group of Caproni aircraft. In the summer of 1917, he joined the Bersaglieri, earning a Silver Medal for fighting on the Karst. Promoted to major, from October to January he was the first commander of the XIX Assault Unit, later renumbered XXIII. With the rank of lieutenant colonel, on May 1st, 1918 he commanded the 1st Battalion of the 242nd Infantry Regiment of the "Teramo" Brigade, taking part in the Battle of the Solstice in Col del Rosso, where he was wounded in the face by a grenade fragment. For that action he earned a Silver and a Bronze Medal. After the war he was awarded the title of Knight of the Order of the Crown of Italy. In Albania he received another Bronze Medal for his feats of arms on Mount Messovum in July 1920. Despite his Italian name, he was Eritrean, of Tigrinya ethnicity. He was adopted in 1891 by Colonel Attilio Mondelli during the retreat following the defeat of Adua and brought to Italy in 1900. His military career came to an abrupt halt during the fascist period, and only resumed, albeit in the reserves, with the advent of the Republic. He obtained the rank of general of the Army Corps in 1968.

Pursuit of the rebels by the XXII in trucks and two squadrons in armoured cars was suspended by orders from higher up. Two Albanian MPs had asked for the armistice.
On 19 August the Regiment was repatriated on the steamer "Bormida" and based in Palmanova, where the IX and XXII were housed, with the X detached in Medea and the XX in Cormons.
In grandfather's service record and in his papers, there is no trace of the mission to Albania. It's my guess that he was among those who for some reason were not embarked either before or after.
November 17, 1920 marked a historic date: the breaking up of the Assault Regiment and its three heroic units: IX, X and XXII.
General Caviglia, commanding the royal troops of Venezia-Giulia, issued the following communication:
"It is not without deep regret that in obedience to higher organic needs I must order the suppression of the three assault battalions and the command of the Regiment. Conceived in a solemn and grave hour of our war, they experienced its culminating and decisive phase; short but intense and luminous life; the glorious memory of which will remain forever in the minds and the history of our epic struggle. My heartfelt and grateful farewell goes to them and to those who had the honour of being part of it."
As soon as Gabriele d'Annunzio heard of the dissolution of the departments, he sent the following message to Colonel Bassi:
"To the Chief of the Arditi. This is neither an incitement nor an appeal. It is a silent farewell, a farewell from an Italian heart that bleeds from warrior to warrior, from Flame to Flame".
The name of the XXII survived for a few more months.
The distinctive numbers of the four units, which had been part of the Regiment (IX, X, XX and XXII), were assigned to the four companies of the XX Assault Unit, the last in existence.
Grandfather was sent on unlimited leave on December 23, 1920.
For more than five years he had served in the Royal Army "with fidelity and honour", as stated in his service record.
The XX Assault Unit was disbanded on February 28, 1921.

Thus ended the epic of the Arditi of the Great War.

Chapter 17.V

It is estimated that between 1917 and 1918 the number of men enlisted in the Assault Units ranged from 30,000 to 35,000.[598]
At the end of the war, around 24,000 were still in service.

What happened to them after the dissolution of their Units?
Why were they forgotten?
Why do the few who do retain a vague memory associate them with fascism?

After reading and rereading my grandfather's diary and after consulting numerous history books on that period, tragic and glorious at the same time, I felt the need to investigate further.
I'm not a historian. Nor do I claim to have made a perfect synthesis of all the historical material existing on the subject.
I just wrote down the facts and opinions which impressed me most, trying to find my own answers to these questions.

The Arditi in the post-war period

After the battle of Vittorio Veneto the assessments of the behaviour of the Arditi were extremely positive.

General Caviglia, commander of the 8th Army, wrote:
"Among the troops placed at my disposal was the Army Assault Corps.
I have never known such a formidable organism of warfare, and I don't know if any have ever existed in the world. For individual and collective instruction, for physical training, for quality of decision, of will, of impulse, of intelligent daring, both personal and collective, it was truly an exceptional organisation of war: certainly, I could not have found better shock troops than they".

---

[598] This estimate does not include those who were called Arditi without having full title because they served in the platoons of Regimental Arditi or in the units of the various weapons and services in the two Assault Divisions.

On November 12, 1918, General Ottavio Zoppi, commander of the 1st Assault Division, directed this proclamation to his troops:

"My victorious warriors!

We have entered a period of waiting. We must wait until the complete execution of the armistice imposed on our enemies, whom we have beaten, has matured.

Since we can't rule out that it might still be necessary to throw a few petards here and there, we must also consider that the mere fact that we are always ready and competent inspires our enemies with that worthy respect and due obedience which should encourage them to sign both the armistice, and after it the peace, that we desire, as Italy's victory deserves.

In the meantime, stay trained and disciplined, and keep that ardent Italian spirit that constitutes one of your strongest and most admired treasures.

At the same time, be merry. Your commanders and I will help you to spend this waiting period well. Make good music, organize pleasant theatrical entertainments, drink (but never go overboard!) good wine (I will always do my best not to let you go without it).

[...]

Men! Let us thank God we were born Italian, and let the first glass you drink, of the wine I am sending you, be a toast to the health, the glory and the future of our Italy."

General Oreste De Gaspari wrote in his report on the battle:

"Events and results were preceded, let me say it, by this mass of enthusiastic souls, with tenacious will and breasts of steel, who, although new to the arena of a grandiose battle, under its guise of great unity, threw themselves into it with old daring, but new discipline, overwhelming everything with their mighty impact, symbol of a new strength and of a new age. Any judgement on my part of these troops, whom I had the great satisfaction of commanding for the first time in combat, would be to impair their value, to tarnish the halo of glory that envelops them all.

In their simplicity, in the naturalness of their value, they were great and it is fitting to bow before them and admire their greatness."

Despite this high praise, by the end of November 1918, General Francesco Saverio Grazioli, who had made large contributions to the development and the achievements of the Assault Units, was already proposing their dissolution to the High Command as soon as peace was certain.

"Now that the war has ceased, and there are no more opportunities for fist-fights, flaunting their daring, looting or swagger, their disorderly and exuberant nature will either be lost and they will return to being ordinary soldiers with no justification for the external forms and their official title (assault troops), or it will persist and thus be extremely difficult to contain, and avoid regrettable disciplinary offenses and even crimes, which would obscure their own glorious fame earned in the war."

The general precluded the possibility of their use in public security duties, fearing that "a kind of pretorianism" might be established.
He suggested they be used in the colony, saving draft troops from being sent to Africa on an unattractive mission.
These indications were accepted by his superior, General Caviglia, and also by the military leadership. In fact, despite being exalted by the press and official communiqués, the Arditi were looked upon with suspicion by the top army officers for a lack of respect for formal discipline and for their privileges no longer justified by greater risk.
The debate within the High Command ended in mid-December 1918.
Badoglio communicated to the Ministry of War the advisability of not wasting the experience of the assault units. The Arditi had been the most ground-breaking organic innovation in the Royal Army during the conflict, developed in an original and autonomous way in comparison to the Austro-German model of the Stürmtruppen and with no equal among the Allies.
Yet, he decided to progressively reduce the number of the assault units and send the ones left to Libya. He feared that a sudden and contextual suppression of the Black Flames could result in uprisings and incidents, in consideration of their very strong "esprit de corps".
Thus, the command of the Assault Army Corps was dissolved first of all (November 28, 1918) and then, between January and February 1919, it was the turn of the units contained in the various armies.
The 2nd Assault Division was dissolved on February 25, 1919.
A few months after the end of the war, only the 1st Assault Division with 6 units was still in existence.
In parallel, the Minister of War, General Albricci, ordered that the personnel of the Infantry Regiments should no longer include platoons of Arditi, nor Stokes and flamethrower sections, nor 37 mm cannons. In August 1919, the Infantry returned to its pre-war situation.

Except for rhetorical and superficial acknowledgments, first liberal and later fascist Italy learned nothing from the experience of the Assault Units nor from the lessons of this world war.

Disappointment at how the Arditi were liquidated at the end of the war clearly transpires from some of their books and writings. One illuminating example is that of Paolo Giudici, who was an officer of the IV Assault Unit at Sdricca, later renumbered I and finally XX.
"After the war, no one cared about us, despite having given the best part of ourselves, despite having sacrificed our lives on the altar of Italy.
No one.
We saw the regiments returning from the new borders one by one to a well-deserved rest. And crowds in the cities welcomed and cheered them.
They all had their day of triumph and marched under arches of marble or oak, under a forest of flags, between the festive wings of the people.
No one welcomed the Black Flames.
Yet we had voluntarily consecrated ourselves to death, we were, always and everywhere, the first in furious assaults; yet in the moments of disaster we did not waver for a moment, the Homeland looked to us as its last defense and we saved it; and yet we flourished because every victory was heralded by our cry and at our cry, from Grappa to the mouth of the Piave, the enemy armies fell apart.
No one welcomed us.
And one fine day they dissolved us, they sent us away, just as the municipalities and lords of Italy used to dismiss the mercenaries hired by them, when they no longer needed their sword.
They disbanded us without even a thank-you for what we had done, without saying goodbye, not even in a coldly polite way; they did it on the sly, almost as if they were afraid of making any noise around us."

Not even the overseas missions were well received.
"They disbanded us, but not all of us. They still needed us, so they sent the 1st Assault Division to Libya, to enjoy the cool of next summer and to cool the boiling spirits of the Arabs, just like they send out coloured troops, like Eritrean battalions.
This was the reward that official Italy attributed to us."

In the immediate aftermath of the war, some Black Flames tried to find a political voice, summoning their ex-comrades and leveraging their discontent.
On the political right, they found the support of Marinetti's futurists, but with few followers, despite the efforts of Mario Carli, a former Arditi officer, who on 1st January 1919 founded the Association of the Arditi of Italy in Rome. The support of Mussolini in Milan was more successful.
First, he published many articles extolling the Black Flames in his newspaper, "Il Popolo d'Italia", then promoted the birth of the Milanese section of the Association in via Cerva, the only one that played any role. In exchange for political, propagandistic and economic support, the Milanese Arditi agreed to become the armed wing of nascent fascism.
This role had its most sensational manifestation on April 15, 1919. With the consent of the police, several dozen Arditi, led by Ferruccio Vecchi and Tommaso Marinetti, confronted a procession of thousands of striking socialist workers at the entrance to Piazza Duomo, forcing them to flee with petards and revolver shots.
Then they tried to attack the headquarters of the socialist newspaper «L'Avanti!», even if it was manned by military troops. When a gunshot from the newspaper office struck one of the soldiers from the security detail, the military no longer resisted the entry of the Arditi, who killed two socialists, devastated the editorial offices, destroyed the machinery and set fire to the premises. Political and military authorities did not prosecute those responsible for the attack. Vecchi and Marinetti, summoned by General Caviglia, at the time Minister of War, were even praised, because their gesture had "saved the nation".
Those months saw the formation of the national association of combatants (ANC) and association of the war-mutilated and disabled (ANMIG); these were patriotic and liberal-democratic, with a program of reforms guaranteeing greater social justice and participation in government, which men of all branches of the military joined.
The Arditi Association, instead, made an elitist choice, consistent with the attitude of detachment and superiority demonstrated during the war. Although no one questioned its representativeness and legitimacy, it had little follow-up: only a few hundred militants throughout Italy.
Thanks to the financing of the industrialists, who saw in them possible "White Guards" against the growing workers' forces, Carli and Vecchi founded the weekly "L'Ardito", in which they reaffirmed the political role of the Black Flames through verbal aggression and demagoguery.

However, the Association was unable to grow significantly, not even with the progressive demobilization of the Assault Units, and it was losing ground in a period when organizations based on large masses of members were emerging in the political struggle.
A violent article, denouncing the intention to use the Assault Units for police duties ("Arditi, not Gendarmes!"), led General Caviglia to prohibit "the sale and reading in the barracks of the Bolshevik newspaper L'Ardito".
Another event worked against them.
In the summer of 1919, a strong popular protest, with little distinctions between parties, called to account the ruling classes on who had wanted the war and how it had been conducted. Overcoming internal polemics between interventionists and neutralists, all political forces except the socialists closed ranks in consensus on the way the war had been waged and on the patriotic celebration of its victory.
This process reduced the political role of the Arditi, as well as that of the Futurists and, seemingly, of the fascists as well. It is no coincidence that in the November elections the three movements all together obtained only a few thousand preferences out of 270,000 voters in Milan.
Too associated with the Great War, "Arditism" was destined to play a marginal role on the political scene, as the war experience was filed away and gradually forgotten. In addition, there were violent internal conflicts, accompanied by expulsions and mutual accusations.
It thus ended up as a minor movement of ex-combatants, squeezed between the followers of d'Annunzio[599]*, who was monopolizing attention with the issue of Fiume, and fascism, which managed to resist and overcome the critical phase thanks to Mussolini's charisma, his national daily newspaper and his contacts with industry.*
The defeat of the workers' movement in the autumn of 1920, after the so-called "Biennio Rosso" (Red Biennium), opened the way for a resurgence of the right wing, offering a great opportunity to boost the Association, re-

[599] Gabriele d'Annunzio also drew heavily on the Arditi heritage. He almost always wore their uniform, he wanted his personal guard to be Arditi, he called his followers "Arditi" and "Fiamme" ("Flames"), he used the war cries and songs of the Arditi, so much so that public opinion ended up attributing to the Arditi a far greater role than they had actually played in the Fiume exploit. Some historians believe that the sedition of Fiume convinced the high commanders of the army to definitively dissolve the Assault Units, fearing the risks of their politicization. It had been tolerated, if not encouraged, in 1919 when turned against socialist forces and workers' subversive actions. Whereas in Fiume, however, it had profoundly threatened the unity of the armed forces.

constituted by the Milanese section and called ANAI, or National Arditi Association of Italy. To widen its membership base, the obligation of having served in the Arditi was dropped (it was enough to be politically allied fighters), but d'Annunzio's followers, accused of socialism and internationalism, were excluded, and any mention of the leading role of the "Vate" (the Poet) disappeared. [600]

After a short period of alliance with the fascist movement, given the concrete danger of absorption in the summer of 1921, the ANAI Congress established autonomy from all parties, invited its members to resign from the Italian Fasci of Combat and realigned with d'Annunzio, who emerged humbled from the experience of Fiume.

The detachment from fascism, reiterated in the National Council of 19 March 1922, is well clarified in the text of a national conference held in October of the same year:

"We felt the need for violence against all the enemies of the homeland until 1919. Now the political situation is greatly changed. The Arditi d'Italia were the true founders of fascism. But in the fascism of the first hour which was the avenger of the revolutionary war and was the most daring movement toward the left and which promised, among other things, to give the land to the peasants and the management of the factories to the workers. On the other hand, the danger of Bolshevism was imminent, with its demonstrations of scorn on the part of the combatants and of exaltation on the part of the deserters. That period has been surpassed for some time through the efforts of the daring minority who made up the first fascist nuclei, which no longer have anything to do with the fascist national party. We now intend to guarantee the freedom of organization of all unions.

---

[600] The legionaries of Fiume were no longer attributed the Arditi status. The government of Fiume was the first in the world to recognize the legitimacy of the Russian Soviet Federative Socialist Republic, led by Lenin, which in turn was the only one in the world to recognize Fiume's state independence. With the treaty of Rapallo (November 12, 1920) Fiume was declared a free city, while Zara passed to Italy. D'Annunzio did not accept the agreement and then the Italian government of Giolitti ordered General Caviglia to clear the legionaries by force. The attack started at 5pm on December 24th. In the five days of combat, the so-called "Natale di Sangue" (Bloody Christmas), 22 legionaries, 5 civilians and 17 Italian soldiers died. After the arms truce of 29, an agreement was signed for the exodus of the legionaries starting from 4 January 1921. D'Annunzio left Fiume on 18 January bound for Venice and then to Gardone Riviera on the Brescia side of Lake Garda. What was supposed to be a stay of a few weeks to complete the drafting of the "Notturno", became definitive instead with the creation of the Vittoriale degli Italiani. With the advent of fascism, in 1924 the free state of Fiume was annexed to Italy, remaining so until 1945.

We do not want to make war on fascism, but we consider ourselves as equidistant from fascists, who for us are a degeneration of fascism, as from communism, which is an aberration of the socialist ideal. Our position is that of a balanced term in the midst of the current chaos created in particular by the absence of responsibility on the part of government bodies. This function of ours is clearly summarized in the thought of d'Annunzio, the man whom the workers trust".

Actually, the ANAI not only had a very limited political space, but also faced competition from the FNAI, the National Federation of the Arditi d'Italia: [601]

"The FNAI was born mainly to counter the ANAI, which, degenerating into pseudo-D'Annunzian unions, might still be a force to fear, if other Arditi had not disavowed their attitudes".

Although it recognized fascist hegemony, the FNAI also sought to carve out its own political space and freedom of action, which Mussolini, however, did not concede.

"Arditism" was now viewed with annoyance and suspicion, with no distinctions between supporters (FNAI) and dissidents (ANAI). The activities and methods of the two organizations were very similar, so much so that the prefectures often confused the two. Moreover, it was not uncommon for the local sections to split due to personal rivalries and pass from one association to the other, a particularly intense phenomenon in the regions of the south.

With the affirmation of fascism, the FNAI eventually prevailed, but it lost any autonomous political capacity. In any case, the overall number of members of the two associations was always relatively limited.

On the left, the "Arditi del Popolo", founded by a handful of Arditi headed by Lieutenant Argo Secondari enjoyed greater success.

At the end of June 1921, the Roman section of ANAI was reconstituted with the aim of defending with force the working masses from the increasingly frequent attacks by fascist action squadrons. The establishment of a Battalion was decided, divided into three companies, the "Temeraria", the "Disperata" and the "Folgore".

The emergence of an organization, which theorized preventive or retaliatory attacks against the fascists action squadrons, not only attracted more than a thousand members in Rome in a short time, mostly construction

[601] FNAI was formed with a national convention in Bologna in October 1922.

workers, railway workers and post-telegraphers, but quickly spread to all of Italy, welcoming to its paramilitary formations anarchists and republicans as well as leftist militants. By the summer of 1921, there were 144 sections in Italy for a total of over 20,000 members.
Obviously, the great majority had not served in the Arditi. The element of unity was the armed resistance to fascism, seen as an anti-proletarian movement.
Armed with daggers, muskets, bombs, revolvers, hunting rifles, sticks and iron clubs, they wore black sweaters with red cockade on their breasts. Their symbol was a laurel-crowned skull with a dagger between its teeth above the motto "A Noi!".
Among their many clashes with the fascists, the one in Sarzana stands out. Six hundred Tuscan "squadrists", that is members of action squadrons, had arrived there to force the release of their Carrara comrades who, some days earlier, had clashed with the "Arditi del Popolo". The latter, aided by the population, chased them away, killing eighteen and injuring thirty.
Despite their initial success and the tumultuous increase in their members, the experience of the "Arditi del Popolo" was short-lived.
Disowned by the ANAI for their proletarian and subversive character, with no support from any political force, repudiated by socialists and communists alike as provocateurs of the police, severely repressed by both the police and the judiciary who were much more tolerant of fascist squadrism, the "Arditi del Popolo" were unable to establish themselves and disappeared after a few months.[602]

In a nutshell, the existence of the Arditi was brilliant, but as short as that of a meteor. Admired and celebrated when their courage was needed, they were quickly put aside and disbanded.
Government and military leaders made the serious mistake of not being able or not wanting to exploit the value of these troops, even after the war.
The Arditi had no future as an autonomous political force, both for lack of strong leadership and for their values which were too bound to wartime and therefore destined to be removed and forgotten.
The facts have amply demonstrated this.

---

[602] According to a circular from the Ministry of the Interior, the "Arditi del Popolo" were considered a criminal association with criminal purposes. After August 1921, the authorities intervened heavy-handedly with charges, searches, captures, arrests and disbandment against them alone, leaving the fascist squadrons free to continue their terrorist actions undisturbed.

The Arditi = Fascists equation is incorrect.
It is true that fascism drew liberally on the symbolism and rituals of the Arditi and some of their values.[603]
With the affirmation of fascism many Arditi joined it, no differently from many other ex-combatants, "imboscati" and civilians. In its path of growth, fascism assimilated the elements it considered useful and discarded or suffocated all the others, opening the way for the oblivion of the assault troops.
The culture of peace after the Second World War, as well as the passage of time, further contributed to reducing the word "Arditi" to the role of an archaic and little used noun in current language, depriving it of the aura and significance it had possessed during the fourth and last Risorgimental war of Italy.

A rediscovery and re-evaluation of the Arditi is only fitting, certainly not for any deplorable celebration of violence, but in order to recover a little national pride, too often dramatically eroded by the behaviour of Italians themselves, as well as for reasons of history and the proper remembrance of these heroes.

[603] As for the symbology, just think of the black colour, the fez, the open jacket, the skulls, the dagger, the mottos ("A Noi!", "Me ne frego") and even the hymn "Giovinezza".

CHAPTER 18.V

As for my grandfather's family, unfortunately I was unable to gather much information.
Like all the other refugees, his mother and brothers probably managed to return home by the summer of 1919.
Attilia did not return, as she died in Tuscany, probably because of the so-called "Spanish" flu. She was born in 1889.
I have no idea in what condition they found their house in the hamlet of Vidali.
Agostino, born in 1901, appears to have died of tuberculosis while he was in Trentino, but the year is unknown.
My grandfather's mother, Perpetua, died in 1937 at the age of seventy-two. Her husband, Mattia, died in 1921, at the age of sixty-seven.
Noè, born in 1899, obtained a pension as an invalid of war for a lung problem. He had two children, Edda and Italo. He died in 1960 in Udine, fatally struck by a car.
Girardo, born in 1907, worked for forty years in Genoa. Upon reaching retirement age, he returned to the old house in Vidali. He had to abandon it in 1976 because of the earthquake which devastated Friuli. From then on until 1979 he lived in Gemona in the house of his niece, Lucia's daughter. Lucia passed away prematurely in 1943 at the age of thirty-four, leaving two children, Attilia and Agostino.
Margherita was almost ninety-seven when she passed away in June 2000. She had remained in Vidali until the 1950s working as a seamstress. Then she moved to Udine with her daughter Marta, who found work as a nurse at the hospital.
As regards Amabile, Mattia's mother, we only know that she was born in 1887 and that she married in Chiusaforte in 1908.
Mattia, born in 1909, worked for many years in Chiasso at the Customs. He had four children. He lived until 1985.
Unfortunately, fate saw to it that neither my father Sergio nor his brother Mario were able to finally learn the war story of their heroic and bold father Pietro, "L'Ardito".

Chapter 19.V

I'll never forget a night some years ago.
I was returning by plane from a trip to Fuerteventura.
About an hour before arriving in Bergamo, suddenly I saw the oxygen masks drop down, one after the other in sequence from the first row to the last, where I was sitting.
At the same time a siren began to sound and a metallic voice, certainly recorded many years earlier, invited passengers to put out their cigarettes and put on the masks!
Panic immediately spread on board.
This was also because stewards and hostesses were racing like mad up and down the corridor without giving us any explanation of what was going on.
We all figured it was something really serious.
There was an excruciating pain growing inside my ears, so bad that I had to concentrate in order to bear it.
We were losing altitude quickly.
I was sure we were about to crash.
I waited for the final impact from one moment to the next.
My face had turned green, according to an eyewitness, who transformed a lively concern into pure terror upon seeing the colour of my face.
While I waited for the impact that was slow in coming, my brain was engaged in a battle with the pain.
After about fifteen minutes the alarm fell silent and they finally explained to us that the pressurization system had failed and the plane had been forced to descend very quickly.
Once I landed, I literally kissed the ground under my feet.
We may not have actually risked what I had feared in the first few minutes of danger, but my brain had decided to register that I had escaped death.
From that day on, I began to appreciate the so-called little things of life much more.

Every now and then, when I'm on the train or subway and watching my contemporaries, immersed in their digital worlds, I think that some of them might also descend from a Great War soldier, who escaped death by chance like my grandpa.

Who knows if their grandfather or their great-grandfather was an Infantryman, an Alpino, a Bersagliere, an Artilleryman or even an Ardito?
I wonder if he told them anything about his war experience.
Who knows if he too left a diary or some writings?
I also think that in the midst of these contemporaries of mine, immersed in their digital worlds, there are surely some grandchildren of the "imboscati" or the "sharks", who got rich thanks to the war.
I often wonder if these contemporaries of mine, immersed in their digital worlds, know something about that period and understand how fortunate and privileged our generation is compared to that of our ancestors.
I am convinced that a flight like mine from Fuerteventura or, alternatively, a book on the Great War would be useful for everyone.

As fate would have it, a bullet, a shrapnel or a simple fragment of a shell didn't end my grandfather's life.
As fate would have it, my father, too, emerged unscathed from the fury of the following war.
As fate would have it, I was able to recover the story of my grandfather and that of my family.
An infinitesimal story like a drop in the murky and dark sea of History.
The telling of it has perhaps given it the property of mercury and thus the possibility of exciting readers, both of current and future generations.
This, too, will certainly depend on fate.

Bergamo, 14 January 2015

P.S. After I finished writing this book, I was tidying up a drawer and I found the will that my grandfather had typed on October 17, 1959, four years before his death. I vaguely remembered it.
I had only read it once many years ago and I was deeply moved.
I got goosebumps and a lump in my throat reading his words:
"I wish the funeral to be simple with a single pillow of flowers on the coffin and accompanied to the grave by the WW1 Combatants' flag or the flag of the Arditi".

EPILOGUE

THE ARRIVAL OF THE LAST SCREENSHOT BROUGHT ME BACK TO REALITY, AS A DIVER SEES THE SUNLIGHT AND STARTS BREATHING AGAIN AFTER A LONG APNOEA.
FOR THREE DAYS I WAS TOTALLY IMMERSED IN A WORLD LIGHT-YEARS AWAY FROM OURS AND I FELT AS IF I WERE RELIVING THE INTENSE EMOTIONS THAT THOSE MEN MUST HAVE FELT.

WHEN I TURNED OFF THE OLD E-READER, I LOOKED WITH EMOTION AND ADMIRATION AT THE MEDALS LINED UP ON THE DESK.
GRANDPA DID A GREAT JOB.
I REMEMBER HE WAS VERY PRECISE IN EVERYTHING HE DID.

WHAT I FOUND IN THIS OLD GREY TRUNK IS FURTHER PROOF, IF EVER IT WAS NEEDED.
THE WINCHESTER IS ON THE BOTTOM, ALWAYS WRAPPED IN THAT STRANGE WRINKLED PAPER, TOGETHER WITH A DOUBLE-BARRELLED SHOTGUN, AN OFFICER'S SABRE AND A SWORD.
THE DAGGER, THE CURVED KNIFE AND THE SPEAR POINTS ARE STORED IN A WOODEN BOX.
ON THE SIDE, WELL FOLDED AND WRAPPED IN CELLOPHANE, THERE ARE A CAMOUFLAGE SUIT AND TWO GREY UNIFORMS (SUMMER AND WINTER) OF THE GUARDIA DI FINANZA.
RESTING ON TOP ARE THE STATIONMASTER'S RED CAP AND THE INFANTRY OFFICER'S CAP, TWO LIEUTENANT'S CAPS AND A GREEN BERET OF THE GUARDIA DI FINANZA.

ANOTHER BOX IS FULL OF HARD-DISKS, WITH ALL THE AUDIO AND VIDEO MEMORIES THAT GRANDFATHER COLLECTED OVER THE YEARS, HIS HUGE PHOTOGRAPHIC ARCHIVE OF TRAVEL AND CREATIVE IMAGES, AS HE USED TO CALL THEM, SCANS OF HIS DRAWINGS AND ALL THE MUSIC HE LOVED, CLASSICAL, OPERA, PROGRESSIVE ROCK AND SO ON.

IT WILL TAKE MONTHS TO SEE AND LISTEN TO EVERYTHING.
I'M SURE I'LL FIND LOTS OF OTHER INTERESTING THINGS FROM THAT LONG-AGO AGE.

IN THE UPPER SHELF OF THE TRUNK THERE ARE NUMEROUS BOXES FULL OF ANCIENT OBJECTS: WATCHES, INK NIBS, COINS FROM VARIOUS YEARS, RAZOR BLADES, PEBBLES OF VARIOUS SHAPES AND COLOURS, VIALS FULL OF SAND.

IN A BEAUTIFUL TIN BOX THERE ARE MANY FAMILY PHOTOS, ALMOST ALWAYS WITH AN INDICATION OF THE YEAR AND THE NAME OF THE PERSON PORTRAYED.

VARIOUS DOCUMENTS AND DIPLOMAS ARE KEPT INSIDE A YELLOW ENVELOPE. THERE ARE ALSO MILITARY SERVICE RECORDS AND A TYPED WILL.

IN THE MIDST OF ALL THESE THINGS SO SCRUPULOUSLY PRESERVED, HOWEVER, THE ORIGINAL NOTEBOOKS ARE NOT TO BE FOUND.
THIS SEEMS VERY ODD TO ME.
SO MUCH SO AS TO RAISE MY SUSPICIONS.
PERHAPS MY GRANDFATHER'S DESIRE TO KNOW WHAT HE HAD NEVER BEEN TOLD WAS SO GREAT THAT HE RECONSTRUCTED WHAT MIGHT HAVE BEEN HIS GRANDFATHER'S, THAT IS MY GREAT-GREAT-GRANDFATHER'S, WAR JOURNAL.

BY THE WAY, THE DAY BEFORE YESTERDAY WAS THE 200TH ANNIVERSARY OF HIS BIRTH.

BORDEAUX, DECEMBER 3RD, 2096

Photo Book

Camposanpiero, September 1918
from left to right Sergente (Pietro Roseano), Lu-Lupo and Faro

REGOLAM. PER LE MATRICOLE (§ 91)

N. 61 del Catal. (R. 1926)

(1) ....

N. di matricola 7319 *del distretto di* Udine (96)

COPIA DEL FOGLIO MATRICOLARE

di Roseano Pietro *di* Mattia
e di Bearzi Angelina *nato il* 1 Dicembre 1896 *a* Chiusaforte
mandamento di Moggio *circondario di* Udine
inscritto nel comune di Chiusaforte *mandamento di* Moggio
circondario di Udine

Contrassegni personali, cognizioni speciali, matrimoni e vedovanze		
Statura m. 1,63 *Torace m.* 0,82	*Bocca*	*Professione o mestiere* muratore
Qualità fisiche in genere	*Dentatura* sana	*Grado d'istruzione*
Capelli { *colore* Neri / *forma* lisci	*Mento*	
Viso	*Segni particolari*	
Colorito pallido	*All'atto dell'arruolamento sapeva* { *leggere? scrivere?* Si	
Occhi castani		*Cognizioni extra professionali*
Sopracciglia		
Fronte		
Naso		

Ammogliato con .... *il* .... (2) *autorizzazione del Comandante del Corpo d'Armata di* .... *in data* .... *n.* ....
Rimasto vedovo il ....

ARRUOLAMENTO, SERVIZI, PROMOZIONI ED ALTRE VARIAZIONI MATRICOLARI	DATA		
Soldato di leva 1a categ. classe 1896 Distretto di Udine e lasciato in congedo illimitato li	22	Settembre	1915
Chiamato alle armi e giunto	26	Novembre	1915
Tale nel 57° Regg.to Fanteria	4	Dicembre	1915
Caporale in detto	25	Marzo	1916
Giunto in territorio dichiarato in istato di guerra	1	Aprile	1916
Tale nel 207° Regg.to Fanteria	19	Maggio	1916
Caporale maggiore in detto	11	Luglio	1917
Sergente in detto	30	Luglio	1917
Tale nel 6° Reparto d'assalto	16	Settembre	1917
Tale nel 2° Regg.to Fanteria (2° Reparto d'assalto)	30	Dicembre	1917
Sergente maggiore in detto	19	Giugno	1918
Tale nel 22° Reparto d'assalto	1	Luglio	1918

(1) Corpo o Ministero. — (2) Per coloro che contrassero matrimonio prima di giungere alle armi cancellare le parole che seguono e sostituire: *prima di giungere alle armi.*

Service record of Pietro Roseano, page 1

ARRUOLAMENTO, SERVIZI, PROMOZIONI ED ALTRE VARIAZIONI MATRICOLARI — DATA

Partito per la Libia	21	marzo	1919
Rientrato in Italia	27	luglio	1919
Inviato in congedo illimitato	23	dicembre	1920
[illegible] il pagamento delle indennità (o dei premi) di cui alla circolare 114 del giornale militare del 1919 in Lire 300			
22° Regg.to Cavalleria	23	12	1920
Dispensato dalla chiamata alle armi ai sensi delle disposizioni riguardanti le dispense (art. 11) [illegible]	1	ottobre	192[illegible]
Concessa dichiarazione di aver tenuto buona condotta aver servito con fedeltà ed onore			

CAMPAGNE, AZIONI DI MERITO, DECORAZIONI, ENCOMI, FERITE, LESIONI, FRATTURE MUTILAZIONI IN GUERRA OD IN SERVIZIO

Campagna di Guerra 1916 - 1917 - 1918

Autorizzato a fregiarsi della medaglia commemorativa Nazionale della guerra 1915-18 istituita con R. decreto N. 1241 in data 29 Luglio 1920 ed apporre sul nastro della medaglia le fascette corrispondenti agli anni di campagna 1916 1917 1918.

Autorizzato a fregiarsi della medaglia Interalleata della Vittoria, R. decreto N.° 918 del 16 dicembre 1920.

Autorizzato a fregiarsi della medaglia ricordo dell'Unità d'Italia di cui al R. decreto 9 ottobre 1922 N.° 135.

Udine (1) 7 GENNAIO 1929 Anno VII

IL MAGGIORE CAPO SEZIONE
Carro Francesco

(2) DISTRETTO MILITARE DI UDINE — RECLUTAMENTO E MOBILITAZIONE

IL MAGGIORE
Capo Uff. Reclut. Mobilitazione
(Luigi Chamard)

(1) Data. — (2) Firme.

Service record of Pietro Roseano, pages 2-3

War Merit Crosses

Commemorative Medal for the Italo-Austrian War 1915-1918

Commemorative Medal for the War 1915-1918 and the Unity of Italy

Allied Victory Medal ***of the Great War for civilization***

Commemorative Medal of the Libyan campaign 1919

Medals awarded to Pietro Roseano

Tripoli, 15 June 1919

Medal commemorating the "Umbria" steamer (*Nicola Gabriele collection*)
and postcard of the XXII Assault Unit (*Stacconeddu family collection*)

Pin of the II-XXII Assault Unit (*Nicola Gabriele collection*)

Postcard and medal commemorating the II-XXII Assault Unit
(Nicola Gabriele collection)

Pietro Roseano with two comrades after returning from Libya, 24 August 1919

Concessione N° 10 2419 Classe 1896

IL MINISTRO DELLA GVERRA

DECRETA

IL Caporal Maggiore

Roseano Pietro di Mattia

È AVTORIZZATO A FREGIARSI DELLA

MEDAGLIA ISTITVITA A RICORDO
DELLA GVERRA MCMXV-MCMXVIII

AVTORIZZATO A FREGIARSI DELLA MEDAGLIA INTERALLEATA
DELLA VITTORIA (R.D. N°637 DEL 6-4-1922)

IL COMANDANTE

TENENTE COLONNELLO

ROMA, ADDÌ 13 luglio 1921

IL MINISTRO

Gasparotto

Editori Alfieri & Lacroix - Roma-Milano

Certificate of Recognition released with the Commemorative Medal for the Italo-Austrian War 1915-1918 and the Allied Victory Medal.

cl. 96 mat. 1319 Pontebba

Numero d'ordine del Registro delle concessioni 357341

Regio Esercito Italiano

Il Ministro della Guerra

Visto il R. Decreto 19 Gennaio 1918, n. 205

Determina:

È concessa al sergente magg.re 22° Reparto d'assalto

Roseano Pietro di Mattia

la Croce al Merito di Guerra

Roma, addì 21 Marzo 1929 A VII

Il Ministro

Certificate of Recognition released with the Italian War Merit Cross, awarded to members of the armed forces with a minimum of one year's service in contact with an enemy and who received a promotion.

Pontebba li 22 Giugno 1928-VI°

Al Comando del Distretto Militare di

UDINE

in risposta alla nota N° 3847 di Cotesto On Comando mi pregio informare quanto segue:

I - Raggiunsi il fronte (ad Ala) il 25-3-1916, col Battaglione di Marcia del 57° Regg. Fanteria comandato dal Sig. Tenente Gorbin. Il 1-5-916 venni trasferito al 207° Regg. Fanteria, 2° Comp. comandata dal Sig. Capitano Fiore. Il Comandante del Battaglione era il Sig. Maggiore Binacchi.

2 - Partecipai col plotone d'assalto del I° Battaglione del 207° Fant. ai combattimenti della Bainzizza (20-8-1917) a quell'epoca avevo il gradó di Sergente.

3 - N. N. sempre in zona d'operazioni

4 - Il 5-9-1917 passai al 6° Battaglione d'Assalto che venne pure denominato 2° e 22° Reparto d'Assalto. Venni assegnato alla 3° Comp. comandata dal Sig. Capitano [illegible]elchi mentre il predetto battaglione era comandato dal Sig. Capitano Abbondanza.
Con detto Reparto presi parte ai combattimenti di Monte Val Bella (28-1-1918) Zenzon di Piave e Fornaci (dal 16 al 19-6-1918)
La 3° Compagnia del 22° Reparto d'Assalto venne poi comandata dal Tenente Sig. Meloni con il quale presi parte ai combattimenti di Moriago, Fontigo e Sernaglia (dal [illegible]-10-1918 all'armistizio)

5 - N. N.

6 - N. N.

7 - N. N.

8 - N. N.

Pietro Roseano: Declaration of military units served and battles

Pietro Roseano, after his appointment as 2nd lieutenant in reserve
2nd Infantry Regiment, "Re" Brigade - year 1937

Pietro Roseano, stationmaster in the 1950s

Xmas 1959. Pietro with wife, sons, daughters-in-law and grandson.

ACKNOWLEDGEMENTS

I would like to mention and thank all the people who have made important contributions to this book.

Andor Kiss (Udine) for his books on the Great War.
Antonio Miotello (Vicenza) for his book on the Battaglia dei Tre Monti.
Antonio Mucelli (San Donà di Piave) for information on the Assault Units.
Carlo Bianchi (Volpago del Montello) for information on the Assault Units.
Christian Lai (La Maddalena) for information on the Arditi gold medals.
Dani Pagnucco (Arzene) for translations into the Friulan language.
Elena Guida (Salzano) for her help in the editing phase.
Federico Stefani (Meolo) for information on Fosso Palumbo.
Colonel Filippo Cappellano (Rome) for info on the events of 2-10-1917.
Gabriele Esposito La Rossa (Napoli) for translations into the Neapolitan dialect.
Gerardo Unia (Cuneo) for information on the 207th Infantry Regiment.
Giacomo and Giampaolo Stacconeddu (Palau) for the postcard of the XXII.
Gianni Pisoni (Bergamo) for translations into the Bergamo dialect.
Grazia Maria Manetti (Firenze) for translations into the Tuscan dialect.
The Moretti family (Venice) for information on sergeant Pietro Moretti.
Marcello Mussolin (Palermo) for translations into the Sicilian dialect.
Nicola Gabriele (Bologna) for the images of the medals of the XXII.
Rossana Giaffreda (Venezia) for translations into the Venetian dialect.
Stefano Costantini (Treviso) for the consultation of the book by Radicati.
Tiziana and Attilia Gubiani (Gemona) for information on the Roseano family.
Umberto Chiaruttini (Udine) for a picture of the 2nd lieutenant Pietro Roseano.

Before going to print, I asked three experts on the Great War and Arditi history, Aldo Gambardella, Antonio Mucelli and Carlo Bianchi, to read the drafts of the novel in order to get their feedback from an historical point of view.
To get feedback from those who knew little about the history of the Arditi but are frequent readers of novels, I involved Emanuela Cattaneo, Laura Finotto, Orsola Saporiti, Paola Agostinis and Walter Pancini.
I thank them all for reading the work and for their useful advice.

Last but not least, I would like to thank Carole McGrath for the remarkable help she has given me in translating this book into English.

BIBLIOGRAPHY

- Baj-Macario Gianni - Von Pitreich Anton, *Prima di Caporetto Gorizia, Libreria Editrice Goriziana, 2007*
- Bernardi Mario, *Di qua e di là del Piave Milano, Ugo Mursia Editore, 1989*
- Bultrini Nicola, *L'ultimo fante, La Grande Guerra sul Carso nelle memorie di Carlo Orelli, Chiari (BS), Nordpress Edizioni, 2004*
- Caccia Dominioni Paolo, *Diario di guerra 1915-1919 Milano, Ugo Mursia Editore, 1993*
- Canale Dario - Margutti Francesco, *Le Battaglie sui Tre Monti Vicenza, Editrice Veneta, 2008*
- Canepari Egidio, *Diario di un fante 1914-1918 Milano, Ugo Mursia Editore, 2014*
- Cappellano F. - Di Martino B., *I reparti d'assalto italiani nella grande guerra Roma, Stato Maggiore dell'Esercito, 2007*
- Cervone Pier Paolo, *Vittorio Veneto, l'ultima battaglia Milano, Ugo Mursia Editore, 1994*
- Ceschin Daniele, *Gli esuli di Caporetto, Roma, Giuseppe Laterza & Figli, 2006*
- Cicchino A. - Olivo R., *La grande guerra dei piccoli uomini Milano, Ancora Editrice, 2005*
- Cordenos Giuseppe, *La fotografia di guerra sul Piave Udine, Paolo Gaspari Editore, 2005*
- Cordova Ferdinando, *Arditi e legionari dannunziani Roma, Manifestolibri, 2007*
- De Simone Cesare, *L'Isonzo mormorava, fanti e generali di Caporetto Milano, Ugo Mursia Editore, 1995*
- Ellero Elpidio, *Storia di un esodo, i Friulani dopo la rotta di Caporetto Udine, Istituto Friulano per la Storia del Movimento di Liberazione, 2001*
- Fadini Francesco, *Caporetto dalla parte del vincitore Milano, Ugo Mursia Editore, 1992*
- Filastò Gaetano, *Diario di un assistente di sanità 1915-16 Chiari (BS), Nordpress Edizioni, 2008*
- Forcella Enzo - Monticone Alberto, *Plotoni di esecuzione Roma-Bari, Giuseppe Laterza & Figli, 1968*
- Garofalo Damiano, *Arditi del popolo: storia della prima lotta armata al fascismo (1917-1922)*

- Gaspari Paolo, *La battaglia dei capitani, Udine 28 ottobre 1917*
  Udine, Gaspari Editore, 2014
- Gasparotto Luigi, *Diario di un fante*
  Chiari (BS), Nordpress Edizioni, 2002
- Gibelli Antonio, *L'officina della guerra*
  Torino, Bollati Boringhieri Editore, 2007
- Giudici Paolo, *Reparti d'assalto*
  Milano, Casa Editrice Alpes, 1928
- Giuliani Reginaldo, *Gli Arditi. Breve storia dei reparti d'assalto della*
  Terza Armata, Milano, Treves, 1919
- Killian Hans, *Attacco* a *Caporetto*
  Gorizia, Libreria Editrice Goriziana, 2005
- Labanca Nicola, *Caporetto storia di una disfatta*
  Firenze, Giunti Gruppo Editoriale, 1997
- Lussu Emilio, *Un anno sull'Altipiano*
  Torino, Giulio Einaudi Editore, 2000
- Magli Massimiliano, *Fucilazioni di guerra*
  Chiari (BS), Nordpress Edizioni, 2007
- Magnifici Alessandro, *La censura di trincea, il regime postale nella G. Guerra*
  Chiari (BS), Nordpress Edizioni, 2008
- Malaparte Curzio, *Viva Caporetto! La rivolta dei santi maledetti*
  Milano, Oscar Mondadori, 1981
- Maranesi Nicola, *Avanti sempre*
  Bologna, Società Editrice il Mulino, 2014
- Melograni Piero, *Storia politica della Grande Guerra 1915-18*
  Milano, Oscar Storia Mondadori, 1998
- Meregalli Carlo, *Grande Guerra: "omini di ferro" contro un Impero*
  Bassano del Grappa (VI), Ghedina & Tassotti Editori, 1996
- Mirijello Saverio, *1914-18 Parole dal fronte*
  Bassano del Grappa (VI), Attilio Fraccaro Editore, 2014
- Monti Buzzetti Sisto, *Scusate la calligrafia - Lettere dal fronte*
  Milano, Terre di Mezzo, 2008
- Morali Enrico, *In guerra con i lupi di Toscana*
  Bassano del Grappa (VI), Itinera Progetti, 2010
- Pirocchi Angelo Luigi, *Arditi - Le truppe d'assalto italiane 1917-20*
  Gorizia, Libreria Editrice Goriziana, 2011
- Pust Ingomar, *1915-1918 Il fronte di pietra, la guerra sulle Alpi Giulie e*
  dal Carso al Grappa, Milano, Ugo Mursia Editore, 1987
- Radicati di Primeglio Maggiorino, *I Reparti d'assalto nella guerra 15-18*
  Torino, Edizioni Superga, 1957
- Rochat Giorgio, *Gli Arditi della Grande Guerra*
  Gorizia, Libreria Editrice Goriziana, 1990

- Rosa Ermes Aurelio, *Arditi sul Grappa*
  Bassano del Grappa (VI), Itinera Progetti, 2003
- Salsa Carlo, *Trincee. Confidenze di un fante*
  Milano, Ugo Mursia Editore, 1982
- Schachinger Werner, *I Bosniaci sul fronte italiano 1915-18*
  Gorizia, Libreria Editrice Goriziana, 2008
- Schaumann Walther - Schubert Peter, *Isonzo, là dove morirono*
  Bassano del Grappa (TV), Ghedina & Tassotti Editori, 1990
- Schemfil Viktor, *La Grande Guerra sul Pasubio 1916-18*
  Milano, Ugo Mursia Editore, 1985
- Schneller Karl, *1916 Mancò un soffio*
  Milano, Ugo Mursia Editore, 1984
- Silvestri Mario, *Isonzo 1917*
  Milano, RCS Libri, 2001
- Soffici Ardengo, *Kobilek*
  Firenze, Vallecchi Editore, 1966
- Tenente Anonimo, *Arditi in guerra*
  Chiari (BS), Nordpress Edizioni, 2000
- Unia Gerardo, *L'undicesima battaglia*
  Cuneo, Nerosubianco, 2013
- Ventrone Angelo, *Piccola storia della Grande Guerra*
  Roma, Donzelli Editore, 2005
- Volpato Paolo, *Asolone, monte di fuoco - Alpini, Fanti e Arditi nell'anno della vittoria, Chiari (BS), Nordpress Edizioni, 2008*
- Volpato Paolo, *Vittoria ad ogni costo, Le battaglie dei Tre Monti*
  Bassano del Grappa (VI), Itinera Progetti, 2009
- Weber Fritz, *Dal Monte Nero a Caporetto, le dodici battaglie dell'Isonzo*
  Milano, Ugo Mursia Editore, 1967
- Weber Fritz, *Guerra sulle Alpi (1915-17)*
  Milano, Ugo Mursia Editore, 1978
- Weber Fritz, *Tappe della disfatta*
  Milano, Ugo Mursia Editore, 1965
- Wilks John & Wilks Eileen, *Rommel a Caporetto*
  Chiari (BS), Nordpress Edizioni, 2004

AUTHOR PROFILE

Roberto Roseano was born in Gemona del Friuli (Udine) in 1958. He took his degree in Statistical Sciences in Padua and since 1986 has been working in Milan in the advertising industry.
He lives in Bergamo. In 2014-15 he wrote his first book, ***"L'Ardito - Romanzo storico"***, set in the First World War. Published later by Itinera Progetti (Bassano del Grappa), in autumn 2017 it won the 50th edition of the prestigious *Premio Acqui Storia*, historical novel section, surpassing established authors and great publishing houses in the final.
In 2020 his book won the XI edition of the *General Amedeo De Cia* award.
He has written several other books on the assault units of the Great War.

"Arditi - Decorati e Caduti, 1917-20"
The result of meticulous historical research lasting over a year in collaboration with Giampaolo Stacconeddu, it collects, separately by unit and chronologically by fact of arms, the 3,625 citations for the medals of military value awarded on 3,142 Arditi and the list of the 3,145 fallen. *(year 2016)*

"Carlo Sabatini - Diario di Guerra 1915-1919"
Based on the unedited diary of one of the most famous recipients of the Gold Medal of Military Valour of the Arditi for his conquest of Mount Corno after climbing a 50-metre overhanging wall; each event has been historically framed and enriched by unpublished images. *(year 2018)*

"II-XXII Reparto d'assalto"
It narrates in historical form the birth and actions of one of the longest-running and fiercest assault units, integrating them with the diaries of two combatants and with biographies, photos, documents and memories of officers and soldiers who fought in the II-XXII. *(year 2018)*

"Cuore Ardito"
The sequel to the novel "L'Ardito". It narrates the events of the XXII Assault Unit in the two-year period 1919-20: missions in Libya and Albania, the enterprise of Fiume. *(year 2019)*

"Giovanni Degli Esposti - Diario di Guerra 1915-1945"
The unedited diary of another highly decorated Ardito, one of the heroes of the conquest of Mount Corno. The text is enriched by a large number of photos and documents. *(year 2020)*

He conceived, promoted and coordinated nine other authors in the creation of the book ***"Arditi d'Oro"***, in which the facts of arms that led to the awarding of the gold medal to twenty men from the assault units are narrated in a romanticized form; for this project he also wrote three short stories. *(year 2018)*
Following the success of that book, he released ***"Arditi d'Argento"***, dedicated to 20 Arditi decorated with a silver medal, coordinating the work of 13 other authors and writing three stories. *(year 2020)*

He is the administrator of the Facebook page ***"Arditi of the XXII Assault Unit"***, with over 6,500 followers, through which he collects and shares photos and documents on the Arditi of the Great War. https://www.facebook.com/ArditiXXII

Printed in July 2020

Printed in Great Britain
by Amazon

25002709R00238